A MAN WAS IN THE CELL

on all fours, circling like a beast. His head thrown back, a man. The moonlight showed his face. It cannot be described—not, at least, by me. A man past death might look like this, a victim of the Inquisition rack, the stake, the pincers: not a human in the twentieth century, surely. I had never seen such suffering within two eyes, such lost, mad suffering. Naked, he crawled about the dirt, cried, leaped up to his feet and clawed the hard stone walls in fury.

Then he saw me.

"[Charles Beaumont was] one of *the* seminal influences on writers of the fantastic and macabre."

—Dean R. Koontz

CHARLES BEAUMONT

THE HOWLING MAN

TOR
HORROR

A TOM DOHERTY ASSOCIATES BOOK
NEW YORK

THE HOWLING MAN

Originally published as CHARLES BEAUMONT: SELECTED STORIES
Reprinted by arrangement with Dark Harvest Inc.

A Tor Book
Published by Tom Doherty Associates, Inc.
175 Fifth Avenue
New York, N.Y. 10010

TOR® is a registered trademark of Tom Doherty Associates, Inc.

Cover art by Peter Scanlan

ISBN: 0-812-50552-2

First mass market printing March 1992

Printed in the United States of America

0 9 8 7 6 5 4 3 2 1

PERMISSIONS

In memory of
Nick and Ria Anker
and of
Chuck and Helen Beaumont

Thanks are due to the following for their help in bringing this book to publication:

Robert Bloch, Ray Bradbury, Howard Browne, Roger Corman, Saul David, Harlan Ellison, Charles E. Fritch, George Clayton Johnson, Richard Matheson, Chad Oliver, Frank M. Robinson, Ray Russell, Jerry Sohl and John Tomerlin.

For friendship, advice and support:

Cathy, Elizabeth and Gregory Beaumont, Larry Anker, Bill Farley, Edward Gorman, Dean R. Koontz, Joe R. Lansdale, Robert R. McCammon, Dave McDonnell, Paul Mikol, Scot Stadalsky, William Relling Jr., Darrell, Donna and Jason Rossi, Peter Straub, Robert Vaillancourt, Stanley Wiater and Douglas E. Winter.

And a very special thanks to the following for the endless hours of driving, interviewing, conversing, all-night coffee shops and encouragement:

Christopher Beaumont, Richard Christian Matheson, William F. Nolan and Dennis Etchison.

TABLE OF CONTENTS

TABLE OF CONTENTS

INTRODUCTION
by Roger Anker

THOUGH BEST REMEMBERED for his short fiction and nostalgic essays in *Playboy*, teleplays for *The Twilight Zone*; and his screenplay adaptation, *The Seven Faces of Dr. Lao*, Charles Beaumont's creative talents have been evidenced in such diverse fields as science fiction, horror, whimsy, crime-suspense, and film criticism.

His prolific output also reflects his many interests and hobbies, including motor racing, music, hi-fidelity equipment, cartooning, and travel.

Tall, lean and bespectacled, Beaumont was always full of a thousand ideas and a thousand projects, and approached them all with what was fantastic energy. In a career which spanned a brief thirteen years, he'd written and sold ten books, seventy-four short stories, thirteen screenplays (nine of which were produced), two dozen articles and profiles, forty comic stories, fourteen columns, and over seventy teleplays.

Some of his books were inspired by his adventurous personal experiences. *Omnibus of Speed* and *When Engines Roar* (both co-edited with William F. Nolan) are about auto racing; *The Intruder*, a novel concerning Southern integration in the early sixties, was drawn from his extensive research on the subject.

Beaumont could never write fast enough to keep up with his ideas. A self-educated man, learning for him was never confined to a classroom; life had much to teach.

He was born Charles Leroy Nutt in Chicago on January 2, 1929, and grew up on that city's North side.

Of his early childhood, he wrote, "Football, baseball and dimestore cookie thefts filled my early world, to the exclusion of Aesop, the brothers Grimm, Dr. Doolittle and even Bullfinch. The installation by my parents of 'library wall-paper' in the house ('A room-full of books for only 70¢ a yard!') convinced me that literature was on the way out anyway, so I lived in illiterate contentment until laid low by spinal meningitis. This forced me to less strenuous forms of entertainment. I discovered Oz; then Burroughs; then Poe—and the jig was up. Have been reading ever since, feeling no pain."

The only child of Charles H. and Letty Nutt, young Charlie Nutt was "fairly outgoing," yet very sensitive about his name. He once expressed to boyhood acquaintance Frank M. Robinson (co-author of *The Glass Inferno* and *The Gold Crew*) his hatred for the continuous name teasing he'd endured: ". . . the kids in school would call him 'Ches' or 'Wall' or would ask 'Is your father some kind of a nut?' " He later changed his name to Charles *Mc*Nutt, but when that didn't satisfy the situation, he changed it finally, legally, to Beaumont.

At an early age, he'd often "haunt" the editorial offices of the Ziff-Davis Publishing Company—publishers of *Amazing Stories* and other pulp magazines—and, from an outer office, would gaze at the group of employees typing busily. To young Charlie Nutt, these people were giants, editing manuscripts, and building a small empire, at that time, in Chicago. "I used to stand there and watch them slamming out 10,000 words a day," he once wrote. "They were Gods to me . . ." Ironically, his first professional sale, "The Devil, You Say?", would appear in the January, 1951 issue of *Amazing Stories*.

At age twelve, mid-way through his two year bout with meningitis, Beaumont's parents sent him to what they considered to be a better climate. In July, 1960, he told the *San Diego Union*, "I lived with five widowed aunts who ran a rooming house near a train depot in the state of Washington. Each night we had the ritual of gathering around the stove and there I'd hear stories about the strange death of each of their husbands."

During this period in Everett, he published his own fan magazine, *Utopia*, and soon became an avid fan of science fiction, writing letters to almost every magazine of this genre. By the time he was thirteen he had broken into print 25 times in almost as many magazines with these resumes and editorial criticisms.

His interests then shifted from typewriter to drawing board and his illustrations began to appear in a number of pulp magazines under the brush name E.T. Beaumont. His first cartoon, done in collaboration with his friend and fellow artist, Ronald Clyne, appeared in *Fantastic Adventures* in October, 1943.

In the early months of 1944, Charlie McNutt turned to drama and radio work, beginning as a featured actor on "Drama Workshop," a West coast show, and soon moved on to write and direct his own spot, "Hollywood Hi-Lights," a 15 minute show of movieland chatter and shop talk.

His formal education was sparse, of which, he wrote, "[I] barely nosed through the elementary grades and gained a certain notoriety in high school as a wastrel, dreamer, could-do-the-work-if-he'd-only-tryer and general lunkhead." He left high school a year short of graduation for a four month period of Army service (Infantry) before he was medically discharged for a bad back. This led to his enroll-

ment into the Bliss-Hayden Acting School in California
under the GI Bill. After starring in a local version of the
Hecht-MacArthur play, *Broadway*, he was signed by Universal Studio as an actor, and was scheduled for a co-
starring role in a Universal-International film. But despite
much "hullabaloo in film magazines and newspapers," this
never materialized, and Beaumont reluctantly gave up a
theatrical career for one in commercial art. Soon he was
sketching cartoons for MGM's animation studio and working as a part-time illustrator for FPCI (Fantasy Publishing
Company) in Los Angeles. Beaumont later wrote, "[I]
worked hard, managed to crack most of the pulp magazines
with illustrations, graduated to book jackets and slick magazine cartoons. But [was] forced, finally, to admit total lack
of any real talent in the field."

When this failed, Beaumont turned to writing.

It was in the summer of 1946, that he met twenty-six-
year-old Ray Bradbury (author of numerous screenplays,
teleplays, essays, poems, and works of fiction, including
Farenheit 451 and *The Martian Chronicles*) in Fowler Brothers Book Store in downtown Los Angeles, and began talking about his comic collection. Remembers Bradbury: "He
said he had a lot of *Steve Canyon*, and I told him I had a
lot of *Prince Valiants* and some Hannes Bok photographs;
so we decided to get together.

"Out of that beginning, of our mutual interest in comic
strips, a friendship blossomed."

Bradbury began to read Beaumont's short fiction and
quickly became a major influence in Beaumont's life—a
mentor. "When I read the first one, I said: 'Yes. Very
definitely. You are a writer,'" recalls Bradbury. "It showed
immediately. It's not like so many people who come to you
with stories and you say, 'Well, they're okay,' You know,
if they keep working they'll make it. Chuck's talent was
obvious from that very first story."

For reasons of economic survival, Beaumont moved to

Mobile, Alabama in 1948, where his father had obtained employment for him as a clerk for the Gulf, Mobile & Ohio Railroad. It was there that he met Helen Broun, and wrote in a notebook: "She's incredible. Intelligent *and* beautiful. This is the girl I'm going to marry!" A year later, they were married and moved to California. Their son, Christopher, was born in December of 1950; they would later parent three more children: Catherine, Elizabeth, and Gregory.

As Beaumont's early writing brought him little more than rejection slips, he worked at a number of jobs, including that of a piano player ("Studied piano for six years, decided [I] couldn't squeak by owing to immensely talented right hand and nowhere left") and, in 1949, a tracing clerk for California Motor Express, where he met John Tomerlin. When the two discovered they shared a passion for words (as well as a skill for "geting out of work"), they quickly cultivated what was to become a lifelong friendship.

In mid-1951, another special friendship was made when Beaumont met a young, struggling writer by the name of Richard Matheson (who, in addition to many screenplays, teleplays and short stories, is known for works such as *I Am Legend* and *The Shrinking Man*). As their families became very close, there soon developed between Beaumont and Matheson a constant interchange of ideas, out of which a number of varied and imaginative stories would emerge. Says writer Dennis Etchison (*Darkside* and *Cutting Edge*), who'd attended Beaumont's UCLA writing class in 1963, "It's pretty difficult to consider Beaumont and Matheson separately because as short story writers they came out at the same time; they worked together, they both came out of an influence from Bradbury, and they both had such a close friendship. I think there are great similarities, trade-offs, and variations between their stories. They were just two of a kind that came up at one time."

As their careers grew, Beaumont and Matheson acted as "spurs" to one another. "He and I, in a very nice way, of course, were very competitive," says Matheson. "At first, I was a little ahead of him in sales. I'd call him on the phone and say, 'I just sold a collection of short stories to Bantam,' and he'd say, 'Thanks a lot, thanks a lot,' and hang up. [laughs] He wasn't serious about it though. But he caught up to me. My first collection of stories [*Born of Man and Woman*, 1954] spurred him on to his first collection [*The Hunger and Other Stories*, 1957]. Then we both did a so-called 'straight' novel just about the same time [Beaumont's *The Intruder*, 1959 and Matheson's *The Beardless Warriors*, 1960]."

But the success which was to come their way, was still in the future. For now, Beaumont was working hard to break through. Says Ray Bradbury, "I was at Universal in 1952 on my very first screen project, *It Came From Outer Space*. And Chuck, coincidentally, was working there in the music department, handling a multilith machine, copying the musical scores. I would see him and have lunch with him there at the studio and encourage him. Those were hard years for him; he didn't want to be in the music department doing all this 'stupid' work. He wanted to *write*."

During this period, Beaumont was writing feverishly, but meeting with little success. His agent at the time, Forrest J. Ackerman, recalls: "I made approximately 78 submissions for him, but nothing happened for quite sometime."

When fired from Universal in June of 1953, Beaumont took the plunge into fulltime writing.

Late 1953 saw the Beaumonts in disastrous financial shape; Chuck's typewriter was in hock and the gas had been shut off in their apartment. Writer William F. Nolan (co-author of *Logan's Run* and biographer of Dashiell Hammett) remembers Beaumont "breaking the seal and turning it back on; Chris required heat, and damn the gas company! Chris got what he needed."

Nolan had met Beaumont, briefly, in 1952 at Universal, when introduced by Ray Bradbury. "I recall Chuck's sad face and ink-stained hands. The first Beaumont story had already appeared (in *Amazing Stories*) and within a few more months, when I saw Chuck again, half a dozen others had been sold. Forry Ackerman got us together early in 1953, and our friendship was immediate and lasting. I found, in Chuck, a warmth, a vitality, an honesty and depth of character which few possess. And, most necessary, a wild, wacky, irreverant sense of humor."

In February, 1954, Beaumont and Nolan began writing comics for Whitman Publication. Together they turned out ten stories, after which Beaumont sold another thirty to become employed at Whitman as co-editor, where he helped to "guide the destinies of such influential literary figures as Bugs Bunny, Mickey Mouse, Donald Duck and Andy Panda."

Finally, in September of that year, Beaumont's first major sale appeared in *Playboy*. "Black Country," a 10,000-word novella about a terminally ill jazzman, is considered by Ray Russell (*Playboy* editor during the 1950s, and author of many works of fiction, including *Incubus* and *Sardonicus*), the best story *Playboy* ever bought. "Beaumont manages to set up a rhythm and sustain a pitch, a concert pitch—to use a musical term—and sustain that from the very beginning to the very end," says Russell. "It almost never relaxes. You're on a beat throughout the entire story until *whhhh*, it's over. There are very few stories that have that, by Beaumont or anybody else."

Playboy soon placed Beaumont on a five-hundred-dollar monthly retainer for first refusal right to his manuscripts, and later listed him as a contributing editor.

Beaumont had reached the turning point in his career.

His stories began to appear in the most prestigious magazines in the nation, including *Esquire*, *Collier's* and *The Saturday Evening Post*. 1954 also marked the beginning of his career in television when, in April, his teleplay "Masquerade" aired on *Four Star Playhouse*. In the years to follow, he would write a number of scripts, many in collaboration with Richard Matheson. "For a year or two, we wrote together on all sorts of projects: we did a couple of *Have Gun, Will Travels*, an old Western series, *Buckskin*, and there was *Philip Marlowe*, and the *D.A.'s Man*. Real crap, most of it," says Matheson, laughingly. "But it was fun, because we had never done this before . . . But eventually we decided that we really didn't need to collaborate, and chose to go our own ways."

Beaumont's entry into television, coupled with his success at *Playboy*, soon enabled him to participate in what was to become a new and exciting hobby—auto racing. In February, 1955, Beaumont and Nolan attended their first sports car race in Palm Springs (an event in which actor James Dean was driving, and with whom Beaumont would later share a maintenance pit). The sport instantly became one of the great fascinations of their lives—a fascination which quickly carried over to John Tomerlin as well. "Chuck was marvelous at talking people into doing things they had not thirty seconds before ever dreamed they wanted to do, and suddenly discovered that it was their lifelong ambition," says Tomerlin. "And the next thing you knew, you'd be off and on your way doing it!"

The trio could soon be found attending and competing in weekend racing events on the West Coast, at an average of one event per month, and writing voluminously for motoring journals such as *Road & Track*, *Autosport*, *The Motor*, *Sports Car Illustrated*, and *Autocar*. A favorite hangout became the Grand Prix—A Hollywood restaurant which catered to the sports car enthusiast and professional alike, and featured racing music, racing records, and 8mm racing films, which were shown over the walls by multiple projectors. Of their racing abilities, Nolan says: "We weren't great, by any means, but we were fairly good, fairly fast, and totally crazy—which means we weren't afraid of anything."

Later this year, Beaumont made a major—as well as difficult—decision to act on his growing concern over the way his fiction was being handled by the Forrest Ackerman agency—an agency which dealt, almost exclusively, in science fiction markets. With increasing regularity, Beaumont had found himself turning toward "mainstream" storytelling and, in July, signed with Don Congdon, of the Harold Matson agency in new York. The move proved to be a beneficial one, and quickly helped in establishing Beaumont's versatility. As Richard Matheson observes, "Chuck had no genre; he was not a science fiction writer, he was not a fantasy writer—although he did write some wonderful science fiction and fantasy stories—he wrote all kinds of fiction. A *lot* of the stuff he wrote—for *Playboy*, what have you—was just flat, good-out fiction. Straight fiction. So there's no category. His mind jumped from place to place."

Beaumont's first short fiction collection, *The Hunger and Other Stories* (G.P. Putnam's Sons) was released in April of 1957 to favorable reviews. "The first sixteen tales of the book are interesting as instruments which reveal the scope and proclivities of a highly individual mind," says the *New York Herald Tribune*. "One is impressed by the creative gymnastics of the author . . . But in 'Black Country,' Beaumont, the author, is forgotten . . . Among all the stories it is this extraordinary work that passionately tears into the heart of jazz which gives Mr. Beaumont undeniable stature as an artist."

In addition to the previously mentioned periodicals, Beaumont's stories—both fiction and non fiction—were appearing in publications as *The Magazine of Fantasy and Science Fiction*, *Fortnight*, and *Rogue*. (In *Rogue*, due to his *Playboy* commitment, he appeared as "C.B. Lovehill" and "Michael Philips.") Other collections soon followed—

Yonder: Stories of Fantasy and Science Fiction (Bantam, 1958), *Night Ride and Other Journeys* (Bantam, 1960), and *The Fiend in You*, a Beaumont-edited anthology (Ballantine Books, 1962). In September of 1957, his first novel was published, *Run From the Hunter* (written in collaboration with John Tomerlin under the joint pseudonym "Keith Grantland").

Though he employed many writing styles, the distinct Beaumont "signature" was always in evidence. "His writing was brisk and very terse," says Bradbury. "There's a great similarity to John Collier. Collier rubbed off on him, just as Collier rubbed off on me. And it was all to the good: good, short, to the point, imaginative storytelling. A lot of us are Collier's indirect sons, but you learn as the years pass, to shake the influence. But it's certainly there. I also see carryovers from my work in Chuck. It's inevitable, because we were around each other so much. I told him about Eudora Welty and Katherine Anne Porter. I think that also shows. And it's all to the good."

By 1958, Beaumont had firmly established himself in television, scripting episodes for shows such as *Alfred Hitchcock Presents*, *One Step Beyond*, *Naked City*, *Thriller* and *Wanted Dead or Alive*. Recalls Jerry Sohl, author of numerous scripts and novels, and with whom Beaumont had collaborated on several screen projects, including an unproduced version of *The Dunwich Horror*, "Chuck was the kind of person who could go in [to a producer's office] and absolutely flabbergast you. He'd do what you'd call 'Blue Sky'—he'd pitch this story and no one would say that's no good, because they'd be so fascinated with Chuck. He had this ability to absolutely overpower you with what it was that he was doing. The trouble with most writers is that they may be good writers, but they can't sell themselves in television. Chuck Beaumont was able to do both; plus he could deliver the goods when the chips were down."

In 1958, Beaumont also saw the film release of his first

produced screenplay, *Queen of Outer Space*. (Two earlier screenplays, *Confession of a Teen-Ager* and *Invaders from 7000 A.D.*, both written in 1956–7, went unproduced.) Of the film, Beaumont says: "[The] studio called me in to do what I'd thought was to be a serious study of a group of men who take a space ship to Venus. But how serious can a picture be when the part of the world's biochemist is played by Zsa Zsa Gabor? The picture [is] about these men who land on Venus and find a planet inhabited entirely by beautiful women.

"Naturally, I wrote the thing as a big spoof. Only trouble was the director and some of the cast didn't realize it."

When Rod Serling's *Twilight Zone* made its network debut in 1959, Beaumont became one of the show's principal writers, scripting 22 of its 156 episodes. Richard Matheson explains his and Beaumont's involvement with the celebrated series. "The show was just getting started and Chuck and I had just joined this agency which was quite good at the time (we'd never had a good film agency before this), so they immediately started getting us appointments. There was a lot of work going on in television—half-hour television—and *Twilight Zone* was about to screen their pilot episode. So Chuck and I went to pitch some ideas to Rod [Serling] and [producer] Buck Houghton." Beaumont and Matheson went on to become second and third, respectively, in production of *Twilight Zone* scripts behind Serling, and were largely responsible for some of the series' classic episodes.

Beaumont was also responsible for bringing a young, untried talent to *Twilight Zone*'s core of principal writers. While George Clayton Johnson's story output was relatively minor (four stories and four teleplays), when compared to that of Serling, Beaumont and Matheson, it was the *quality* of his work which soon placed him on a level with the other three.

By now a close-knit "brotherhood" had formed between

Beaumont and his friends—many of whom considered him the cornerstone or "electric center" of the group. "Chuck was like the hub of the wheel," explains Nolan, "And you had all these different spokes going out: Richard Matheson, John Tomerlin, George Clayton Johnson, OCee Ritch, Chad Oliver, Ray Russell, Rod Serling, Frank Robinson, Charles Fritch, myself. Spokes. All connected to Beaumont. He energized us. Fired us. Made us stretch our creative and writing muscles. He was always encouraging us to do better. It was a very stimulating period in our lives."

The summer of 1961 found Beaumont involved in an explosively-controversial project: the first motion picture to deal with the volatile problem of Southern school integration, based on his novel *The Intruder*.

The factual springboard for both novel and film was an article on rabble-rousing John Kasper in *Look* magazine, printed in 1957 as "Intruder in the South," which described a power-hungry Kasper's efforts to sabotage school integration in Clinton, Tennessee. Adam Cramer, the central figure in Beaumont's story (portrayed by actor William Shatner), is on a similar mission and also uses integration as a ready lever in an attempt to gain personal power. He fails, as Kasper failed, but not before mob violence has taken its ugly toll, as it actually did in Clinton; by the time Kasper left, a week after his arrival, bombings, acts of terror, and attacks on integrationists had become common in the small community.

Intrigued by Kasper, Beaumont packed a suitcase and flew to Clinton to interview him.

A year and a half later his novel was finished, and Beaumont was subsequently hired to do the screenplay adaptation for director Roger Corman.

When Corman, whose forte had long been science fiction-horror, was unable to obtain studio backing, he financed *The Intruder* on an independent basis. Filmed on location in and near Charleston, Missouri, on a shoestring budget of $100,000, and utilizing some 300 local townspeople in its cast, Beaumont went along to oversee his script and to essay the cameo role of school principal Harley Paton.

The film was never successful in general release due to complications over its controversial nature, but it was later exploited under the misnomer, *I Hate Your Guts*, and, later, *Shame*.

The early Sixties also saw the production of seven other Beaumont screenplays: *The Premature Burial* (written in collaboration with Ray Russell); *Burn, Witch, Burn* (with Richard Matheson); *The Wonderful World of the Brothers Grimm* (with David P. Harmon and William Roberts); *The Haunted Palace*; *The Seven Faces of Dr. Lao*; *The Masque of the Red Death* (with R. Wright Campbell); and *Mr. Moses* (with Monja Danischevsky). In 1959, Beaumont also worked with Otto Preminger on *Bunny Lake is Missing*; however, Beaumont's script was never used and he remained uncredited on the film.

By now, film and television offers were flooding in. At times Beaumont juggled as many as ten projects simultaneously, and would have to farm the extra work out to fellow writers William F. Nolan, Jerry Sohl, John Tomerlin, Ray Russell and OCee Ritch. "I gather Chuck did too much, didn't he?" observes Bradbury. "He overloaded himself; then had to farm the extra work out to his friends. I think there's a similarity here to Rod Serling—Rod could never resist temptation. In other words, you've been neglected a good part of your life and no one is paying attention to you, and all of a sudden, people *are* paying attention: they're offering you jobs here and there. And the temptation is: Jeez! I never had anything. I better take that because it may not last! And that happens to all of us. So Chuck, I think suffered from 'Serling Syndrome.' Rod, in the last year of his life, did all those commercials, which he didn't have to do. But he couldn't resist, and I gather Chuck couldn't resist all these things; then it got to be a

real burden and he had to do something with it. So his
friends had to come to his aid."

Although he'd attained a high-level of creative and financial success in film and television, Beaumont had often
confided to close friends his desire to return to novel writing, and, in 1963, decided to finish *Where No Man Walks*—
a novel he'd begun in mid-1957. John Tomerlin explains,
"Once you begin working in Hollywood, unless you enter
it through the back door of doing novels and then writing
the screenplays and stories that you want to, you end up
taking assignments; usually, to a large extent, those assignments are other people's—you're meeting their requirements. Even if the story is original, you must adapt it to
their requirements. I think Chuck didn't like doing that,
and wanted very much to write books that he had seen
himself writing."

But time was running out on Beaumont.

By mid-1963, his concentration began to slip; he was
using Bromo Seltzer constantly to cope with ever increasing
headaches. Friends remarked he looked notably older than
his thirty-four years of age. By 1964, he could no longer
write. Meetings with producers turned disastrous. His
speech became slower, more deliberate. His concentration
worsened. Meanwhile, his family and friends desperately
tried to understand and treat his symptoms.

In the summer of 1964, after a battery of tests at UCLA,
Beaumont was diagnosed as having Alzheimer's Disease; he
faced premature senility, aging, and an early death. "The
saving grace to it," says Tomerlin, "if there is one, in a
disease like that, is he was not really aware, after the very
beginning, that there was anything wrong with him. When
he first began to show strong symptoms of it, he would
have kind of momentary flashes of great concern, as though
he saw something happening and couldn't understand what
it was. But it was a fairly gentle process."

Charles Beaumont died February 21, 1967 at the age of thirty-eight, his full potential never realized.

His last hardcover book was *Remember? Remember?*, and as Bill Nolan observes, "there is so *much* to remember about Charles Beaumont: [a] midnight call to California— Chuck calling from Chicago to tell me he planned to spend the day with Ian Fleming and why not join them? . . . the frenzied, nutty nights when we plotted Mickey Mouse adventures for the Disney Magazines . . . the bright, hot, exciting racing weekends at Palm Springs, Torrey Pines, Pebble Beach . . . the whirlwind trips to Paris and Nassau and New York . . . the sessions on the set at *Twilight Zone* when he'd exclaim, 'I write it and they create it in three dimensions. God, but it's *magic!*' . . . the fast, machinegun rattle of his typewriter as I talked to Helen in the kitchen while he worked in the den . . . the rush to the newsstand for the latest Beaumont story . . ."

Yet, Beaumont's magic is still with us, evidenced by the four children who survived him, and in the stories which follow. He was a craftsman, the kind of writer who could be relied upon to perform the ultimate function of fiction—entertainment—adding always some ambiance, echoing, indefinable, the reflection of a storyteller who was more than a voice . . .

Roger Anker
Los Angeles, California
January, 1987

PREFACE
by Christopher Beaumont

ROGER ANKER HAS put together a good and varied collection of Beaumont short stories. But he's done something more. He's wrapped each and every story in the loving embrace of a friend. Matheson, Tomerlin, Bradbury, Nolan; all names I grew up with. Each one a distinct and pleasant piece of my memory. A memory that includes the picture of a young boy falling asleep, night after night, to the sound of his father's typewriter, the keys finally becoming a familiar lullaby.

Do not think for a minute that the style and clarity found in these stories was not the result of countless hours spent shaping and reshaping, and then reshaping again, the words.

But somehow, in the midst of his passion for the words, he found time enough, and love enough to be a father. And such is the quality of that love that it sustained his children; Catherine, Elizabeth, Gregory and myself, through the stormy weather that followed his death and the death of our mother.

Not only sustained, but inspired and confirmed our suspicions that certain things never die: a story well told, the steadfast loyalty of a good and true friend, and the memory of a father who somewhere knew that his time was short, and so passionately shared all that he had to share.

And even now, some nights, I vaguely hear the typewriter keys tapping in the other room. The single bell at the end of the carriage. The sound of the roller twisting another lucky page into the works. And then the tapping starts again and I begin to drift to sleep.

Good night, Father

THE HOWLING MAN

MISS GENTILBELLE

Introduction by Ray Bradbury

It has been too many years. Quite suddenly I realize the old memory is failing.

I say this because I thought I remembered everything there was to remember about Charles Beaumont and "Miss Gentilbelle." Not so.

For some letters have come into my hands from that time more than 30 years ago, when Charles Beaumont was a young father and a more-than-aspiring writer. Those were the years when I promised Chuck if he showed up at my house every Wednesday evening with a new story, I would read it. It was a way of forcing him, and several other writer friends, to do one story a week, 52 weeks a year. Quality, I told them and him, came out of quantity. The more you wrote, the better you got. That is if your intentions were honorable and your dreams high and wondrous.

Chuck did just that. He not only wrote 52 short stories a year, but he revised them during the same weeks.

"Miss Gentilbelle" must have come under my eye on not just one or two, but three or four occasions. With this, and other stories, I wanted Chuck to learn how to cut his stories. Like every writer in the history of the world, including myself, his stories ran long, and needed shaves and haircuts.

I wish I had some of the original versions of "Miss Gentilbelle"

*in front of me. For it is obvious, in re-reading our old letters, that
he revised and cut the story three or four times. At one point, I
rather rigorously insisted that if he didn't edit his stories, I wouldn't
read them. That seems terribly harsh, now that I look back. But
young writers are often stubborn, and remembering my own stubbornness about my immortal prose, I had to nag Chuck.*

*It was all worth while, as can be seen by the story here. Chuck
revised it at least four times, and I became its friendly agent to
several magazines. My luck was not good. When I had sent it
around five or six times, I passed the story on to other hands,
and it finally sold.*

*Further results can be seen in dozens and then scores of his
future tales. He became, in a very short while, not only my hon-
orary son, but first cousin to John Collier, Roald Dahl, Nigel
Kneale, and a lot of other story tellers that we admired together.
Until, at last, he became and stayed the one and only Charles
Beaumont.*

*I am glad that we were friends. I am proud that I gently
nagged "Miss Gentilbelle" at various times. Long after the nags
are forgotten, the story will stand. Here is the early Chuck Beaumont, promising even greater things that he lived just long enough,
thank God, to do.*

———

ROBERT SETTLED ON his favorite branch of the old elm
and watched Miss Gentilbelle. The night was very black,
but he was not afraid, although he was young enough to
be afraid. And he was old enough to hate, but he didn't
hate. He merely watched.

Miss Gentilbelle sat straight and stiff in the faded chair
by the window. The phonograph had been turned down
and she sat, listening. In her hands were a teacup, faintly
flowered, and a saucer that did not match. She held them

with great care and delicacy and the tea had long ago turned cold.

Robert decided to watch Miss Gentilbelle's hands.

They were thin and delicate, like the cup and saucer. But he saw that they were also wrinkled and not smooth like his own. One of the fingers was encircled by a tarnished yellow band and the skin was very, very white.

Now the phonograph began to repeat toward the end of the record and Miss Gentilbelle let it go for a while before she moved.

When she rose, Robert became frightened and cried loudly. He had forgotten how to climb down from the tree. Miss Gentilbelle heard him crying and after she had replaced the record in its album she went to the window and raised it halfway to the top.

"Roberta," she said. "I'm surprised. Quite surprised." She paused. "Trees are for monkeys and birds, not little girls. Do you remember when I told you that?"

The soft bayou wind took Miss Gentilbelle's words and carried them off. But Robert knew what had been said.

"Yes, Mother. Trees are for monkeys and birds."

"Very well. Come down from there. I wish to speak with you."

"Yes, Mother." Robert remembered. Cautiously at first, and then with greater daring, he grasped small limbs with his hands and descended to the ground. Before the last jump a jagged piece of bark caught on his gown and ripped a long hole in the gauzy cloth.

The jump hurt his feet but he ran up the splintery steps fast because he had recognized the look in Miss Gentilbelle's eyes. When he got to the living room, he tried nervously to hold the torn patch of cloth together.

He knocked.

"Come in, Roberta." The pale woman beckoned, ges-

tured. "Sit over there, please, in the big chair." Her eyes
were expressionless, without color, like clots of mucus. She
folded her hands. "I see that you have ruined your best
gown," she whispered. "A pity, it once belonged to your
grandmother. You should have been in bed asleep, but instead you were climbing trees and that is why you ruined
your gown. It's made of silk—did you know that, Roberta?
Pure silk. Soft and fragile, like the wings of a dove; not
the coarse burlap they're using nowadays. Such a pity . . .
It can never be replaced." She was quiet for a time; then
she leaned forward. "Tell me, Roberta—what did you
promise when I gave you the gown?"

Robert hesitated. There were no words to come. He
stared at the frayed Oriental rug and listened to his heart.

"Roberta, don't you think you ought to answer me?
What did you promise?"

"That—" Robert's voice was mechanical. "That I would
take good care of it."

"And have you taken good care of it?"

"No, Mother, I . . . haven't."

"Indeed you have not. You have been a wicked girl."

Robert bit flesh away from the inside of his mouth.
"Can't it be mended?" he asked.

Miss Gentilbelle put a finely woven handkerchief to her
mouth and gasped. "Mended! Shall I take it to a tailor and
have him sew a patch?" Her eyes came to life, flashing.
"When a butterfly has lost its wing, what happens?"

"It can't fly."

"True. It cannot fly. It is dead, it is no longer a butterfly. Roberta—there are few things that can ever be
mended. None of the really worthwhile things can be." She
sat thoughtfully silent for several minutes, sipping her cold
tea.

Robert waited. His bladder began to ache.

"You have been an exceedingly wicked girl, Roberta,

and you must be punished. Do you know how I shall punish you?"

Robert looked up and saw his mother's face. "Shall you beat me?"

"Beat you? Really, do I seem so crude? When have I ever beaten you? No. What are a few little bruises. They disappear and are forgotten. You must be taught a lesson. You must be taught never to play tricks again."

The hot night air went through the great house and into his body, but when Miss Gentilbelle took his hand in hers, he felt cold. Her fingers seemed suddenly to be made of iron. They hurt his hand.

Then, in silence, the two walked from the living room, down the vast, dark hall, past the many dirty doorways and, finally, into the kitchen.

"Now, Roberta," Miss Gentilbelle said, "run up to your room and bring Margaret to me. Instantly."

He had stopped crying: now he felt ill. Robert knew what his mother was going to do.

He reached up and clutched her arm. "But—"

"I shall count up to thirty-five."

Robert ran out of the room and up the stairs, counting quickly to himself. When he entered his bedroom he went to the small cage and took it from the high shelf. He shook it. The parakeet inside fluttered white and green wings, moved its head in tiny machine movements.

Twenty seconds had passed.

Robert inserted his finger through the slender bars, touched the parakeet's hard bill. "I'm sorry, Margaret," he said. "I'm sorry." He put his face up close to the cage and allowed the bird to nip gently at his nose.

Then he shook the confusion from his head, and ran back downstairs.

Miss Gentilbelle was waiting. In her right hand was a large butcher knife. "Give Margaret to me," she said.

Robert gave the cage to do his mother.

"Why do you force me to do these things, child?" asked Miss Gentilbelle.

She took the parakeet from its cage and watched the bird struggle.

Robert's heart beat very fast and he couldn't move; but, he did not hate, yet.

Miss Gentilbelle held the parakeet in her left hand so that one wing was free. The only sound was the frantic fluttering of this wing.

She put the blade of the knife up close to the joint of the wing.

Robert tried not to look. He managed to stare away from Margaret's eyes; his gaze held on his mother's hands.

She held the knife stationary, frozen, touching the feathers.

Why didn't she do it! Get it over with! It was like the time she had killed Edna, holding the knife above the puppy's belly until—

"And now, when you wish you had your little friend, perhaps you will think twice before you climb trees."

There was a quick movement, a glint of silver, an unearthly series of small sounds.

The wing fluttered to the floor.

"Margaret!"

The parakeet screamed for a considerable time before Miss Gentilbelle pressed the life from it. When it was silent, as last, the white fingers that clutched it were stained with a dark, thin fluid.

Miss Gentilbelle put down the butcher knife, and took Robert's hand.

"Here is Margaret," she said. "Take her. Yes. Now: Shall we mend Margaret?"

Robert did not answer.

"Shall we put her together again, glue back her pretty little wing?"

"No, Mother. Nothing can be mended."

"Very good. Perhaps you will learn." Miss Gentilbelle smiled. "Now take the bird and throw it into the stove."

Robert held the dead parakeet gently in his hands, and secretly stroked its back. Then he dropped it into the ashes.

"Take off your gown and put it in, also."

As Robert drew off the thin blue nightgown, he looked directly into his mother's eyes.

"Something you would like to say to me, Roberta?"

"No, Mother."

"Excellent. Put in some papers and light them. And when you've finished that, get a rag from the broom closet and wipe the floor. Then put the rag into the stove."

"Yes, Mother."

"Roberta."

"Yes?"

"Do you understand why Margaret was killed?"

This time he wanted to say no, he did not understand. Not at all. There was such confusion in his head.

"Yes, Mother. I understand."

"And will you climb trees any more when you ought to be in bed?"

"No. I won't climb any more trees."

"I think that is true. Good night, Roberta. You may go up to your room, afterwards."

"Good night, Mother."

Miss Gentilbelle walked to the sink and carefully washed her hands. She then returned to the living room and put a record on the phonograph.

When Robert went upstairs, she smiled at him.

He lay still in the bed. The swamp wind was slamming shutters and creaking boards throughout the house, so he could not sleep. From a broken slat in his own shutter, moonlight shredded in upon the room, making of everything dark shadows.

He watched the moonlight and thought about the things he was beginning to know.

They frightened him. The books—The pictures of the people who looked like him and were called boys, and who looked like Miss Gentilbelle and were called girls, or ladies, or women . . .

He rose from the bed, put his bathrobe about him, and walked to the door. It opened noiselessly, and when it did, he saw that the entire hallway was streaming with dark, cold light. The old Indian's head on the wall looked down at him with a plaster frown, and he could make out most of the stained photographs and wrinkled paintings.

It was so quiet, so quiet that he could hear the frogs and crickets outside; and the moths, bumping and thrashing against the walls, the windows.

Softly he tiptoed down the long hall to the last doorway and then back again to his room. Perspiration began to form under his arms and between his legs, and he lay down once more.

But sleep would not come. Only the books, the knowledge, the confusion. Dancing. Burning.

Finally, his heart jabbing, loud, Robert rose and silently retraced his footsteps to the door.

He rapped, softly, and waited.

There was no answer.

He rapped again, somewhat harder than before; but only once.

He cupped his hands to his mouth and whispered into the keyhole: *"Drake!"*

Silence. He touched the doorknob. It turned.

He went into the room.

A large man was lying across a bulky, posterless bed. Robert could hear the heavy guttural breathing, and it made him feel good.

"Drake. Please wake up."

Robert continued to whisper. The large man moved, jerked, turned around. "Minnie?"

"No, Drake. It's me."

The man sat upright, shook his head violently, and pulled open a shutter. The room lit up.

"Do you know what will happen if she finds you here?"

Robert sat down on the bed, close to the man. "I couldn't sleep. I wanted to talk to you. She won't hear—"

"You shouldn't be here. You know what she'll say."

"Just a little while. Won't you talk a little while with me, like you used to?"

The man took a bottle from beneath the bed, filled a glass, drank half. "Look here," he said. "Your mother doesn't like us to be talking together. Don't you remember what she did last time? You wouldn't want that to happen again, would you?"

Robert smiled. "It won't. I don't have anything left for her to kill. She could only hit me now and she wouldn't hit you. She never hits you."

The man smiled, strangely.

"Drake."

"What?"

"Why doesn't she want me to talk to you?"

The man coughed. "It's a long story. Say I'm the gardener and she's the mistress of the house and you're her . . . daughter, and it isn't right that we should mix."

"But why?"

"Never mind."

"Tell me."

"Go back to bed, Bobbie. I'll see you next week when your mother takes her trip into town."

"No, Drake, please talk a little more with me. Tell me about town; please tell me about town."

"You'll see some day—"

"Why do you always call me 'Bobbie'? Mother calls me Roberta. Is my name Bobbie?"

The man shrugged. "No. Your name is Roberta."

"Then why do you call me Bobbie? Mother says there is no such name."

The man said nothing, and his hand trembled more.

"Drake."

"Yes?"

"Drake, am I *really* a little girl?"

The man got up and walked over to the window. He opened the other shutter and stood for a long while staring into the night. When he turned around, Robert saw that his face was wet.

"Bobbie, what do you know about God?"

"Not very much. It is mentioned in the George Bernard Shaw book I am reading, but I don't understand."

"Well, God is who must help your mother now, Bobbie boy!"

Robert's fists tightened. He knew—he'd known it for a long time. A *boy* . . .

The man had fallen onto the bed. His hands reached for the bottle, but it was empty.

"It's good," the man said. "Ask your questions. But don't ask them of me. Go away now. Go back to your room!"

Robert wondered if his friend were ill, but he felt too strange to be with anyone. He opened the door and hurried back to his room.

And as he lay down, his brain hurt with the new thoughts. He had learned many wonderful things this night. He could almost identify the feeling that gnawed at the pit of his stomach whenever he thought of Miss Gentilbelle . . .

Robert did not sleep before the first signs of dawn appeared. And then he dreamed of dead puppies and dead birds.

They were whispering something to him.

"Why, Roberta," said Miss Gentilbelle, in a soft, shocked voice. "You haven't worn your scent this morning. Did you forget it?"

"Yes."

"A pity. There's nothing like the essence of blossoms to put a touch of freshness about everything."

"I'm sorry."

"I should be displeased if you were to forget your scent again. It's not ladylike to go about smelling of your flesh."

"Yes, Mother."

Miss Gentilbelle munched her toast slowly and looked into Robert's flushed face.

"Roberta, do you feel quite well?"

"Yes."

Miss Gentilbelle put her hand to Robert's forehead. "You do seem somewhat feverish. I think we will dispense with today's lesson in Jeanne d'Arc. Immediately following your criticism on the Buxtehude you will go to bed."

The breakfast was finished in silence as Miss Gentilbelle read a book. Then they went into the living room.

Robert hated the music. It sounded in the faded room like the crunch of shoes on gravel, and the bass notes were all dissolved into an ugly roar.

They listened for one hour without speaking, and Robert moved only to change the records.

"Now, then, Roberta," Miss Gentilbelle said. "Would you agree with Mr. Locke that Buxtehude in these works surpasses the bulk of Bach's organ music?"

Robert shook his head. He knew he would have to answer. "I think Mr. Locke is right."

And then it struck him that he had actually lied before,

many times. But perhaps he never knew before that he disliked music.

"Very good. No need to continue. The facts are self-evident. Go to your room and undress. Dinner will be prepared at twelve-thirty."

Robert curtsied and began to walk to the stairway.

"Oh, Roberta."

"Yes, Mother?"

"Did you by any chance see Mr. Franklin last night?"

Robert's throat went dry. It was difficult to hold on to his thoughts. "No, Mother, I did not."

"You know you should never see that evil man, don't you? You must always avoid him, never speak a word to him. You remember when I told you that, don't you?"

"Yes, Mother."

"You disobeyed me once. You would never dream of doing that again, would you, Roberta?"

"No, Mother."

"Very good. Retire to your room and be dressed for dinner by twelve."

Robert went up the stairs slowly, for he could not see them. Tears welled in his eyes and burned them, and he thought he would never reach the top.

When he went into his room he saw Margaret for a moment and then she was gone.

He sat on the bed and proceeded to remove his clothes. They were dainty clothes, thin and worn, demanding of great care. He took them off lightly with a touch and looked at each garment for a long time.

The patent leather shoes, the pink stockings, the pale yellow dress—he laid them neatly on the sofa and looked at them. Then, when all the clothes had been removed, he went to the mirror and looked into it.

Robert didn't know what he saw and he shook his head. Nothing seemed clear; one moment he felt like shouting and another, like going to sleep. Then he became fright-

ened and leapt into the large easy chair, where he drew his
legs and arms about him. He sat whimpering softly, with
his eyes open, dreaming.

A little bird flew out of a corner and fluttered its wings
at him. Margaret's wing, the one Miss Gentilbelle had cut
off, fell from the ceiling into his lap and he held it to his
face before it disappeared.

Presently the room was full of birds, all fluttering their
wings and crying, crying to Robert. He cried, too, but
softly.

He pulled his arms and legs closer to him and wrenched
at the blond curls that fell across his eyes. The birds flew
at him and around him and then their wings started to fall
off. And as they did, the brown liquid he remembered
soaked into all the feathers. Some of it got on Robert and
when it did, he cried aloud and shut his eyes.

Then the room seemed empty. There were no birds. Just
a puppy. A little dog with its belly laid open, crawling up
to Robert in a wake of spilled entrails, looking into his
eyes.

Robert fell to the floor and rolled over several times, his
body quivering, flecks of saliva streaming from his lips.

"Edna, Edna, don't go away."

The puppy tried to walk further but could not. Its round
low body twitched like Robert's, and it made snuffling
noises.

Robert crawled to a corner.

"Edna, please. It wasn't me, it wasn't, really . . ."

And then a cloud of blackness covered Robert's mind,
and he dropped his head on his breast.

When he awakened he was in bed and Drake was standing over him, shaking his shoulders.

"Bobbie, what is it?"

"I don't know. All of sudden I saw Margaret and Edna
and all the birds. They were mad, Drake. They were mad!"

The man stroked Robert's forehead gently.

"It's all right. You don't have to be afraid now. You just had a bad nightmare, that's all. I found you laying on the floor."

"It seemed very real this time."

"I know. They sometimes do. Why, I could hear you crying all the way down the hall!"

"She didn't hear me, did she?"

"No, she didn't hear you."

Then Robert saw the heavy brown bag. "Drake, why have you got that suitcase?"

The man coughed and tried to kick the bag underneath the bed. "It's nothing. Just some equipment for the yard."

"No, no it isn't, Drake. I can tell. You're going away!"

"It's equipment for the yard, I tell you."

"Please don't go away, Drake. Please don't. Please don't."

The man tightened his fists and coughed again.

"Now you look, Bobbie. I've just got to go away for a little trip, and I'll be back before you know it. And maybe then we can go off somewhere together. I'm going to find out about it, but you mustn't say a word to your mother. Hear?"

Robert looked up, confused. Something fluttered. He could see it, from the corner of his eye.

The man was dirty and he smelled of alcohol, but it made Robert feel good when he touched him.

"Really? You mean *us*?"

"Bobbie. You've got to tell me something first. Do you love your mother?"

He didn't have to think about it. "No, she always kills things, and always hurts things. I don't love her."

The man spoke under his breath. "I've wanted to do this for a long time."

Something crawled in a corner. Robert could almost see it. "Drake," he said, "have you ever killed anything?"

Perspiration stood out on the man's forehead. He answered as if he had not heard.

"Only once, Bobbie. Only once did I kill."

"What was it? An animal?"

"No. It was worse, Bobbie. I killed a human spirit—a soul."

"Mother does it all the time!"

"I know. There's been a lot of death in this house . . . But here now, lad, are you over your nightmare?"

Robert tried not to look up.

"Are we really going away when you get back? Away from Mother and this place, just you and me, Drake? Promise me?"

"Yes, boy. Yes, we are!"

The man took Robert's hand in his and held it hard.

"Now you see here. If she learns of this there'll be a lot of trouble. Something might go wrong. So, whatever you do, don't you let on to her what's happened. I'll see the authorities and tell them everything and you'll get out of here. And we'll be free, you and me, boy!"

Robert didn't say anything. He was looking at a corner.

"Bobbie, you're not old enough yet to know everything about your mother. She wasn't always like she is now. And I wasn't, either. Something just happened and . . . well, I'll tell you about it later so you'll understand. But right now, I want you to do something. After I leave, you get yourself another little pet, a frog or something. Keep it in this room. She'll know nothing's changed, then. She'll know you haven't been talking to me. Get that frog, Bobbie, and I'll be back so that you can have it always as a friend. Always.

"Goodbye, lad. You'll not be staying with that crazy woman much longer, I promise you."

Robert smiled and watched Drake go toward the door.

"Will you really come back, Drake?"

"Nothing on earth is going to stop me, son. I knew that

when I saw you last night; I knew it when you asked me those questions. The first normal things I'd heard for . . . Yes, son, I'll be back for you."

Robert did not understand much. Only about the frog. He would find himself a pet and keep it.

The movement in the corners had stopped, and Robert could think for only a little while before he fell into a sound sleep. So sound a sleep that he did not hear Miss Gentilbelle coming up the stairs and he did not see her face when she stepped into the room.

"Roberta, you're late. You were told to be downstairs promptly at twelve-thirty and instead I find you resting like a lady of great leisure. Get up, girl!"

Robert's eyes opened and he wanted to scream.

Then he apologized, remembering to mention nothing of Drake. He put on his dress quickly and went downstairs after Miss Gentilbelle.

He scarcely knew what he was eating; the food was tasteless in his mouth. But he remembered things and answered questions as he always had before.

During dessert Miss Gentilbelle folded her book and laid it aside.

"Mr. Franklin has gone away. Did you know that?"

"No, Mother, I did not. Where has he gone?"

"Not very far—he will be back. He's sure to come back; he always does. Roberta, did Mr. Franklin say anything to you before he left?"

"No, Mother, he did not. I didn't know Mr. Franklin had gone away."

Robert looked at Miss Gentilbelle's hands, watched the way the thin fingers curled about themselves, how they arched delicately in the air.

He looked at the yellow band and again at the fingers. Such white fingers, such dry, white fingers . . .

"Mother."

"Yes?"

"May I go into the yard for a little while?"

"Yes. You have been naughty and kept me waiting dinner but I shall not punish you. See you remember the kindness and be in the living room in one half hour. You have your criticism to write."

"Yes, Mother."

Robert walked down the steps and into the yard. A soft breeze went through his hair and lifted the golden curls and billowed out his dress. The sun shone hotly but he did not notice. He walked to the first clump of trees and sat carefully on the grass. He waited.

And then, after a time, a plump frog hopped into the clearing and Robert quickly cupped his hands over it. The frog leapt about violently, bumping its body against Robert's palms, and then it was still.

Robert loosened the thin cloth belt around his waist and put the frog under his dress, so that it did not protrude noticeably.

Then he stroked its back from outside the dress. The frog did not squirm or resist.

Robert thought a while.

"I shall call you Drake," he said.

When Robert re-entered the kitchen he saw that Miss Gentilbelle was still reading. He excused himself and went up to his bedroom, softly, so that he would not be heard, and hid the frog in his dresser.

He began to feel odd then. Saliva was forming inside his mouth, boiling hot.

The corners of his room looked alive.

He went downstairs.

". . . and Jeanne d'Arc was burned at the stake, her body consumed by flames. And there was only the sound of the flames, and crackling straw and wood: she did not cry out once." Miss Gentilbelle sighed. "There was punishment for you, Roberta. Did you profit from her story?"

Robert said yes, he had profited.

"So it is with life. The Maid of Orleans was innocent of any crime; she was filled with the greatest virtue and goodness, yet they murdered her. Her own people turned upon her and burnt the flesh away from her bones! Roberta—this is my question. What would *you* have done if you'd been Jeanne d'Arc and could have lived beyond the stake?"

"I—don't know."

"That," said Miss Gentilbelle, "is your misfortune. I must speak with you now. I've purposely put off this discussion so that you might think. But you've thought and remain bathed in your own iniquity. Child, did you honestly suspect that you could go babbling about the house with that drunken fool without my knowledge?"

Robert's heart froze; the hurting needles came.

"I listened to you, and heard a great deal of what was said. First, let us have an answer to a question. Do you think that you are a boy?"

Robert did not answer.

"You do." Miss Gentilbelle moved close. "Well, as it happens, you are not. Not in any sense of the word. For men are animals—do you understand? Tell me, are you an animal or a human being, Roberta?"

"A human being."

"Exactly! Then obviously you cannot be a boy, isn't that so? You are a girl, a young lady: never, never forget that. Do you hear?"

"Yes, Mother."

"That, however, is not the purpose of this discussion." Miss Gentilbelle calmed swiftly. "I am not disturbed that your mind plays tricks on you. No. What does disturb me is that you should lie and cheat so blatantly to your mother. You see, I heard you talking."

Robert's head throbbed uncontrollably. His temples seemed about to burst with pain.

"So—he has gone to get the authorities to take you away from me! Because your mother is so cruel to you, so viciously cruel to the innocent young child! And you will both ride off on a white horse to wonderful lands where no one is mean . . ." Her cheeks trembled. Her eyes seemed glazed. "Roberta, can you be so naive? Mr. Franklin is *accustomed* to such promises: I know." She put a hand to her brow, moved thin fingers across the flesh. "At this moment," she said, distantly, "he is in a bar, drinking himself into a stupor. Or perhaps one of the Negro brothels—I understand he's a well-known figure there."

Miss Gentilbelle did not smile. Robert was confused: this was unlike her. He could catch just a little something in her eyes.

"And so you listened to him and loved him and you wait for him. I understand, Roberta; I understand very well indeed. You love the gardener and you will go away with him!" Something happened; her tone changed, abruptly. It was no longer soft and distant. "You must be punished. It ought to be enough when you finally realize that your Drake will never come back to carry you off. But—it is not enough. There must be more."

Robert heard very little now.

"Stop gazing off as if you didn't hear me. Now—bring your little friend here."

Robert felt the seed growing within him. He could feel it hard and growing inside his heart. And he couldn't think now.

Miss Gentilbelle took Robert's wrist in her hand and clutched it until her nails bit deep into the flesh. "I saw you put that animal in your dress and take it upstairs. Fetch it to me this instant."

Robert looked into his mother's eyes. Miss Gentilbelle stood above him, her hands clasped now to the frayed white collars of her dress. She was trembling and her words did not quite knit together.

"Get it, bring it to me. Do you hear?"

Robert nodded dumbly, and went upstairs to his room. It was alive. Birds filled it, and puppies. Little puppies, crying, whimpering with pain.

He walked straight to the dresser and withdrew the frog, holding it securely in his hand.

Green and white wings brushed his face as he went back toward the door.

He walked downstairs and into the living room. Miss Gentilbelle was standing in the doorway; her eyes danced over the wriggling animal.

Robert said nothing as they walked into the kitchen.

"I am sure, Roberta, that when you see this—and when you see that no one ever comes to take you away—that the best thing is merely to be a good girl. It is enough. To be a good girl and do as Mother says."

She took the frog and held it tightly. She did not seem to notice that Robert's mouth was moist, that his eyes stared directly through her.

She did not seem to hear the birds and the puppies whispering to Robert, or see them clustering about him.

She held the frog in one hand, and with the other pulled a large knife from the knife-holder. It was rusted and without luster, but its edge was keen enough, and its point sharp.

"You must think about this, child. About how you forced your mother into punishing you." She smiled. "Tell me this: have you named your little friend?"

"Yes. His name is Drake."

"Drake! How very appropriate!"

Miss Gentilbelle did not look at her son. She put the

frog on the table and turned it over on its back. The creature thrashed violently.

Then she put the point of the knife on the frog's belly,
paused, waited, and pushed inwards. The frog twitched as
she held it and drew the blade slowly across, slowly, deep
inside the animal.

In a while, when it had quieted, she dropped the frog
into a box of kindling.

She did not see Robert pick up the knife and hold it in
his hand.

Robert had stopped thinking. Snowy flecks of saliva dotted his face, and his eyes had no life to them. He listened
to his friends. The puppies, crawling about his feet, yipping
painfully. The birds, dropping their bloody wings, flying
crazily about his head, screaming, calling. And now the
frogs, hopping, croaking . . .

He did not think. He listened.

"Yes . . . yes."

Miss Gentilbelle turned quickly, and her laughter died
as she did so. She threw her hands out and cried—but the
knife was already sliding through her pale dress, and
through her pale flesh.

The birds screeched and the puppies howled and the frogs
croaked. Yes, yes, yes, yes!

And the knife came out and went in again, it came out
and went in again.

Then Robert slipped on the wet floor and fell. He rolled
over and over, crying, softly, and laughing, and making
other sounds.

Miss Gentilbelle said nothing. Her thin white fingers
were curled about the handle of the butcher knife, but she
no longer tried to pull it from her stomach.

Presently her wracked breathing stopped.

Robert rolled into a corner, and drew his legs and arms
about him, tight.

He held the dead frog to his face and whispered to it . . .

The large red-faced man walked heavily through the cypressed land. He skillfully avoided bushes and pits and came, finally, to the clearing that was the entrance to the great house.

He walked to the wrought-iron gate that joined to the high brick wall that was topped with broken glass and curved spikes.

He opened the gate, crossed the yard, and went up to the decaying, splintered steps.

He applied a key to the old oak door.

"Minnie!" he called. "Got a little news for you! Hey, Minnie!"

The silent stairs answered him.

He went into the living room, upstairs to Robert's room. "Minnie!"

He walked back to the hallway. An uncertain grin covered his face. "They're not going to let you keep him! How's that? How do you like it?"

The warm bayou wind sighed through the shutters.

The man made fists with his fingers, paused, walked down the hall, and opened the kitchen door.

The sickly odor went to his nostrils first. The words "Jesus God" formed on his lips, but he made no sound.

He stood very still, for a long time.

The blood on Miss Gentilbelle's face had dried, but on her hands and where it had gathered on the floor, it was still moist.

Her fingers were stiff around the knife.

The man's eyes traveled to the far corner. Robert was huddled there, chanting softly—flat, dead, singsong words.

". . . wicked . . . must be punished . . . wicked girl . . ."

Robert threw his head back and smiled up at the ceiling.

The man walked to the corner and lifted Robert to his chest and held him tightly, crushingly.

"Bobbie," he said. "Bobbie. Bobbie. Bobbie."

The warm night wind turned cold.

It sang through the halls and through the rooms of the great house in the forest.

And then it left, frightened and alone.

THE VANISHING AMERICAN

Introduction by John Tomerlin

On his way home, after working late at the office, Mr. Minchell discovers that he is, in fact, vanishing. To his employer, store clerks, bartenders—even his own family—he either has become literally invisible, or so insignificant that his presence no longer can be detected. Only through an act of daring, an assertion of his individuality, does Mr. Minchell reappear; gain attention; prove his existence.

The pun is a recurrent theme in Charles Beaumont's titles—"Fair Lady" being another, obvious, example; "Point of Honor" and "Black Country" two less apparent ones—and is some indication of the sort of writer he was. A storyteller, a spinner of yarns, balladeer, prophet; a discoverer of the wondrous amidst the commonplace. His ideas sprang from the germinal "What if . . . ?"

What if homosexuality were the norm instead of inversion; what if a woman sought rape instead of avoiding it; and what if, in lieu of the assimilation of aboriginals, an American actually did vanish?

The sometimes-obvious answers were couched in terms of characters and events so unexpected (occasionally unpleasant, frequently macabre, yet invariably real) that they laid bare new truths and new dimensions of understanding.

*This is because the pure act of imagination that is a Beaumont
story is deeply rooted in personal history. The office where Mr.
Minchell works adding up figures on a manifest, is the office of
a southern California trucking firm for which Charles performed
similar, agonizing services in 1950. "King Richard" is one of the
stone lions at the entrance to the public library on 5th Avenue
near 42nd Street, which he often visited while living in New York.*

*To those who knew him best, the trappings and imagery of his
stories are funhouse mirrors through which his real life can be
glimpsed: people, places, actual events. There was the early loss
of his father, and strained relationships with his mother; a pair
of maiden aunts in Washington who raised him—eccentrics to
say the least; and periods of serious illnesses as a child. All appear repeatedly in his stories.*

*The most familiar character of all, though, one that appears
time and again in different guises, is alone or has only one other
equally powerless person to talk to; is sometimes the possessor of
a unique gift or talent, sometimes not; and must, through an act
of daring or personal risk, achieve recognition and appreciation.*

*"I'll be seeing you," the stranger in the crowd says. "That's
right," Mr. Minchell says from his seat atop the lion. "You'll be
seeing me."*

Fear not, old friend, we see you still.

HE GOT THE notion shortly after five o'clock; at least, a
part of him did, a small part hidden down beneath all the
conscious cells—*he* didn't get the notion until some time
later. At exactly five P.M., the bell rang. At two minutes
after, the chairs began to empty. There was the vast slamming of drawers, the straightening of rulers, the sound of
bones snapping and mouths yawning and feet shuffling
tiredly.

Mr. Minchell relaxed. He rubbed his hands together and relaxed and thought how nice it would be to get up and go home, like the others. But of course there was the tape, only three-quarters finished. He would have to stay.

He stretched and said good night to the people who filed past him. As usual, no one answered. When they had gone, he set his fingers pecking again over the keyboard. The *click-clicking* grew loud in the suddenly still office, but Mr. Minchell did not notice. He was lost in the work. Soon, he knew, it would be time for the totaling, and his pulse quickened at the thought of this.

He lit a cigarette. Heart tapping, he drew in smoke and released it.

He extended his right hand and rested his index and middle fingers on the metal bar marked TOTAL. A mile-long ribbon of paper lay gathered on the desk, strangely festive. He glanced at it, then at the manifest sheet. The figure 18037448 was circled in red. He pulled breath into his lungs, locked it there; then he closed his eyes and pressed the TOTAL bar.

There was a smooth low metallic grinding, followed by absolute silence.

Mr. Minchell opened one eye, dragged it from the ceiling on down to the adding machine.

He groaned, slightly.

The total read: 18037447.

"God." He stared at the figure and thought of the fifty-three pages of manifest, the three thousand separate rows of figures that would have to be checked again "God."

The day was lost, now. Irretrievably. It was too late to do anything. Madge would have supper waiting, and F.J. didn't approve of overtime; also . . .

He looked at the total again. At the last two digits.

He sighed. Forty-seven. And thought, startled: Today, for the Lord's sake, is my birthday! Today I am forty—

what?—forty-seven. And that explains the mistake, I suppose. Subconscious kind of thing . . .

Slowly he got up and looked around the deserted office.

Then he went to the dressing room and got his hat and his coat and put them on, carefully.

"Pushing fifty now . . ."

The outside hall was dark. Mr. Minchell walked softly to the elevator and punched the *Down* button. "Forty-seven," he said, aloud; then, almost immediately, the light turned red and the thick door slid back noisily. The elevator operator, a bird-thin, tan-fleshed girl, swiveled her head, looking up and down the hall. "Going down," she said.

"Yes," Mr. Minchell said, stepping forward.

"Going down." The girl clicked her tongue and muttered, "Damn kids." She gave the lattice gate a tired push and moved the smooth wooden-handled lever in its slot.

Odd, Mr. Minchell decided, was the word for this particular girl. He wished now that he had taken the stairs. Being alone with only one other person in an elevator had always made him nervous: now it made him very nervous. He felt the tension growing. When it became unbearable, he cleared his throat and said, "Long day."

The girl said nothing. She had a surly look, and she seemed to be humming something deep in her throat.

Mr. Minchell closed his eyes. In less than a minute—during which time he dreamed of the cables snarling, of the car being caught between floors, of himself trying to make small talk with the odd girl for six straight hours—he opened his eyes again and walked into the lobby, briskly.

The gate slammed.

He turned and started for the doorway. Then he paused, feeling a sharp increase in his heartbeat. A large, red-faced, magnificently groomed man of middle years stood directly beyond the glass, talking with another man.

Mr. Minchell pushed through the door, with effort. He's

seen me now, he thought. If he asks any questions, though, or anything, I'll just say I didn't put it on the time card; that ought to make it all right . . .

He nodded and smiled at the large man. "Good night, Mr. Diemel."

The man looked up briefly, blinked, and returned to his conversation.

Mr. Minchell felt a burning come into his face. He hurried on down the street. Now the notion—though it was not even that yet, strictly: it was more a vague feeling—swam up from the bottom of his brain. He remembered that he had not spoken directly to F.J. Diemel for over ten years, beyond a "Good morning" . . .

Ice-cold shadows fell off the tall buildings, staining the streets, now. Crowds of shoppers moved along the pavement like juggernauts, exhaustedly, but with great determination. Mr. Minchell looked at them. They all had furtive appearances, it seemed to him suddenly, even the children, as if each was fleeing from some hideous crime. They hurried along, staring.

But not, Mr. Minchell noticed, at him. Through him, yes. Past him. As the elevator operator had done, and now F.J. And had anyone said good night?

He pulled up his coat collar and walked toward the drugstore, thinking. He was forty-seven years old. At the current life-expectancy rate, he might have another seventeen or eighteen years left. And then death.

If you're not dead already.

He paused and for some reason remembered a story he'd once read in a magazine. Something about a man who dies and whose ghost takes up his duties, or something; anyway, the man didn't know he was dead—that was it. And at the end of the story, he runs into his own corpse.

Which is pretty absurd: he glanced down at his body. Ghosts don't wear $36 suits, nor do they have trouble pushing doors open, nor do their corns ache like blazes, and what the devil is wrong with me today?

He shook his head.

It was the tape, of course, and the fact that it was his birthday. That was why his mind was behaving so foolishly.

He went into the drugstore. It was an immense place, packed with people. He walked to the cigar counter, trying not to feel intimidated, and reached into his pocket. A small man elbowed in front of him and called loudly; "Gimme coupla nickels, will you, Jack?" The clerk scowled and scooped the change out of his cash register. The small man scurried off. Others took his place. Mr. Minchell thrust his arm forward. "A pack of Luckies, please," he said. The clerk whipped his fingers around a pile of cellophaned packages and, looking elsewhere, droned: "Twenty-six." Mr. Minchell put his twenty-six-cents-exactly on the glass shelf. The clerk shoved the cigarettes toward the edge and picked up the money, deftly. Not once did he lift his eyes.

Mr. Minchell pocketed the Luckies and went back out of the store. He was perspiring now, slightly, despite the chill wind. The word "ridiculous" lodged in his mind and stayed there. Ridiculous, yes, for heaven's sake. Still, he thought—now just answer the question—isn't it true? Can you honestly say that that clerk saw you?

Or that anybody saw you today?

Swallowing dryly, he walked another two blocks, always in the direction of the subway, and went into a bar called the Chez When. One drink would not hurt, one small, stiff, steadying shot.

The bar was a gloomy place, and not very warm, but there was a good crowd. Mr. Minchell sat down on a stool and folded his hands. The bartender was talking animatedly with an old woman, laughing with boisterous good humor from time to time. Mr. Minchell waited. Minutes passed. The bartender looked up several times, but never made a move to indicate that he had seen a customer.

Mr. Minchell looked at his old gray overcoat, the humbly floraled tie, the cheap sharkskin suit-cloth, and became aware of the extent to which he detested this ensemble. He sat there and detested his clothes for a long time. Then he glanced around. The bartender was wiping a glass, slowly.

All right, the hell with you. I'll go somewhere else.

He slid off the stool. Just as he was about to turn he saw the mirrored wall, pink-tinted and curved. He stopped, peering. Then he almost ran out of the bar.

Cold wind went into his head.

Ridiculous. The mirror was curved, you jackass. How do you expect to see yourself in curved mirrors?

He walked past high buildings, and now past the library and stone lion he had once, long ago, named King Richard; and he did not look at the lion, because he'd always wanted to ride the lion, ever since he was a child, and he'd promised himself he would do that, but he never did.

He hurried on to the subway, took the stairs by twos, and clattered across the platform in time to board the express.

It roared and thundered. Mr. Minchell held onto the strap and kept himself from staring. No one watched him. No one even glanced at him when he pushed his way to the door and went out onto the empty platform.

He waited. Then the train was gone, and he was alone.

He walked up the stairs. It was fully night now, a soft, unshadowed darkness. He thought about the day and the strange things that were gouging into his mind and thought about all this as he turned down a familiar street which led to his familiar apartment.

The door opened.

His wife was in the kitchen, he could see. Her apron flashed across the arch, and back, and across. He called: "Madge, I'm home."

Madge did not answer. Her movements were regular.

Jimmy was sitting at the table, drooling over a glass of pop, whispering to himself.

"I said—" Mr. Minchell began.

"Jimmy, get up and go to the bathroom, you hear? I've got your water drawn."

Jimmy promptly broke into tears. He jumped off the chair and ran past Mr. Minchell into the bedroom. The door slammed viciously.

"Madge."

Madge Minchell came into the room, tired and lined and heavy. Her eyes did not waver. She went into the bedroom, and there was a silence; then a sharp slapping noise, and a yelling.

Mr. Minchell walked to the bathroom, fighting down the small terror. He closed the door and locked it and wiped his forehead with a handkerchief. Ridiculous, he thought, and ridiculous and ridiculous. I am making something utterly foolish out of nothing. All I have to do is look in the mirror, and—

He held the handkerchief to his lips. It was difficult to breathe.

Then he knew that he was afraid, more so than ever before in a lifetime of being afraid.

Look at it this way, Minchell: why shouldn't *you vanish?*

"Young man, just you wait until your father gets here!"

He pushed the handkerchief against his mouth and leaned on the door and gasped.

"What do you mean, vanish?"

Go on, take a look. You'll see what I mean.

He tried to swallow, couldn't. Tried to wet his lips, found that they stayed dry.

"Lord—"

He slitted his eyes and walked to the shaving mirror and looked in.

His mouth fell open.

The mirror reflected nothing. It held nothing. It was dull and gray and empty.

Mr. Minchell stared at the glass, put out his hand, drew it back hastily.

He squinted. Inches away. There was a form now: vague, indistinct, featureless: but a form.

"Lord," he said. He understood why the elevator girl hadn't seen him, and why F.J. hadn't answered him, and why the clerk at the drugstore and the bartender and Madge . . .

"I'm not dead."

Of course you're not dead—not that way.

"—tan your hide, Jimmy Minchell, when he gets home."

Mr. Minchell suddenly wheeled and clicked the lock. He rushed out of the steam-filled bathroom, across the room, down the stairs, into the street, into the cool night.

A block from home he slowed to a walk.

Invisible! He said the word over and over, in a half-voice. He said it and tried to control the panic that pulled at his legs, and at his brain, and filled him.

Why?

A fat woman and a little girl passed by. Neither of them looked up. He started to call out and checked himself. No. That wouldn't do any good. There was no question about it now. He was invisible.

He walked on. As he did, forgotten things returned; they came and they left, too fast. He couldn't hold onto them. He could only watch, and remember. Himself as a youngster, reading: the Oz books, Tarzan, and Mr. Wells. Himself going to the University, wanting to teach, and meeting Madge; then not planning any more, and Madge changing, and all the dreams put away. For later. For the right time. And then Jimmy—little strange Jimmy, who ate filth and picked his nose and watched television, who had never read books, never; Jimmy, his son, whom he would never understand . . .

He walked by the edge of the park now. Then on past the park, through a maze of familiar and unfamiliar neighborhoods. Walking, remembering, looking at the people and feeling pain because he knew that they could not see him, not now or ever again, because he had vanished. He walked and remembered and felt pain.

All the stagnant dreams came back. Fully. The trip to Italy he'd planned. The open sports car, bad weather be damned. The firsthand knowledge that would tell him whether he did or did not approve of bullfighting. The book . . .

Then something occurred to him. It occurred to Mr. Minchell that he had not just suddenly vanished, like that, after all. No; he had been vanishing gradually for a long while. Every time he said good morning to that bastard Diemel he got a little harder to see. Every time he put on his horrible suit he faded. The process of disappearing was set into action every time he brought his pay check home and turned it over to Madge, every time he kissed her, or listened to her vicious unending complaints, or decided against buying that novel, or punched the adding machine he hated so, or . . .

Certainly.

He had vanished for Diemel and the others in the office years ago. And for strangers right afterwards. Now even Madge and Jimmy couldn't see him. And he could barely see himself, even in a mirror.

It made terrible sense to him. *Why* shouldn't *you disappear*? Well, why, indeed? There wasn't any very good reason, actually. None. And this, in a nightmarish sort of a way, made it as brutally logical as a perfect tape.

Then he thought about going back to work tomorrow and the next day and the day after that. He'd have to, of course. He couldn't let Madge and Jimmy starve; and, besides, what else would he do? It wasn't as if anything important had changed. He'd go on punching the clock and saying good morning to people who didn't see him, and he'd run the tapes and come home beat, nothing altered, and some day he'd die and that would be that.

All at once he felt tired.

He sat down on a cement step and sighed. Distantly he realized that he had come to the library. He sat there, watching the people, feeling the tiredness seep through him, thickly.

Then he looked up.

Above him, black and regal against the sky, stood the huge stone lion. Its mouth was open, and the great head was raised proudly.

Mr. Minchell smiled. King Richard. Memories scattered in his mind: old King Richard, well, my God, here we are.

He got to his feet. Fifty thousand times, at least, he had passed this spot, and every time he had experienced that instant of wild craving. Less so of late, but still, had it ever completely gone? He was amazed to find that now the childish desire was welling up again, stronger than ever before. Urgently.

He rubbed his cheek and stood there for several minutes. It's the most ridiculous thing in the world, he thought, and I must be going out of my mind, and that must explain everything. But, he inquired of himself, even so, why not?

After all, I'm invisible. No one can see me. Of course, it didn't have to be this way, not really. I don't know, he went on, I mean, I believed that I was doing the right thing. Would it have been right to go back to the University and the hell with Madge? I couldn't change that, could I? Could I have done anything about that, even if I'd known?

He nodded sadly.

All right, but don't make it any worse. Don't for God's sake *dwell* on it!

To his surprise, Mr. Minchell found that he was climbing up the concrete base of the statue. It ripped the breath

from his lungs—and he saw that he could much more easily
have gone up a few extra steps and simply stepped on—
but there didn't seem anything else to do but just this,
what he was doing. Once upright, he passed his hand over
the statue's flank. The surface was incredibly sleek and
cold, hard as a lion's muscles ought to be, and tawny.

He took a step backwards. Lord! Had there ever
been such power? Such marvelous downright power and—
majesty, as was here? From stone—no, indeed. It fooled a
good many people, but it did not fool Mr. Minchell. He
knew. This lion was no mere library decoration. It was an
animal, of deadly cunning and fantastic strength and unbelievable ferocity. And it didn't move for the simple reason that it did not care to move. It was waiting. Some day
it would see what it was waiting for, its enemy, coming
down the street. Then look out, people!

He remembered the whole yarn now. Of everyone on
Earth, only he, Henry Minchell knew the secret of the lion.
And only he was allowed to sit astride this mighty back.

He stepped onto the tail, experimentally. He hesitated,
gulped, and swung forward, swiftly, on up to the curved
rump.

Trembling, he slid forward, until finally he was over the
shoulders of the lion, just behind the raised head.

His breath came very fast.

He closed his eyes.

It was not long before he was breathing regularly again.
Only now it was the hot, fetid air of the jungle that went
into his nostrils. He felt the great muscles ripple beneath
him and he listened to the fast crackle of crushed foliage,
and he whispered:

"Easy, fellow."

The flying spears did not frighten him; he sat straight,
smiling, with his fingers buried in the rich tawny mane of
King Richard, while the wind tore at his hair . . .

Then, abruptly, he opened his eyes.

The city stretched before him, and the people, and the lights. He tried quite hard not to cry, because he knew that forty-seven-year-old men never cried, not even when they had vanished, but he couldn't help it. So he sat on the stone lion and lowered his head and cried.

He didn't hear the laughter at first.

When he did hear it, he thought that he was dreaming. But it was true: somebody was laughing.

He grasped one of the statue's ears for balance and leaned forward. He blinked. Below, some fifteen feet, there were people. Young people. Some of them with books. They were looking up and smiling and laughing.

Mr. Minchell wiped his eyes.

A slight horror came over him, and fell away. He leaned farther out.

One of the boys waved and shouted: "Ride him, Pop!"

Mr. Minchell almost toppled. Then, without understanding, without even trying to understand—merely knowing—he grinned widely, showing his teeth, which were his own and very white.

"You—see me?" he called.

The young people roared.

"You do!" Mr. Minchell's face seemed to melt upwards. He let out a yell and gave King Richard's shaggy stone mane an enormous hug.

Below, other people stopped in their walking and a small crowd began to form. Dozens of eyes peered sharply, quizzically.

A woman in gray furs giggled.

A thin man in a blue suit grunted something about these damned exhibitionists.

"You pipe down," another man said. "Guy wants to ride the goddamn lion it's his own business."

There were murmurings. The man who had said pipe down was small and he wore black-rimmed glasses. "I used to do it all the time." He turned to Mr. Minchell and cried: "How is it?"

Mr. Minchell grinned. Somehow, he realized, in some mysterious way, he had been given a second chance. And this time he knew what he would do with it. "Fine!" he shouted, and stood upon King Richard's back and sent his derby spinning out over the heads of the people. "Come on up!"

"Can't do it," the man said. "Got a date." There was a look of profound admiration in his eyes as he strode off. Away from the crowd he stopped and cupped his hands and cried: "I'll be seeing you!"

"That's right," Mr. Minchell said, feeling the cold new wind on his face. "You'll be seeing me."

Later, when he was good and ready, he got down off the lion.

PLACE OF MEETING

It swept down from the mountains, a loose, crystal-smelling wind, an autumn chill of moving wetness. Down from the mountains and into the town, where it set the dead trees hissing and the signboards creaking. And it even went into the church, because the bell was ringing and there was no one to ring the bell.

The people in the yard stopped their talk and listened to the rusty music.

Big Jim Kroner listened too. Then he cleared his throat and clapped his hands—thick hands, calloused and work-dirtied.

"All right," he said loudly. "All right, let's settle down now." He walked out from the group and turned. "Who's got the list?"

"Got it right here, Jim," a woman said, coming forward with a loose-leaf folder.

"All present?"

"Everybody except that there German, Mr. Grunin—Grunger—"

Kroner smiled; he made a megaphone of his hands. "Grüninger—Bartold Grüninger?"

A small man with a mustache called out excitedly, "Ja, ja! . . . s'war schwer den Friedhof zu finden."

"All right. That's all we wanted to know, whether you was here or not." Kroner studied the pages carefully. Then he reached into the pocket of his overalls and withdrew a stub of pencil and put the tip in his mouth.

"Now, before we start off," he said to the group, "I want to know is there anybody here that's got a question or anything to ask?" He looked over the crowd of silent faces. "Anybody don't know who I am? No?"

Then came another wind, mountain-scattered and fast: it billowed dresses, set damp hair moving; it pushed over pewter vases, and smashed dead roses and hydrangeas to swirling dust against the gritty tombstones. Its clean rain smell was gone now, though, for it had passed over the fields with the odors of rotting life.

Kroner made a check mark in the notebook. "Anderson," he shouted. "Edward L."

A man in overalls like Kroner's stepped forward.

"Andy, you covered Skagit valley, Snohomish and King counties, as well as Seattle and the rest?"

"Yes, sir."

"What you got to report?"

"They're all dead," Anderson said.

"You looked everywhere? You was real careful?"

"Yes, sir. Ain't nobody alive in the whole state."

Kroner nodded and made another check mark. "That's all, Andy. Next: Avakian, Katina."

A woman in a wool skirt and gray blouse walked up from the back, waving her arms. She started to speak.

Kroner tapped his stick. "Listen here for a second, folks," he said. "For those that don't know how to talk English, you know what this is all about—so when I ask my question, you nod up-and-down for yes (like this) and sideways (like this) for no. Makes it a lot easier for those of us as don't remember too good. All right?"

There were murmurings and whispered consultations and for a little while the yard was full of noise. The woman called Avakian kept nodding.

"Fine," Kroner said. "Now, Miss Avakian. You covered what? . . . Iran, Iraq, Turkey, Syria. Did you—find—an-ybody a-live?"

The woman stopped nodding. "No," she said. "No, no."

Kroner checked the name. "Let's see here. Boleslavsky, Peter. You can go on back now, Miss Avakian."

A man in bright city clothes walked briskly to the tree clearing. "Yes, sir," he said.

"What have you got for us?"

The man shrugged. "Well, I tell you; I went over New York with a fine-tooth comb. Then I hit Brooklyn and Jersey. Nothin', man. Nothin' nowhere."

"He is right," a dark-faced woman said in a tremulous voice. "I was there too. Only the dead in the streets, all over, all over the city; in the cars I looked even, in the *offices*. Everywhere is people dead."

"Chavez, Pietro. Baja, California."

"All dead, señor chief."

"Ciodo, Ruggiero. Capri."

The man from Capri shook his head violently.

"Denman, Charlotte. Southern United States."

"Dead as doornails . . ."

"Elgar, Davis S . . .

"Ferrazio, Ignatz . . .

"Goldfarb, Bernard . . .

"Halpern . . .

"Ives . . . Kranek . . . O'Brian . . ."

The names exploded in the pale evening air like deep gunshots; there was much head-shaking, many people saying, "No. No."

At last Kroner stopped marking. He closed the notebook and spread his big workman's hands. He saw the round eyes, the trembling mouths, the young faces; he saw all the frightened people.

A girl began to cry. She sank to the damp ground, and covered her face and made these crying sounds. An elderly man put his hand on her head. The elderly man looked sad. But not afraid. Only the young ones seemed afraid.

"Settle down now," Kroner said firmly. "Settle on down. Now, listen to me. I'm going to ask you all the same question one more time, because we got to be sure." He waited for them to grow quiet. "All right. This here is all of us, everyone. We've covered all the spots. Did anybody here find one single solitary sign of life?"

The people were silent. The wind had died again, so there was no sound at all. Across the corroded wire fence the gray meadows lay strewn with the carcasses of cows and horses and, in one of the fields, sheep. No flies buzzed near the dead animals; there were no maggots burrowing. No vultures; the sky was clean of birds. And in all the untended rolling hills of grass and weeds which had once sung and pulsed with a million voices, in all the land there was only this immense stillness now, still as years, still as the unheard motion of the stars.

Kroner watched the people. The young woman in the gay print dress; the tall African with his bright paint and cultivated scars; the fierce-looking Swede looking not so fierce now in this graying twilight. He watched all the tall and short and old and young people from all over the world, pressed together now, a vast silent polyglot in this country meeting place, this always lonely and long-deserted spot— deserted even before the gas bombs and the disease and the flying pestilences that had covered the earth in three days and three nights. Deserted. Forgotten.

"Talk to us, Jim," the woman who had handed him the notebook said. She was new.

Kroner put the list inside his big overalls pocket.

"Tell us," someone else said. "How shall we be nourished? What will we do?"

"The world's all dead," a child moaned. "Dead as dead, the whole world . . ."

"Todo el mund—"

"Monsieur Kroner, Monsieur Kroner, what will we do?"

Kroner smiled. "Do?" He looked up through the still-hanging poison cloud, the dun blanket, up to where the moon was now risen in full coldness. His voice was steady, but it lacked life. "What some of us have done before," he said. "We'll go back and wait. It ain't the first time. It ain't the last."

A little fat bald man with old eyes sighed and began to waver in the October dusk. The outline of his form wavered and disappeared in the shadows under the trees where the moonlight did not reach. Others followed him as Kroner talked.

"Same thing we'll do again and likely keep on doing. We'll go back and—sleep. And we'll wait. Then it'll start all over again and folks'll build their cities—new folks with new blood—and then we'll wake up. Maybe a long time yet. But it ain't so bad; it's quiet, and time passes." He lifted a small girl of fifteen or sixteen with pale cheeks and red lips. "Come on, now! Why, just think of the appetite you'll have all built up!"

The girl smiled. Kroner faced the crowd and waved his hands, large hands, rough from the stone of midnight pyramids and the feel of muskets, boil-speckled from night hours in packing plants and trucking lines; broken by the impact of a tomahawk and machine-gun bullet; but white where the dirt was not caked, and bloodless. Old hands, old beyond years.

As he waved, the wind came limping back from the mountains. It blew the heavy iron bell high in the steepled white barn, and set the signboards creaking, and lifted ancient dusts and hissed again through the dead trees.

Kroner watched the air turn black. He listened to it fill with the flappings and the flutterings and the squeakings. He waited; then he stopped waving and sighed and began to walk.

He walked to a place of vines and heavy brush. Here he paused for a moment and looked out at the silent place of high dark grass, of hidden huddled tombs, of scrolls and stone-frozen children stained silver in the night's wet darkness; at the crosses he did not look. The people were gone, the place was empty.

Kroner kicked away the foliage. Then he got into the coffin and closed the lid.

Soon he was asleep.

THE DEVIL, YOU SAY?

Introduction by Howard Browne

In 1951, as the then editor of the Ziff-Davis Fiction Group, I bought "The Devil, You Say?"—Charles Beaumont's first story sale. This obviously made me the first to recognize his unique talents as a writer.

Not true. As I recall, TDYS came into our editorial offices via the "slush pile," i.e. the daily raft of unsolicited submissions to the several fiction magazines the company published at the time. It was the staff's job to go through the pile in the unlikely chance of coming across something we could use.

At the time Lila Shaffer—a gifted young woman with an unerring ability to separate the occasional grain of wheat from all that chaff—was associate editor of both Amazing Stories and Fantastic Adventures.

As I recall, she plunked the Beaumont story on the desk in front of me, said something like, "This is the best thing I've come across in I don't know how long. You've got to read it. Right now!", and sat down.

I said, "Since you put it that way," and began reading.

After the first four or five pages, I looked up at her, said, "You know damned well I don't like stories that open with someone saying 'Let me tell you what happened to me a while back.' Lacks immediacy."

"Read," she said.

I read the rest of it, handed her the pages, said, "Who is this guy?"

She said, "I don't know. I never heard of him before."

"Send a check," I said. "And a letter saying we want first crack at anything else he writes."

Unfortunately nothing came of it. Playboy and Rogue paid better rates than we did.

A few years later I was brought to Hollywood to write for motion pictures and television. Shortly after I got there, I met Charles Beaumont and told him the whole story. I'm not sure he believed me, but he laughed and bought me a drink.

And we raised our glasses in a toast. To Lila Shaffer.

———————————————

IT WAS TWO o'clock in the morning when I decided that my attendance at a meeting of the International Newspapermen's Society for the Prevention of Thirst was a matter of moral necessity. This noble Brotherhood, steeped in tradition and by now as immortal as the institution of the public press, has always been a haven, a refuge and an inspiration to weary souls in the newspaper profession. Its gatherings at Ada's Bar & Grill—Open 24 Hours A Day— have made more than a few dismiss their woes for a while.

I had just covered a terrifically drab story which depended nine tenths upon the typewriter for its effect, and both brain and throat had grown quite dry in consequence. The extra block and a half over to Ada's was a completely natural detour.

As usual at this time of day, the only customers were newspapermen.

Joe Barnes of the *Herald* was there, also Marv Kepner

and Frank Monteverdi of the *Express*. Warren Jackson, the *Globe*'s drama critic, sat musing over a cigar, and Mack Sargent, who got paid for being the *New*'s sports man, seemed to be fascinated by improvising multiple beer rings on the table cloth.

The only one I was surprised to see was Dick Lewis, a featured columnist for the *Express* who'd lately hit the syndicates. He usually didn't drop in to Ada's more than two or three times a month, and then he never added much to the conversation.

Not that he wasn't likeable. As a matter of fact, Dick always put a certain color into the get-togethers, by reason of being such a clam. It gave him a secretive or "Mystery-Man" appearance, and that's always stimulating to gabfests which occasionally verge towards the monotonous.

He sat in one of the corner booths, looking as though he didn't give a damn about anything. A little different this time, a little lower at the mouth. Having looked into mirrors many times myself, I'd come to recognize the old half-closed eyelids that didn't result from mere tiredness. Dick sat there considering his half-empty stein and stifling only a small percentage of burps. Clearly he had been there some time and had considered a great many such half-empty steins.

I drew up a chair, tossed off an all-inclusive nod of greeting and listened for a few seconds to Frank's story of how he had scooped everybody in the city on the *Lusitania* disaster, only to get knocked senseless by an automobile ten seconds before he could get to a phone. The story died in the mid-section, and we all sat for a half hour or so quaffing cool ones, hiccoughing and apologizing.

One of the wonderful things about beer is that a little bit, sipped with the proper speed, can give one the courage to do and say things one would ordinarily not have the courage to even dream of doing and saying. I had absorbed, *presto*, sufficient of the miracle drug by the time the clock got to three A.M., to do something I guess I'd wanted to do in the back of my mind for a long time. My voice was loud and clear and charged with insinuation. Everybody looked up.

"Dammit, Lewis," I said, pointing directly at him, "in order to be a member in good standing of this Society, you've just got to say something interesting. A guy simply doesn't look as inscrutable as you do without having something on his mind. You've listened to our stories. Now how about one of your own?"

"Yeah," joined Monteverdi, "Ed's right. You might call it your dues."

Jackson looked pleased and put in: "See here, Lewis, you're a newsman, aren't you? Surely you have *one* halfway diverting story." "If it's personal," I said, "so much the better. I mean, after all, we're a Brotherhood here."

And that started it. Pretty soon we were all glaring at poor Dick, looking resentful and defiant.

He then surprised us. He threw down the last of his drink, ordered three more, stared us each in the face one by one and said:

"Okay. All right. You're all just drunk enough to listen without calling for the boys in white, though you'll still think I'm the damndest liar in the state. All right, I admit it. I do have something on my mind. Something you won't believe worth beans. And let me tell you something else. I'm quitting this screwball racket, so I don't care what you think."

He drained another stein-full.

"I'm going to tell you why as of tomorrow I start looking for some nice quiet job in a boiler factory. Or maybe as a missionary."

And this is the story Dick Lewis told that night. He was either mightily drunk or crazy as a coot, because you could tell he believed every word he said.

I'm not sure about any of it, myself. All I know for

certain is that he actually did quit the game just as he said he would, and since that night I haven't even heard his name.

When my father died he left me a hundred and twenty-two dollars, his collection of plastic-coated insects and complete ownership of the *Danville Daily Courier*. He'd owned and edited the *Courier* for fifty-five years and although it never made any money for him, he loved it with all his heart. I sometimes used to think that it was the most precious thing in life to him. For whenever there wasn't any news—which was all the time—he'd pour out his inner thoughts, his history, his whole soul into the columns. It was a lot more than just a small town newspaper to Dad: it was his life.

I cut my first teeth on the old hand press and spent most of my time in the office and back room. Pop used to say to me, "You weren't born, lad, you appeared one day out of a bottle of printer's ink." Corny, but I must have believed him, because I grew up loving it all.

What we lived on those days was a mystery to me. Not enough issues of the *Courier* were sold even to pay for the paper stock. Nobody bought it because there was never anything to read of any interest—aside from Dad's personal column, which was understandably limited in its appeal. For similar reasons, no one ever advertised. He couldn't afford any of the press services or syndicates, and Danville wasn't homebody enough a town to give much of a darn how Mrs. Piddle's milk cows were coming along.

I don't even know how he managed to pay the few hands around the place. But Dad didn't seem to worry, so I never gave the low circulation figures a great deal of thought.

That is, I didn't until it was my turn to take over.

After the first month I began to think about it a lot. I remember sitting in the office alone one night, wondering just how the hell Dad ever did it. And I don't mind saying,

I cussed his hide for not ever telling me. He was a queer old duck and maybe this was meant as a test or something.

If so, I had flunked out on the first round.

I sat there staring dumbly at the expense account and wondering, in a half-stupid way, how such a pretty color as red ever got mixed up with so black a thing as being broke.

I wondered what earthly good a newspaper was to Danville, It was a town unusual only because of its concentrated monotony: nothing ever happened. Which is news just once, not once a day. Everybody was happy, nobody was starving; everlasting duties were tended to with a complete lack of reluctance. If every place in the world had been like Danville, old Heraclitus wouldn't have been given a second thought. It hadn't had so much as a drunken brawl since 1800.

So I figured it all out that night. I'd take the sheets of paper in front of me and pitch them into the waste basket. Within an hour I'd call up everyone who worked with me, including the delivery boys, and tell them that the *Danville Daily Courier* had seen its day. Those people with subscriptions, I thought, would have to try to find me. I had about ten dollars left and owed twenty times that in rent and credit.

I suppose you just don't decide to close up business and actually close it up—right down to firing all the help—in an hour's time. But that's what I was going to do. I didn't take anything into consideration except the fact that I had to go somewhere and get a job quick, or I'd end being the first person in Danville's history to die of starvation. So I figured to lock up the office, go home and get my things together and leave the next afternoon for some nearby city.

I knew that if I didn't act that fast, if I stayed and tried to sell the office and the house, I'd never get out of Danville. You don't carry out flash decisions if you wait around to weigh their consequences. You've got to act. So that's what I started to do.

But I didn't get far. About the time I had it all nicely resolved and justified, I was scared out of my shoes by a polite sort of cough, right next to me. It was after midnight and subconsciously I realized that this was neither the time nor the place for polite coughs—at least ones I didn't make. Especially since I hadn't heard anyone come in.

An old boy who must have been crowding ninety stood in front of the desk, staring at me. And I stared right back. He was dressed in the sporty style of the eighteen nineties, with whiskers all over his face and a little black derby which canted jauntily over his left eye.

"Mr. Lewis?" he said, hopping on the side of the desk and taking off his white gloves, finger by finger. "Mr. Richard Lewis?"

"Yes, that's right," is what I said.

"The son of Elmer Lewis?"

I nodded, and I'll bet my mouth was wide open. He took out a big cigar and lit it.

"If I may be so rude," I finally managed to get out, "who the hell are you and how did you get in here?"

His eyes twinkled and immediately I was sorry for having been so abrupt. I don't know why, but I added, "After all, y'know, it's pretty late."

The old geezer just sat there smiling and puffing smoke into the air.

"Did you want to see me about something, Mr.—"

"Call me Jones, my boy, call me Jones. Yes, as a matter of fact, I do have some business with you. Y'see, I knew your father quite well once upon a time—might say he and I were very close friends. Business partners too, you might say. Yes. Business partners. Tell me, Richard, did you ever know your father to be unhappy?"

It was an odd conversation, but Mr. Jones was far too

friendly and ingratiating to get anything but courtesy out of me. I answered him honestly.

"No, Dad was always about the happiest person I've ever seen. Except when Mother died, of course."

Jones shifted and waved his cane in the air.

"Of course, of course. But aside from that. Did he have any grievances about life, any particular concern over the fact that his newspaper was never very, shall we say, successful? In a word, Richard, was your father content to the day he died?"

"Yes, I'd say he was. At least I never heard him complain. Dad never wanted anything but a chance to putter around the office, write his column and collect bugs."

At this he whacked the desk and grinned until all I could see was teeth.

"Ah, that's very good, m'boy, very good. Times haven't been like they were in the old days. I'd begun to wonder if I was as good as I made out to be. Why, do you know that Elmer was my first customer since that time Dan'l Webster made such a fool of me! Oh, that was rich. You've got to hand it to those New Hampshire lawyers, you've just got to hand it to them."

He sat chuckling and puffing out smoke, and, looking squarely at the situation, I began to get a very uncomfortable sensation along the back of my spine.

"Your dad wasn't any slouch, though, let me tell you, Dick. That part of the deal is over. He got what he wanted out of his life on Earth and now he's—what's that wonderful little expression somebody started a few centuries ago?—oh yes, he's paying the fiddler. But things were almost as bad then as they are now, I mean as far as signed, paid-up contracts go. Oh, I tell you, you humans are getting altogether too shrewd for your own good. What with wars and crime and politicians and the like, I scarcely have anything to do these days. No fun in merely shoveling 'em in."

A long, gassy sigh.

"Yes sir, Elmer was on to me all right. He played his cards mighty clever. Included you, Dick m'boy. So all I have to do is make you happy and, well then, the deal's closed."

By this time I felt pretty much like jumping out the window, but shot nerves or not, I was able to say:

"Look, Grandpa, I don't know what in hell you're talking about. I'm in no mood for this sort of thing and don't particularly care to be. If you were a friend of Pop's I'm glad to see you and all that, but if you came here for hospitality I'm afraid you're out of luck. I'm leaving town tomorrow. If you'd like, I'll walk you to a nice clean hotel."

"Ah," he said, pushing me back into my chair with his cane, "you don't understand. Lad, I've not had much practice lately and may be a trifle on the rusty side, but you must give me my dues. Let me see—if I remember correctly, the monthly cash stipend was not included and therefore was not passed on to you."

"Look—"

"The hundred and fifty a month your father got, I mean. I see you know nothing of it. Cautious one, Elmer. Take it easy, son, take it easy. Your troubles are over."

This was too much. I got up and almost shouted at him.

"I've got enough troubles already, without a loony old bird like you busting in on me. Do we take you to a hotel, or do you start traveling?"

He just sat there and laughed like a jackass, poking me with his cane and flicking cigar ashes all over the floor.

"Dick m'boy, it's a pity you don't want out of life what your father did. In a way, that would have simplified things. As it is, I'm going to have to get out the old bag of tricks and go to work. Answer one more question and you may go your way."

I said, "All right, make it snappy, Pop. I'm getting tired of this game."

"Am I right in assuming that your principal unhappiness lies in the fact that your newspaper is not selling as you would like it to, and that this is due to the categorical fact that nothing newsworthy ever takes place in this town?"

"Yeah, that's right on the button. Now—"

"Very well, Dick. That's what I wanted to know. I advise you to go home now and get a good night's sleep."

"Exactly what I plan to do. It's been charming, Mr. Jones. I don't mind saying I think you're a nosy galoot with squirrels in the head. Anyway, do you want to go to a hotel?"

He jumped down off the desk and started to walk with me toward the front door.

"No thank you, Richard lad; I have much work to do. I tell you, stop worrying. Things are going to be rosy for you and, if you watch your step, *you'll* have no fiddler to pay. And now, good night."

Jones then dug me in the ribs with his cane and strode off, whistling "There'll Be a Hot Time in the Old Town Tonight."

He was headed straight for the Little Creek bridge, which gradually opened off into flap pastures and a few farm houses. Nothing lay beyond that except the graveyard.

I suppose he didn't know where he was going, but I was too confused and tired to care much. When I looked again there wasn't hide nor hair of Mr. Jones.

He was promptly forgotten. Almost, anyway. When you're broke and owe everybody in town, you're able to forget just about anything. Except, of course, that you're broke and owe everybody in town.

I locked up the office and started for home. The fire and fury were gone: I couldn't get up the gall to phone everyone and do all the things I'd planned to do.

So, miserable as a wet dog, I trudged a few blocks to the

house, smoked a half dozen cigarettes and went to bed, hoping I'd have the guts to get on the train the next day.

I woke up early feeling like a fish left out in the sun too long. It was six o'clock and, like always at this time, I wished that I had a wife or a mistress to get me a big breakfast. Instead I hobbled downstairs and knew exactly what Mother Hubbard felt like. I fixed a lousy cup of coffee and sat down to a glorious dish of corn flakes. I knew that train was mighty far away and that in a little while I'd go to the office, reach in the filler box and help set up another stinking issue of the *Daily Courier*. Then would come the creditors and the long line of bushwa. Even the corn flakes tasted rancid.

Then I heard a distinct thud against the front door. It struck me as being odd, because there had never before been any thuds at that particular front door, which made precisely that sound.

I opened it, looked around and finally at my feet. There, folded magnificently and encircled with a piece of string, was a newspaper.

Since the *Courier* was the only paper Danville had ever known, and since I never read the thing anyway, it all looked very peculiar. Besides, none of my delivery boys ever folded in such a neat, professional manner.

There wasn't anybody in sight, but I noticed, before I picked it up, that there was a paper on the doorstep of every house and store around. Then people started coming out and noticing the bundles, so I gathered it up and went back inside. Maybe I scratched my head. I know I felt like it.

There was a little card attached to the string. It read:

COMPLIMENTARY ISSUE
If You Desire To Begin Or Rebegin Your Subscription, Send Checks Or Cash To The Office Of

The Danville Daily Courier. Rates Are Listed
Conveniently Within.

That was a laugh, but I didn't. Something was screwy
somewhere. In the first place, there weren't supposed to be
any morning deliveries. I, Ernie Meyer and Fred Scarborough (my staff) started the edition around eight o'clock,
and it didn't get delivered until six that night. Also, since
no one was in the office after I left and nothing whatsoever
had been done on the next days issue—let alone the fancy
printing on that card, which could have been done only on
a large press—well, I got an awfully queer feeling in the
pit of my stomach.

When I opened up the paper I about yelled out loud. It
looked like the biggest most expensive highfalutin' city paper ever put together. The legend still read—*Danville Daily
Courier*, but I'd have felt better if it had said the *Tribune*.

Immediately upon reading the double-inch headlines, I
sat down and started to sweat. There in black, bold letters
were the words:

MAYOR'S WIFE GIVES BIRTH
TO BABY HIPPOPOTAMUS

And underneath:

At three A.M. this morning, Mayor and Mrs.
Fletcher Lindquist were very much startled to find
themselves the parents of a healthy, 15 pound baby
hippo. Most surprising is the fact that nowhere in
the lineage of either the Mayor or his wife is there
record of a hippopotamus strain. Mrs. Lindquist's
great-grandfather, reports show, was a raving lunatic from the age of twenty-three to the time of
his death, fifty years later, but it is biologically
unsound to assume that such ancestral proclivities

would necessarily introduce into later generations
so unusual a result.

Therefore, Danville's enterprising, precedent-
setting Mayor Lindquist may be said to have
proved his first campaign promise, to wit, "I will
make many changes!"

Continued on page 15

I don't have to recount what I did or thought at all this.
I merely sat there and numbly turned to page fifteen.

Displaying his usual cool and well-studied philosophy, the Mayor announced that, in view of the
fact that the Lindquists' expected baby was to have
been called either Edgar Bernhardt or Louisa Ann,
and inasmuch as the hippopotamus was male in
sex, the name Edgar Bernhardt would be employed as planned.

When queried, the Mayor said simply, "I do not
propose that our son be victim to unjudicious slan-
der and stigmatic probings. Edgar will lead a
healthy, normal life." He added brusquely: "I have
great plans for the boy!"

Both Mrs. Lindquist and the attending physician, Dr. Forrest Peterson, refrained from comment, although Dr. Peterson was observed in a
corner from time to time, mumbling and striking
his forehead.

I turned back to the front page, feeling not at all well.
There, 3 inches by 5 inches was a photograph of Mrs.
Fletcher Lindquist, holding in her arms (honest to God!) a
pint-sized hippopotamus.

I flipped feverishly to the second sheet, and saw:

FARMER BURL ILLING COMPLAINS
OF MYSTERIOUS APPEARANCE
OF DRAGONS IN BACK YARD.

And then I threw the damn paper as far as I could and
began pinching myself. It only hurt; I didn't wake up. I
closed my eyes and looked again, but there it was, right
where I'd heaved it.

I suppose I should have, but I didn't for a moment get
the idea I was nuts. A real live newspaper had been delivered at my door. I owned the only newspaper in town and
called it the *Danville Daily Courier*. This paper was also
called the *Danville Daily Courier*. I hadn't put together an
issue since the day before. This one was dated today. The
only worthwhile news *my* paper had ever turned out was a
weather report. This one had stuff that would cause the
Associated Press to drop its teeth.

Somebody, I concluded, was nuts.

And then I slowly remembered Mr. Jones. That screwy
Mr. Jones, that loony old bird-brain.

He'd broken into the office after I'd left and somehow
put together this fantastic issue. Where he got the photograph I didn't know, but that didn't bother me. It was the
only answer. Sure—who else would have done such a thing?
Thought he'd help me by making up a lot of tall tales and
peddling them to everyone in town.

I got sore as hell. So this was how he was going to "help"
me! If he'd been there at the moment I would have broken
every bone in his scrawny old body. My God, I thought,
how'll I get out of this? What would I say when the Mayor
and Illing and Lord knows how many others got wind of
it?

Dark thoughts of me, connected to a long rail, coated
from head to toe with a lot of tar and lot of feathers,
floated clearly before my eyes. Or me at the stake, with
hungry flames lapping up . . . Who could blame them? *Some*

big time magazine or tabloid would get a copy—they'd never miss a story like this. And then Danville would be the laughing stock of the nation, maybe of the world. At the very best, I'd be sued blue.

I took one last look at that paper on the floor and lit out for the office. I was going to tear that old jerk limb from limb—I was going to make some *real* news.

Halfway there the figure of Fred Scarborough rushed by me a mile a minute. He didn't even turn around. I started to call, but then Ernie Meyer came vaulting down the street. I tried to dodge, but the next thing I knew Ernie and I were sitting on top of each other. In his eyes was an insane look of fear and confusion.

"Ernie," I said, "what the devil's the matter with you? Has this town gone crazy or have I?"

"Don't know about that, Mr. Lewis," he panted, "but I'm headin' for the hills."

He got up and started to take off again. I grabbed him and shook him till his teeth rattled.

"What *is* the matter with you? Where's everybody running? Is there a fire?"

"Look, Mr. Lewis, I worked for your dad. It was a quiet life and I got paid regular. Elmer was a little odd, but that didn't bother me none, because I got paid regular, see. But things is happening at the office now that I don't have to put up with, 'cause, Mr. Lewis, I don't get paid at all. And when an old man dressed like my grandfather starts a lot of brand new presses running all by himself and, on top of that, chases me and Fred out with a pitchfork, well, Mr. Lewis, I'm quittin'. I resign. Goodbye, Mr. Lewis. Things like this just ain't ever happened in Danville before."

Ernie departed in a hurry, and I got madder at Mr. Jones.

When I opened the door to the office, I wished I was either in bed or had a drink. All the old hand-setters and presses were gone. Instead there was a huge, funny looking machine, popping and smoking and depositing freshly folded newspapers into a big bin. Mr. Jones, with his derby still on his head, sat at my desk pounding furiously at the typewriter and chuckling like a lunatic. He ripped a sheet out and started to insert another, when he saw me.

"Ah, Dick m'boy! How are you this morning? I must say, you don't look very well. Sit down, won't you. I'll be finished in a second."

Back he went to his writing. All I could do was sit down and open and close my mouth.

"Well," he said, taking the sheets and poking them through a little slot in the machine. "Well, there's tomorrow's edition, all—how does it go?—all put to bed. They'll go wild over that. Just think, Reverend Piltzer's daughter was found tonight with a smoking pistol in her hand, still standing over the body of her—"

I woke up.

"Jones!"

"Of course, it's not front page stuff. Makes nice filler for page eight, though."

"Jones!"

"Yes, m'boy?"

"I'm going to kill you. So help me, I'm going to murder you right now! Do you realize what you've done? Oh Lord, don't you know that half the people in Danville are going to shoot me, burn me, sue me and ride me out on a rail? Don't you—but they won't. No sir. I'll tell them everything. And you're going to stick right here to back me up. All of the—"

"Why, what's the matter, Dick? Aren't you happy? Look at all the news your paper is getting."

"Hap-Happy? You completely ruin me and ask if I'm happy! Go bar the door, Jones; they'll be here any second."

He looked hurt and scratched the end of his nose with his cane.

"I don't quite understand, Richard. *Who* will be here? Out of town reporters?"

I nodded weakly, too sick to talk.

"Oh no, they won't arrive until tomorrow. You see, they're just getting this morning's issue. Why are you so distraught? Ah, I know what will cheer you up. Take a look at the mail box."

I don't know why, but that's what I did. I knew the mail wasn't supposed to arrive until later, and vaguely I wanted to ask what had happened to all the old equipment. But I just went over and looked at the mail box, like Mr. Jones suggested. I opened the first letter. Three dollars dropped out. Letter number two another three bucks. Automatically I opened letter after letter, until the floor was covered with currency. Then I imagined I looked up piteously at Mr. J.

"Subscriptions, m'boy, subscriptions. I hurried the delivery a bit, so you'd be pleased. But that's just a start. Wait'll tomorrow, Dick. This office will be knee-deep in money!"

At this point I finally did begin to think I was crazy.

"What is all this about, Jones? *Please* tell me, or call the little white wagon. Am I going soggy in the brain?"

"Come, come! Not a bit of it! I've merely fulfilled my promise. Last night you told me that you were unhappy because the *Courier* wasn't selling. Now, as you can see, it *is* selling. And not only in Danville. No sir, the whole world will want subscriptions to your paper, Richard, before I'm through."

"But you don't understand, Jones. You just can't make up a lot of news and expect to get by with it. It's been tried a hundred different times. People are going to catch on. And you and me, we're going to be jailed sure as the devil. Do you see now what you've done?"

He looked at me quizzically and burst out laughing.

"Why, Dick, you *don't* understand yet, do you! Come

now, surely you're not such a dunce. Tell me, exactly what do you think?"

"Merely that an old man stepped into my life last night and that my life has been a nightmare ever since."

"But beyond that. Who am I and why am I here?"

"Oh, I don't know, Mr. Jones. You're probably just a friend of Dad's and thought you could help me out by this crazy scheme. I can't even get angry with you anymore. Things were going to hell without you—maybe I can get a job on the prison newspaper."

"Just a queer old friend of Elmer's, eh? And you think I did no more than 'make up' those headlines. You don't wonder about this press—" he waved his cane toward the large machine which had supplanted the roll-your-own—"or how the papers got delivered or why they look so professional? Is that press your imagination?"

I looked over at the machine. It was nothing I'd ever seen before. Certainly it was not an ordinary press. But it was real enough. Actual papers were popping out of it at the rate of two or three a second. And then I thought of that photograph.

"My God, Jones, do you mean to tell me that you're—"

"Precisely, my lad, precisely. A bit rusty, as I said, but with many a unique kick left."

He kicked his heels together and smiled broadly.

"Now, you can be of no help whatever. So, since you look a bit peaked around the face, it is my suggestion that you go home and rest for a few days."

"That news . . . those things in the paper, you mean they were—"

"Absolutely factual. Everything that is printed in the *Danville Daily Courier*," he said gaily, "is the, er, the gospel truth. Go home, Dick: I'll attend to the reporters and editors and the like. When you're feeling better, come back and we'll work together. Perhaps you'll have a few ideas."

He put another sheet in the typewriter, rested his bushy chin on the head of the cane for a moment, twinkled his eyes and then began typing like mad.

I staggered out of the office and headed straight for Barney's Grill. All I had was beer, but that would have to do. I had to get drunk: I knew that.

When I got to Barney's, the place was crowded. I ordered a beer and then almost dropped it when the waiter said to me:

"You certainly were right on the ball, Mr. Lewis, you and your paper. Who'd a'ever thought the Mayor's wife would have a hippopotamus? Yes sir, right on the ball. I sent in my subscription an hour ago!"

Then Mrs. Olaf Jaspers, a quiet old lady who always had her coffee and doughnut at Barney's before going to work at the hospital, said:

"Oh, it was certainly a sight to see. Miz Lindquist is just as proud. Fancy, a hippopotamus!"

I quickly gulped the beer.

"You mean you actually saw it, Mrs. Jaspers?"

"Oh my yes," she answered. "I was there all the time. We can't any of us figure it out, but it was the cutest thing you ever did see. Who was that old fellow that took the picture, Richard? A new man?"

Everyone began talking to me then, and my head swam around and around.

"Mighty quick of you, Lewis! You've got *my* subscription for two years!"

"Poor Burl never did catch those pesky dragons. Ate up every one of his turnips, too."

"You're a real editor, Mr. Lewis. We're all going to take the *Courier* from now on. Imagine; all these funny things happen and you're right there to get all the news!"

I bought a case of beer, excused myself, went home and got blind drunk.

* * *

It was nice to wake up the next morning, because, even though my head split I felt sure this was every bit a dream. The hope sank fast when I saw all the beer bottles lying on the floor. With an empty feeling down below, I crawled to the front door and opened it.

No dream.

The paper lay there, folded beautifully. I saw people running down the streets, lickity split, toward Main Street.

Thinking was an impossibility. I made for the boy's room, changed clothes, fixed some breakfast and only then had the courage to unfold the issue. The headlines cried: EXTRA!! Underneath, almost as large:

S.S. QUEEN MARY DISCOVERED ON MAIN STREET

An unusual discovery today made Danville, U.S.A., a center of world-wide attention. The renowned steam ship, the S.S. *Queen Mary*, thought previously to be headed for Italy enroute from Southampton, appeared suddenly in the middle of Main Street in Danville, between Geary and Orchard Ave.

Imbedded deep in the cement so that it remains upright, the monstrous vessel is proving a dangerous traffic hazard, causing many motorists to go an entire mile out of their way.

Citizens of Danville view the phenomenon with jaundiced eyes, generally considering it a great nuisance.

Empty whiskey bottles were found strewn about the various decks, and all the crew and passengers remain under the influence of heavy intoxication.

In the words of the Captain, J.E. Cromerline:

"I din' have a thing to do with it. It was that damned navigator, all his fault."

Officials of the steam ship line are coming from London and New York to investigate the situation.

Continued on page 20

That's what it said, and, so help me, there was another photograph, big and clear as life.

I ran outside, and headed for Main Street. But the minute I turned the corner, I saw it.

There, exactly as the paper had said, was the *Queen Mary*, as quiescent and natural as though she'd been in dock. People were gathered all around the giant ship, jabbering and yelling.

In a dazed sort of way, I got interested and joined them.

Lydia Murphy, a school teacher, was describing the nautical terms to her class, a gang of kids who seemed happy to get out of school.

Arley Taylor, a fellow who used to play checkers with Dad, walked over to me.

"Now, ain't that something, Dick! I ask ya, ain't that something!"

"That, Arley," I agreed, "is something."

I saw Mr. Jones standing on the corner, swinging his cane and puffing his cigar. I galloped over to him.

"Look, Jones, I believe you. Okay, you're the devil. But you just can't do this. First a hippopotamus, now the world's biggest ocean liner in the middle of the street—You're driving me nuts!"

"Why, hello Dick. Say, you ought to see those subscriptions now! I'd say we have five thousand dollars' worth. They're beginning to come in from the cities now. Just you wait, boy, you'll have a newspaper that'll beat 'em all!"

Arguing didn't faze him. I saw then and there that Mr. Jones wouldn't be stopped. So I cussed a few times and

started off. Only I was stopped short by an expensive looking blonde, with horn-rimmed glasses and a notebook.

"Mr. Richard Lewis, editor of the *Danville Courier*?" she
said.

"That's me."

"My name is Elissa Traskers. I represent the *New York
Mirror*. May we go somewhere to talk?"

I mumbled, "Okay," and took one more look at the
ship.

Far up on the deck I could see a guy in a uniform chasing
what couldn't have been anything else but a young lady
without much clothes on.

When two big rats jumped off the lowest port hole and
scampered down the street, I turned around sharply and
almost dragged the blonde the entire way to my house.

Once inside, I closed the door and locked it. My nerves
were on the way out.

"Mr. Lewis, why did you do that?" asked the blonde.

"Because I like to lock doors, I *love* to lock doors. They
fascinate me."

"I see. Now then, Mr. Lewis, we'd like a full account,
in your own words, of all these strange happenings."

She crossed a tan leg and that didn't help much to calm
me down.

"Miss Traskers," I said, "I'll tell you just once, and then
I want you to go away. I'm not a well man.

"My father, Elmer Lewis, was a drifter and a floater all
his life, until he met the devil. Then he decided what would
really make him happy. So he asked the devil to set him
up in a small town with a small town newspaper. He asked
for a monthly cash stipend. He got all this, so for fifty years
he sat around happy as a fool, editing a paper which didn't
sell and collecting lousy bugs—"

The blonde baby looked worried because I must have
sounded somewhat unnatural. But maybe the business with

the boat had convinced her that unusual things do, occasionally, happen.

"Mr. Lewis," she said sweetly, "before you go on, may I offer you a drink?".

And she produced from her purse a small, silver flask. It had scotch in it. With the elan of the damned, I got a couple of glasses and divided the contents of the flask into each.

"Thanks."

"Quite all right. Now, enough kidding, Mr. Lewis. I must turn in a report to my paper."

"I'm *not* kidding, honey. For fifty-five years my dad did this, and my mother stuck right by him. The only thing out of the ordinary they ever had was me."

The scotch tasted wonderful. I began to like Miss Traskers a lot.

"All this cost Pop his soul, but he was philosophic and I guess that didn't matter much to him. Anyway, he tricked the devil into including me into the bargain. So after he died and left the paper to me, and I started to go broke, Mr. Jones appeared and decided to help me out."

"To help you out?"

"Yeah. All this news is his work. Before he's done he'll send the whole world off its rocker, just so I can get subscriptions."

She'd stopped taking it down a long time ago.

"I'd think you were a damned liar, Mr. Lewis—"

"Call me Dick."

"—if I hadn't seen the *Queen Mary* sitting out there. Frankly, Mr. Lew—Dick, if you're telling the truth, something's got to be done."

"You're darn right it does, Elissa. But *what*? The old boy is having too much fun now to be stopped. He told me himself he hasn't had anything to do like this for centuries."

"Besides," she said, "how did I get here so quickly? The

ship was discovered only this morning, yet I can't remember—"

"Oh, don't worry about it, kid. From now on *anything* is likely to happen."

Something did. I went over and kissed her, for no apparent reason except that she was a pretty girl and I was feeling rotten. She didn't seem to mind.

Right on cue, the doorbell rang.

"Who is it?" I shouted.

"We're from the Associated Press. We want to see Mr. Richard Lewis," came a couple of voices. I could hear more footsteps coming up the front porch.

"I'm sorry," I called, "he's just come down with Yellow Fever. He can't see anybody."

But is wasn't any use. More and more steps and voices, and I could see the door being pushed inward. I grabbed Elissa's hand and we ran out the back way, ran all the way to the office.

Strangely, there weren't many people around. We walked in, and there, of course, was Mr. Jones at the typewriter. He looked up, saw Elissa and winked at me.

"Listen to this, boy. BANK PRESIDENT'S WIFE CLAIMS DIVORCE—EXPLAINS CAUGHT HUSBAND TRIFLING WITH THREE MERMAIDS IN BATHTUB. 'Course, it's rather long, but I think we can squeeze it in. Well, well, who have you there?"

I couldn't think of anything else, so I introduced Elissa.

"Ah, from the *Mirror*! I got you down here this morning, didn't I?"

Elissa looked at me and I could tell she didn't think I had been trying to fool her.

"Have you turned in your report yet, Miss?"

She shook her head.

"Well, do so immediately! Why do you think I took the trouble of sending you in the first place? Never mind, I'll attend to it. Oh, we're terribly busy here. But a shapely lass like you shouldn't have to work for a living, now should she, Dick?"

And with this, Jones nudged Elissa with his cane, in a spot which caused me to say:

"Now see here Jones—this is going too far! Do that again and I'll punch you in the snoot."

"I must say, Richard, you're just like your father. Don't lose a minute, do you!"

I reached out to grab him, but the second afterwards he was over on the other side of the room.

"Tut tut, m'boy, not a very nice way to treat your benefactor! Look at that basket there."

I looked and so did Elissa. She looked long and hard. The room was full of money and checks, and Mr. Jones danced over with a mischievous glint in his eyes.

"Bet a couple could take just what's there and live comfortably for a year on it. That is, if they were sure there would be more to come."

He sidled over to Elissa and nudged her again, and I started swinging.

Before I landed on my face, a thought came to me. It was a desperate, long-odds, crazy thought, but it seemed the answer to everything.

"Tell you what, Jones," I said, picking myself up off the floor and placing Elissa behind me. "This is a little silly after all. I think you're right. I think I've acted in a very ungrateful fashion and I want to apologize. The *Courier* is really selling now, and it appears that it'll make me a lot of money. All thanks to you. I'm really sorry."

He put the chair down and seemed pleased.

"Now then, that's more like it, Dick. And, er, I apologize, young lady. I was only being devilish."

Elissa was a sophisticated girl: she didn't open her mouth.

"I can see that you're busy, Mr. Jones, so if you don't mind, Elissa and I will take a little walk."

I gave him a broad wicked wink, which delighted him.

"That's *fine*, m'boy. I want to get this evening's edition ready. Now let's see, where was I . . ."

By this time it was getting dark. Without saying a word, I pushed Elissa into the alley behind the shop. You could hear the press chugging away inside, so I began to talk fast.

"I like you," I said, "and maybe after all this is over, we can get together somewhere. But right now the important thing is to stop that bird."

She looked beautiful there in the shadows, but I couldn't take the time to tell her so. Vaguely I sensed that I'd somehow fallen in love with this girl whom I'd met that same day. She looked in all ways cooperative.

I did manage to ask: "You got a boyfriend?"

Again she shook that pretty blonde head, so I got right back to the business at hand.

"Jones *has* to be stopped. What he's done so far is fantastic, all right, but comparatively harmless. However, we've got to remember that he's the devil after all, and for sure he's up to something. Things won't stay harmless, you can count on that. Already he's forgotten about the original idea. Look at him in there, having the time of his life. This was all he needed to cut loose. Dad made the mistake of leaving the *idea* of my happiness up to Mr. Jones' imagination."

"All right, Dick, but what do we do?"

"Did you notice that he read aloud what's *going* to happen tonight, Elissa?"

"You mean about the mermaids in the bathtub?"

"Yes. Don't you get it? That hasn't happened yet. He thinks up these crazy ideas, types 'em out, gets 'em all printed and *then* they take place. He goes over, takes a few pictures and in some way gets the papers delivered a few minutes later, complete with the news. Don't ask me why he doesn't just snap his fingers—maybe he enjoys it this way more."

"I suppose that's, uh, sensible. What do you want me to do, Dick?"

"It's asking a lot, I suppose, but we can't let him wreck the whole world. Elissa, do you think you could divert the devil for about a half hour?"

Looking at her, I knew she could.

"I get it now. Okay, if you think it'll work. First, do me a favor?"

"Anything."

"Kiss me again, would you?"

I complied, and let me tell you, there was nothing crazy about that kiss. I was honestly grateful to Mr. Jones for *one* thing at least.

Elissa opened the front door of the office, threw back her hair and crooked a finger at the devil.

"Oh Mr. Jones!"

From the alley I could see him stop typing abruptly. More than abruptly. So would I.

"Why, my dear! Back from your walk so soon? Where is Richard?"

"I don't know—he just walked off and didn't say anything. Now I'm all alone."

The devil's eyes looked like tiny red hot coals, and he bit clean through his cigar.

"Well," he said. "Well, well, *well!*"

"You wouldn't like to take me out for a few drinks, would you, Mr. Jones?"

The way she moved her hips would have made me bite through my cigar, if I'd had a cigar. She was doing beautifully.

"Well, I had planned to—no, it can wait. Certainly, Miss Traskers, I'd be pleased, more than pleased, oh, *very* pleased to accompany you somewhere for a spot. Richard has probably gone home to talk to other reporters."

With this he hopped over the desk and took Elissa's arm.

"Oh, my dear girl, it has been so long, so very long. Voluntarily, I mean."

She smiled at the old goat and in a few minutes they were headed straight for Barney's Grill. I almost chased them when I heard him say, "And afterwards, perhaps we could take a stroll through the woods, eh?"

As soon as they were out of sight, I ran into the office, took his material out of the typewriter and inserted a new sheet.

I thought for a few minutes, and then hurriedly typed:

DEVIL RETURNS HOME

The devil, known also as Mr. Jones, cut short his latest visit to Earth because of altercations in Gehenna. Mr. Elmer Lewis, for some years a resident of the lower regions, successfully made his escape and entry into heaven, where he joined his wife, Elizabeth. The devil can do nothing to alter this, but has decided to institute a more rigorous discipline among his subjects still remaining.

And then, on another sheet I wrote:

OFFICE OF DANVILLE DAILY
COURIER DISAPPEARS

The citizens of Danville were somewhat relieved this morning as they noticed the disappearance of the office of the town's only newspaper, the *Courier*. All the news reported in the pages of this tabloid since April 11, furthermore, was found to be totally false and misrepresentational, except the information printed in this edition. Those who paid for subscriptions have all received their money in full.

> Richard Lewis, the editor, is rumored to be in New York, working for one of the large metropolitan newspapers.
>
> The community of Danville continues a normal, happy existence, despite the lack of a news organ.

I walked over to the machine, which still ejected papers, and quickly inserted the two sheets into the slot, exactly as I'd observed Jones do.

At which point the universe blew up in my face. The entire office did a jig and then settled gently but firmly, on top of my head.

When things unfuzzed and I could begin to see straight, I found myself sitting at a typewriter in a very large and very strange office.

A fellow in shirt-sleeves and tortoise-shells ambled over and thumped me on the back.

"Great work, Dick," he said. "Great job on that city hall fire. C'mon, break down, you set it yourself?"

Of course, as was becoming a habit, I stared dumbly.

"Always the dead-pan—wotta joker! So now you're in the syndicates. Some guys are just plain old lucky, I guess. Do *I* ever happen to be around when things like that bust out? Huh!"

He walked away, and by degrees, very carefully, I learned that I'd just scooped everybody on a big fire that had broken out in the city hall.

I was working for the *Mirror*, making $75.00 per week. I'd been with them only a few days, but everyone seemed very chummy.

It had worked. I'd outsmarted the devil! I'd gotten rid of him and the paper and everything. And then I remembered.

I remembered Elissa. So, come quitting time, I asked the first guy I saw:

"Where does Miss Elissa Traskers work, you know?"

The fellow's eyes lit up and he looked melancholy.

"You mean the Blonde Bomber? Whatta gal, whatta gal! Those legs, those—"

"Yeah—where does she work?"

"Second floor. Flunks for Davidson, that lucky—"

I got down to the second floor quick. There she was, as pretty as I remembered her. I walked up and said:

"Hello, honey. It worked!"

"I beg your pardon?"

She didn't have to say any more. I realized with a cold heartless feeling what it was I'd forgotten. I'd forgotten Elissa. Didn't even mention her on either of those sheets, didn't ever mention her!

"Don't you remember, honey? You were doing me a favor, coaxing the devil to buy you a few drinks . . ."

It was there in her eyes. She could have been staring at an escaped orangoutang.

"Excuse me," she said, picked up her coat and trotted out of the office. And out of my life.

I tried to get in touch with her any number of times after that, but she didn't know me each time. Finally I saw it was no good. I used to sit by the window and watch her leave the building with some other guy or another, sit there and wish I'd just left things like they were while Mr. Jones was having fun.

It wasn't very peaceful, but so what. I ask you, so what?"

Dick sat in his corner, looked serious as a lawyer. We'd all stopped laughing quite a while back, and he was actually so convincing that I piped up:

"Okay, what happened then? That why you want to quit newspaper work—because of her?"

He snickered out the side of his mouth and lit another cigarette.

"Yeah, that's why. Because of her. But that isn't all.

You guys remember what happened to the Governor's wife last week?"

We remembered. Governor Parker's spouse had gone berserk and run down Fifth Avenue without a stitch on.

"You know who covered that story, who was right there again?"

It had been Lewis. That story was what had entrenched him solidly with the biggest syndicate in the country.

"All right. Can any of you add two and two?"

We were all silent.

"What are you talking about?" Jackson asked.

Dick threw down a beer and laughed out loud, though he didn't seem particularly amused.

"I wasn't so smart. I didn't stop the devil; I just stalled him awhile. He's back, y'understand, he's back! And this time he's going to get mad. That's why I'm quitting the newspapers. I don't know what I'll do, but whatever it is Mr. Jones is going to do his damndest to make me successful."

I was about to start the laughter, when I saw something that cut it off sharp.

I saw a very old gentleman, with derby, spats and cane, leaning against the bar and winking at me.

It didn't take me long to get home.

FREE DIRT

Introduction by Dennis Etchison

In the fifties and sixties Charles Beaumont's name was magic. With a style so smooth and polished that it could be published in Playboy and the slicks as easily as in the genre magazines, he was a singular inspiration. Ray Bradbury had achieved some degree of detente with the literary mainstream years earlier; now there was a new champion and role model, one with a unique aura of glamour, confidence and apparently unlimited potential who would surely succeed in elevating imaginative writing from its adolescent ghetto to a position of respectability in the real world. His method was facile and yet sophisticated, accessible and esoteric, readable and technically impeccable, and somehow never superficial or calculated but deeply personal, sincere and committed in the manner of any serious art. The field has not known his like before or since.

In 1963 the UCLA Extension catalogue listed an Advanced Science Fiction Workshop, one of the first of its kind anywhere, to be taught by Beaumont himself. I was still living at home and had no job or money other than the small checks I had begun to receive for my fiction. But UCLA was within driving distance of Lynwood, and I did own a 1950 Ford, bought with my first short story sale, that might get me there if I carried an extra quart of oil in the trunk and stayed off the freeway. So I signed up as quickly as I could borrow the enrollment fee from my parents, and set out on the long haul down Imperial Highway for ten weeks of evening sessions.

I had seen him before, at the World Science Fiction Convention in 1958, where he and Richard Matheson shared the spotlight, and at the Pacific Coast Writers Conference, where he appeared along with the likes of Christopher Isherwood, Anais Nin, Ray Bradbury and Rod Serling. He was as I remembered him, though his sandy hair was no longer bright and his eyes showed signs of sleeplessness. There he sat behind his desk, dignified beyond reproach, chain-smoking Pall Malls so deeply that nothing reemerged after he inhaled. He spoke quietly and charmingly on a level perfectly adjusted to the needs of the class. He suggested that we submit stories, read them or allow him to read them aloud if he wanted an oral critique, and entertained us with anecdotes. From time to time friends of his would drop by, lecture or answer questions if they felt like it—William Shatner, who had starred in the film of The Intruder, stayed to give a cold dramatic reading of one of the student stories; William F. Nolan taught us the value of notebooks; Ron Goulart remained in the background shy and self-effacing. Our teacher honored us by sharing a new manuscript of his own, and went so far as to offer us an idea that he had never gotten around to writing but which, he said, was ours to use as we liked. It was about a man who is killed in an accident but revived after being dead for several minutes—long enough to develop a ghost. Several in the class wrote about this premise. I did not, but the idea remained with me, and in the late sixties I used it as the basis for a pseudonymous novel. Later, in the eighties, a variation became the core of my novel Darkside. A definitive version has yet to be written, but someday one of us may get it right enough to do Beaumont justice.

He even took us to the movies one session for a sneak preview of The Haunted Palace, which he had scripted from work of Lovercraft's but which was presented by AIP as another Edgar Allen Poe adaptation. We were encouraged to invite friends, and when two or three times as many people as were in the class gathered around Beaumont in front of the World Theater on Hollywood Boulevard, he reached for his wallet without hesitation and purchased a kitetail of tickets several feet long. Needless to say we applauded when his name came on the screen.

One night Ray Bradbury spoke to our group. It came out in passing reference that Bradbury was ten years older than Beaumont, who was then only thirty-four. I remember my shock, since Ray looked healthy enough to pass for ten years younger than our teacher. Had they misspoken, reversing the order? Later I learned of the illness that had already begun to take its debilitating toll, and wondered if on some molecular level Beaumont had understood how short his time was and that he must compress a lifetime's achievement into only a few years . . .

All that remains now is the memory of that summer as it exists unchanged in the minds of those who were there, and the typed comments he handed back with our assignments. I have carefully saved mine, a brief page on "Wet Season." Not long after the class ended I sent the story to Nolan, who was then editing the magazine Gamma. He rejected it with the longest and kindest such letter I would ever receive. He said that he did not quite understand the story but that it reminded him of "Free Dirt," another tale he could not grasp logically but which he found haunting and compelling. I was overwhelmed, particularly since the Beaumont story was a favorite of mine. My piece had nothing to do with it in either style or substance, and the comparison was certainly unwarranted as an assessment of quality, but Nolan had detected Beaumont's influence. Six months later Nolan wrote asking to see the story again, claiming that he could not get it out of his mind. This time he did publish it, something that would not have happened had it not been for the class.

There is more to tell, but this book is supposed to be by and about Beaumont, not his fans and camp followers. So let me just say that there were other lessons I am only now beginning to understand. Over the years I have come to see that summer as immeasurably richer than it seemed at the time, one of the cornerstone events of my life and career. Twenty years later I decided

to try in my own small way to pay back the debt by teaching
my version of the same class for UCLA Extension. I do not have
Charles Beaumont's talent, but I have done my best to inspire
students as young as I was then, and to retell as much of the
advice from 1963 as I can remember. Nolan has dropped by
several times, as have Bradbury and Matheson and many others
who have become my friends, including Beaumont's son Chris,
now a successful writer, producer. And on those nights when my
class lets out after three all-too-short hours, I wish that I had
taken Chuck up on his repeated offers to join him for a drink at
the Cock & Bull on Sunset. I never did, because I was embar-
rassed to be only twenty and poorly dressed with barely enough
gas money in my jacket pocket, and because I did not know that
that time would never come again. The only thing I can do now
is to buy my own students a drink while they are still mine to
know, and to ask them to raise their glasses with me in tribute
to the living memory of the man they should have known.

No FOWL HAD ever looked so posthumous. Its bones lay
stacked to one side of the plate like kindling: white, dry
and naked in the soft light of the restaurant. Bones only,
with every shard and filament of meat stripped methodically off. Otherwise, the plate was a vast glistening plain.

The other, smaller dishes and bowls were equally virginal. They shone fiercely against one another. And all a
pale cream color fixed upon the snowy white of a tablecloth
unstained by gravies and unspotted by coffee and free from
the stigmata of breadcrumbs, cigarette ash and fingernail
lint.

Only the dead fowl's bones and the stippled traceries of
hardened red gelatine clinging timidly to the bottom of a

dessert cup gave evidence that these ruins had once been a dinner.

Mr. Aorta, not a small man, permitted a mild belch, folded the newspaper he had found on the chair, inspected his vest for food leavings and then made his way briskly to the cashier.

The old woman glanced at this check.

"Yes, sir," she said.

"All righty," Mr. Aorta said and removed from his hip pocket a large black wallet. He opened it casually, whistling The Seven Joys of Mary through the space provided by his two front teeth.

The melody stopped, abruptly. Mr. Aorta looked concerned. He peered into his wallet, then began removing things; presently its entire contents was spread out.

He frowned.

"What seems to be the difficulty, sir?"

"Oh, no difficulty," the fat man said, "exactly." Though the wallet was manifestly empty, he flapped its sides apart, held it upside down and continued to shake it, suggesting the picture of a hydrophobic bat suddenly seized in mid-air.

Mr. Aorta smiled a weak harassed smile and proceeded to empty all of his fourteen separate pockets. In a time the counter was piled high with miscellany.

"Well!" he said impatiently. "What nonsense! What bother! Do you know what's happened? My wife's gone off and forgotten to leave me any change! Heigh-ho, well—my name is James Brockelhurst: I'm with the Pliofilm Corporation. I generally don't eat out, and—here, no, I insist. This is embarrassing for you as well as for myself. I *insist* upon leaving my card. If you will retain it, I shall return tomorrow evening at this time and reimburse you."

Mr. Aorta shoved the pasteboard into the cashier's hands, shook his head, shoveled the residue back into his pockets and, plucking a toothpick from a box, left the restaurant.

He was quite pleased with himself—an invariable reaction to the acquisition of something for nothing in return. It had all gone smoothly, and what a delightful meal!

He strolled in the direction of the streetcar stop, casting occasional licentious glances at undressed mannequins in department store windows.

The prolonged fumbling for his car token worked as efficiently as ever. (Get in the middle of the crowd, look bewildered, inconspicuous, search your pockets earnestly, the while edging from the vision of the conductor—then, take a far seat and read a newspaper.) In four years' traveling time, Mr. Aorta computed he had saved a total of $211.20.

The electric's ancient list did not jar his warm feeling of serenity. He studied the amusements briefly, then went to work on the current puzzle, whose prize ran into the thousands. Thousands of dollars, actually for nothing. Something for nothing. Mr. Aorta loved puzzles.

But the fine print made reading impossible.

Mr. Aorta glanced at the elderly woman standing near his seat; then, because the woman's eyes were full of tired pleading and insinuation, he refocused out the wire crosshatch windows.

What he saw caused his heart to throb. The section of town was one he passed every day, so it was a wonder he'd not noticed it before—though generally there was little provocation to sightsee on what was irreverently called "Death Row"—a dreary round of mortuaries, columbariums, crematories and the like, all crowded into a five-block area.

He yanked the stop-signal, hurried to the rear of the streetcar and depressed the exit plate. In a few moments he had walked to what he'd seen.

It was a sign, artlessly lettered though spelled correctly enough. It was not new, for the white paint had swollen and cracked and the rusted nails had dripped trails of dirty orange over the face of it.

The sign read:

FREE DIRT
Apply Within
Lilyvale
Cemetery

and was posted upon the moldering green of a woodboard wall.

Now Mr. Aorta felt a familiar sensation come over him. It happened whenever he encountered the word FREE—a magic word that did strange and wonderful things to his metabolism.

Free. What was the meaning, the *essence* of free? Why, something for nothing. And to get something for nothing was Mr. Aorta's chiefest pleasure in this mortal life.

The fact that it was dirt which was being offered Free did not oppress him. He seldom gave more than a fleeting thought to these things; for, he reasoned, nothing is without its use.

The other, subtler circumstances surrounding the sign scarcely occurred to him: why the dirt was being offered, where free dirt from a cemetery would logically come from; et cetera. In this connection he considered only the probable richness of the soil, for reasons he did not care to speculate upon.

Mr. Aorta's solitary hesitation encircled such problems as: Was this offer an honest one, without strings where he would have to buy something? Was there a limit on how much he could take home? If not, what would be the best method of transporting it?

Petty problems: all solvable.

Mr. Aorta did something inwardly that resembled a
smile, looked about and finally located the entrance to the
Lilyvale Cemetery.

These desolate grounds, which had once accommodated
a twine factory, an upholstering firm and an outlet for
ladies' shoes, now lay swathed in a miasmic vapor—
accreditable, in the absence of nearby bogs, to a profusion
of windward smokestacks. The blistered hummocks, peaked
with crosses, slabs and stones, loomed gray and sad in the
gloaming: withal, a place purely delightful to describe, and
a pity it cannot be—for how it looked there that evening
has little to do with the fat man and what was to become
of him.

Important only that it was a place full of dead people on
their backs under ground, moldering and moldered.

Mr. Aorta hurried because he despised to waste, along
with everything else, time. It was not long before he had
encountered the proper party and had this sort of conversation.

"I understand you're offering free dirt."

"That's right."

"How much may one have?"

"Much as one wants."

"On what days?"

"Any days; most likely there'll always be some fresh."

Mr. Aorta sighed in the manner of one who has just
acquired a lifetime inheritance or a measured checking account. He then made an appointment for the following Saturday and went home to ruminate agreeable ruminations.

At a quarter past nine that night he hit upon an excellent
use to which the dirt might be put.

His back yard, an ochre waste, lay chunked and dry, a
barren stretch repulsive to all but the grossest weeds. A
tree had once flourished there, in better days, a haven for

suburbanite birds, but then the birds disappeared for no good reason except that this was when Mr. Aorta moved into the house, and the tree became an ugly naked thing.

No children played in this yard.

Mr. Aorta was intrigued. Who could say? Perhaps something might be made to grow! He had long ago written an enterprising firm for free samples of seeds, and received enough to feed an army. But the first experiment had shriveled into hard useless pips and, seized by lassitude, Mr. Aorta had shelved the project. Now . . .

A neighbor named Joseph William Santucci permitted himself to be intimidated. He lent his old Reo truck, and after a few hours the first load of dirt had arrived and been shoveled into a tidy mound. It looked beautiful to Mr. Aorta, whose passion overcompensated for his weariness with the task. The second load followed, and the third, and the fourth, and it was dark as a coalbin out when the very last was dumped.

Mr. Aorta returned the truck and fell into an exhausted, though not unpleasant, sleep.

The next day was heralded by the distant clangor of church bells and the *chink-chink* of Mr. Aorta's spade, leveling the displaced graveyard soil, distributing it and grinding it in with the crusty earth. It had a continental look, this new dirt: swarthy, it seemed, black and saturnine: not at all dry, though the sun was already quite hot.

Soon the greater portion of the yard was covered, and Mr. Aorta returned to his sitting room.

He turned on the radio in time to identify a popular song, marked his discovery on a post card and mailed this away, confident that he would receive either a toaster or a set of nylon hose for his trouble.

Then he wrapped four bundles containing respectively: a can of vitamin capsules, half of them gone; a half-tin of coffee; a half-full bottle of spot remover; a box of soap flakes with most of the soap flakes missing. These he mailed, each with a note curtly expressing his total dissatisfaction, to the companies that had offered them to him on a money-back guarantee.

Now it was dinnertime, and Mr. Aorta beamed in anticipation. He sat down to a meal of sundry delicacies such as anchovies, sardines, mushrooms, caviar, olives and pearl onions. It was not, however, that he enjoyed this type of food for any aesthetic reasons: only that it had all come in packages small enough to be slipped into one's pocket without attracting the attention of busy grocers.

Mr. Aorta cleaned his plates so thoroughly no cat would care to lick them; the empty tins also looked new and bright: even their lids gleamed irridescently.

Mr. Aorta glanced at his checkbook balance, grinned indecently, and went to look out the back window.

The moon was cold upon the yard. Its rays passed over the high fence Mr. Aorta had constructed from free rocks, and splashed moodily onto the new black earth.

Mr. Aorta thought a bit, put away his checkbook and got out the boxes containing the garden seeds.

They were good as new.

Joseph William Santucci's truck was in use every Saturday thereafter for five weeks. This good man watched curiously as his neighbor returned each time with more dirt and yet more, and he made several remarks to his wife about the oddness of it all, but she could not bear even to talk about Mr. Aorta.

"He's robbed us blind," she said. "Look! He wears your old clothes, he uses my sugar and spices and borrows everything else he can think of! Borrows, did I say? I mean *steals*. For years! I have not seen the man pay for a thing yet! Where does he work that he makes so little money?"

Neither Mr. nor Mrs. Santucci knew that Mr. Aorta's daily labors involved sitting on the sidewalk downtown, with dark glasses on and a battered tin cup in front of him. They'd both passed him several times, though, and given him pennies, both unable to penetrate the clever disguise. It was all kept, the disguise, in a free locker at the railroad terminal.

"Here he comes again, that loony!" Mrs. Santucci wailed.

Soon it was time to plant the seeds, and Mr. Aorta went about this with ponderous precision, after having consulted numerous books at the library. Neat rows of summer squash were sown in the richly dark soil; and peas, corn, beans, onions, beets, rhubarb, asparagus, water cress and much more, actually. When the rows were filled and Mr. Aorta was stuck with extra packs, he smiled and dispersed strawberry seeds and watermelon seeds and seeds without clear description. Shortly the paper packages were all empty.

A few days passed and it was getting time to go to the cemetery again for a fresh load, when Mr. Aorta noticed an odd thing.

The dark ground had begun to yield to tiny eruptions. Closer inspection revealed that things had begun to grow. In the soil.

Now Mr. Aorta knew very little about gardening, when you got right down to it. He thought it strange, of course, but he was not alarmed. He saw things growing, that was the important point. Things that would become food.

Praising his good fortune, he hurried to Lilyvale and there received a singular disappointment: Not many people had died lately. There was scant little dirt to be had: hardly one truckful.

Ah well, he thought, things are bound to pick up over the holidays; and he took home what there was.

Its addition marked the improvement of the garden's growth. Shoots and buds came higher, and the expanse was far less bleak.

He could not contain himself until the next Saturday, for obviously this dirt was acting as some sort of fertilizer on his plants—the free food called out for more.

But the next Saturday came a cropper. Not even a shovel's load. And the garden was beginning to desiccate . . .

Mr. Aorta's startling decision came as a result of trying all kinds of new dirt and fertilizers of every imaginable description (all charged under the name of Uriah Gringsby). Nothing worked. His garden, which had promised a full bounty of edibles, had sunk to new lows: it was almost back to its original state. And this Mr. Aorta could not abide, for he had put in considerable labor on the project and this labor must not be wasted. It had deeply affected his other enterprises.

So—with the caution born of desperateness, he entered the gray quiet place with the tombstones one night, located freshly dug but unoccupied graves and added to their six-foot depth yet another foot. It was not noticeable to anyone who was not looking for such a discrepancy.

No need to mention the many trips involved: it is enough to say that in time Mr. Santucci's truck, parked a block away, was a quarter filled.

The following morning saw a rebirth in the garden.

And so it went. When dirt was to be had, Mr. Aorta was obliged; when it was not—well, it wasn't missed. And the garden kept growing and growing, until—

As if overnight, everything opened up! Where so short a time past had been a parched little prairie, was now a multifloral, multi-vegetable paradise. Corn bulged yellow from its spiny green husks; peas were brilliant green in their half-split pods, and all the other wonderful foodstuffs glowed full rich with life and showcase vigor. Rows and rows of them, and cross rows!

Mr. Aorta was almost felled by enthusiasm.

A liver for the moment and an idiot in the art of canning, he knew what he had to do.

It took a while to systematically gather up the morsels, but with patience, he at last had the garden stripped clean of all but weeds and leaves and other unedibles.

He cleaned. He peeled. He stringed. He cooked. He boiled. He took all the good free food and piled it geometrically on tables and chairs and continued with this until it was all ready to be eaten.

Then he began. Starting with the asparagus—he decided to do it in alphabetical order—he ate and ate clear through beets and celery and parsley and rhubarb, paused there for a drink of water, and went on eating, being careful not to waste a jot, until he came to water cress. By this time his stomach was twisting painfully, but it was a sweet pain, so he took a deep breath and, by chewing slowly, did away with the final vestigial bit of food.

The plates sparkled white, like a series of bloated snowflakes. It was all gone.

Mr. Aorta felt an almost sexual satisfaction—by which is meant, he had had enough . . . for now. He couldn't even belch.

Happy thoughts assailed his mind, as follows: His two greatest passions had been fulfilled; life's meaning acted out symbolically, like a condensed *Everyman*. These two things only are what this man thought of.

He chanced to look out the window.

What he saw was a bright speck in the middle of blackness. Small, somewhere at the end of the garden—faint yet distinct.

With the effort of a brontosaurus emerging from a tar pit Mr. Aorta rose from his chair, walked to the door and went out into his emasculated garden. He lumbered past dangling grotesqueries formed by shucks and husks and vines.

The speck seemed to have disappeared, and he looked carefully in all directions, slitting his eyes, trying to get accustomed to the moonlight.

Then he saw it. A white fronded thing, a plant, perhaps only a flower; but there, certainly, and all that was left.

Mr. Aorta was surprised to see that it was located at the bottom of a shallow declivity in the ground, very near the dead tree. He couldn't remember how a hole could have got dug in his garden, but there were always neighborhood kids and their pranks. A lucky think he'd grabbed the food when he did!

Mr. Aorta leaned over the edge of the small pit and reached down his hand toward the shining plant. It resisted his touch, somehow. He leaned farther over and still a little farther, and still he couldn't lay fingers on the thing.

Mr. Aorta was not an agile man. However, with the intensity of a painter trying to cover one last tiny spot awkwardly placed, he leaned just a mite farther and plosh! he'd toppled over the edge and landed with a peculiarly wet thud. A ridiculous damned bother, too: now he'd have to make a fool of himself, clambering out again. But, the plant: He searched the floor of the pit, and searched it, and no plant could be found. Then he looked up and was appalled by two things: Number One, the pit had been deeper than he'd thought; Number Two, the plant was wavering in the wind above him, on the rim he had so recently occupied.

The pains in Mr. Aorta's stomach got progressively worse. Movements increased the pains. He began to feel an overwhelming pressure in his ribs and chest.

It was at this moment of his discovery that the top of the hole was up beyond his reach that he saw the white plant in full moonglow. It looked rather like a hand, a big human hand, waxy and stiff and attached to the earth. The wind hit it and it moved slightly, causing a rain of dirt pellets to fall upon Mr. Aorta's face.

He thought a moment, judged the whole situation, and

began to climb. But the pains were too much and he fell, writhing.

The wind came again and more dirt was scattered down into the hole: soon the strange plant was being pushed to and fro against the soil, and dirt fell more and more heavily. More and more, more heavily and more heavily.

Mr. Aorta, who had never up to this point found occasion to scream, screamed. It was quite successful, despite the fact that no one heard it.

The dirt came down, and presently Mr. Aorta was to his knees in damp soil. He tried rising, and could not.

And the dirt came down from that big white plant flip-flopping in the moonlight and the wind.

After a while Mr. Aorta's screams took on a muffled quality.

For a very good reason.

Then, some time later, the garden was just as still and quite as it could be.

Mr. and Mrs. Joseph William Santucci found Mr. Aorta. He was lying on the floor in front of several tables. On the tables were many plates. The plates on the tables were clean and shining.

Mr. Aorta's stomach was distended past burst belt buckle, popped buttons and forced zipper. It was not unlike the image of a great white whale rising curiously from placid, forlorn waters.

"Ate hisself to death," Mrs. Santucci said in the fashion of the concluding line of a complex joke.

Mr. Santucci reached down and plucked a tiny ball of soil from the fat man's dead lips. He studied it. And an idea came to him . . .

He tried to get rid of the idea, but when the doctors found Mr. Aorta's stomach to contain many pounds of dirt—and nothing else, to speak of—Mr. Santucci slept badly, for almost a week.

They carried Mr. Aorta's body through the weeded but otherwise empty and desolate back yard, past the mournful dead tree and the rock fence.

They gave him a decent funeral, out of the goodness of their hearts, since no provision had been made.

And then they laid him to rest in a place with a moldering green woodboard wall: the wall had a little sign nailed to it.

And the wind blew absolutely Free.

SONG FOR A LADY

THE TRAVEL AGENT had warned us. It was an old ship, very old, very tired. And slow. "In fact," said Mr. Spierto, who had been everywhere and knew all about travel, "there's nothing slower afloat. Thirteen days to Le Havre, fourteen to Southampton. Provided there are favorable winds, of course! No; I doubt that we'll spend our honeymoon on her. Besides, this will be her last crossing. They're going to scrap the old relic in a month." And I think that's the reason we picked the *Lady Anne* for our first trip abroad. There was something appealing about taking part in a ship's last voyage, something, Eileen said, poignant and special.

Or maybe it was simply the agent's smirk. He might have been able to talk us out of it otherwise, but he had to smirk—the veteran of Katmandu and the innocent untraveled Iowans—and that got us mad. Anyway, we made two first class reservations, got married and caught a plane for New York.

What we saw at the dock surprised us. Spierto's horrified descriptions of the ship had led us to expect something between a kayak and The Flying Dutchman, whereas at first glance the *Lady Anne* seemed to be a perfectly ordinary ocean liner. Not that either of us had ever actually *seen* an ocean liner, except in films; but we decided what one should look like, and this looked like one. A tall giant of a vessel, it was, with a bright orange hull and two regal smokestacks; and a feeling of lightness, of grace, almost, despite the twenty thousand tons.

Then we got a little closer. And the *Lady Anne* turned into one of those well-dressed women who look so fine a block away and then disintegrate as you approach them. The orange on the hull was bright, but it wasn't paint. It was rust. Rust, like fungus, infecting every inch, trailing down from every port hole. Eating through the iron.

We gazed at the old wreck for a moment, then resolutely made our way past some elderly people on the dock and, at the gangplank, stopped. There was nothing to say, so Eileen said: "It's beautiful."

I was about to respond when a voice snapped: "No!" An aged man with thin but fierce red hair was standing behind us, bags in hand. "Not 'it'," he said, angrily. "*She*. This ship is a lady."

"Oh, I'm sorry." My wife nodded respectfully. "Well, then *she's* beautiful."

"Indeed she is!" The man continued to glare, not malevolently, not furiously, but with great suspicion. He stared up the plank, then paused. "You're seeing someone off?"

I told him no.

"Visitors, then."

"No," I said. "Passengers."

The old man's eyes widened. "How's that?" he said, exactly as if I'd just admitted that we were Russians spies. "You're what?"

"Passengers," I said again.

"Oh, no," he said, "no, no, I hardly think so. I hardly think that. This, you see is the *Lady Anne*. There's been a mistake."

"Jack, please!" A small square woman with thick glasses shook her head reproachfully.

"Be still," the old man snapped at her. His voice was becoming reedy with excitement. "If you'll consult your tickets, young fellow, I think you'll find that a serious error has occurred here. I repeat, this is the *Lady Anne*—"

"—and I repeat," I said, not too patiently, "that we're passengers." However, he didn't move, so I fished the tickets out of my pockets and shoved them at him.

He stared at the papers for a long time; then, sighing, handed them back. "Private party," he muttered; "excursion, might say. Planned so long. Outsiders! I . . ." And without another word, he turned and marched stiffly up the gangplank. The small square woman followed him, giving us a thin, curious smile.

"Well!" Eileen grinned, after the slightest hesitation. "I guess that means 'Welcome Aboard' in British."

"Forget it." I took her hand and we went directly to the cabin. It was small, just as the friendly travel agent had prophesied: two bunks, an upper and lower, a sink, a crown-shaped *pot du chambre*. But it wasn't stark. Incredible fat cupids stared blindly from the ceiling, the door was encrusted with flaked gold paint, and there was a chipped chandelier. Grotesque, but cheerful, somehow. Of course, it would have been cheerful at half the size—with a few rats thrown in—because we'd gotten ourselves into this mess against everyone's advice and, one way or another, we were determined to prove that our instincts had been right.

"Nice," said Eileen, reaching up and patting a cupid's belly.

I kissed her and felt, then, that things wouldn't be too bad. It would take more than a grumpy old Englishman and a crazy stateroom to spoil our trip. A lot more.

Unfortunately, a lot more was fast in coming.

When we took our stroll out on deck, we noticed a surprisingly large number of elderly people standing at the rail; but, we were excited, and somehow this didn't register. We waved at the strangers on the dock, watched the passengers still coming aboard, and began to feel the magic. Then I saw the old red-headed gentleman tottering toward us, still glaring and blinking. In a way he looked like the late C. Aubrey Smith, only older and thinner. Just as straight, though, and just as bushy in the eyebrows.

"See here," he said, pointing at me with his cane, "you aren't really serious about this, are you?"

"About what?" I said.

"Traveling on the *Lady Anne*. That is, hate to sound cliqueish and all that, but—"

"We're serious," Eileen said, curtly.

"Dear me." The old man clucked his tongue. "Americans, too. British ship, y'know. Sort of reunion and—" He motioned toward another man in tweeds. "Burgess! Over here!" The man, if anything older than our friend, caned his way across the wooden planks. "Burgess, these are the ones I mean. They've tickets!"

"No, no, no," said the man with the cane. "Whole thing obviously a ghastly blunder. Calm yourself, McKenzie: we've time yet. Now then." He gave us a crafty, crooked smile. "No doubt you young people aren't aware that this is rather a, how shall I put it, private, sort of, cruise; d'ye see? Very tight. Dear me, yes. Unquestionably a slip-up on the part of—"

"Look," I said, "I'm getting tired of this routine. There hasn't been any slip-up or anything else. This is our ship and by God we're sailing to Europe on it. Her."

"That," said Burgess, "is bad news indeed."

I started to walk away, but the old man's fingers gripped my arm. "Please," he said. "I expect this may seem odd to you, quite odd, but we're actually trying to be of help."

"Exactly so," said the redheaded man, McKenzie.

"There are," he whispered darkly, "things you don't know about this ship."

"For example," Burgess cut in, "she is over sixty-five years old. No ventilation, y'know; no modern conveniences whatever on her. And she takes forever to cross."

"And dangerous," said the redheaded man. "Dear me, yes."

The two old fellows pulled us along the deck, gesturing with their canes.

"Look at those deck chairs, just look at 'em. Absolute antiques. Falling to pieces. Wouldn't trust the best of 'em to hold a baby."

"And the blankets, as you see, are rags. Quite threadbare."

"And look at that staircase. Shameful! Shouldn't be at all surprised to see it collapse at any moment."

"Oh, we can tell you, the *Lady Anne* is nothing but an ancient rust bucket."

"So you see, of course, how impractical the whole idea is."

They looked at us.

Eileen smiled her sweetest smile. "As a matter of fact," she said, "I think this is the most darling little boat I've ever seen. Don't you agree, Alan?"

"Definitely," I said.

The old men stared in disbelief; then Burgess said: "You'll get bored."

"We never get bored," Eileen said.

McKenzie said, "You'll get sick, then!"

"Never."

"Wait!" Burgess was frowning. "We're wasting time. Look here, why you are both so damned determined to travel on an outdated ship when there are dozens of fine modern vessels available, I shan't pretend to understand. Perhaps it is typical American stubbornness. Flying in the face of convention, that sort of thing. Eh? Admirable!

However, we must insist that you overcome this determination."

Eileen opened her mouth, then shut it when she saw the roll of money clutched in the old man's fist.

"I am prepared," he said, in a firm voice, "to pay you double the amount you spent for your tickets, provided you will abandon your plan."

There was a short silence.

"Well?"

I glanced at Eileen. "Not a chance," I said.

"Triple the amount?"

"No."

"Very well. I am forced to extremes. If you will leave the *Lady Anne* now, I will give you the equivalent of five thousand American dollars."

"Which," McKenzie said, "I will meet."

"Making it ten thousand dollars."

Eileen seemed almost on the edge of tears. "Not for a million," she said. "Now let me tell you gentlemen something. Ever since we picked this ship, people have been doing their best to discourage us. I don't know why and I don't care. If you're so afraid the brash Americans are going to upset your British tea—"

"My good lady, we—"

"—you can forget it. We won't go near you. But we paid for our tickets and that gives us every bit as much right to the *Lady Anne* as you have! Now just go away and leave us alone!"

The conversation ended. We walked back to the bow and waited, in silence, until the line had been cast off and the tugs had begun to pull us out to sea; then, still not mentioning the episode, we wandered around to the other side of the ship. I know now that there were elderly people there, too, and only elderly people, but again, we were too sore—and the adventure was too new—to notice this.

It wasn't, in fact, until the fire drill, with the corridor

packed, that it first began to sink in. There weren't any young people to be seen. No students. No children. Only old men and old women, most of them walking, but several on canes and on crutches, a few in wheel chairs. And, judging from the number of tweed suits, pipes, mustaches, and woolen dresses, mostly all British.

I was thinking about the two weeks to Southampton and the ten thousand dollars, when Eileen said, "Look."

I looked. And ran into hundreds of unblinking eyes, turned directly on us. Staring as though we were a new species.

"Don't worry," I whispered, without much assurance, "we'll find somebody our age on board. It stands to reason."

And it did stand to reason. But although we looked everywhere, everywhere it was the same: old men, old women. British. Silent. Staring.

Finally we got tired of the search and walked into the ship's single public room. It was called the Imperial Lounge: a big hall with hundreds of chairs and tables, a tiny dance floor, a podium for musicians, and a bar. All done in the rococo style you'd expect to find on the *Titanic*: purples and greens, faded to gray, and chipped gold. People sat in the chairs, neither reading nor playing cards nor talking. Just sitting, with hands folded. We tiptoed across a frayed rug to the bar and asked the grandfather in charge for two double-Scotches; then we ordered two more.

"Housie-Housie tonight," Eileen said, gesturing toward a blackboard. "That's British bingo. But I suppose we won't be invited."

"Nuts to 'em," I said. We looked at each other, then out over the white-thatched balding sea of heads—some dropping in afternoon sleep already—and back at each other; and I'm proud to say that neither of us wept.

After the drinks we exited the Imperial Lounge, softly, and queued up for lunch. The restaurant was Empire style, the silks smelling of age and dust, the tapestries blurred. We ordered something called Bubble and Squeak because it sounded jolly, but it wasn't. And neither were the diners surrounding us. Particularly those who sat alone. They all had an air of melancholy, and they stared at us throughout the meal, some surreptitiously, some openly.

Finally we gave up trying to eat and fled back to the Imperial Lounge, because where else was there to go?

The sea of heads was calm. Except for one. It was red, and when we entered it nodded and bounced up.

Mr. Friendly's eyes were snapping. "I beg your pardon," he said. "Hate to bother you. But my wife, Mrs. McKenzie, over there—she, uh, points out that I've been rude. Quite rude. And I expect I ought to apologize."

"Do you?" I asked.

"Oh, yes! But there is something more important. Really good news, in fact." It was strange to see the old boy smiling so happily; the frown seemed to have been a fixture. "Mr. Burgess and I talked the whole thing over," he said, "and we've decided that you won't have to leave the ship after all."

"Say," I said, a trifle bitterly, "that *is* good news. We were afraid we'd have to swim back and it's had us sick with worry."

"Really?" Mr. McKenzie cocked his head to one side. "Sorry about that, my boy. But we were quite concerned, all of us, as I daresay you gathered. Y'see, it simply hadn't occurred to us that an *outsider* would ever want to go on the *Lady*. I mean, she's primarily a freighter, as it were; and the last time she took on a new passenger was, according to Captain Protheroe, the summer of '48. So you can understand—but never mind that, never mind that. It's all settled now."

"*What's* all settled?" asked my wife.

"Why, everything," said the old man, expressively. "But come, you really must join Mrs. McKenzie and me for a bit of tea. That's one thing that hasn't changed on the *Lady*. She still has the finest tea of any ship afloat. Eh, my dear?"

The small square woman nodded.

We exchanged introductions as if we were meeting for the first time. The man named Burgess extended his hand and shook mine with real warmth, which was quite a shock. His wife, a quiet, pale woman, smiled. She stared at her cup for a moment, then said, "Ian, I expect the Ransomes are wondering a bit about your and Mr. McKenzie's behavior this morning."

"Eh?" Burgess coughed. "Oh, yes. But it's all right now, Cynthia; I told you that."

"Still—"

"Perhaps I can help," said Mrs. McKenzie, who had not yet spoken. Her voice was a lovely soft thing, yet, oddly, commanding. She looked at Eileen. "But first you must tell us why you chose the *Lady Anne*."

Eileen told them.

Mrs. McKenzie's smile changed her face, it washed away the years and she became almost beautiful. "My dear," she said, "you were quite right. The *Lady* is special. More special, I should say, than either you or your husband might imagine. You see, this is the ship Jack and I sailed on when we were married—which would be fifty-six years ago."

"Fifty-five," said the redheaded man. He took a drink of tea and set the cup down gently. "She was a splendid thing then, though. The ship, I mean!"

"Jack, really."

Eileen looked at McKenzie and said, in an even voice: "I thought you told us that it was an old rust bucket."

"Not 'it.' *She*." Burgess blushed. "Should both have been struck down by lightning," he said. "Greatest lie ever uttered. Mrs. Ransome, mark this: the *Lady Anne* was and is now the finest ship that ever crossed the sea. Queen of the fleet, she was."

"And quite unusual," put in McKenzie. "Only one of her kind, I believe. Y'see, she specialized in honeymooners. That was her freight then: young people in love; aye. That's what makes your presence so—what shall I say—ironic? Eh? No, that isn't it. Not ironic. Sally, what is the damned word I'm looking for?"

"Sweet," said his wife, smiling.

"No, no. Anyway, that was it. A regular floating wedding suite, y'might say. Young married couples, that's all you'd ever see on her. Full of juice and the moon in their eyes. Dear me. It was funny, though. All those children trying to act grown-up and worldly, trying to act married and used to it, d'you see, and every one of 'em as nervous as a mouse. Remember, Burgess?"

"I do. Of course, now, that only lasted for a few days, McKenzie. The *Lady Anne* gave 'em time to know each other." The old man laughed. "She was a wise ship. She understood such things."

Mrs. McKenzie lowered her eyes, but not, I thought, out of embarrassment. "At any rate," she said, "although it was, needless to say, unofficial, that did seem to be the policy of the owners, then. *Everything* arranged for young people. For anyone else, I imagine the ship must have been a bit on the absurd side. Love has its own particular point of view, you know: it sees everything larger than life. Nothing too ornate for it, or too fancy, or too dramatic. If it is a good love, it demands the theatrical—and then transfigures it. It turns the grotesque into the lovely, as a child does . . ." The old woman raised her eyes. "Where a shipping line ever found that particular vision, I shall never know. But they made the *Lady Anne* into an enchanted gondola and took that moment of happiness and—pure—sweet pain that all lovers have and made the moment live for two really unspeakably pleasant weeks . . ."

The redheaded McKenzie cleared his throat loudly. "Quite so," he said, glancing at his wife, who smiled secretly. "Quite so. I expect they get the drift, my dear. No need to go sticky."

"But," said his wife, "I feel sticky."

"Eh? Oh." He patted her hand. "Of course. Still—"

Burgess removed his pipe. "The point is," he said, "that we spent a good many fine hours aboard this old scow. The sort of hours one doesn't forget. When we heard that they were going to . . . retire . . . the *Lady*, well, it seemed right, somehow, that we should join her on her last two-way sailing. And that, I think accounts for the number of old parties aboard. Most of 'em here for the same reason, actually. Boshier-Jones and his wife over there, sound asleep: the bald chap. Engineer in his day, and a good one. The White-aways, just past the column. They were on our first sailing. Innes Champion, the writer: quite a droll fellow most of the time, though you wouldn't guess it now. A widower, y'know. Wife passed on in '29. They had their honeymoon on the *Lady*—a better one, if possible, than ours: propeller fell off—that would be in 1906—and they were four days in repairing it, so he says. Terrible liar, though. Don't know that chap in the wheel-chair; do you, McKenzie?"

"Brabham. Nice enough, but getting on, if you know what I mean. Tends to tremble and totter. Still, a decent sort."

"Alone?"

"I fear so."

Mrs. McKenzie took a sip of cold tea and said: "I hope you understand a bit more of our attitude, Mrs. Ransome. And I do hope you will forgive us for staring at you and your husband occasionally. It's quite impolite, but I think we are not actually seeing *you* so much as we are seeing ourselves, as we were fifty years ago. Isn't that foolish?"

Eileen tried to say something, but it didn't work. She shook her head.

"One other thing," Mrs. McKenzie said. "You *are* in love with each other, aren't you?"

"Yes," I said. "Very much."

"Splendid. I told Jack that when I first saw you this morning. But, of course, that wasn't the point. I'd forgotten the plan."

"Sally!" McKenzie frowned. "Do watch it."

The old woman put a hand to her mouth, and we sat there quietly. Then Burgess said, "I think it's time for the men to adjourn for a cigar. With your permission?"

We walked to the bar and Burgess introduced me around. "Van Vlyman, this is Ransome. He's American but he's all right. Nothing to worry about." "Sanders, shake hands with young Ransome. He and his wife are on their honeymoon, y'know. Picked the *Lady Anne*! No, no, I tell you: it's all been straightened out." "Fairman, here now, wake up; this is—"

The warmth of these men suddenly filled me, and after a while it seemed as though, magically, I wasn't thirty-two at all, but seventy-two, with all the wisdom of those years.

The man called Sanders insisted upon buying a round and raised his glass. "To the finest, loveliest, happiest ship that ever was!" he said, and we drank, solemnly.

"Pity," someone said.

"No!" The portly ex-colonel, Van Vlyman, crashed his fist down upon the polished mahogany. "Not a 'pity'! A *crime*. An evil, black-hearted crime, perpetrated by stupid little men with bow ties."

"Easy, Van Vlyman. Nothing to get heated over now."

"Nothing, indeed!" roared the old soldier. "Easy, indeed! God Almighty, are all of you so ancient, so feeble that you can't see the truth? Don't you know why they want to scrap the *Lady*?"

Sanders shrugged. "Outlived her usefulness," he said.

"Usefulness? Usefulness to whom, sir? Nonsense! D'you hear? She's the best ship on the sea." Van Vlyman scowled darkly. "A little slow, perhaps—but, I put it to you, Sanders, by whose standards? Yours? Mine? Thirteen, fourteen days for a crossing is fast enough for anyone in his right mind. Only people aren't in their right minds any more, that's the trouble. That's the core of it right there. People, I say, have forgotten how to relax. They've forgotten how to appreciate genuine luxury. Speed: that's all that counts nowadays. Get it over with! Why? Why are they in such a hurry?" He glared at me. "What's the damned rush?"

Burgess looked sad. "Van Vlyman, aren't you being a bit—"

"To the contrary. I am merely making an observation upon the state of the world today. Also, I am attempting to point out the true reason for this shameful decision."

"Which is?"

"A plot, *doubt*less of Communist origin," declared the colonel.

"Oh, really, Van Vlyman—"

"Haven't you eyes? Are you all that senile? The *Lady Anne* was condemned because she represents a way of life. A better way of life, by God, sir, than anything they're brewing up today; and they can't stand that. She's not just a ship, I tell you; she's the old way. She's grace and manners and tradition. Don't you see? She's the Empire!"

The old man's eyes were flashing.

"Nothing," he said, in a lower voice, "is sacred any more. The beasts are at the gate, and we're all too old to fight them. Like the *Lady* herself, too old and too tired. So we stand about in stone fury like pathetic statues with our medals gone to rust and our swords broken while the vandals turn our castles into sideshows, put advertisements for soap along our roads, and—wait! the time is soon!—reach up their hairy hands and pull the Queen down from her throne. Scrap the *Lady*! No. But how are we to stop them from scrapping England?"

The old man stood quite still for several minutes, then he turned and walked away; and McKenzie said, beneath his breath: "Poor chap. He'd planned this with his wife, and then she had to go and die on him."

Burgess nodded. "Well, we'll have some cards tonight and he'll feel better."

We drank another; then Eileen and I had dinner with the McKenzies and retired to our cabin.

Mrs. McKenzie had been right. Love does have its own particular vision: the plaster cupids and golden door didn't seem grotesque at all; in fact, very late at night, with the moon striping the calm black ocean, it seemed to me that there could hardly be a nicer room.

The next twelve days were like a lazy, endless dream. We had trouble, at first, adjusting to it. When you've lived most of your life in a city, you forget that leisure can be a creative thing. You forget that there is nothing sinful in relaxation. But the *Lady Anne* was good to us. She gave us time, plenty of time. And on the fourth day I stopped fidgeting and began to enjoy the pleasures of getting to know the woman I'd married. Eileen and I talked together and made love together and walked the ancient deck together, hoping that it would never end, secure in the knowledge that it would . . . but not for a while.

We forgot, too, that the other passengers were in their seventies and eighties. It wasn't important, any longer. They were married couples, as we were, and in a very real way, they were on their honeymoons, too. Twice we surprised McKenzie and his wife on the promenade deck well after midnight, and the Burgesses hardly ever stopped holding hands. The women and men who were alone looked melancholy, but somehow not sad. Even the old colonel, Van Vlyman, had stopped being angry. We'd see him every now and then seated on the deck, his eyes looking out over the Atlantic, dreaming.

Then, treacherously, as if it sneaked up on us, the twelfth day came, and the smell of land was in the air. Far in the distance we could see the gray spine of Cherbourg, and we wondered what had happened to the hours.

McKenzie stopped us in The Imperial Lounge. His face wore a slightly odd expression. "Well," he said, "it's almost over. I expect you're glad."

"No," I told him. "Not really."

That pleased him. "The *Lady*'s done her job for you, then?"

"She has," said Eileen, a different, softer, more feminine Eileen than I'd known two weeks before.

"Well, then; you'll be coming to the dance tonight?"

"Wouldn't miss it."

"Capital! Uh . . . one thing. Have you packed your luggage?"

"No. I mean, we don't dock till tomorrow night, so—"

"Quite. Still, it would do no harm to pack them anyhow," said McKenzie. "See you at the dance!"

Like so many others, the things he said frequently sounded peculiar and meant nothing. We went outside and stood at the rail and watched the old sailors—who were all part of the original crew—scrubbing down the ship. They seemed to be working especially hard, removing every trace of dirt, scraping the rails with stiff wire brushes, getting things neat.

At eight we went back to the cabin and changed into our evening dress; and at nine-thirty joined the others in the Imperial Lounge.

The incredible little band was playing antique waltzes and fox trots, and the floor was filled with dancing couples. After a few drinks, we became one of the couples. I danced with Eileen for a while, then with almost every other woman aboard. Everyone seemed to be happy again. Eileen was trying to rumba with Colonel Van Vlyman, who kept sputtering that he didn't know how, and Mrs. McKenzie taught me a step she'd learned in 1896. We drank some more and danced more and laughed, and then the clock struck midnight and the band stood up and played Auld Lang Syne and the people held hands and were quiet.

McKenzie and Burgess walked up then, and Burgess said: "Mr. Ransome, Mrs. Ransome: we'd like you to meet our captain, Captain Protheroe. He's been here as long as the *Lady* has; isn't that right, sir?"

An unbelievably old man in a neat blue uniform nodded his head. His hair was thin and white, his eyes were clear.

"A most unusual man, the captain," said Burgess. "He understand things. Like the rest of us, actually—except that his wife is a ship. Still, I doubt I love my Cynthia more than he loves the *Lady Anne*."

The captain smiled and looked directly at us. "You've had a pleasant voyage?" he asked, in a good strong voice.

"Yes, sir," I said. "We're grateful to have been part of it."

"Indeed? Well, that's very nice."

There was a pause, and I suddenly became aware of a curious fact. The vibration of the engines, deep below us, had stopped. The ship itself had stopped.

Captain Protheroe's smile broadened. "Very nice, indeed," he said. "As Mr. McKenzie pointed out to me earlier, your presence aboard has been rather symbolic, if I may use the word. Us ending, you beginning; that sort of thing, eh?" He rose from the chair. "Now then. I'm afraid that I must say good bye to you. We've radioed your position and you oughtn't to be inconvenienced for more than a few hours."

"Beg pardon?" I said.

Burgess coughed. "They don't know," he said. "Thought it would be better that way."

"Eh? Oh, yes, how stupid of me. Of course." Captain Protheroe turned his clear eyes back to us. "You won't mind obliging us," he said, "by gathering up your things?"

"Gathering up our things?" I parroted, stupidly. "Why?"

"Because," he said, "we are going to put you off the ship."

Eileen grabbed my arm, but neither of us could think of a thing to say. I was vaguely conscious of the stillness of the boat, of the people in the room, staring at us.

"I'm very much afraid that I shall have to ask you to hurry," said the captain, "for it is getting rather late. The rescue vessel is already on its way, you see. You, uh, *do* understand?"

"No," I said, slowly, "we don't. And we're certainly not going anywhere until we do."

Captain Protheroe drew up to his full height and glanced sharply at McKenzie. "Really," he said, "I should've thought you'd have anticipated this."

McKenzie shrugged. "Didn't want to worry them."

"Indeed. And now we're in a mess, for, of course, we've no time at all for lengthy explanations."

"In that case," said Burgess, "let's skip them." His eyes were twinkling. "I rather think they'll understand eventually."

The captain nodded. He said. "Excuse me," walked out of the room, returned a moment later with a pistol. Then, aiming the pistol at me: "Sorry, but I must insist you do as we say. McKenzie, take this thing and see to it that the Ransomes are ready within ten minutes."

McKenzie nodded, brandished the gun. "Come along," he said. "And don't take it too hard, my boy."

He prodded us down to the cabin and kept waving the pistol until we'd packed our bags. He seemed hugely delighted with his new role.

"Now, gather up the life jackets and follow me."

We returned to the boat station, where almost everyone on the ship had gathered.

"Lower away!" cried the captain, and a useless-looking white lifeboat was cranked over the side.

"Now then, if you will please climb down that ladder . . ."

"For God's sake," I said. "This—"

"The *ladder*, Mr. Ransome. And do be careful!"

We clambered down into the lifeboat, which was rocking gently, and watched them raise the rope.

We could see the McKenzies, the Burgesses, Van Vlyman, Sanders and Captain Protheroe standing by the rail, waving. They had never looked so pleasant, so happy.

"Don't worry," one of them called, "you'll be picked up in no time at all. Plenty of water and food there; and a light. You're sure you have all your luggage?"

I heard the ship's engines start up again, and I yelled some idiotic things; but then the *Lady Anne* began to pull away from us. The old people at the rail, standing very close to one another, waved and smiled and called: "Good bye! Good bye!"

"Come back!" I screamed, feeling, somehow, that none of this was actually happening. "Damn it, come back here!" Then Eileen touched my shoulder, and we sat there listening to the fading voices and watching the immense black hull drift away into the night.

It became suddenly very quiet, very still. Only the sound of water slapping against the lifeboat.

We waited. Eileen's eyes were wide; she was staring into the darkness, her hand locked tightly in mine.

"Shhh," she said.

We sat there for another few minutes, quietly, rocking; then there was a sound, soft at first, hollow, but growing.

"Alan!"

The explosion thundered loose in a swift rushing fury, and the water began to churn beneath us.

Then, as suddenly, it was quiet again.

In the distance I could see the ship burning. I could feel the heat of it. Only the stern was afire, though: all the rest of it seemed untouched—and I was certain, oddly certain that no one had been harmed by the blast.

Eileen and I held each other and watched as, slowly, as gracefully and purposefully, the *Lady Anne* listed on her side. For an eternity she lay poised, then the dark mass of her slipped into the water as quickly and smoothly as a giant needle into velvet.

It could not have taken more than fifteen minutes. Then the sea was calm and as empty as it ever was before there were such things as ships and men.

We waited for another hour in the lifeboat, and I asked Eileen if she felt cold but she said no. There was a wind across the ocean, but my wife said that she had never felt so warm before.

LAST RITES

Introduction by
Richard Matheson

I have referred (in print) to Chuck Beaumont's stories with such phrases as "alight with the magic of a truly extraordinary imagination," "shot through with veins of coruscating wit," "feather light and dancing on a wind of jest" and "flashes of the wondrous and delightful."

All true; and this may well be the over-riding image of his work.

But there is more. Other stories which cut deeper. Which move the reader and speak of things profound.

Such a story is "Last Rites."

I don't know whether Chuck was raised as a Catholic. I don't think so but I'm not positive. I know he married a woman who was deeply committed to Catholicism. Perhaps his knowledge—and insight—into the religion came from his relationship with his wife Helen.

Wherever it came from, there is a sense of truth to it. For my money, Graham Greene never wrote a story any more perceptive about Catholicism than "Last Rites." I find it extremely moving, shot through not with "veins of coruscating wit" but with a deep vein of humanity and love.

What more could any reader ask of a story? What greater legacy could any writer leave?

———————————————————————

SOMEWHERE IN THE church a baby was shrieking. Father Courtney listened to it, and sighed, and made the Sign of the Cross. Another battle, he thought, dismally. Another grand tug of war. And who won this time, Lord? Me? Or that squalling infant, bless its innocence?

"In the Name of the Father, and of the Son, and of the Holy Ghost. Amen."

He turned and made his way down the pulpit steps, and told himself, Well, you ought to be used to it by now, Heaven knows. After all, you're a priest, not a monologist. What do you care about "audience reaction?" And besides, who ever listens to these sermons of yours, anyway—even under the best of conditions? A few of the ladies in the parish (though you're sure they never hear or understand a word), and, of course, Donovan. But who else?

Screech away, little pink child! Screech until you—no. No, no. Ahhh!

He walked through the sacristy, trying not to think of Donovan, or the big city churches with their fine nurseries, and sound-proof walls, and amplifiers that amplified . . .

One had what one had: it was God's will.

And were things really so bad? Here there was the smell of forests, wasn't there? And in what city parish could you see wild flowers growing on the hills like bright lava? Or feel the earth breathing?

He opened the door and stepped outside.

The fields were dark-silver and silent. Far above the

fields, up near the clouds, a rocket launch moved swiftly, dragging its slow thunder behind it.

Father Courtney blinked.

Of course things were not so bad. Things would be just fine, he thought, and I would not be nervous and annoyed at little children, if only—

Abruptly he put his hands together. "Father," he whispered, "let him be well. Let that be Your will!"

Then, deciding not to wait to greet the people, he wiped his palms with a handkerchief and started for the rectory.

The morning was very cold. A thin film of dew coated each pebble along the path, and made them all glisten like drops of mercury. Father Courtney looked at the pebbles and thought of other walks down this path, which led through a woods to Hidden River, and of himself laughing; of excellent wine and soft cushions and himself arguing, arguing; of a thousand sweet hours in the past.

He walked and thought these things and did not hear the telephone until he had reached the rectory stairs.

A chill passed over him, unaccountably.

He went inside and pressed a yellow switch. The screen blurred, came into focus. The face of an old man appeared, filling the screen.

"Hello, Father."

"George!" the priest smiled and waved his fist, menacingly. "George, why haven't you contacted me?" He sputtered. "Aren't you out of that bed yet?"

"Not yet, Father."

"Well, I expected it, I knew it. *Now* will you let me call a doctor?"

"No—" The old man in the screen shook his head. He was thin and pale. His hair was profuse, but very white, and there was something in his eyes. "I think I'd like you to come over, if you could."

"I shouldn't," the priest said, "after the way you've been

treating all of us. But, if there's still some of that Chianti left . . ."

George Donovan nodded. "Could you come right away?"

"Father Yoshida won't be happy about it."

"Please. Right away."

Father Courtney felt his fingers draw into fists. "Why?" he asked, holding onto the conversational tone. "Is anything the matter?"

"Not really," Donovan said. His smile was brief. "It's just that I'm dying."

"And I'm going to call Doctor Ferguson. Don't give me any argument, either. This nonsense has gone far—"

The old man's face knotted. "No," he said, loudly. "I forbid you to do that."

"But you're ill, man. For all we know, you're *seriously* ill. And if you think I'm going to stand around and watch you work yourself into the hospital just because you happen to dislike doctors, you're crazy."

"Father, listen—*please*. I have my reasons. You don't understand them, and I don't blame you. But you've got to trust me. I'll explain everything, if you'll promise me you won't call *anyone*."

Father Courtney breathed unsteadily; he studied his friend's face. Then he said, "I'll promise this much. I won't contact a doctor until I've seen you."

"Good." The old man seemed to relax.

"I'll be there in fifteen minutes."

"With your Little Black Bag?"

"Certainly not. You're going to be all right."

"Bring it, Father. Please. Just in case."

The screen blurred and danced and went white.

Father Courtney hesitated at the blank telephone.

Then he walked to a table and raised his fists and brought them down hard, once.

You're going to get well, he thought. It isn't going to be too late.

Because if you are dying, if you really are, and I could have prevented it . . .

He went to the closet and drew on his overcoat.

It was thick and heavy, but it did not warm him. As he returned to the sacristy he shivered and thought that he had never been so cold before in all his life.

The Helicar whirred and dropped quickly to the ground. Father Courtney removed the ignition key, pocketed it, and thrust his bulk out the narrow door, wheezing.

A dull rumbling sifted down from the sky. The wake of fleets a mile away, ten miles, a hundred.

It's raining whales in our backyard, the priest thought, remembering how Donovan had described the sound once to a little girl.

A freshet of autumn leaves burst against his leg, softly, and for a while he stood listening to the rockets' dying rumble, watching the shapes of gold and red that scattered in the wind, like fire.

Then he whispered, "Let it be Your will," and pushed the picket gate.

The front door of the house was open.

He walked in, through the living-room, to the study.

"George."

"In here," a voice answered.

He moved to the bedroom, and twisted the knob.

George Donovan lay propped on a cloudbank of pillows, his thin face white as the linen. He was smiling.

"I'm glad to see you, Father," he said, quietly.

The priest's heart expanded and shrank and began to thump in his chest.

"The Chianti's down here in the night-table," Donovan gestured. "Pour some: morning's a good enough time for a dinner wine."

"Not now, George."

"Please. It will help."

Father Courtney pulled out the drawer and removed the

half-empty bottle. He got a glass from the bookshelf, filled it. Dutifully, according to ritual, he asked, "For you?"

"No," Donovan said. "Thank you all the same." He turned his head. "Sit over there, Father, where I can see you."

The priest frowned. He noticed that Donovan's arms were perfectly flat against the blanket, that his body was rigid, outlined beneath the covering. No part of the old man moved except the head, and that slowly, unnaturally.

"That's better. But take off your coat—it's terribly hot in here. You'll catch pneumonia."

The room was full of cold winds from the open shutters.

Father Courtney removed his coat.

"You've been worried, haven't you?" Donovan asked.

The priest nodded. He tried to sense what was wrong, to smell the disease, if there was a disease, if there was anything.

"I'm sorry about that." The old man seemed to sigh. His eyes were misted, webbed with distance, lightly. "But I wanted to be alone. Sometimes you have to be alone, to think, to get things straight. Isn't that true?"

"Sometimes, I suppose, but—"

"No. I know what you're going to say, the questions you want to ask. But there's not enough time . . ."

Father Courtney arose from the chair, and walked quickly to the telephone extension. He jabbed a button. "I'm sorry, George," he said, "but you're going to have a doctor."

The screen did not flicker.

He pressed the button again, firmly.

"Sit down," the tired voice whispered. "It doesn't work. I pulled the wires ten minutes ago."

"Then I'll fly over to Milburn—"

"If you do, I'll be dead when you get back. Believe this: I know what I'm talking about."

The priest clenched and unclenched his stubby fingers, and sat down in the chair again.

Donovan chuckled. "Drink up," he said. "We can't have good wine going to waste, can we?"

The priest put the glass to his lips. He tried to think clearly. If he rushed out to Milburn and got Doctor Ferguson, perhaps there'd be a chance. Or—He took a deep swallow.

No. That wouldn't do. It might take hours.

Donovan was talking now; the words lost—a hum of locusts in the room, a far-off murmuring; then, like a radio turned up: "Father, how long have we been friends, you and I?"

"Why . . . twenty years," the priest answered. "Or more."

"Would you say you know me very well by now?"

"I believe so."

"Then tell me first, right now, would you say that I've been a good man?"

Father Courtney smiled. "There've been worse," he said and thought of what this man had accomplished in Mount Vernon, quietly, in his own quiet way, over the years. The building of a decent school for the children—Donovan had shamed the people into it. The new hospital—Donovan's doing, his patient campaigning. Entertainment halls for the young; a city fund for the poor; better teachers, better doctors—all, all because of the old man with the soft voice, George Donovan.

"Do you mean it?"

"Don't be foolish. And don't be treacly, either. Of course I mean it."

In the room, now, a strange odor fumed up, suddenly.

The old man said, "I'm glad." Still he did not move. "But, I'm sorry I asked. It was unfair."

"I don't have the slightest idea what you're talking about."

"Neither do I, Father, completely. I thought I did, once, but I was wrong."

The priest slapped his knees, angrily. "Why won't you let me get a doctor? We'll have plenty of time to talk afterwards."

Donovan's eyes narrowed, and curved into what resembled a smile. "You're a doctor," he said. "The only one who can help me now."

"In what way?"

"By making a decision." The voice was reedy: it seemed to waver and change pitch.

"What sort of a decision?"

Donovan's head jerked up. He closed his eyes and remained this way for a full minute, while the acrid smell bellied and grew stronger and whorled about the room in invisible currents.

" '. . . the gentleman lay braveward with his furies . . .' Do you remember that, Father?"

"Yes," the priest said. "Thomas, isn't it?"

"Thomas. He's been here with me, you know, really; and I've been asking him things. On the theory that poets aren't entirely human. But he just grins. 'You're dying of strangers,' he says; and grins. Bless him." The old man lowered his head. "He disappointed me."

Father Courtney reached for a cigarette, crumpled the empty pack, laced and unlaced his fingers. He waited, remembering the times he had come to this house, all the fine evenings. Ending now?

Yes, whatever else he would learn, he knew that, suddenly: they were ending.

"What sort of a decision, George?"

"A theological sort."

Father Courtney snorted and walked to a window. Outside, the sun was hidden behind a curtain of gray. Birds sat black and still on the telephone lines, like notes of music; and there was rain.

"Is there something you think you haven't told me?" he asked.

"Yes."

"I don't think so, George." Father Courtney turned. "I've known about it for a long time."

The old man tried to speak.

"I've known very well. And now I think I understand why you've refused to see anyone."

"No," Donovan said. "You don't. Father, listen to me: it isn't what you think."

"Nonsense." The priest reverted to his usual gruffness. "We've been friends for too many years for this kind of thing. It's *exactly* what I think. You're an intelligent, well-read, mule-stubborn old man who's worried he won't get to Heaven because sometimes he has doubts."

"That isn't—"

"Well, rubbish! Do you think I don't ask questions, myself, once in a while? Just because I'm a priest, do you think I go blindly on, never wondering, not even for a minute?"

The old man's eyes moved swiftly, up and down.

"Every intelligent person doubts, George, once in a while. And we all feel terrible about it, and we're terribly sorry. But I assure you, if this were enough to damn us, Heaven would be a wilderness." Father Courtney reached again for a cigarette. "So you've shut yourself up like a hermit and worried and stewed and endangered your life, and all for nothing." He coughed. "Well, that's it, isn't it?"

"I wish it were," Donovan said, sadly. His eyes kept dancing. There was a long pause; then he said, "Let me pose you a theoretical problem, Father. Something I've been thinking about lately."

Father Courtney recalled the sentence, and how many times it had begun the evenings of talk—wonderful talk!

These evenings, he realized, were part of his life now. An important part. For there was no one else, no one of Donovan's intelligence, with whom you could argue any subject under the sun—from Frescobaldi to baseball, from colonization on Mars to the early French symbolists, to agrarian reforms, to wines, to theology . . .

The old man shifted in the bed. As he did, the acrid odor diminished and swelled and pulsed. "You once told me," he said, "that you read imaginative fiction, didn't you?"

"I suppose so."

"And that there were certain concepts you could swallow—such as parallel worlds, mutated humans, and the like—, but that other concepts you couldn't swallow at all. Artificial life, I believe you mentioned, and time travel, and a few others."

The priest nodded.

"Well, let's take one of these themes for our problem. Will you do that? Let's take the first idea."

"All right. Then the doctor."

"We have this man, Father," Donovan said, gazing at the ceiling. "He looks perfectly ordinary, you see, and it would occur to no one to doubt this; but he is not ordinary. Strictly speaking, he isn't even a man. For, though he lives, he isn't alive. You follow? He is a thing of wires and coils and magic, a creation of other men. He is a machine . . ."

"George!" The priest shook his head. "We've gone through this before: it's foolish to waste time. I came here to help you, not to engage in a discussion of science fiction themes!"

"But that's how you *can* help me," Donovan said.

"Very well," the priest sighed. "But you know my views on this. Even if there were a logical purpose to which such a creature might be put—and I can't think of any—I still say they will never create a machine that is capable of abstract thought. Human intelligence is a spiritual thing—and spiritual things can't be duplicated by men."

"You really believe that?"

"Of course I do. Extrapolation of known scientific advances is perfectly all right; but this is something else entirely."

"Is it?" the old man said. "What about Pasteur's discovery? Or the X-Ray? Did Roentgen correlate a lot of embryonic data, Father, or did he come upon something brand new? What do you think even the scientists themselves would have said to the idea of a machine that would see through human tissue? They would have said it's fantastic. And it was, too, and is. Nevertheless, it exists."

"It's not the same thing."

"No . . . I suppose that's true. However, I'm not trying to convince you of my thesis. I ask merely that you accept it for the sake of the problem. Will you?"

"Go ahead, George."

"We have this man, then. He's artificial, but he's perfect: great pains have been taken to see to this. Perfect, no detail spared, however small. He looks human, and he acts human, and for all the world knows, he *is* human. In fact, sometimes even he, our man, gets confused. When he feels a pain in his heart, for instance, it's difficult for him to remember that he has no heart. When he sleeps and awakes refreshed, he must remind himself that this is all controlled by an automatic switch somewhere inside his brain, and that he doesn't *actually* feel refreshed. He must think, I'm not real, I'm not real, I'm not real!

"But this becomes impossible, after a while. Because he doesn't believe it. He begins to ask, Why? *Why* am I not real? Where is the difference, when you come right down to it? Humans eat and sleep—as I do. They talk—as I do. They move and work and laugh—as I do. What they think, I think, and what they feel, I feel. Don't I?

"He wonders, the mechanical man does, Father, what

would happen if all the people on earth were suddenly
to discover they were mechanical also. Would they feel
any the less human? Is it likely that they would rush off to
woo typewriters and adding machines? Or would they
think, perhaps, of revising their definition of the word,
'Life'?

"Well, our man thinks about it, and thinks about it, but
he never reaches a conclusion. He doesn't believe he's
nothing more than an advanced calculator, but he doesn't
really believe he's human, either: not completely.

"All he knows is that the smell of wet grass is a fine
smell to him, and that the sound of the wind blowing
through the trees is very sad and beautiful, and that he
loves the whole earth with an impossible passion . . ."

Father Courtney shifted uncomfortably in his chair. If
only the telephone worked, he thought. Or if he could be
sure it was safe to leave.

". . . other men made the creature, as I've said; but many
more like him were made. However, of them all, let's say
only he was successful."

"Why?" the priest asked, irritably. "Why would this be
done in the first place?"

Donovan smiled. "Why did we send the first ship to the
moon? Or bother to split the atom? For no good reason,
Father. Except the reason behind all of science: Curiosity.
My theoretical scientists were curious to see if it could be
accomplished, that's all."

The priest shrugged.

"But perhaps I'd better give our man a history. That
would make it a bit more logical. All right, he was born a
hundred years ago, roughly. A privately owned industrial
monopoly was his mother, and a dozen or so assorted tech-
nicians his father. He sprang from his electric womb fully
formed. But, as the result of an accident—lack of knowledge, what have you—he came out rather different from
his unsuccessful brothers. A mutant! A mutated robot,

Father—now there's an idea that ought to appeal to you! Anyway, *he* knew who, or what, he was. He remembered. And so—to make it brief—when the war interrupted the experiment and threw things into a general uproar, our man decided to escape. He wanted his individuality. He wanted to get out of the zoo.

"It wasn't particularly easy, but he did this. Once free, of course, it was impossible to find him. For one thing, he had been constructed along almost painfully ordinary lines. And for another, they couldn't very well release the information that a mechanical man built by their laboratories was wandering the streets. It would cause a panic. And there was enough panic, what with the nerve gas and the bombs."

"So they never found him, I gather."

"No," Donovan said, wistfully. "They never found him. And they kept their secret well: it died when they died."

"And what happened to the creature?"

"Very little, to tell the truth. They'd given him a decent intelligence, you see—far more decent, and complex, then they knew—so he didn't have much trouble finding small jobs. A rather old-looking man, fairly strong—he made out. Needless to say, he couldn't stay in a town for more than twenty years or so, because of his inability to age, but this was all right. Everyone makes friends and loses them. He got used to it."

Father Courtney sat very still now. The birds had flown away from the telephone lines, and were at the window, beating their wings, and crying harshly.

"But all this time, he's been thinking, Father. Thinking and reading. He makes quite a study of philosophy, and for a time he favors a somewhat peculiar combination of Russell and Schopenhauer—unbitter bitterness, you might say. Then this phase passes, and he begins to search through the vast theological and metaphysical literature. For what? He isn't sure. However, he is sure of one thing, now: He *is*, indubitably, human. Without breath, without heart, without blood or bone, artificially created, he thinks this and believes it, with a fair amount of firmness, too. Isn't that remarkable!"

"It is indeed," the priest said, his throat oddly tight and dry. "Go on."

"Well," Donovan chuckled, "I've caught your interest, have I? All right, then. Let us imagine that one hundred years have passed. The creature has been able to make minor repairs on himself, but—at last—he is dying. Like an ancient motor, he's gone on running year after year, until he's all paste and hairpins, and now, like the motor, he's falling apart. And nothing and no one can save him."

The acrid aroma burned and fumed.

"Here's the real paradox, though. Our man has become religious. Father! He doesn't have a living cell within him, yet he's concerned about his soul!"

Donovan's eyes quieted, as the rest of him did. "The problem," he said, "is this: Having lived creditably for over a century as a member of the human species, can this creature of ours hope for Heaven? Or will he 'die' and become only a heap of metal cogs?"

Father Courtney leapt from the chair, and moved to the bed. "George, in Heaven's name, let me call Doctor Ferguson!"

"Answer the question first. Or haven't you decided?"

"There's nothing to decide," the priest said, with impatience. "It's a preposterous idea. No machine can have a soul."

Donovan made the sighing sound, through closed lips. He said, "You don't think it's conceivable, then, that God could have made an exception here?"

"What do you mean?"

"That He could have taken pity on this theoretical man of ours, and breathed a soul into him after all? Is that so impossible?"

Father Courtney shrugged. "It's a poor word, impossible," he said. "But it's a poor problem, too. Why not ask me whether pigs ought to be allowed to fly?"

"Then you admit it's conceivable?"

"I admit nothing of the kind. It simply isn't the sort of question any man can answer."

"Not even a priest?"

"Especially not a priest. You know as much about Catholicism as I do, George; you ought to know how absurd the proposition is."

"Yes," Donovan said. His eyes were closed.

Father Courtney remembered the time they had argued furiously on what would happen if you went back in time and killed your own grandfather. This was like that argument. Exactly like it—exactly. It was no stranger than a dozen other discussions. (What if Mozart had been a writer instead of a composer? If a person died and remained dead for an hour and were then revived, would he be haunted by his own ghost?) Plus, perhaps, the fact that Donovan might be in a fever. Perhaps and might and why do I sit here while his life may be draining away . . .

The old man made a sharp noise. "But you can tell me this much," he said. "If our theoretical man were dying, and you knew that he was dying, would you give him Extreme Unction?"

"George, you're delirious."

"No, I'm not: please Father! Would you give this creature the Last Rites? If, say, you knew him? If you'd known him for years, as a friend, as a member of the parish?"

The priest shook his head. "It would be sacrilegious."

"But why? You said yourself that he might have a soul, that God might have granted him this. Didn't you say that?"

"I—"

"Father, remember, he's a friend of yours. You know

him *well.* You and he, this creature, have worked together, side by side, for years. You've taken a thousand walks together, shared the same interests, the same love of art and knowledge. For the sake of the thesis, Father. Do you understand?"

"No," the priest said, feeling a chill freeze into him. "No, I don't."

"Just answer this, then. If your friend were suddenly to reveal himself to you as a machine, and he was dying, and wanted very much to go to Heaven—what would you do?"

The priest picked up the wine glass and emptied it. He noticed that his hand was trembling. "Why—" he began, and stopped, and looked at the silent old man in the bed, studying the face, searching for madness, for death.

"What would you do?"

An unsummoned image flashed through his mind. Donovan, kneeling at the altar for Communion, Sunday after Sunday; Donovan, with his mouth firmly shut, while the others yawned; Donovan, waiting to the last moment, then snatching the Host, quickly, dartingly, like a lizard gobbling a fly.

Had he ever seen Donovan eat?

Had he seen him take one glass of wine, ever?

Father Courtney shuddered slightly, brushing away the images. He felt unwell. He wished the birds would go elsewhere.

Well, answer him, he thought. *Give him an answer. Then get in the helicar and fly to Milburn and pray it's not too late . . .*

"I think," the priest said, "that in such a case, I would administer Extreme Unction."

"Just as a precautionary measure?"

"It's all very ridiculous, but—I think that's what I'd do. Does that answer the question?"

"It does, Father. It does." Donovan's voice came from

nowhere. "There is one last point, then I'm finished with my little thesis."

"Yes?"

"Let us say the man dies and you give him Extreme Unction; he does or does not go to Heaven, provided there is a Heaven. What happens to the body? Do you tell the towns-people they have been living with a mechanical monster all these years?"

"What do you think, George?"

"I think it would be unwise. They remember our theoretical man as a friend, you see. The shock would be terrible. Also, they would never believe he was the only one of his kind; they'd begin to suspect their neighbors of having clockwork interiors. And some of them might be tempted to investigate and see for sure. And, too, the news would be bound to spread, all over the world. I think it would be a bad thing to let anyone know, Father."

"How would I be able to suppress it?" the priest heard himself ask, seriously.

"By conducting a private autopsy, so to speak. Then, afterwards, you could take the parts to a junkyard and scatter them."

Donovan's voice dropped to a whisper. Again the locust hum.

". . . and if our monster had left a note to the effect he had moved to some unspecified place, you . . ."

The acrid smell billowed, all at once, like a steam, a hiss of blinding vapor.

"George."

Donovan lay unstirring on the cloud of linen, his face composed, expressionless.

"George!"

The priest reached under the blanket and touched the heart-area of Donovan's chest. He tried to pull the eyelids up: they would not move.

He blinked away the burning wetness. "Forgive me!" he said, and paused, and took from his pocket a small white jar and a white stole.

He spoke softly, under his breath, in Latin. While he spoke, he touched the old man's feet and head with glistening fingertips.

Then, when many minutes had passed, he raised his head.

Rain sounded in the room, and swift winds, and far-off rockets.

Father Courtney grasped the edge of the blanket.

He made the Sign of the Cross, breathed, and pulled downward, slowly.

After a long while he opened his eyes.

THE HOWLING MAN
Introduction by Harlan Ellison

No one—not critics or savants of semiotics or even readers of the most sensitive sort—can know how good Chuck Beaumont was at putting words on paper. Only other writers can feel the impulse that beats in his work as strongly as it beats in themselves. Good writers love him and what he did; mediocre writers envy and marvel and even hate him a little because he heard the music denied them; bad writers are simply overwhelmed and are left desolate at the realization that, like Salieri, they can never be Mozart. Charles Beaumont was truly one in a million. A million men and women fighting that battle waged every time they sit down to work, on a battlefield 8½ × 11, in conflict not only with themselves and the best they've ever done personally, but with all the best who went before.

We try to avoid such statements, because they reek of the worst pronouncements of Hemingway getting into the ring with Chekhov (that snappy little counterpuncher). But any writer worth the name, unless he or she is totally daft, knows that it's true: comparisons will eventually be made, and one has to go up against the highest standards of literature if one hopes to be read fifteen minutes after final blackout. Even John Simon knows it: ". . . there is no point in saying less than your predecessors have said."

So we pick our icons. And we pick them carefully, in hopes that we haven't been spotted so many balls that beating the competition is a hollow victory. Mine have been Kafka and Poe and Borges . . . and Beaumont. (Arrogance had long been my prime character flaw.) Thus far I don't think their shades need worry.

And though I know the former three only through their work, Chuck Beaumont was my friend for about nine years, and I had the honor of buying and publishing quite a bit of his stuff.

From April Fool's Day 1959, my separation date from the U.S. Army, till August of 1960, yoked with the excellent novelist Frank M. Robinson, I was editor of Rogue, a slick men's magazine published out of Evanston, Illinois—only a few miles and even fewer dissimilarities from Playboy's offices on Ohio Street in Chicago's Loop. The magazine was published by one of the industry's great characters, William L. Hamling.

Now, Mr. Hamling, early in his publishing career, circa 1950, had worked in Skokie, Illinois for a man named George von Rosen, publisher of (among other titles, such as Art Photography, which Bill worked on) Modern Man, arguably the first true men's magazine.

(Let me backtrack for a moment. I hadn't really intended to get into this much ancient history, simply to make a point about origins, but it occurs to me that this is the kind of publishing history minutiae that gets lost forever unless someone accidentally manages to commit it to paper before the memories blur. Some archivist may one day need this series of linkages, which are kinda sorta fascinating inbf themselves, so excuse the digression.

(Hamling had worked under editor Raymond A. Palmer at Ziff-Davis Publishing in Chicago during the '40s, winding up as managing editor of the pulp science fiction magazines Amazing Stories and Fantastic Adventures in 1948. When Z-D decided to move the operation to New York in 1950, both Palmer and Hamling chose to stay in Evanston. Palmer started Other Worlds *and Imagination, digest-sized genre magazines, and Hamling got a job with von Rosen.*

(In 1951, Ray Palmer fronted Hamling financially and Bill bought Imagination, later adding Imaginative Tales and, in 1955, branching out of the sf digest idiom to start a semi-slick men's magazine, Rogue. Which circles us back out of the digression to the element of Hamling's stint at von Rosen's magazine factory that resulted in Beaumont working for us at Rogue.)

In the accounting department at von Rosen's happy little nudery, was a guy who had been fired from Esquire (which also, at that time, had its office in Chicago.) His name was Hugh Hefner, and his aspirations were only slightly higher than those of his co-worker, William L. Hamling ... though his taste and inventiveness were infinitely greater. Hamling and Hefner were friendly acquaintances. Not buddies, but chummy enough that when Hamling saw Hefner start Playboy on his kitchen table (with a capital investment of $600 of his own money and loans from friends that brought the seed total to between $7000$8000) and quickly achieve high-profile success, his own sense of home-grown American venality was piqued.

By 1953, when Hefner started Playboy and began gathering around him the core talents who would form the basis of the magazine's non-public popularity—Beaumont, Matheson, Herbert Gold, Ken Purdy and others—Hamling had become financially solvent with the sf magazines, and he burned with envy at the way in which that no-name guy from von Rosen's accounting department had passed him at a dead run. Playing his acquaintance with Hefner to get basic start-up information, Hamling began Rogue, ripping off as many aspects of the original as he could on a lower budget. The paper wasn't slick, the photos weren't in color, the nudes weren't as stunning, but it was the second men's magazine (excluding Modern Man, which was mostly nudes, with prose that might have included some fiction and contemporary articles, but if it did, I can't remember any.) And in 1955 when Rogue debuted, the market was so new that there was plenty of room for a Playboy competitor, despite its ragtag look.

But Hamling had a plethora of blind spots. The most interesting, of concern to us here, was that though he envied Hefner to a degree that consumed him, he also admired him and sought to emulate Hefner's every move. By 1959, when Hamling hired me straight out of my honorable discharge to edit Rogue, he had decided to go whole hog and turn Rogue into a full slick magazine. So he needed professional talent—both as editorial staff and as contributors—to supplement his own iron will at the conceptual stages. After Frank Robinson and I came on board, Hamling set about (from the vantage point behind that blind spot) coopting everyone of talent who worked for Hefner, on the theory that they must be the best . . . after all, wasn't Hefner publishing them? Don't ask.

The problem for Bill was that most of those people were under exclusive contract to Hefner, with restrictions against their publishing anywhere else in competing markets that were Draconian. (Once, a model who had appeared in Playboy had the bad fortune to allow a photo set of leftovers appear in Rogue. The woman's personal services contract with HMH was voided and she lost thousands of dollars' worth of personal appearance gigs, not to mention the succoring warmth of the Playboy Mansion.)

But Bill was determined. The two most prominent contributors to Playboy whose acquisition obsessed Hamling, were artist Ron Bradford and writer Charles Beaumont. So Bill made the acquaintance of Chuck, and made him money offers Chuck couldn't refuse, and before I arrived at Rogue Chuck was already doing profiles of show biz personalities and sports car pieces under the house pseudonyms "Michael Phillips" and "Robert Courtney." (These names were used by others, as well. My own "The Case for Our College Bohemians"—about which the less said, the better—was published in the August 1959 Rogue bylined "Robert Courtney.")

But on the day that Chuck delivered into my hands the manuscript of "The Howling Man," which Hefner had rejected for heaven-only-knows-what-reason, I realized instantly that we had been proffered a small literary miracle, and that a house pseudonym would not suffice. Another "Courtney" or "Phillips" piece meant nothing. But if we could create a separate nom-de-plume persona for Beaumont's fiction, we might be able to raise out of the mire of non-entities a penname creation that might have as much serious literary coin as Beaumont himself.

The Evan HunterEd McBain Theory.

Bill Hamling, of course, thought "The Howling Man" was much too dangerous a piece for us to publish. Frank Robinson and I beat him mercilessly, day after day, until he finally capitulated; and I set about preparing a showcase for the work that would set it off for special attention.

First, I achieved one of Bill's dreams by getting to artist Ron Bradford, who had been doing the most memorable feature art for Hefner. Through the then-art director, Richard A. Thompson, who knew Bradford in the Chicago art community, I met and cajoled Ron by using the one tool I knew was perfect: I let him read "The Howling Man."

Bradford was as knocked out by the story as Frank and I had been, and he agreed to do the art. I invented the name "Corey Summerwell" for Bradford and he created a style of collage entirely different from what he was doing for Playboy so Hefner would not be able to make the connection. Ironically, a second piece of Bradford art, for a story titled "Manny" by Raymond Passacantando, got into print a month before the Summerwell painting for "The Howling Man" in the November 1959 Rogue.

All that remained was to invent a pseudonym for Beaumont. We wanted it to be a subterfuge, but we also wanted those who were on to such things to know who was behind the pen-name. I invented C.B. Lovehill. The C and the B are obvious; beau I twisted out the French to get love, though idiomatically it was a stretch; and mont became hill. On the meet the authors page that issue (called "Rogue Notes"), my attempts to keep Beaumont out of trouble with Hefner by making no allusions to the pseudonym, were defeated by Hamling who, with typical disregard for anyone else's personal danger, rewrote my copy and damned surely indicated Lovehill was Beaumont to all but the dopiest reader. I was furious with Hamling, as was Beaumont, but life with Hamling in it was like having a nagging summer flu that simply will not go away; and finally, we just had to accept it.

The story was published, it drew huge amounts of laudatory mail, and Chuck went on to do (if memory serves) another half dozen stories for me, stories like "Dead, You Know" and "Genevieve, My Genevieve."

Funnily, in the same "Rogue Notes" where Chuck was betrayed, we ran a photo of "Lovehill." It is a snapshot of Frank Robinson in his summer straw hat, talking on the phone with his back to the camera. (In another issue, "Courtney" is seen in photo closeup. He looks a lot like Ellison.)

The story that lies at the heart of all this history has gone on to be recognized as a modern fantasy classic. Chuck scripted it for the original Twilight Zone and its television incarnation plays and replays endlessly in syndication; and each time it airs we realize anew how deft, how sinister, how universal in its message it is.

But beyond the simple plot structure and horrendous implications of characterization, "The Howling Man" recommends itself, and the wonders of Beaumont's muse, because it is the rare fiction that we cannot forget. It touches places in the soul that resonate purely, almost thirty years after it first appeared, as strongly as in 1959. It is, for me, not merely a point of pride to be able to say that I was privileged to publish the work of one of the best writers this country ever produced, but it is a way of saying thank you to a man who was my friend and who influenced not only my own writing but my life in ways he would recognize were he still with us.

Yet on this 20th anniversary of Chuck's passing (as I write this introduction to what I think is his finest short story), it takes on

considerable import for anyone who looks toward the icons for
the tap roots of contemporary American fiction.

Charles Beaumont was one in a million, and perhaps rereading
"The Howling Man" will remind the other 999,999 that what
they do, when they do it with honor and high craft, has been
profoundly influenced by what Chuck taught us in the pages of
magazines now three decades gone.

THE GERMANY OF that time was a land of valleys and
mountains and swift dark rivers, a green and fertile land
where everything grew tall and straight out of the earth.
There was no other country like it. Stepping across the
border from Belgium, where the rain-caped, mustached
guards saluted, grinning, like operetta soldiers, you entered
a different world entirely. Here the grass became as rich
and smooth as velvet; deep, thick woods appeared; the air
itself, which had been heavy with the French perfume of
wines and sauces, changed: the clean, fresh smell of lakes
and pines and boulders came into your lungs. You stood a
moment, then, at the border, watching the circling hawks
above and wondering, a little fearfully, how such a thing
could happen. In less than a minute you had passed from
a musty, ancient room, through an invisible door, into a
kingdom of winds and light. Unbelievable! But there, at
your heels, clearly in view, is Belgium, like all the rest of
Europe, a faded tapestry from some forgotten mansion.

In that time, before I had heard of St. Wulfran's, of the
wretch who clawed the stones of a locked cell, wailing in
the midnight hours, or of the daft Brothers and their mad
Abbott, I had strong legs and a mind on its last search, and
I preferred to be alone. A while and I'll come back to this
spot. We will ride and feel the sickness, fall, and hover on

the edge of death, together. But I am not a writer, only one who loves wild, unhousebroken words; I must have a real beginning.

Paris beckoned in my youth. I heeded, for the reason most young men just out of college heed, although they would never admit it: to lie with mysterious beautiful women. A solid, traditional upbringing among the corseted ruins of Boston had succeeded, as such upbringings generally do, in honing the urge to a keen edge. My nightly dreams of beaded bagnios and dusky writhing houris, skilled beyond imagining, reached, finally, the unbearable stage beyond which lies either madness or respectibility. Fancying neither, I managed to convince my parents that a year abroad would add exactly the right amount of seasoning to my maturity, like a dash of curry in an otherwise bland, if not altogether tasteless, chowder. I'm afraid that Father caught the hot glint in my eye, but he was kind. Describing, in detail, and with immense effect, the hideous consequences of profligacy, telling of men he knew who'd gone to Europe, innocently, and fallen into dissolutions so profound they'd not been heard of since, he begged me at all times to remember that I was an Ellington and turned me loose. Paris, of course, was enchanting and terrifying, as a jungle must be to a zoo-born monkey. Out of respect to the honored dead, and Dad, I did a quick trot through the Tuileries, the Louvre, and down the Champs Elysées to the Arc de Triomphe; then, with the fall of night, I cannoned off to Montmartre and the Rue Pigalle, embarking on the Grand Adventure. Synoptically, it did not prove to be so grand as I'd imagined; nor was it, after the fourth week, so terribly adventurous. Still: important to what followed, for what followed doubtless wouldn't have but for the sweet complaisant girls.

Boston's Straights and Narrows don't, I fear, prepare one—except psychologically—for the Wild Life. My health broke in due course and, as my thirst had been well and

truly slaked, I was not awfully discontent to sink back
into the contemplative cocoon to which I was, apparently, more suited. Abed for a month I lay, in celibate silence
and almost total inactivity. Then, no doubt as a final
gesture of rebellion, I got my idea—got? or had my concentrated sins received it, like a signal from a failing
tower?—and I made my strange, un-Ellingtonian decision.
I would explore Europe. But not as tourist, safe and fat in
his fat, safe bus, insulated against the beauty and the ug-
liness of changing cultures by a pane of glass and a room
at the English-speaking hotel. No. I would go like an un-
protected wind, a seven-league-booted leaf, a nestless bird,
and I would see this dark strange land with the vision of a
boy on the last legs of his dreams. I would go by bicycle,
poor and lonely and questing—as poor and lonely and
questing, anyway, as one can be with a hundred thousand
in the bank and a partnership in Ellington, Carruthers &
Blake waiting.

So it was. New England blood and muscles wilted on
that first day's pumping, but New England spirit tough-
ened as the miles dropped back. Like an ant crawling over
a once lovely, now decayed and somewhat seedy Duchess, I
rode over the body of Europe. I dined at restaurants
where boar's heads hung, all vicious-tusked and blind; I
slept at country inns and breathed the musty age, and
sometimes girls came to the door and knocked and asked
if I had everything I needed ("Well . . .") and they were
better than the girls in Paris, though I can't imagine why.
No matter. Out of France I pedaled, into Belgium, out,
and to the place of cows and forest, mountains, brooks and
laughing people: Germany. (I've rhapsodized on purpose
for I feel it's quite important to remember how completely
Paradisical the land was then, at that time.)

I looked odd, standing there. The border guard asked
what was loose with me, I answered Nothing—grateful for
the German, and the French, Miss Finch had drummed

into me—and set off along the smallest, darkest path. I serpentined through forests, cities, towns, villages, and always I followed its least likely appendages. Unreasonably, I pedaled as if toward a destination: into the Moselle Valley country, up into the desolate hills of emerald.

By a ferry, fallen to desuetude, the reptile drew me through a bosky wood. The trees closed in at once. I drank the fragrant air and pumped and kept on pumping, but a heat began to grow inside my body. My head began to ache. I felt weak. Two more miles and I was obliged to stop, for perspiration filmed my skin. You know the signs of pneumonia: a sapping of the strength, a trembling, flashes of heat and of cold; visions. I lay in the bed of damp leaves for a time. At last a village came to view. A thirteenth-century village, gray and narrow-streeted, cobbled to the hidden store fronts. A number of old people in peasant costumes looked up as I bumped along and I recall one ancient tallow-colored fellow—nothing more. Only the weakness, like acid, burning off my nerves and muscles. And an intervening blackness to pillow my fall.

I awoke to the smells of urine and hay. The fever had passed, but my arms and legs lay heavy as logs, my head throbbed horribly, and there was an empty shoveled-out hole inside my stomach somewhere. For a while I did not move or open my eyes. Breathing was a major effort. But consciousness came, eventually.

I was in a tiny room. The walls and ceiling were of rough gray stone, the single glassless window was arch-shaped, the floor was uncombed dirt. My bed was not a bed at all but a blanket thrown across a disorderly pile of crinkly straw. Beside me, a crude table; upon it, a pitcher; beneath it, a bucket. Next to the table, a stool. And seated there, asleep, his tonsured head adangle from an Everest of robe, a monk.

I must have groaned, for the shorn pate bobbed up precipitately. Two silver trails gleamed down the corners of the suddenly exposed mouth, which drooped into a frown. The slumbrous eyes blinked.

"It is God's infinite mercy," sighed the gnomelike little man. "You have recovered."

"Not as yet," I told him. Unsuccessfully, I tried to remember what had happened; then I asked questions.

"I am Brother Christophorus. This is the Abbey of St. Wulfran's. The Burgemeister of Schwartzhof, Herr Barth, brought you to us nine days ago. Father Jerome said that you would die and he sent me to watch, for I have never seen a man die, and Father Jerome holds that it is beneficial for a Brother to have seen a man die. But now I suppose that you will not die." He shook his head ruefully.

"Your disappointment," I said, "cuts me to the quick. However, don't abandon hope. The way I feel now, it's touch and go."

"No," said Brother Christophorus sadly. "You will get well. It will take time. But you will get well."

"Such ingratitude, and after all you've done. How can I express my apologies?"

He blinked again. With the innocence of a child, he said, "I beg your pardon?"

"Nothing." I grumbled about blankets, a fire, some food to eat, and then slipped back into the well of sleep. A fever dream of forests full of giant two-headed beasts came, then the sound of screaming.

I awoke. The scream shrilled on—Klaxon-loud, high, cutting, like a cry for help.

"What is that sound?" I asked.

The monk smiled. "Sound? I hear no sound," he said.

It stopped. I nodded. "Dreaming. Probably I'll hear a good deal more before I'm through. I shouldn't have left Paris in such poor condition."

"No," he said. "You shouldn't have left Paris."

Kindly now, resigned to my recovery, Brother Christophorus became attentive to a fault. Nurselike, he spooned thick soups into me, applied compresses, chanted soothing prayers, and emptied the bucket out the window. Time passed slowly. As I fought the sickness, the dreams grew less vivid—but the nightly cries did not diminish. They were as full of terror and loneliness as before, strong, real in my ears. I tried to shut them out, but they would not be shut out. Still, how could they be strong and real except in my vanishing delirium? Brother Christophorus did not hear them. I watched him closely when the sunlight faded to the gray of dusk and the screams began, but he was deaf to them—if they existed. If they existed!

"Be still, my son. It is the fever that makes you hear these noises. That is quite natural. Is that not quite natural? Sleep."

"But the fever is gone! I'm sitting up now. Listen! Do you mean to tell me you don't hear *that*?"

"I hear only you, my son."

The screams, that fourteenth night, continued until dawn. They were totally unlike any sounds in my experience. Impossible to believe they could be uttered and sustained by a human, yet they did not seem to be animal. I listened, there in the gloom, my hands balled into fists, and knew, suddenly, that one of two things must be true. Either someone or something was making these ghastly sounds, and Brother Christophorus was lying, or—I was going mad. Hearing-voices mad, climbing-walls and frothing mad. I'd have to find the answer: that I knew. And by myself.

I listened with a new ear to the howls. Razoring under the door, they rose to operatic pitch, subsided, resumed, like the cries of a surly, hysterical child. To test their reality, I hummed beneath my breath, I covered my head with a blanketing, scratched at the straw, coughed. No difference. The quality of substance, of existence, was there. I tried, then, to localize the screams; and, on the fifteenth

night, felt sure that they were coming from a spot not far
along the hall.

"The sounds that maniacs hear seem quite real to them."

I know. I know!

The monk was by my side, he had not left it from the
start, keeping steady vigil even through Matins. He joined
his tremulous soprano to the distant chants, and prayed
excessively. But nothing could tempt him away. The food
we ate was brought to us, as were all other needs. I'd see
the Abbot, Father Jerome, once I was recovered. Meanwhile . . .

"I'm feeling better, Brother. Perhaps you'd care to show
me the grounds. I've seen nothing of St. Wulfran's except
this little room."

"There is only this little room multiplied. Ours is a rigorous order. The Franciscans, now, they permit themselves
esthetic pleasure; we do not. It is, for us, a luxury. We
have a single, most unusual job. There is nothing to see."

"But surely the Abbey is very old."

"Yes, that is true."

"As an antiquarian—"

"Mr. Ellington—"

"What is it you don't want me to see? What are you
afraid of, Brother?"

"Mr. Ellington? I do not have the authority to grant
your request. When you are well enough to leave, Father
Jerome will no doubt be happy to accommodate you."

"Will he also be happy to explain the screams I've heard
each night since I've been here?"

"Rest, my son. Rest."

The unholy, hackle-raising shriek burst loose and
bounded off the hard stone walls. Brother Christophorus
crossed himself, apropros of nothing, and sat like an ancient Indian on the weary stool. I knew he liked me. Especially, perhaps. We'd got along quite well in all our talks,
but this—*verboten*.

I closed my eyes. I counted to three hundred. I opened my eyes.

The good monk was asleep. I blasphemed, softly, but he did not stir, so I swung my legs over the side of the straw bed and made my way across the dirt floor to the heavy door. I rested there a time, in the candleless dark, listening to the howls; then, with Bostonian discretion, raised the bolt. The rusted hinges creaked, but Brother Christophorus was deep in celestial marble: his head drooped low upon his chest.

Panting, weak as a landlocked fish, I stumbled out into the corridor. The screams became impossibly loud. I put my hands to my ears, instinctively, and wondered how any-one could sleep with such a furor going on. It *was* a furor. In my mind? No. Real. The monastery shook with these shrill cries. You could feel their realness with your teeth.

I passed a Brother's cell and listened, then another; then I paused. A thick door, made of oak or pine, was locked before me. Behind it were the screams.

A chill went through me on the edge of those unutterable shrieks of hopeless, helpless anguish, and for a moment I considered turning back—not to my room, not to my bed of straw, but back into the open world. But duty held me. I took a breath and walked up to the narrow bar-crossed window and looked in.

A man was in the cell. On all fours, circling like a beast, his head thrown back, a man. The moonlight showed his face. It cannot be described—not, at least, by me. A man past death might look like this, a victim of the Inquisition rack, the stake, the pincers: not a human in the third de-cade of the twentieth century, surely. I had never seen such suffering within two eyes, such lost, mad suffering. Naked, he crawled about the dirt, cried, leaped up to his feet and clawed the hard stone walls in fury.

Then he saw me.

The screaming ceased. He huddled, blinking, in the corner of his cell. And then, as though unsure of what he saw, he walked right to the door.

In German, hissing: "Who are you?"

"David Ellington," I said. "Are you locked in? Why have they locked you in?"

He shook his head. "Be still, be still. You are not German?"

"No." I told him how I came to be at St. Wulfran's.

"Ah!" Trembling, his horny fingers closing on the bars, the naked man said: "Listen to me, we have only moments. They are mad. You hear? All mad. I was in the village, lying with my woman, when their crazy Abbot burst into the house and hit me with his heavy cross. I woke up here. They flogged me. I asked for food, they would not give it to me. They took my clothes. They threw me in this filthy room. They locked the door."

"Why?"

"Why?" He moaned. "I wish I knew. That's been the worst of it. Five years imprisoned, beaten, tortured, starved, and not a reason given, not a word to guess from— Mr. Ellington! I have sinned, but who has not? With my woman, quietly, alone with my woman, my love. And this God-drunk lunatic, Jerome, cannot stand it. Help me!"

His breath splashed on my face. I took a backward step and tried to think. I couldn't quite believe that in this century a thing so frightening could happen. Yet, the Abbey was secluded, above the world, timeless. What could not transpire here, secretly?

"I'll speak to the Abbot."

"No! I tell you, he's the maddest of them all. Say nothing to him."

"Then how can I help you?"

He pressed his mouth against the bars. "In one way only. Around Jerome's neck, there is a key. It fits this lock. If—"

"Mr. Ellington!"

I turned and faced a fierce El Greco painting of a man. White-bearded, prow-nosed, regal as an Emperor beneath the gray peaked robe, he came out of the darkness. "Mr. Ellington, I did not know that you were well enough to walk. Come with me, please."

The naked man began to weep hysterically. I felt a grip of steel about my arm. Through corridors, past snore-filled cells, the echoes of the weeping dying, we continued to a room.

"I must ask you to leave St. Wulfran's," the Abbot said. "We lack the proper facilities for care of the ill. Arrangements will be made in Schwartzhof—"

"One moment," I said. "While it's probably true that Brother Christophorus's ministrations saved my life—and certainly true that I owe you all a debt of gratitude—I've got to ask for an explanation of that man in the cell."

"What man?" the Abbot said softly.

"The one we just left, the one who's screamed all night long every night."

"No man has been screaming, Mr. Ellington."

Feeling suddenly very weak, I sat down and rested a few breaths' worth. Then I said, "Father Jerome—you are he? I am not necessarily an irreligious person, but neither could I be considered particularly religious. I know nothing of monasteries, what is permitted, what isn't. But I seriously doubt you have the authority to imprison a man against his will."

"This is quite true. We have no such authority."

"Then why have you done so?"

The Abbot looked at me steadily. In a firm, inflexible voice, he said: "No man has been imprisoned at St. Wulfran's."

"He claims otherwise."

"Who claims otherwise?"

"The man in the cell at the end of the corridor."

"There is no man in the cell at the end of the corridor."

"I was talking with him!"

"You were talking with no man."

The conviction in his voice shocked me into momentary silence. I gripped the arms of the chair.

"You are ill, Mr. Ellington," the bearded holy man said. "You have suffered from delirium. You have heard and seen things which do not exist."

"That's true," I said. "But the man in the cell—whose voice I can hear now!—is not one of those things."

The Abbot shrugged. "Dreams can seem very real, my son."

I glanced at the leather thong about his turkey-gobbler neck, all but hidden beneath the beard. "Honest men make unconvincing liars," I lied convincingly. "Brother Christophorus has a way of looking at the floor whenever he denies the cries in the night. You look at me, but your voice loses its command. I can't imagine why, but you are both very intent upon keeping me away from the truth. Which is not only poor Christianity, but also poor psychology. For now I am quite curious indeed. You might as well tell me, Father; I'll find out eventually."

"What do you mean?"

"Only that. I'm sure the police will be interested to hear of a man imprisoned at the Abbey."

"I tell you, *there is no man!*"

"Very well. Let's forget the matter."

"Mr. Ellington—" The Abbot put his hands behind him. "The person in the cell is, ah, one of the Brothers. Yes. He is subject to . . . seizures, fits. You know fits? At these times, he becomes intractable. Violent. Dangerous! We're obliged to lock him in his cell, which you can surely understand."

"I understand," I said, "that you're still lying to me. If the answer were as simple as that, you'd not have gone through the elaborate business of pretending I was deliri-

ous. There'd have been no need. There's something more
to it, but I can wait. Shall we go on to Schwartzof?"

Father Jerome tugged at his beard viciously, as if it were
some feathered demon come to taunt him. "Would you
truly go to the police?" he asked.

"Would you?" I said. "In my position?"

He considered that for a long time, tugging the beard,
nodding the prowed head; and the screams went on, so
distant, so real. I thought of the naked man clawing in his
filth.

"Well, Father?"

"Mr. Ellington, I see that I shall have to be honest with
you—which is a great pity," he said. "Had I followed my
original instinct and refused to allow you in the Abbey to
begin with . . . but, I had no choice. You were near death.
No physician was available. You would have perished. Still,
perhaps that would have been better."

"My recovery seems to have disappointed a lot of people," I commented. "I assure you it was inadvertent."

The old man took no notice of this remark. Stuffing his
mandarin hands into the sleeves of his robe, he spoke with
great deliberation. "When I said that there was no man in
the cell at the end of the corridor, I was telling the truth.
Sit down, sir! Please! Now." He closed his eyes. "There is
much to the story, much that you will not understand or
believe. You are sophisticated, or feel that you are. You
regard our life here, no doubt, as primitive—"

"In fact, I—"

"In fact, you do. I know the current theories. Monks
are misfits, neurotics, sexual frustrates, and aberrants. They
retreat from the world because they cannot cope with the
world. Et cetera. You are surprised I know these things?
My son, I was told by the one who began the theories!"
He raised his head upward, revealing more of the leather
thong. "Five years ago, Mr. Ellington, there were no
screams at St. Wulfran's. This was an undistinguished little

Abbey in the wild Black Mountain region, and its inmates'
job was quite simply to serve God, to save what souls they
could by constant prayer. At that time, not very long after
the great war, the world was in chaos. Schwartzhof was
not the happy village you see now. It was, my son, a resort
for the sinful, a hive of vice and corruption, a pit for the
unwary—and the wary also, if they had not strength. A
Godless place! Forsaken, fornicators paraded the streets.
Gambling was done. Robbery and murder, drunkenness,
and evils so profound I cannot put them into words. In all
the universe you could not have found a fouler pesthole,
Mr. Ellington! The Abbots and the Brothers at St. Wulfran's succumbed for years to Schwartzhof, I regret to say.
Good men, lovers of God, chaste good men came here and
fought but could not win against the black temptations.
Finally it was decided that the Abbey should be closed. I
heard of this and argued. 'Is that not surrender?' I said.
'Are we to bow before the strength of evil? Let me try, I
beg you. Let me try to amplify the word of God that all in
Schwartzhof shall hear and see their dark transgressions
and repent!' "

The old man stood at the window, a trembling shade.
His hands were now clutched together in a fervency of
remembrance. "They asked," he said, "if I considered myself more virtuous than my predecessors that I should hope
for success where they had failed. I answered that I did
not, but that I had an advantage. I was a convert. Earlier
I had walked with evil, and knew its face. My wish was
granted. For a year. One year only. Rejoicing, Mr. Ellington, I came here; and one night, incognito, walked the
streets of the village. The smell of evil was strong. Too
strong, I thought—and I had reveled in the alleys of Morocco, I had seen the dens of Hong Kong, Paris, Spain.
The orgies were too wild, the drunkards much too drunk,
the profanities a great deal too profane. It was as if the
evil of the world had been distilled and centered here, as

if a pagan tribal chief, in hiding, had assembled all his
rituals about him . . ." The Abbot nodded his head. "I
thought of Rome, in her last days; of Byzantium; of—Eden.
That was the first of many hints to come. No matter what
they were. I returned to the Abbey and donned my holy
robes and went back into Schwartzhof. I made myself con-
spicuous. Some jeered, some shrank away, a voice cried
'Damn your foolish God!' And then a hand thrust out from
darkness, touched my shoulder, and I heard: 'Now, Father,
are you lost?' "

The Abbot brought his tightly clenched hands to his
forehead and tapped his forehead.

"Mr. Ellington, I have some poor wine here. Please have
some."

I drank, gratefully. Then the priest continued.

"I faced a man of average appearance. So average, indeed, that I felt I knew, then. 'No,' I told him, 'but you
are lost!' He laughed a foul laugh. 'Are we not all, Father?'
Then he said a most peculiar thing. He said his wife was
dying and begged me to give her Extreme Unction. 'Please,'
he said, 'in God's sweet name!' I was confused. We hurried
to his house. A woman lay upon a bed, her body nude. 'It
is a different Extreme Unction that I have in mind,' he
whispered, laughing. 'It's the only kind, dear Father, that
she understands. No other will have her! Pity! Pity on the
poor soul lying there in all her suffering. Give her your
Sceptre!' And the woman's arms came snaking, supplicat-
ing toward me, round and sensuous and hot . . ."

Father Jerome shuddered and paused. The shrieks, I
thought, were growing louder from the hall. "Enough of
that," he said. "I was quite sure then. I raised my cross
and told the words I'd learned, and it was over. He
screamed—as he's doing now—and fell upon his knees. He
had not expected to be recognized, nor should he have
been normally. But in my life, I'd seen him many times, in
many guises. I brought him to the Abbey. I locked him in

the cell. We chant his chains each day. And so, my son, you see why you must not speak of the things you've seen and heard?''

I shook my head, as if afraid the dream would end, as if reality would suddenly explode upon me. "Father Jerome," I said, "I haven't the vaguest idea of what you're talking about. Who is the man?''

"Are you such a fool, Mr. Ellington? That you must be told?''

"Yes!''

"Very well," said the Abbot. "He is Satan. Otherwise known as the Dark Angel, Asmodeus, Belial, Ahriman, Diabolus—the Devil.''

I opened my mouth.

"I see you doubt me. That is bad. Think, Mr. Ellington, of the peace of the world in these five years. Of the prosperity, of the happiness. Think of this country, Germany, now. Is there another country like it? Since we caught the Devil and locked him up here, there have been no great wars, no overwhelming pestilences: only the sufferings man was meant to endure. Believe what I say, my son; I beg you. Try very hard to believe that the creature you spoke with is Satan himself. Fight your cynicism, for it is born of him; he is the father of cynicism, Mr. Ellington! His plan was to defeat God by implanting doubt in the minds of Heaven's subjects!'' The Abbot cleared his throat. "Of course," he said, "we could never release anyone from St. Wulfran's who had any part of the Devil in him.''

I stared at the old fanatic and thought of him prowling the streets, looking for sin; saw him standing outraged at the bold fornicator's bed, wheedling him into an invitation to the Abbey, closing that heavy door and locking it, and, because of the world's temporary postwar peace, clinging to his fantasy. What greater dream for a holy man than actually capturing the Devil!

"I believe you," I said.

"Truly?"

"Yes. I hesitated only because it seemed a trifle odd that Satan should have picked a little German village for his home."

"He moves around," the Abbot said. "Schwartzhof attracted him as lovely virgins attract perverts."

"I see."

"Do you? My son, do you?"

"Yes. I swear it. As a matter of fact, I thought he looked familiar, but I simply couldn't place him."

"Are you lying?"

"Father, I am a Bostonian."

"And you promise not to mention this to anyone?"

"I promise."

"Very well." The old man sighed. "I suppose," he said, "that you would not consider joining us as a Brother at the Abbey?"

"Believe me, Father, no one could admire the vocation more than I. But I am not worthy. No; it's quite out of the question. However, you have my word that your secret is safe with me."

He was very tied. Sound had, in these years, reversed for him: the screams had become silence, the sudden cessation of them, noise. The prisoner's quiet talk with me had awakened him from deep slumber. Now he nodded wearily, and I saw that what I had to do would not be difficult after all. Indeed, no more difficult than fetching the authorities.

I walked back to my cell, where Brother Christophorus still slept, and lay down. Two hours passed. I rose again and returned to the Abbot's quarters.

The door was closed but unlocked.

I eased it open, timing the creaks of the hinges with the screams of the prisoner. I tiptoed in. Father Jerome lay snoring in his bed.

Slowly, cautiously, I lifted out the leather thong, and was

a bit astounded at my technique. No Ellington had ever burgled. Yet a force, not like experience, but like it, ruled my fingers. I found the knot. I worked it loose.

The warm iron key slid off into my hand.

The Abbot stirred, then settled, and I made my way into the hall.

The prisoner, when he saw me, rushed the bars. "He's told you lies, I'm sure of that!" he whispered hoarsely. "Disregard the filthy madman!"

"Don't stop screaming," I said.

"What?" He saw the key and nodded, then, and made his awful sounds. I thought at first the lock had rusted, but I worked the metal slowly and in time the key turned over.

Howling still, in a most dreadful way, the man stepped out into the corridor. I felt a momentary fright as his clawed hand reached up and touched my shoulder; but it passed. "Come on!" We ran insanely to the outer door, across the frosted ground, down toward the village.

The night was very black.

A terrible aching came into my legs. My throat went dry. I thought my heart would tear loose from its moorings. But I ran on.

"Wait."

Now the heat began.

"Wait."

By a row of shops I fell. My chest was full of pain, my head of fear: I knew the madmen would come swooping from their dark asylum on the hill. I cried out to the naked hairy man: "Stop! Help me!"

"Help you?" He laughed once, a high-pitched sound more awful than the screams had been; and then he turned and vanished in the moonless night.

I found a door, somehow.

The pounding brought a rifled burgher. Policemen came at last and listened to my story. But of course it was denied by Father Jerome and the Brothers of the Abbey.

"This poor traveler has suffered from the vision of pneumonia. There was no howling man at St. Wulfran's. No, no, certainly not. Absurd! Now, if Mr. Ellington would care to stay with us, we'd happily—no? Very well. I fear that you will be delirious a while, my son. The things you see will be quite real. Most real. You'll think—how quaint!—that you have loosed the Devil on the world and that the war to come—what war? But aren't there always wars? Of course!—you'll think that it's your fault"—those old eyes burning condemnation! Beak-nosed, bearded head atremble, rage in every word!—"that you'll have caused the misery and suffering and death. And nights you'll spend, awake, unsure, afraid. How foolish!"

Gnome of God, Christophorus, looked terrified and sad. He said to me, when Father Jerome swept furiously out: "My son, don't blame yourself. Your weakness was *his* lever. Doubt unlocked that door. Be comforted: we'll hunt *him* with our nets, and one day . . ."

One day, what?

I looked up at the Abbey of St. Wulfran's, framed by dawn, and started wondering, as I have wondered since ten thousand times, if it weren't true. Pneumonia breeds delirium; delirium breeds visions. Was it possible that I'd imagined all of this?

No. Not even back in Boston, growing dewlaps, paunches, wrinkles, sacks and money, at Ellington, Carruthers & Blake, could I accept that answer.

The monks were mad, I thought. Or: The howling man was mad. Or: The whole thing was a joke.

I went about my daily work, as every man must do, if sane, although he may have seen the dead rise up or freed a bottled djinn or fought a dragon, once, quite long ago.

But I could not forget. When the pictures of the carpenter from Braumau-am-Inn began to appear in all the papers, I grew uneasy; for I felt I'd seen this man before. When the carpenter invaded Poland, I was sure. And when the world was plunged into war and cities had their entrails blown asunder and that pleasant land I'd visited became a place of hate and death, I dreamed each night.

Each night I dreamed, until this week.

A card arrived. From Germany. A picture of the Moselle Valley is on one side, showing mountains fat with grapes and the dark Moselle, wine of these grapes.

On the other side of the card is a message. It is signed *"Brother Christophorus"* and reads (and reads and reads!): *"Rest now, my son. We have him back with us again."*

THE DARK MUSIC

IT WAS NOT a path at all but a dry white river of shells, washed clean by the hot summer rain and swept by the winds that came over the gulf from Mexico: a million crushed white shells, spread quietly over the cold earth, for the feet of Miss Lydia Maple.

She'd never seen the place before. She'd never been told of it. It couldn't have been purposeful, her stopping the bus at the unmarked turn, pausing, then inching down the narrow path and stopping again at the tree-formed arch; on the other hand, it certainly was not impulse. She had recognized impulsive actions for what they were years ago: animal actions. And, as she was proud to say, Miss Maple did not choose to think of herself as an animal. Which the residents of Sand Hill might have found a slightly odd attitude for a biology teacher, were it not so characteristic.

Perhaps it was this: that by its virginal nature, the area promised much in the way of specimens. Frogs would be here, and insects, and, if they were lucky, a few garden snakes for the bolder lads.

In any case, Miss Maple was well satisfied. And if one could judge from their excited murmurings, which filtered through the thickness of trees, so were the students.

She smiled. Leaning against the elm, now, with all the forest fragrance to her nostrils, and the clean gulf breeze cooling her, she was suddenly very glad indeed that she had selected today for the field trip. Otherwise, she would be at this moment seated in the chalky heat of the classroom. And she would be reminded again of the whole nasty business, made to defend her stand against the clucking tongues, or to pretend there was nothing to defend. The newspapers were not difficult to ignore; but it was impossible to shut away the attitude of her colleagues; and—no: one must not think about it.

She looked at the shredded lace of sunlight.

It was a lovely spot! Not a single beer can, not a bottle nor a cellophane wrapper nor even a cigarette to suggest that human beings had ever been here before. It was—*pure*.

In a way, Miss Maple liked to think of herself in similar terms. She believed in purity, and had her own definition of the word. Of course she realized—how could she doubt it now?—she might be an outmoded and slightly incongruous figure in this day and age; but that was all right. She took pride in the distinction. And to Mr. Owen Tracy's famous remark that hers was the only biology class in the world where one would hear nothing to discourage the idea of the stork, she had responded as though to a great compliment. The Lord could testify, it hadn't been easy! How many, she wondered, would have fought as valiantly as she to protect the town's children from the most pernicious and evil encroachment of them all?

Sex education, indeed!

By all means, let us kill every last lovely dream; let us destroy the only trace of goodness and innocence in this wretched, guilty world!

Miss Maple twitched, vaguely aware that she was dozing. The word *sex* jarred her toward wakefulness, but *purity* pulled her back again. What a pity, in a way, she thought, that I was born so late . . .

She had no idea what the thought meant; only that, for all the force of good she might be in Sand Hill, her battle was probably a losing one; and she was something of a dinosaur. In earlier, unquestionably better times, how different it would have been! Her purity would have then served a very real and necessary function, and would not have called down charges from the magazines that she was "hindering education." She might have been born in pre-Dynastian Egypt, for instance, and marched at the forefront of the court maidens toward some enormously important sacrifice. Or in the early Virginia, when the ladies were ladies and wore fifteen petticoats and were cherished because of it. Or in New England. In any time but this!

A sound brushed her ear.

She opened her eyes, watched a fat wren on a pipestem twig, and settled back to the half-sleep, deciding to dream a while now about Mr. Hennig and Sally Barnes. They had been meeting secretly after three o'clock, Miss Maple knew. She'd waited, though, and taken her time, and then struck. And she'd caught them, in the basement, doing unspeakable things.

Mr. Hennig would not be teaching school for a while now.

She stretched, almost invisible against the forest floor. The mouse-colored dress covered her like an embarrassed hand, concealing, not too successfully, the rounded hills of her breasts, keeping the secret of her slender waist and full hips, trailing down below the legs she hated because they were so smooth and white and shapely, down to the plain black leather shoes. Her face was pale and naked as a nun's, but the lips were large and moist and the cheekbones high, and it did not look very much like a nun's face. Miss Maple fought her body and her face every morning, but she was not victorious. In spite of it all, and to her eternal dismay, she was an attractive woman.

The sound came again, and woke her.

It was not the fat bird and it was not the children. It was music. Like the music of flutes, very high-pitched and mellow, yet sharp; and though there was a melody, she could not recognize it.

Miss Maple shook her head, and listened.

The sound was real. It was coming from the forest, distant and far off, and if you did not shut out the other noises, you could scarcely hear it. But it was there.

Miss Maple rose, instantly alert, and brushed the leaves and pine needles away. For some reason, she felt a chill.

Why should there be music in a lost place like this?

She listened. The wind cooled through the trees and the piping sound seemed to be carried along with it, light as shadows. Three quick high notes; a pause; then a trill, like an infant's weeping; and a pause. Miss Maple shivered and started back to the field where the children were. She took three steps and did not take any more in that direction.

The music changed. Now it did not weep, and the notes were not so high-pitched. They were slow and sinuous, lower to the ground.

Imploring. Beckoning . . .

Miss Maple turned and, without having the slightest notion why, began to walk into the thickness. The foliage was wet, glistening dark green, and it was not long before her thin dress was soaked in many places, but she understood that she must go on. She must find the person who was making such beautiful sounds.

In minutes she was surrounded by bushes, and the trail had vanished. She pushed branches aside, walked, listened.

The music grew louder. It grew nearer. But now it was fast, yelping and crying, and there was great urgency in it. Once, to Miss Maple's terror, it sounded, for a brief moment, like chuckling; still, there was no note that was not lonely, and sad.

She walked, marveling at her foolishness. It was, of course, not proper for a school teacher to go tumbling through the shrubbery, and she was a proper person. Besides—she stopped, and heard the beating of her heart—what if it were one of those horrid men who live on the banks of rivers and in woods and wait for women? She'd heard of such men.

The music became plaintive. It soothed her, told her not to be afraid; and some of the fear drained away.

She was coming closer, she knew. It had seemed vague and elusive before, now it thrummed in the air and encircled her.

Was there ever such lonely music?

She walked carefully across a webwork of stones. They protruded like small islands from the rushing brook, and the silver water looked very cold, but when her foot slipped and sank, she did not flinch.

The music grew impossibly loud. Miss Maple covered her ears with her hands, and could not still it. She listened and tried to run.

The notes rolled and danced in her mind; shrill screams and soft whispers and silences that pulsed and roared.

Beyond the trees.

Beyond the trees; another step; one more—

Miss Maple threw her hands out and parted the heavy green curtain.

The music stopped.

There was only the sound of the brook, and the wind, and her heart.

She swallowed and let the breath come out of her lungs. Then, slowly, she went through the shrubs and bushes, and rubbed her eyes.

She was standing in a grove. Slender saplings, spotted brown, undulated about her like the necks of restless giraffes, and beneath her feet there was soft golden grass, high and wild. The branches of the trees came together at the top to form a green dome. Sunlight speared the ground.

Miss Maple looked in every direction. Across the grove

to the surrounding dark and shadowed woods, and to all sides. And saw nothing. Only the grass and the trees and the sunlight.

Then she sank to the earth and lay still, wondering why she felt such heat and such fear.

It was at this moment that she became conscious of it: one thing which her vision might deny, and her senses, but which she knew nonetheless to be.

She was not alone.

"Yes?" the word rushed up and then died before it could ever leave her mouth.

A rustle of leaves; tiny hands applauding.

"Who is it?"

A drum in her chest.

"Yes, *please*—who is it? Who's here?"

And silence.

Miss Maple put fisted fingers to her chin and stopped breathing. I'm not alone, she thought. I'm not alone.

No.

Did someone say that?

The terror built, and then she felt something else entirely that wasn't terror and wasn't fear, either. Something that started her trembling. She lay on the grass, trembling, while this new sensation washed over her, catching her up in great tides and filling her.

What was it? She tried to think. She'd known this feeling before, a very long time ago; years ago on a summer night when the moon was a round, unblinking, huge and watchful eye, and that boy—John?—had stopped talking and touched her. And how strange it was then, wondering what his hands were going to do next. John! There's a big eye watching us; take me home, I'm afraid! I'm afraid, John.

If you don't take me home, I'll tell.

I'll tell them the things you tried to do.

Miss Maple stiffened when she felt the nearness, and heard the laughter. Her eyes arced over the grove.

"Who's laughing?"

She rose to her feet. There was a new smell in the air. A coarse animal smell, like wet fur: hot and fetid, thick, heavy, rolling toward her, covering her.

Miss Maple screamed.

Then the pipes began, and the music was frenzied this time. In front of her, in back, to the sides of her; growing louder, growing faster, and faster. She heard it deep in her blood and when her body began to sway, rhythmically, she closed her eyes and fought and found she could do nothing.

Almost of their own volition, her legs moved in quick, graceful steps. She felt herself being carried over the grass, swiftly, light as a blown leaf—

"Stop!"

—swiftly, leaping and turning, to the shaded dell at the end of the grove.

Here, consumed with heat, she dropped to the softness, and breathed the animal air.

The music ceased.

A hand touched her, roughly.

She threw her arms over her face: "No. Please—"

"Miss Maple!"

She felt her hands reaching toward the top button of her dress.

"Miss Maple! What's the matter?"

An infinite moment; then, everything sliding, melting, like a vivid dream you will not remember. Miss Maple shook her head from side to side and stared up at a young boy with straw hair and wide eyes.

She pulled reality about her.

"You all right, Miss Maple?"

"Of course, William," she said. The smell was gone. The music was gone. It was a dream. "I was following a snake, you see—a chicken snake, to be exact: and a nice, long one, too—and I almost had it, but I twisted my ankle on one of the stones in the brook. That's why I called."

The boy said, "Wow."

"Unfortunately," Miss Maple continued, getting to her feet, "it escaped me. You don't happen to see it, do you, William?"

William said no, and she pretended to hobble back to the field.

At 4:19, after grading three groups of tests, Miss Lydia Maple put on her gray cotton coat and flat black hat and started for home. She was not exactly thinking about the incident in the forest, but Owen Tracy had to speak twice. He had been waiting.

"Miss Maple. Over here!"

She stopped, turned and approached the blue car. The principal of Overton High was smiling: he was too handsome for his job, too tall and too young, and Miss Maple resented his eyes. They traveled. "Yes, Mr. Tracy?"

"Thought maybe you'd like a lift home."

"That is very nice of you," she said, "but I enjoy walking. It isn't far."

"Well, then, how about my walking along with you?"

Miss Maple flushed. "I—"

"Like to talk with you, off the record." The tall man got out of his car, locked it.

"Not, I hope, about the same subject."

"Yes."

"I'm sorry. I have nothing further to add."

Owen Tracy fell into step. His face was still pleasant, and it was obvious that he intended to retain his good humor, his charm. "I suppose you read Ben Sugrue's piece in the *Sun-Mirror* yesterday?"

Miss Maple said, "No," perfunctorily. Sugrue was a monster, a libertine: it was he who started the campaign, whose gross libidinous whispers had first swept the town.

"It refers to Overton High as a medieval fortress."

"Indeed? Well," Miss Maple said, "perhaps that's so." She smiled, delicately. "It was, I believe, a medieval fortress that saved the lives of four hundred people during the time of the Black Plague."

Tracy stopped a moment to light a cigarette. "Very good," he conceded. "You're an intelligent person, Lydia. Intelligent and sharp."

"Thank you."

"And that's what puzzles me. This mess over the sex-education program isn't intelligent and it isn't sharp. It's foolish. As a biology teacher you ought to know that."

Miss Maple was silent.

"If we were an elementary school," Tracy said, "well, maybe your idea would make sense. I personally don't think so, but at least you'd have a case. In a high school, though, it's silly; and it's making a laughingstock out of us. If I know Sugrue, he'll keep hammering until one of the national magazines picks it up. And that will be bad."

Miss Maple did not change her expression. "My stand," she said, "ought to be perfectly clear by now, Mr. Tracy. In the event it isn't, let me tell you again. There will be no sex-education program at Overton so long as I am in charge of the biology department. I consider the suggestion vile and unspeakable—and quite impractical—and am not to be persuaded otherwise: neither by yourself, nor by that journalist, nor by the combined efforts of the faculty. Because, Mr. Tracy, I feel a responsibility toward my students. Not only to fill their minds with biological data, but to protect them, also." Her voice was even. "If you wish to take action, of course, you are at liberty to do so—"

"I wouldn't want to do that," Owen Tracy said. He seemed to be struggling with his calm.

"I think that's wise," Miss Maple said. She paused and stared at the principal.

"And what is that supposed to mean?"

"Simply that any measure to interrupt or impede my work, or force changes upon the present curriculum, will prove embarrassing, Mr. Tracy, both to yourself and to Overton." She noticed his fingers and how they were curling.

"Go on."

"I hardly think that's necessary."

"I do. Go on, please."

"I may be . . . old-fashioned," she said, "but I am not stupid. Nor am I unobservant. I happen to have learned some of the facts concerning yourself and Miss Bond . . ."

Owen Tracy's calm fled like a released animal. Anger began to twitch along his temples. "I see."

They looked at one another for a while; then the principal turned and started back in the opposite direction. The fire had gone out of his eyes. After a few steps, he turned again and said, "It may interest you to know that Miss Bond and I are going to be married at the end of the term."

"I wonder why," Miss Maple said, and left the tall man standing in the bloody twilight.

She felt a surge of exultation as she went up the stairs of her apartment. Of course she'd known nothing about them, only guessed: but when you think the worst of people, you're seldom disappointed. It had been true, after all. And now her position was absolutely unassailable.

She opened cans and bottles and packages and prepared her usual supper. Then, when the dishes were done, she read Richard's *Practical Criticism* until nine o'clock. At nine-thirty she tested the doors to see that they were securely locked, drew the curtains, fastened the windows and removed her clothes, hanging them carefully in the one small closet.

The gown she chose was white cotton, chin-high and ankle-low, faintly figured with tiny fleur-de-lis. For a brief moment her naked body was exposed; then, at once, covered up again, wrapped, encased, sealed.

Miss Maple lay in the bed, her mind untroubled.

But sleep would not come.

She got up after a while and warmed some milk; still she could not sleep. Unidentifiable thoughts came, disturbing her. Unnormal sensations. A feeling that was not proper . . .

Then she heard the music.

The pipes: the high-pitched, dancing pipes of the afternoon, so distant now that she felt perhaps she was imagining them, so real she knew that couldn't be true. They were real.

She became frightened, when the music did not stop, and reached for the telephone. But what person would she call? And what would she say?

Miss Maple decided to ignore the sounds, and the hot strange feeling that was creeping upon her alone in her bed.

She pressed the pillow tight against her ears, and held it there, and almost screamed when she saw that her legs were moving apart slowly, beyond her will.

The heat in her body grew. It was a flame, the heat of high fevers, moist and interior: not a warmth.

And it would not abate.

She threw the covers off and began to pace the room, hands clenched. The music came through the locked windows.

Miss Maple!

She remembered things, without remembering them.

She fought another minute, very hard; then surrendered. Without knowing why, she ran to the closet and removed her gray coat and put it on over the nightgown; then she opened a bureau drawer and pocketed a ring of keys, ran out the front door, down the hall, her naked feet silent upon the thick-piled carpet, and into the garage where it was dark. The music played fast, her heart beat fast, and she moaned softly when the seldom-used automobile sat cold and unresponding to her touch.

At last it came to life, when she thought she must go out of her mind; and Miss Maple shuddered at the dry coughs and violent starts and black explosions.

In moments she was out of town, driving faster than she had ever driven, pointed toward the wine-dark waters of the gulf. The highway turned beneath her in a blur and sometimes, on the curves, she heard the shocked and painful cry of the tires, and felt the car slide; but it didn't matter. Nothing mattered, except the music.

Though her eyes were blind, she found the turn-off, and soon she was hurtling across the white path of shells, so fast that there was a wake behind her, then, scant yards from the restless stream, she brought her foot down hard upon the brake pedal, and the car danced to a stop.

Miss Maple rushed out because now the piping was inside her, and ran across the path into the field and across the field into the trees and through the trees, stumbling and falling and getting up again, not feeling the cold sharp fingers of brush tearing at her and the high wet grass soaking her and the thousand stones daggering her flesh, feeling only the pumping of her heart and the music, calling and calling.

There! The brook was cold, but she was across it, and past the wall of foliage. And there! The grove, moon-silvered and waiting.

Miss Maple tried to pause and rest; but the music would not let her do this. Heat enveloped her: she removed the coat; ate her: she tore the tiny pearl buttons of her gown and pulled the gown over her head and threw it to the ground.

It did no good. Proper Miss Lydia Maple stood there, while the wind lifted her hair and sent it billowing like shreds of amber silk, and felt the burning and listened to the pipes.

Dance! they told her. Dance tonight, Miss Maple: now. It's easy. You remember. Dance!

She began to sway then, and her legs moved, and soon she was leaping over the tall grass, whirling and pirouetting.

Like this?

Like that, Miss Maple. Yes, like that!

She danced until she could dance no more, then she stopped by the first tree by the end of the grove, and waited for the music to stop as she knew it would.

The forest became silent.

Miss Maple smelled the goaty animal smell and felt it coming closer; she lay against the tree and squinted her eyes, but there was nothing to see, only shadows.

She waited.

There was a laugh, a wild shriek of amusement; bull-like and heavily masculine it was, but wild as no man's laugh ever could be. And then the sweaty fur odor was upon her, and she experienced a strength about her, and there was breath against her face, hot as steam.

"Yes," she said, and hands touched her, hurting with fierce pain.

"Yes!" and she felt glistening muscles beneath her fingers, and a weight upon her, a shaggy, tawny weight that was neither ghost nor human nor animal, but with much heat; hot as the fires that blazed inside her.

"Yes," said Miss Maple, parting her lips. "Yes! *Yes!*"

The change in Miss Lydia Maple thenceforth was noticed by some but not marked, for she hid it well. Owen Tracy would stare at her sometimes, and sometimes the other teachers would wonder to themselves why she should be looking so tired so much of the time; but since she did not say or do anything specifically different, it was left a small mystery.

When some of the older boys said that they had seen Miss Maple driving like a bat out of hell down the gulf highway at two in the morning, they were quickly silenced:

for such a thing was, on the face of it, too absurd for consideration.

The girls of her classes were of the opinion that Miss Maple looked happier than she had ever been, but this was attributed to her victory over the press and the principal's wishes on the matter of sex-education.

To Mr. Owen Tracy, it seemed to be a distasteful subject for conversation all the way around. He was in full agreement with the members of the school board that progress at Overton would begin only when Miss Maple was removed: but in order to remove her, one would have to have grounds. Sufficient grounds, at that, for there was the business of himself and Lorraine Bond . . .

As for Miss Maple, she developed the facility of detachment to a fine degree. A week went by and she answered the call of the pipes without fail—though going about it in a more orderly manner—and still, wondering vaguely about the spattered mud on her legs, about the grass stains and bits of leaves and fresh twigs, she did not actually believe that any of it was happening. It was fantastic, and fantasy had no place in Miss Maple's life.

She would awaken each morning satisfied that she had had another unusual dream; then she would forget it, and go about her business.

It was on a Monday—the night of the day that she had assembled positive proof that Willie Hammacher and Rosalia Forbes were cutting classes together and stealing away to Dauphin Park; and submitted this proof; and had Willie and Rosalia threatened with expulsion from school—that Miss Maple scented her body with perfumes, lay down and waited, again, for the music.

She waited, tremulous as usual, aching beneath the temporary sheets; but the air was still.

He's late, she thought, and tried to sleep. Often she would sit up, though, certain that she had heard it, and once she got halfway across the room toward the closet; and sleep was impossible.

She stared at the ceiling until three A.M., listening.

Then she rose and dressed and got into her car.

She went to the grove.

She stood under the crescent moon, under the bruised sky.

And heard the wind; her heart; owls high in the trees; the shifting currents of the stream; the stony rustle of the brook; and heard the forest quiet.

Tentatively, she took off her clothes, and stacked them in a neat pile.

She raised her arms from her sides and tried a few steps. They were awkward. She stopped, embarrassed.

"Where are you?" she whispered.

Silence.

"I'm here," she whispered.

Then, she heard the chuckling: it was cruel and hearty, but not mirthless.

Over here, Miss Maple.

She smiled and ran to the middle of the grove. Here?

No, Miss Maple: over here! You're looking beautiful tonight. And hungry. Why don't you dance?

The laughter came from the trees, to the right. She ran to it. It disappeared. It appeared again, from the trees to the left.

What can you be after, madame? It's hardly proper, you know. Miss Maple, where are your clothes?

She covered her breasts with her hands, and knew fear. "Don't," she said. "Please don't." The aching and the awful heat were in her. "Come out! I want—"

You want—?

Miss Maple went from tree to tree, blindly. She ran until pain clutched at her legs, and, by the shadowed dell, she sank exhausted.

There was one more sound. A laugh. It faded.

And everything became suddenly very still and quiet.

Miss Maple looked down and saw that she was naked. It shocked her. It shocked her, also, to become aware that she was Lydia Maple, thirty-seven, teacher of biology at Overton.

"Where are you?" she cried.

The wind felt cold upon her body. Her feet were cold among the grasses. She knew a hunger and a longing that were unbearable.

"Come to me," she said, but her voice was soft and hopeless.

She was alone in the wood now.

And this was the way it had been meant.

She put her face against the rough bark of the tree and wept for the first time in her life. Because she knew that there was no more music for her, there would never be any music for her again.

Miss Maple went to the grove a few more times, late at night, desperately hoping it was not true. But her blood thought for her: What it was, or who it was, that played the pipes so sweetly in the wooded place would play no more; of that she was sure. She did not know why. And it gave her much pain for many hours, and sleep was difficult, but there was nothing to be done.

Her body considered seeking out someone in the town, and rejected the notion. For what good was a man when one had been loved by a god?

In time she forgot everything, because she had to forget. The music, the dancing, the fire, the feel of strong arms about her: everything.

And she might have gone on living quietly, applauding purity, battling the impure, and holding the Beast of Worldliness outside the gates of Sand Hill forever—if a strange thing had not happened.

It happened in a small way.

During dinner one evening Miss Maple found herself craving things. It had been a good day, she found proof that the rumors about Mr. Etlin, the English teacher, were true—he did indeed subscribe to that dreadful magazine; and Owen Tracy was thinking of transferring to another school; yet, as she sat there in her apartment, alone, content, she was hungry for things.

First it was ice cream. Big plates of strawberry ice cream topped with marshmellow sauce.

Then it was wine.

And then Miss Maple began to crave grass . . .

Nobody ever did find out why she moved away from Sand Hill in such a hurry, or where she went, or what happened to her.

But then, nobody cared.

THE MAGIC MAN

Introduction by Charles E. Fritch

At Chuck Beaumont's funeral twenty years ago, a man came up to me and introduced himself. "I'm Bill Shatner," he said. And of course he was—Captain Kirk himself, beamed down to planet Earth for this sad occasion to pay his respects to a fine writer and a nice guy inexplicably cut down in his prime.

Shatner had already appeared in Chuck's film The Intruder. *If fate had played a kinder hand he might also have appeared in television and movie Star Trek adventures with interesting and literate screenplays sculpted by the fine creative hand of Charles Beaumont. What incredible journeys he would have taken us on, what strange new Beaumontian worlds we might have explored. The mind boggles!*

Beaumont is no longer with us (God knows why; I don't), but we do have a wealth of his stories, a literary treasure trove that brings back fond personal memories for me. I remember, for example, the reading of many of these stories in manuscript form to a group of writer-friends gathered around Chuck's table in the kitchen of his North Hollywood apartment. And for those of you who had not the good fortune to know this man, you can discover him through these stories; it will be an effort well worth your time.

"The Magic Man" is one of my favorite pieces. Some stories

written a generation-plus ago date badly, but this one seems timeless. I had not read it in a quarter of a century, but once again, all these years later, I delighted in and admired Chuck's magic in building a story: the smooth phrasings, the just-right metaphor or simile in just the right place, the rhythm of the sentences that makes the images flow with fluid grace even as the story unfolds.

The casual reader would not notice the bricks and the mortar, and a good thing, too, or, as in the story itself, the magic might go away. The story illustrates another truism that Chuck had learned: stories that meant something should be about real people. The pretty word, the clever phrase, the unusual gimmick are fine if they fit, but by themselves they are not enough to sustain the delicate magic for very long, and stories that have only these artificial devices fade quickly and are soon forgotten.

"The Magic Man" is one of Chuck's stories that will not be forgotten. When it came to telling a story, he was a craftsman, a wordsmith, a magician who mesmerized his audience with the tools of his trade: a typewriter, a free-wheeling imagination, and a gift for telling tales about people who lived and breathed in his and their universe. He created a magic that lives on, for just as surely as the character in the story that follows, Chuck Beaumont was himself a magic man!

IN THE CLEAR September moonlight now the prairie lay silent and cool and the color of lakes. Dust coated it like rich fur, and there was only the night wind sliding and sighing across the tabled land, and the wolves—always the wolves—screaming loneliness at the skies: otherwise, silence, as immense as the end of things.

Dr. Silk thought about this as he tried to pull sleep into his head. It had been a long day, full of miles and sweat and blasting sun, and he should be sleeping, like Obadiah, resting for tomorrow, the Lord knew. Why else had the night been created? Yet, here he was, wide awake. Thinking.

With his knife-sharp brittle thigh, the old man sought some supporting softness in the thin straw mattress. Then, at last, feeling the covers slip to the floor, he snorted, swung his feet over the side of the pallet, and sat for a while, rubbing the back of his neck.

"You got troubles, Doctor?" Obadiah's voice was mildly alarmed; if he had been awakened it was impossible to tell. "You sick?"

"No troubles," Dr. Silk said, shaking his head. "Got to get a breath of air is all."

"You want to be careful and not take the cold."

"I'll be careful."

Outside the wagon, the night was chill. Dr. Silk got out his hand-carved pipe and sat down on the wagon steps and watched the wind for a while. He watched it race along the prairie, lifting dust and making little gray dances, and he began to think, as he had many times before on just such nights, of the invisible life that surrounded him, existing in unseen magic.

Magic. He held the word, smiled, and glanced along the wagon. Its colors were faded now, but in the glow of moon they blazed: reds and yellows and oranges and bright greens. And the big-lettered printing, vivid with scrollwork:

THE MAGIC MAN
Wonders Performed Before Your Eyes!

Dr. Silk began to feel good again, after . . . months. It must be months. He forgot about the cold, pulled at his pipe, and let tomorrow take form.

It warmed him.

For something wonderful was going to happen: tomorrow Dr. Silk—no; Micah Jackson—the foolish, cranky, asthmatic old man who creaked when he walked, who snuffled and sneezed and coughed and wandered the land in a wagon, mostly lonely, mostly tired—this prune-wrinkled sack of ancient bones—would disappear. Allakazam! Micah Jackson would disappear. And in his place there would be an elegant gentlemen in a brocade vest and a black top hat and a suit as dark as midnight: *The Magic Man, Doctor Silk—Prince, Emperor, Bringer of Mysteries and Wonders and Miracles.*

Tentatively, his fingers made an invisible coin vanish: he leaned back and thought now of the children. Of their fresh faces and their wide wondering eyes. In a while his pipe died, but he did not notice . . .

Then dawn came, slowly, spilling its cold light over the desert. Leather-toned dust had mounded up around the wagon wheels and the still sleeping mules, high, as if the rig were some forgotten tomb unburied for an hour. Dr. Silk blinked crusted eyelids and wondered whether he'd actually dozed off. It didn't seem so. But, in any case, he felt just fine.

"Obadiah!" It was very early. Far ahead and low he could see the moon, wafer-thin, unreal, ready to wink instantly out. And it was deaf-quiet. "Obadiah!" He knocked the pain out of his bones and moved up the steps. "You aim to sleep all day?"

The old Negro's eyes came open; a sheen of silver covered his face. "Morning," he said, uncertainly.

"Morning. How about some breakfast?"

"You want breakfast?" A glass of applejack usually sufficed for Dr. Silk. He disliked soft foods and was fearful of anything that might cause further damage to his already chipped and cracking plates.

"Of course! Coffee, and beans, and maybe a couple biscuits."

"Yes, sir. Biscuits." Obadiah dressed quickly, and began to rummage. "We must be getting close."

"If we move," Dr. Silk said, "we ought to reach Two Forks by late afternoon: three, four o'clock, the way I see it."

"How about the medicine?" Obadiah gestured toward the rows of empty bottles strapped to the wall. They were labeled: DOCTOR SILK'S *WONDEROL*—A SOOTHING REMEDY FOR HEADACHE, STOMACH CRAMPS, QUINSY, DIZZINESS & OTHER AILMENTS.

"Well, I'll mix up a batch pretty soon."

The Negro paused. "Didn't we sell an awful lot to the people last time we was to Two Forks?"

"We did indeed," Dr. Silk said. He frowned. "Obadiah, how many times have I got to tell you? There's nothing whatsoever harmful in Wonderol. If the folks think it'll cure them, it's got just as good a chance as anything else."

"Yes, sir." Obadiah tottered down the steps. "But one of these here fine days," he muttered, "we going to be running around all covered with a lot of tar and feathers, you see . . ."

Dr. Silk laughed. He walked over to the large brass-bound trunk that sat in the corner and pulled up the lid.

He began to remove things.

Colored squares of cloth came out first, transparent, weightless as gauze. These he transferred to a smaller box. Then serpentines uncoiled from the trunk; and bright gold hoops came out; and decks of cards and rubber bottles and disembodied hands and a stringless banjo that could make sweet music. Wonder followed wonder. The knife that was sharp enough to slice through wire but could not even scratch a child's soft flesh; Black Ben, the wooden bandit who could speak and sometimes did, if you asked him to, politely; the rose bush that grew on the head of a walking stick—all the miracles of Pandora's box, and more, one after another, carefully sorted and placed and made ready.

When he had finished here, Dr. Silk got a stiff brush and went to work on the black suit that hung from a hook. Dust flew and the old man cursed and then it was time for breakfast.

"Hitch up the mules, Obadiah!"

"But you ain't et."

"I'll eat on the way. Hitch 'em up!"

And they traveled, then, groaning and rattling, over the flour-soft desert. Dr. Silk fussed with his food and filled the Wonderol bottles and fussed some more; at last he could wait no longer.

He stripped off the dirty woollen trousers and checkered shirt. He stood before the jouncing mirror. He waxed his mustaches until they were as sharp and wicked and hard as scimitars.

"Easy, Obadiah, dammit. Easy!"

He climbed into the tight black suit. He put on the brocade vest, a dazzle of moss-green.

He looked again into the mirror. *Well, there you are, Doctor, and who says you aren't handsome*—and sighed.

Then, sitting up so as not to wrinkle the suit, bracing himself against the wagon wall, he fell fast asleep.

". . . the Magic Man! The Magic Man!"

"Where?"

"Right there, comin' down the street, can't you see?"

"It *is*, it's him—he's back!"

"Hey, Ma, look! Dr. Silk!"

Drowsing elders leaned forward on torn cane-backed chairs; large women turned their heads and tried to hold onto their children; all over, people came out of doors and peered through windows and stopped what they were doing.

"By God, here we go again!"

And suddenly the street was a tumult of dogs and children, yipping, yelling, running.

"Come back here, James, you listening to me?"

Everyone watched, as the familiar wagon grew larger. And thought: Has a whole year really passed? Has it?

There was Obadiah, sitting erect, expressionless, a dark gentleman with tight white hair, looking exactly as he'd looked the first time; and Dr. Silk—a monarch, an Eastern potentate, a devil and a god—smiling mysteriously at the running people.

"Hi, when's it gonna be?" a young girl cried.

And the others: "When's the show?" "You gonna do magic for us?" "Tonight—it'll be tonight, won't it?"

Dr. Silk smiled and waited until they had crossed the town and reached the open edge; then he nodded to Obadiah and Obadiah squealed the brake blocks and scrambled down, arms filled with cardboard posters.

"Let me take a look at one of them things." One of the men in the gathering crowd came forward.

"What's it say, Mr. Fritch?"

"Tonight," the man read aloud, "at eight o'clock. Says we're all invited to attend a show given by the world's greatest—God Almighty, what's that?"

"Prestidigitator," Dr. Silk supplied. "Magician."

The man scowled, and continued. "Wonders-performed-never-before-seen-by-the-human-eye. All-new. Watch-miracles-as-they-happen. See-the-enchanted-rose-bush. See-rabbits-appear-out-of-empty-air. See-the-great-card-mystery—" The man stopped reading. "Tonight?"

"Tonight. Eight sharp."

"Hiii!" The children began to swarm over the wagon, like mad puppies.

A boy whose face was a violent explosion of brown freckles climbed up and hollered: "Hey, where you been?"

"Traveling, son."

"Like where, for instance?"

Dr. Silk jumped down and started to talk. The crowd parted and formed an aisle; grown-ups mumbled excitedly, striding off, while the children went with the Magic Man—the older, and braver, ones, those who remembered last year, by his side; the younger ones following timidly behind. Obadiah remained. When the posters were all up, he would construct the stages, in secret.

"Traveling like where?"

"Oh," Dr. Silk said, casually but loudly enough for all to hear, "like China."

"China!"

"And Paris-France, and London."

"Really?"

"How about Egypt?" called a voice from the rear: a thin, awkward child, too excited to blush.

"By all means," Dr. Silk laughed. "You don't think I'd miss Egypt, do you?"

"And Germany—was you there?"

"Oh, yes."

"Bet you never went to Africky, with all the cannibals!"

"Now that's where you're wrong, young man. Some of my best friends happen to be cannibals."

"Is your man a cannibal?"

"Obadiah? Well . . ." Dr. Silk stopped, suddenly. "I wouldn't want this to get around, but—" He stopped and turned his head in all directions, while the children held their breath. "Can you all keep a secret?"

Dozens of small heads went up and down, solemnly.

"Well, that man of mine used to be—No; I'd better not tell you."

"Tell us!"

"No. You'd get scared and run home. You'd tell your daddies and then they wouldn't let you come to the show."

"No sir! We wouldn't say a word."

A boy not much larger than a prairie dog tugged at Dr. Silk's black trousers, and said, in a high squeaky voice:

"Honest to *God*!"

The Magic Man sighed, and squatted. He put his arms around nearby slender shoulders. "All right. Now you understand, I wouldn't tell nobody else but you . . . Well, sir, that old man of mine used to be the wildest, fiercest cannibal on the whole Sandwich Island."

"The Sandwich Island? Where's that at?"

"Why, boy, don't they teach geography in the schools any more? That's in Darkest Africa, right near the Indian Ocean."

"Oh."

"We were just passing through, you see, when all of a sudden, our ship was attacked by head-hunters. It was something, all right. Anyone here present ever been attacked by head-hunters?"

No one said a word.

"Seven foot tall they was and blacker than the ace of spades, and ugly? Enough to make a body wake up in the cold sweats of a night. They'd all snuck on board without making a sound, and bust in on us. We didn't have a chance. Them devils had special swords that would slice through a stair-rail in one swipe, while we had our fists and that's all. Plus being outnumbered eleven to one. People, I'm not ashamed to say that I was nervous. Everywhere I looked, heads were flying off from folks I'd been chatting with only a few minutes before. I heard the captain start to yell, 'Git back, ye no-good heathens'—but he never finished what he was going to say, because one of the head-hunters had creeped up and lopped off his head clean as a whistle. Having no weapon, I caught it on the fly—"

"You caught *what* on the fly, Dr. Silk?" a voice quavered.

"The captain's head. Got it by the hair, you see, and started to swing. Luckily Captain Ruyker was a Dutchman, and it's a known fact that Dutchmen have heads as hard as rock. We clouted our way through six or seven of the devils, the captain and me—knocked 'em galley west—but then, when I got to the rail, I seen it was no use. I was a goner. You all know what a crocodile is?"

"Yes, sir."

"Well, that ocean was just crawling with crocs. I couldn't jump in and swim for it or I'd be et in two minutes. And I couldn't turn back, either, because there they was, madder than hornets, them head-hunters, coming at me with their swords. Either way I was due to be *somebody's* dinner."

A girl in a gingham dress whispered: "Why didn't you use your magic?"

Dr. Silk shook his head. "That wouldn't have been fair," he said. "Would it?"

"I guess not," the girl sighed.

Dr. Silk straightened up, careful not to groan. A boy with round eyes and pale cheeks said: "What'd you do then?"

"Well, between crocodiles and cannibals, a smart man will always pick cannibals. That's what I did, too. 'Come on,' I told them. 'I'll fight you by twos or by threes!' But they didn't listen. Just kept coming. Then when I closed my eyes and could almost feel that blade zipping through my neck, they surprised me. Picked me up bodily and threw me in a canoe and we paddled down the Amazon to this here place, the Sandwich Island. That's where they all lived, you see. Well, I got there and in two shakes those head-hunters had me in this pot—great big old pot, like a kettle, rusty, made of iron. My hands was tied, so I couldn't do nothing but watch while they poured in the water and threw in some apples, bunches of carrots, and about ten heads of lettuce . . ."

"What were they aiming to do, Dr. Silk?"

"That's a silly question, boy." Dr. Silk's voice sank to a dreadful murmur. "They were aiming to cook me alive."

A girl put her hands to her lips. Some of the older boys giggled nervously and fell silent again.

Now they were all walking. The grown-ups on the porches didn't bother them because they knew Dr. Silk and they knew what he meant to the children. Secretly, a lot of them wished they could join the crowd and listen to the wonderful stories; but, of course, that would not be fitting.

Passing the Two Forks Feed and Grain Store, mincing along, barely moving at all, Dr. Silk and his parade made those with book learning think of the Pied Piper of Hamelin . . .

"What happened then, sir?"

"Well, you might know that along about now I was beginning to feel pretty low. The flames was crackling and the water was boiling and those seven-foot black demons sat hunched down on their hams, waiting. Just—waiting."

"Did you holler?"

"Wouldn't do no good. Who'd hear me?"

"Goddy."

"I began to sweat some then, and I could see myself all decked out on the table with an apple stuck in my mouth, when there came this eerie kind of scream. Like this"— Dr. Silk cupped his hands around his mouth and emitted a low cry, something like an owl, something like a coyote— "*Owoooo!* 'What's that?' I said, but they just looked sad and wouldn't answer. Then I saw over across the island, by the water, was a great big castle made out of colored rocks."

"That's where the noise was coming from?"

"Right. And it wouldn't stop, either. *Owooo! Owooo!* Sent the cold shivers down my spine. But I seen there was no sense in my worrying about that—not with the water bubbling and boiling all around me like a stew. Finally there was nothing else left to do, except . . ."

"You magicked them!"

"Only a little. I said the magic words that made the

ropes around my hands and feet vanish and in a second I was out of the pot. Say, I want you to know that I did some running then! Dripping carrots and lettuce and what-all, I kept about two feet ahead. Anyone here ever try to dodge a spear while they were running?"

No one ever had.

"It wasn't easy. I could feel them shafts whistling by my ears no more than an inch. Looked like I was done for, when one of the spears got into my shirt: it must of been tossed mighty hard, because it lifted me up off the ground and carried me right across the island like a bird. Probably would of dumped me smackdab in the ocean if I hadn't got off, too. But I did get off, and landed right at the door of the castle. Heard the screaming, then, louder than before, so I rushed in, slammed the door in the nick of time, and went to investigate."

"Was it a haunted castle?"

Dr. Silk frowned. "Boy, I could tell you it was haunted, but that would be a lie."

"Just an ordinary castle?"

"Ordinary as it could be, except for all the shrunk-up heads on the walls. Well, I went through a lot of corridors, and then sure enough, there, laying in state, was the king of Sandwich Island. It didn't take no more than a glance to see he was ailing with a rare tropical disease, the kind that makes your toes drop off. And holler? You'd of thought he was trying to call home a god. And there I was. It was my opportunity to run out the back way and escape to my freedom—but I couldn't do it."

"Why not?" the freckled boy asked.

"Because of the king. You never let a man die without trying to help, do you?"

"But them head-hunters are gonna get you any second!"

"It was a risk I had to take. Moving fast, I reached into my satchel and brought out a bottle of special medicine. I could hear the door splintering, so I cracked the neck of the glass on the wall and opened the king's mouth and poured her all in. And do you know what?"

"What?"

"By the time those cannibals busted in, their ruler was setting up, well as the day he was born. Of course, that changed their attitude in a hurry. They wanted to shake my hand, but I refused, after what they had done to Captain Ruyker and my friends on the boat. Still, they said, I had to be paid back. So the king thought a spell and finally decided to give me his son for a slave."

"Obadiah?"

"None other. He's been with me ever since, and a truer friend you couldn't ask."

There was the sound of held-breath suddenly released.

"Does he ever try to—" The girl in the gingham dress still looked terrified.

Dr. Silk smiled. "It's only happened twice since that day in 1840. You may be sure I made him take back the heads and apologize. I don't think there's anything to worry about now."

Down the street, coming out of a saloon, with his arms full of posters, Obadiah stopped and grinned, widely: a crescent of glittering white shone from the dusky face. He waved.

The children shuddered.

"Well," Dr. Silk said, "you kids run along now. I'll be seeing you tonight."

"You got any new magic for us?"

"Oh, *lots* of new magic, son. You wait."

"We'll be there. We will."

The dust snowed up around all the skinny wool-wrapped legs as the children broke and scattered and ran home to count the minutes.

Dr. Silk chuckled, straightened his shoulders, and walked imperially to the Wild Silver Saloon. Its pleated batwings swung noiselessly inward, and back. He made his way to the stained oak bar and said, "Applejack, please," and began to dig for coins.

The bartender set down the glass. "On the house," he said.

"Thank you very much."

"You're the magician."

"I am."

"I seen you last year when you was in Two Forks, and the year before that." The bartender was a huge man: clumped black hair covered his arms and head, the tops of his fingers, the top of his nose, like the pelt of a muddied coyote. It was strange to see such a man smile. Yet he smiled now, and Dr. Silk wondered for a moment how it would have been if Micah Jackson had just walked in instead of the Magic Man.

"Putting on a show tonight, are you?"

"Yes, indeed. I hope that you can come."

"I'll do that," the bartender said, "if I can get me a substitute." He went over to a thin man at the end of the bar and Dr. Silk watched and listened and forgot that there lived a lonely, withered old man named Micah Jackson, too tired to care, too old to run, ready for death to catch up.

The men in the bar had their eyes fastened on him. As they would if he were the President: more than that, though, more than mere respect. These were adults, some of them with years painted into their faces, tottering grandfathers; and still, were their eyes much different from children's, now? He studied their eyes in the big bar mirror.

There was respect, yes; a little fear, perhaps; and love—certainly there was that, abundantly.

Why? he wondered, as he always did. Was it because he was a man who could fool them with illusions? Only because he knew how to make pigeons fly out of an ordinary hat?

He threw down the rest of the applejack and hoped this wasn't the answer. The liquid warmed a path. Perhaps, he thought, it was because he brought a little honest wonder into their lives one night out of the year . . .

Then he remembered the prairie that surrounded this small and weary town. And the applejack made him want to turn and say something to the men. You don't have to wait for me, he wanted to say. Just open your eyes: there's magic in the air. Show me a tree, I'll show you a trick no magician alive could ever do. The dust underneath your boots is a riddle to keep you up nights: What did it used to be before it was dust? Mountains? And the sun! Hey, keep your eyes on the yellow ball—now it's there, now it isn't. Where does it go to? And why? A stone, a hill, a lake—now there's tricks that are tricks, gentlemen! There is magic for you. And I'd give a lot to figure out how they're done, yes, sir, a lot . . .

But he didn't say any of this. Instead he ordered another drink and reached over and calmly withdrew a bouquet from a small man's vest. The man jumped back and stared.

"Better shut your mouth, Jeff," the bartender said, winking, "or he'll be taking something out of it you won't want to see!"

The man closed his mouth and everybody laughed.

They gathered around, then, at this signal. "Show us another one now, come on. Give us a rabbit."

Dr. Silk vanished the bouquet and pulled a cartwheel from nowhere.

"Give us a rabbit!"

"Now, boys, I got to save something for tonight. Even magicians have to eat, you know."

"That so? I'd of thought you'd conjure up a steak whenever you felt like it!"

"Well, that's true. But they never taste so good, somehow. Though I do remember one experience when I had no choice in the matter. It was in Russia, and I hadn't et anything but bugs for seventeen days and nights . . ."

The bartender leaned forward, wiping slowly at a thick glass mug. "You was in Russia?"

"Oh yes," Dr. Silk said. "Got a good friend there—only man I know who can outshoot me. He once knocked the wings off a beetle at fifty paces. And—well, when things get on the dull side, I take a little trip and visit him. Of course, he's always glad to see me, since if it hadn't been for Doc Silk, he'd probably *still* be sitting on that flag-pole . . ."

Every man in the bar had now joined the group. Dr. Silk looked around, took a breath, and began to talk.

He knew they would believe him. After all, how can you doubt the word of a man who pulls roses out of the air?

Obadiah rang the bells; the crowd hushed; Dr. Silk walked through the curtained tunnel from the wagon to the stage.

He bowed gravely. A creature he was from another world, as strange in this tiny Kansas town as a comet. Oil lamps from below threw unearthly light across his face, curving the shadow of his mustaches up into the squints of his eyes. He was unreal. At any moment he might turn into a hawk or crumble into a little heap of stars or snap his fingers and change night into day.

"Ladies and gentlemen—" His voice was smooth and deep, a roar of ocean. "—and good friends!"

Far away there was the snorting of restless ponies; otherwise the town was silent, gathered here. Children sat on boxes or their father's shoulders: a few were squeezed as close to the platform as they could get, squirrel-eyed already, watching.

"The wonders I have brought to you tonight are here for your edification and enjoyment. They were taught to me by an East Indian princess, in exchange for saving her life. Before that eventful happenstance on the Fiji Isles, I was an ordinary man, possessed of no more powers than you . . . or you . . ." His finger jabbed out, pointing to one and then to another. ". . . or you. Then I learned the Mysteries of the Ages, and dedicated myself to bringing them to the people of the United States, my home. Later on I'll tell you all about a magic remedy that you can't get anywhere else—you all know it by now. But first: On with the show!"

And with a twist of his wrist, Dr. Silk plucked a crimson handkerchief out of the air. While the people watched, he balled the cloth into his fist, held it, and said, "Allakazam!" and shook loose *five* handkerchiefs, all knotted together, all different colors.

Applause tumbled out over the stage. Shouts and laughter and shrill little cries. Micah Jackson's body became inhabited by a demon: the demon made legs hop that could never have hopped otherwise; the old man in the black suit moved about the stage with youthful, fluid grace, prancing, bowing, skittering.

Rapidly, he pulled wonders from his sleeves. He borrowed a young cowboy's hat and broke six eggs into it and then made the eggs disappear: Presto! He showed the people two bright yellow hoops, eternally joined as the links of a chain. Strong men tried to pull the hoops apart. Clever men searched for the tiny hinges that had to be there, and weren't. Ordinary hoops? Very well. *Rickety-rack, pompety-pom!* And with a flourish, Dr. Silk separated the hoops and sent them rolling away.

The applause was guns going off now, it was horses stampeding. Dr. Silk ate it and drank it, and knew that of all the places he had ever been, Two Forks loved him most. He'd actually thought he had been slipping, losing the love that nourished him—and listen to them now!

Obadiah, looking fierce and mysterious in the light, as a head-hunter ought to look, put the miracles away with immense style. Sometimes—on times like this—the old man seemed to forget that he had joined Dr. Silk as the result of a bet: he seemed to remember far-off jungles of Arabian Deserts or floating islands in the clouds. Obadiah was old, he partook of the wonder against his will.

Now Dr. Silk was crawling inside a coffin, and the eyes of the people broadened, and their fists clenched, and their breath stopped in their throats.

Obadiah's voice boomed majestically. "Will somebody from the audience kindly step up and nail down the lid?"

A farmer let friends push him up onto the stage. He grinned foolishly, and winked, and put his shoulders into the hammer. The farmer went back into the crowd, full of triumph. "He's foxed now; you can wager. He's in that box for good!"

Obadiah stretched his arms and held up a lavender curtain and counted: "One! Two! Three! Four! Are you ready, Doctor?"

"Ready!"

And there was Dr. Silk, standing by the coffin, bowing.

The people stomped, shouted, yelled, thumped, while the children kept crying, "How'd you do it? Tell us how you did it!"

The miracles went on, wrapping the people of Two Forks tighter and tighter in the spell. Time ceased to exist, while rabbits hopped out of top hats and cards flew loose like wild pigeons, only to fly back again, and chairs and tables floated on the still night air.

"Pick a card, sir. Any card."

(*The pains were coming back, getting into his bones.*)

"Well, I don't know—"

"Got it?"

(*Hot pains, knifing. Get away!*)

"Yeah, I guess so!"

"Is there—" Dr. Silk had to gasp to keep the hurting from his body "—is there any way I could have seen that card, sir?"

"Not that I know of there ain't."

"Sure about that?"

(*Better now; a little better; passing.*)

"Yeah."

"All right. The card you're holding . . . might it be the ace of spades?"

"God bless us, that's what it is, sure enough!"

"Thank you, sir, thank you. And now—"

The people of Two Forks listened to a speech made by a villainous looking dummy, they watched silver dollars appear from their vests, from their ears, from their hair . . .

(*The pain gathered in his heart, punched, and subsided.*)

"If you found it on me, dammit, then I figure it's mine!"

And all the while, the children screeching, "*Please* tell us! How'd you do that one, Dr. Silk? Did it really come out of nowhere? Show us how! Please!"

Finally, it was time for the last magic. Perspiring, Dr. Silk told them about the years he had spent in Ethiopia, and how the maharaja had refused absolutely and how he'd had to creep into the palace in the dead of night, at great risk to his life, in order to steal the enchanted basket.

"Is it empty, sir?"

"Empty as it can be!"

"Nothing whatever inside? Hold it up for everybody to see, please. Nothing there?"

"Nope."

"I'd like a strong man, please. A man with muscles, who knows how to throw."

"Go on, Doody! Go on."

"Ah, thank you. Now then, I want you to take this empty basket and throw it straight up into the air, as high as you can. Is that clear?"

"Just toss it up in the air, you mean?"

"That's right. Ready? One . . . two . . . three . . . Throw it, sir!"

The man threw the basket: it sailed upward. All eyes held it. Then there was an explosion, and eyes jerked back to Dr. Silk, who stood on the stage with the smoking pistol in his hand. The basket fell back to the stage, rolled, was still.

"Mr. Doody, would you care to remove the lid?"

The man poked tentatively at the basket's woven teapot lid. It fell aside.

"The Lord!"

And out of the basket shot a hundred snakes! Red ones, green ones, yellow ones—jerking, twitching serpentines, like a rainbow come suddenly apart.

Dr. Silk looked over at Obadiah, who grinned and winked and immediately hauled out the boxes of Wonderol.

The people stood smiling out as far as you could see. Bowing, Dr. Silk listened to their applause; he listened and felt the love as it cascaded over the oil lamps. And he knew it was the sweetest, most marvelous feeling that could be: he wished he could do more—something to repay them for this love which, if they knew it, kept him alive, nourished him, let the heart of Micah Jackson beat on. If he could make them see the magic around them, that would be a repayment—but how many ever saw this magic? No, he couldn't do that for the people. Yet—

"How'd you do it?" The high-voiced softly shrill question had become a chant. The children were ecstatic: "Tell us, tell us, please!"

Begging, imploring. Would he do this for them, would he, please?

Dr. Silk felt the applejack—*"Mr. Jackson, if you don't cut it out, you'll be dead in a year, I promise you"*—and his head seemed to dance with the children's question.

Then, all at once, he knew. He knew what he could give the people. He knew how he could say thank you and say good-by, gracefully, forever.

"All right," he called. "Gather round, now!"

"What are you gonna do? You gonna . . . show us how the magic's done? Are you?"

Dr. Silk looked at them. You know better than this, he thought, and he thought: It is because you're going to have the big tricks explained to you in a little while and you know how you'll feel and you want them to feel the same? No. It isn't. And it isn't a test, either. Or anything. Just a way to repay them.

"Yes," Dr. Silk said, "I am."

Obadiah's jaw fell. He walked over quickly. "You ain't really?" he said.

"I am. The children want it, Obadiah. I'll never be able to do anything else for them—you know that. And just look at their eyes."

"I wouldn't Doctor, swear to the Lord."

"He's gonna show us!"

The clapping began again. Everyone pressed close, expectant, waiting.

"Don't do it," Obadiah said. "Let's just sell us some medicine like we always do and scat."

But Dr. Silk was already reaching into the black box.

He removed the enchanted hoops. "Now I want you to pay close attention," he declared.

"We will." "Shhh!"

Carefully, then, with exaggerated simplicity, he showed how there were actually three hoops, how two of them fit together and where the third one came from.

"See?"

The children squealed incredulously and clapped their hands. Someone said, "I'll be damned, I will be damned."

"Show us more!"

Dr. Silk felt the pain again. "You want to see more?" he asked. "You really and truly do?"

"Yes!"

Obadiah grunted and sat down.

"Very well." And Dr. Silk went on to show them the

magic cane, and how it wasn't magic at all. "See," he smiled, "the flowers, which aren't real, they fold up, like this, inside the head. They're there all the time. Then I just press this here spring and it releases them. I bought it in Chicago at a warehouse . . ."

One by one, carefully, Dr. Silk explained his miracles. The deck of cards that contained nothing but aces of spades; the eggs that really weren't eggs at all; the coffin that had no bottom . . .

"Just lift it off, you see, and put it back. Just like that!"

Gradually the squealings died. The audience thinned. But the Magic Man did not notice: he could think of nothing but the love the people had given him and how he *must* repay them. So he did not feel the wrinkles jumping back into his face, or the dust of far-off places falling from his suit, or hear the way the crowd was turning quiet; or see the children's faces, with their hundred dimming lights.

When at last he had come to the enchanted basket— snakes coiled neatly in the false bottom—Dr. Silk stopped, and blinked away the wetness. "We're all magicians now," he said, his smile poised, waiting.

There were murmurs beyond the flickering of the lamps, and shufflings.

The people were silent. They looked at one another furtively, and a few giggled, while a few wore angry expressions.

Slowly, they began to disperse.

The people began to go away.

Dr. Silk felt the pain another time, more strongly than ever before: almost a new kind of pain, wrenching at his heart. He saw the boy with the freckles who had been with him this afternoon. The boy's eyes were moist. He paused, staring, then he wheeled and tore away into the shadows.

"But, I thought you wanted—" Dr. Silk saw the dark night faces clearly. No one looked back.

The bartender from the Wild Silver Saloon seemed about

to say something—his face was red and embarrassed, not angry—but then he turned and walked off too.

In moments the tiny stage, the wagon, stood alone. Dr. Silk did not move. He kept staring over the lights, just standing there, staring.

"Boss, let's go. Let's us go."

"Obadiah—" Dr. Silk took a hold of the Negro's thin shoulders. "They didn't actually believe in me, did they? Did they honestly believe I could—"

Obadiah shrugged. "Let's us get on out of here," he said. Then he began to pick up the tarnished wonders, quickly, and hurl them into the box.

"All right." Dr. Silk looked down at his hands, at the lint-flecked, worn black suit, at the cracking patent-leather shoes. "All right." He thought of the children and all their dying faces, of the men and their faces—hard and astonished and dumbfounded as if they'd heard God snore, and watched Him get drunk, and found that He was no different from them, and so, once more, they were left with nothing to believe in.

He felt the pain come rushing.

"Why? Lord, tell me that."

Dr. Silk went through the curtained tunnel back into the wagon and sat down on the straw pallet and sat there, quietly, and did not move even when the wagon lurched and began to sway.

After a long time, he took off the black suit, the green vest, the white shirt. He got the wax out of his mustaches.

Then he went to the window and stood there, looking out over the prairie, the moon-drenched, cool eternal prairie, moving past him. For hours, for miles.

And while he stood there, the hurting grew; it came back into his body, piercing, hard, familiar hurting.

"Why?"

The wagon stopped.

"You feel all right now, Doctor?" Obadiah held onto the door. He looked frightened and lost.

The Magic Man studied his friend; then he snorted and leaned back and closed his eyes. He tried not to think of the people. He tried not to think of Micah Jackson asking *How's it done?* and then learning as he would, so soon now, so very soon.

"It reminds me of the time," he said softly, "in Calcutta, when I went six months without hearing the sound of a human voice . . ."

Obadiah walked over to the pallet and sat down, smiling. "I don't recall you ever mentioned that experience to me, Dr. Silk," he said. "Tell me about it, would you, please?"

FAIR LADY

Introduction by
George Clayton Johnson

When I was offered an opportunity to select a story of Charles Beaumont's for this collection, I immediately thought of "Fair Lady."

It may seem an odd choice.

As many of you know it is a slight story that takes up only 5 pages in Beaumont's 183 page THE HUNGER And Other Stories, his first story collection. Before being published in THE HUNGER, "Fair Lady" had never been printed before, written while Beaumont was still an unknown young man striving to become a published writer.

A mainstream story like "Fair Lady" has a tough time of it in the marketplace, even though it may have great merit, simply because it doesn't fit into a convenient genre. Its very ordinariness and simplicity works against it. And yet, there is a lot of fragile magic packed in these few plain pages. The story's tone perfectly matches its subject matter, and one feels as he reads it that each word has been chosen with special precision to carry a freightload of delicate associations. Its pace is slow and yet the story is a model of terseness and suspense containing that quality which people call "classic" when they encounter it.

"Fair Lady" is Charles Beaumont's tenderest short story.

It is about the joys and perils of living in a dreamworld and deals in what Beaumont called "The Greater Truth."

Cold facts never had much appeal to Beaumont. He was aware of them, but would search around and over and behind them looking for something better. It was one of his greatest talents as a storymaker, what William F. Nolan called "thinking side-ways"—a way of deliberately ignoring obvious connections to look for the unlikely and to be able to make an emotion-laden case for it—to discover the warm facts that often made the cold ones irrelevant. "If you want your castles to last forever, make them out of sand," he once told me.

I know from my own experience that many of a beginning writer's first stories are written blindly, on speculation, often at night on the kitchen table and submitted, along with a self-addressed stamped envelope to addresses culled from the back pages of popular magazines. When the story comes back more frayed than before with a printed rejection form that gives no reason for the rejection the writer will re-examine the manuscript again seeking the flaw that has betrayed him, trying to see with fresh eyes and, having decided to alter it he must retype it again before submitting it to a new potential market to have it returned again and again.

A would-be writer must be very devoted to his goal of publication and be prepared for a lot of emotional punishment along the way.

If he perseveres he will learn to rewrite, which is the art of it.

As anyone will tell you who has never written a story, it is a simple thing to do. You just put a sheet of paper in a typewriter and let the words flow. The result is a story that reads as though it wrote itself.

As anyone will tell you who has written a story, it is not quite that simple. There are usually many revisions, editings, and re-writings necessary in order to make a story appear as though there were little effort involved in its creation.

"Fair Lady" gives evidence of such close rewriting and, oddly for a story with so few events or characters, is very strongly plotted in that the reader quickly senses that the writer knows his destination exactly although it may be an unexpected one, and, although he may take a deceptive path to get there, and further, that one will learn something important if he reads to the end.

Rereading this story in order to write an introduction to it I was struck by how much of the story I remembered from my first reading of it almost 30 years ago—how much detail, how many dazzling lines and flashes of insight were etched into my mind—to me the sign of a first-rate work.

The ingredients are simple:

Elouise Baker, an elderly schoolteacher (". . . unbeautiful and old. And what is a thing after all, when it is no longer young, if it is not old?"), and Oliver O'Shaugnessy, a genial bus driver (". . . a broad burly man behind the wheel who smiled at her with his eyes."), and an early morning bus ride, but from these familiar elements Beaumont has fashioned a deeply felt excursion into the human heart, reaching out to touch your emotions at will (". . . and who could speak with her about love and be on safe ground?").

And, as sweetly sad and starkly tragic as it is, who can deny that it is a love story with a happy ending?

This introduction to Charles Beaumont's story "Fair Lady" is intended as a tribute to young, unpublished, unknown Charles LeRoy Nutt who became Charles Beaumont.

————————

"Go to Mexico, Elouise," they had told her. "You'll find him there." So she had gone to Mexico and searched the little dry villages and the big dry cities, searched carefully; but she did not find him. So she left Mexico and came home.

Then they said, "Paris! That's the place he'll be. Only, hurry, Elouise! It's getting late." But Paris was across an ocean: it didn't exist, except in young girls' hearts and old women's minds, and if she were to see him there, a *boulevardier*, a gay charmer with a wine bottle—no, they were wrong. He wasn't in Paris.

In fact—it came to her one day in class, when the sun was not bright and autumn was a dead cold thing outside— Duane wasn't anywhere. She knew this to be true because a young man with golden hair and smooth cheeks was standing up reading Agamemnon, and she listened *and did not dream*.

She did not even think of Duane—or, as it may have been, Michael or William or Gregory.

She went home after grading the papers and thought and tried to recall his features. Then she looked about her room, almost, it seemed, for the first time: at the faded orange wallpaper, the darkwood chiffonier, the thin rows of books turned gray and worn by gentle handling over the years. The years . . .

She discovered her wrists and the trailing spongy blue veins, the tiny wrinkled skin that was no longer taut about the hands; and her face, she studied it, too, in the mirror, and saw the face the mirror gave back to her. Not ugly, not hard, but . . . unbeautiful, and old. And what is a thing, after all, when it is no longer young, if it is not old?

She searched, pulled out memories from the cedar chest, and listened in the quiet room to her heart. But he was not there, the tall stranger who waited to love her, only her, Miss Elouise Baker, and she knew now that he never would be. Because he never was.

It was on that night that Miss Elouise wept softly for death to come and take her away.

And it was on the next morning that she met, and fell in love with, Mr. Oliver O'Shaugnessy.

It happened this way. Miss Elouise was seated at the bus

stop waiting for the 7:25, seated there as on years of other mornings; only now she thought of death whereas before she'd thought of life, full and abundant. She was an elderly school-teacher now, dried-up and desiccated, like Mrs. Ritter or Miss Ackwright; cold in the morning air, unwarmed by dreams, cold and heavy-lidded from a night of staring, frightened, into darkness. She sat alone, waiting for the 7:25.

It came out of the mist with ponderous grace, its old motor loud with the cold. It rumbled down the street, then swerved and groaned to a stop before the triangular yellow sign. The doors hissed open and it paused, breathing heavily.

But Miss Elouise stared right into the red paint, sat and stared in the noise and the smoke and didn't move at all or even blink.

The voice came to her soft and unalarmed, almost soothing: "You wouldn't be sitting there thinking up ways to keep the kiddies after school, would you?"

She looked up and saw the driver.

"I'm sorry. I . . . must have dozed off."

She got inside and began to walk to her seat, the one she'd occupied every morning for a million years.

Then it happened. A rushing into existence, a running, a being. Later she tried to remember her impressions of the surrounding few seconds. She recalled that the bus was empty of passengers. That the advertising signs up above had been changed. That the floor had not been properly swept out. Willed or unwilled, it happened then, at the moment she reached her seat and the doors hissed closed. With these words it happened:

Fair Lady.

"What did you say?"

"Unless you're under twelve years of age, which you'd have a hard time persuading me of, miss, I'll have to ask the company's rightful fare." Then gently, softly, like the laughter of elves: "It's a wicked, money-minded world, and me probably the worst of all, but that's what makes it spin."

Miss Elouise looked at the large red-faced man in the early-morning fresh uniform creased from the iron and crisp. The cap, tilted back over the gray locks of hair; the chunks of flesh straining the clothes tight and rolling out over the belt; at the big, broad, burly man behind the wheel who smiled at her with his eyes. She looked at Oliver O'Shaugnessy, whom she'd seen before and before and never seen before this moment.

Then she dropped a dime into the old-fashioned black coin box and sat down.

But not in her usual seat. She sat down in the seat first back from the man who'd said Fair Lady when it took just those words out of a fat dictionary of words to bring her to life.

That's how it happened. As mysteriously, as unreasonably as any great love has ever happened. And Miss Elouise, from that time on, didn't question or doubt or, for that matter, even think about it much. She just accepted.

And it made the old dream an embarrassed little thing. A pale, dated matinee illusion—she couldn't even bear to think of it, now, with its randy smell of shieks on horseback and dark strangers from a cardboard nowhere. Duane . . . what an effete ass *he* turned out to be, and to think: she might actually have met him and been crushed and forsaken and forever lost . . .

Now, she could once again take up her interest in books and art and music, and, in a little while, it all came—she was loving her job—loving it. And before, she hated it with her soul. Since falling in love with Oliver O'Shaugnessy, these things were hers. She grew young and healthy and wore a secret smile wherever she went.

Every morning, then, Miss Elouise would hurry to the bus stop and wait while her heart rattled fast. And, sure

enough, the bus would come and it would be empty—most
of the time, anyway: when it was not empty, she felt that
intruders or in-laws had moved in for a visit. But, mostly
it was empty.

For thirty minutes every morning, she would live years
of life. And slowly, deliciously, she came to know Oliver
as well as to love him. He grew dearer to her as she found,
each day, new sides to him, new facets of his great personality. For example, his moods became more readily apparent, though hidden behind the smile he always wore for
her: she came to know his moods. On some days he felt
perfectly wretched; on others, tired and vaguely disturbed;
still other days found him bursting with spring cheer, happy
as a fed child. Once, even, Oliver was deeply introspective
and his smile was weary and forced as he revolved the large
wedding ring on his third finger left hand. Through all, he
changed and broadened and grew tall, and she loved him
with all her heart.

Of course she never spoke of these things. Ever. In fact,
they conversed practically not at all. He had no way of
guessing the truth, though at times Miss Elouise thought
perhaps he did.

Together, it was perfect. And what more can be said?

For three years Miss Elouise rode with Oliver O'Shaugnessy, her lover, every morning, every morning without
fail. Except for that awful day each week when he did not
work—and these were dark, empty days, full of longing.
But they passed. And it gave such wings to her spirit that
she felt truly no one in the world could be quite so happy.
Fulfillment there was, and quiet contentment. No wife in
bed with her husband had even known one tenth this in-
timacy; no youngsters in the country under August stars
had ever come near to the romance that was hers; nor had
ever a woman known such felicity, unspoken, undemanded,
but so richly there.

For three magic years. And who could speak with her about love and be on fair ground?

Then, there came a morning. A morning cold as the one of years before, when she had thought of death, and Miss Elouise felt a chill enter her heart and lodge there. She glanced at her watch and looked at the street, misted and empty and wet gray. It was not late, it was not Oliver's day off, nothing had happened—therefore, why should she be afraid? Nevertheless, she was afraid.

The bus came. It swung around the corner far ahead and rolled toward her and came to its stop and, without thinking or looking, she got on.

And saw.

Oliver O'Shaugnessy was not there.

A strange young man with blond hair and thick glasses sat at the wheel. Miss Elouise felt everything loosen and break apart and start to drift off. She was terrified, suddenly, frozen like a china figurine, and she did not even try to move or understand.

It was not merely that something had been taken—as her father had been taken, her father whom she loved so very much. Not merely that. It was knowing, all at once, that she *herself* was being taken, pushed out of a world she'd believed in and told to stay away.

Once she'd known a woman who was insane. They would say to this woman, "You were walking through the house last night, and laughing," and the woman, who never laughed, she wouldn't remember and her eyes would widen in fear and she would say, later, in a lost voice: "I wonder what I could have been laughing at . . ."

There was a throaty noise, a loud cough.

"Who are you?" Miss Elouise said.

"Beg pardon?" the young man said.

"Where is Oliver?"

"O'Shaugnessy? Got transferred. Takes the Randolphe route now."

Transferred . . .

Miss Elouise felt that a cageful of little black ugly birds had suddenly been released and that they beat their wings against her heart. She remembered the loneliness and how the loneliness had died and been replaced with something good and clean and fine and built of every lovely dream in all the world.

She got off the bus at the next stop and went home and thought all that day and into the night. Very late into the night . . .

Then, the birds went away.

She smiled, as she had been smiling for these years, and, when the morning came again, she made a telephone call. Retirement—for Miss Elouise? Why certainly she was due it, but—

She worked busily as a housewife, packing, moving, setting straight the vacant room, telling her goodbyes.

It took time. But not much, really, and she worked so fast and so hard she had little time to think. The days flew.

And then it was done.

And, smiling, she sat one morning in new air, on a new corner two blocks from her new home, and she waited for the bus.

And presently, as lovers will, her lover came to her.

A POINT OF HONOR

TODAY MRS. MARTINEZ did not practice on the organ, so St. Christopher's was full of the quiet that made Julio feel strange and afraid. He hated this feeling, and, when he touched the sponge in the fountain of Holy Water—brittle and gray-caked, like an old woman's wrist—he thought of sitting alone in the big church and decided that tomorrow would be time enough to pray. Making the Sign of the Cross, he put a dime and two pennies into the poor box and went back down the stone stairs.

The rain was not much. It drifted in fine mist from the high iron-colored clouds, freckling the dry streets briefly, then disappearing.

Julio wished that it would rain or that it would not rain.

He hurried over to the young man who was still leaning against the fender of a car, still cleaning his fingernails with a pocket knife. The young man looked up, surprised.

"So let's go," Julio said, and they started to walk.

"That was a quickie," the young man said.

Julio didn't answer. He should have gone in and prayed and then he wouldn't be so scared now. He thought of the next few hours, of Paco and what would be said if it were known how scared he really was.

"I could say your mom got sick, or something. That's what Shark pulled and he got out of it, remember."

"So?"

"So nothing, for Chrissakes. You want me to mind my own business—all right."

Danny Arriaga was Julio's best friend. You can't hide things from your best friend. Besides, Danny was older, old enough to start a mustache, and he'd been around: he had even been in trouble with a woman once and there was a child, which had shocked Julio when he first heard about it, though later he was filled with great envy. Danny was smart and he wasn't soft. He'd take over, some day. So Julio would have to pretend.

"Look, I'm sorry—okay by you?"

"Jimdandy."

"I'm nervous is all. Can't a guy get nervous without he's chicken?"

They walked silently for a while. The heat of the sun and the half-rain had left the evening airless and sticky, and both boys were perspiring. They wore faded blue jeans which hung tight to their legs, and leather flying jackets with THE ACES crudely lettered in whitewash on the backs. Their hair was deep black, straight and profuse, climbing down their necks to a final point on each; their shoes were brightly shined, but their T-shirts were grimy and speckled with holes. Julio had poked the holes in his shirt with his finger, one night.

They walked across the sidewalk to a lawn, down the lawn's decline to the artificial lake and along the lake's edge. There were no boats out yet.

"Danny," Julio said, "why you suppose Paco picked me?"

Danny Arriaga shrugged. "Your turn."

"Yeah, but what's it going to be?"

"For you one thing, for another guy something else. Who knows? It's all what Paco dreams up."

Julio stopped when he saw that they were approaching the boathouse. "I don't want to do it, I'm chicken—right?"

Danny shrugged again and took out a cigarette. "I told you what I would've told Paco, but you didn't want to. Now it's too late."

"Gimme a bomb," Julio said.

For the first time, suddenly, as he wondered what he had to do tonight, he remembered a crazy old man he had laughed at once in his father's pharmacy on San Julian Street and how hurt his father had been because the old man was a shellshock case from the first world war and couldn't help his infirmity. He felt like the old man now.

"Better not crap around like this," Danny said, "or Paco'll start wondering."

"Let him wonder! All right, all right."

They continued along the edge of the lake. It was almost dark now, and presently they came to the rear door of the park's boathouse. Danny looked at Julio once, stamped out his cigarette and rapped on the door.

"Check the playboys," somebody said, opening the door.

"Cram it," Danny said. "We got held up."

"That's a switch."

Julio began to feel sick in his stomach.

They were all there. And Julio knew why: to see if he would chicken out.

Lined up against the far wall, Gerry Sanchez, Jesús Rivera, Manuel Morales and his two little brothers who always tagged along wherever he went; seated in two of the battery boats, Hernando and Juan Verdugo and Albert Dominguin. All silent and in their leather-jacket-and-jeans uniforms. In the center of the big room was Paco.

Julio gestured a greeting with his hand, and immediately began to fear the eyes that were turned on him.

Paco Maria Christobal y Mendez was a powerfully muscled, dark and darkhaired youth of seventeen. He sat tipped back in a wicker chair, with his arms stretched behind his head, staring at Julio, squinting through the cigarette smoke.

"What, you stop in a museum on the way?" Paco said. Everybody laughed. Julio laughed.

"What are you talking? I ain't so late as all that."

"Forty-five minutes is too late." Paco reached to the table and moved a bottle forward.

"Speech me," Julio said. "Speech me."

"Hey, listen, you guys! Listen. Julio's cracking wise."

"Who's cracking wise? Look, so I'm here, so what should I do?"

Danny was looking at his shoes.

Paco rubbed his face. It glistened with hot sweat and was inflamed where the light beard had caused irritations. "Got a hot job for Julio tonight," he said. "Know what it is?"

"How should I know?" Julio tried hard to keep his voice steady.

"Great kidders, you English," Paco said. "Hey, you guys, he don't know." He looked over at Danny Arriaga. "You didn't tell him?"

"For Chrissakes," Danny said.

"All right, all right, so. You still want in The Aces?"

Julio nodded.

"By which means you got to do whatever I say you got to do, no matter what, right? Okay." Paco drank from the bottle and passed it to Manuel Morales, who drank and gave the bottle to the younger of his brothers, who only wet his lips and gave it back.

Julio knew he'd have to wait, because he remembered Albert's initiation, and how Paco had stalled and watched to see how scared he got. They'd sent Albert to swipe a car that was owned by the manager of Pacific Fruit who always left the key in. That wasn't so bad, even if Albert did wreck the car the same night, driving it back to the club. Swiping a car would be all right.

But from the way Danny looked, it wasn't going to be anything like that. Paco had it in for him ever since he found out about his going to church. Though there must be more to it, because Julio knew that Hernando and Juan went to church, too.

Something deep and strange, hard to figure.

But strong.

"Pretty soon it's time," Paco said, leaning back in the chair. The others were smiling.

The boats rocked uneasily in the small currents, a short drifting.

Julio thought about Paco, about how he'd come to The Aces. It was Danny who joined first, long before, even before Julio was wearing jeans. Paco was later, a new guy on the street. Mr. Mendez was dead, and his mother worked in the Chinese grocery on Aliso Street with the dead cats in the window. No organization to the club, then. Paco moved in and organized. He beat up Vincente Santa Cruz, who was the strongest guy in the Heights, and he introduced the guys to marijuana and showed them where to get it. He'd been booked three times at the jail and was seen with girls tagging after him, even though he wasn't good-looking, only strong and powerful. Danny admired Paco. Julio didn't, but he respected him.

"Charge up, kid." Paco opened a pill box which contained four crude cigarettes.

"Afterwards," Julio said.

"So okay. Afterwards." Paco grinned and winked at the others.

There was silence again: only the water sloshing against the boats and the painful creak of the wicker chair straining back and forth.

The room was very small. THE ACES was whitewashed on the walls, and initials were carved in various places.

Except Julio's. His were not on any of the walls. That distinction would come only when he'd finished his job.

No one seemed prepared to break the quiet.

Julio thought, Danny knows. He knew all along, but he wouldn't tell me. Danny was a full-fledged member now. He'd had to break windows out of Major Jewelry and swipe enough watches for the gang. A tough assignment, because of the cops who prowled and wandered around all the time. It took nerve. Julio had broken into a store himself, though—a tire shop—and so he knew he could do it again, although he remembered how afraid he had been.

Why wouldn't they tell him, for Chrissakes? Why stall? If they'd only tell him now, he'd go right out, he was sure. But, any later . . .

"Scared?" Paco asked, lighting another cigarette and taking off his jacket.

"Listen close—you'll hear me shaking," Julio said.

Danny smiled.

Paco frowned and brought his chair forward with a loud noise.

"What are you so cocky—I'll give you in the mouth in a minute. I asked a question."

"No. I ain't scared."

"That's a crock of shit. Who are you trying to kid, anyway? Me?"

Suddenly Julio hated this leering, posturing Paco as he had never hated a person before. He looked at his friend Danny, but Danny was looking elsewhere.

"Mackerel snapper, isn't it, Julio?" Paco scratched his leg loudly. "What did you, go to confession today or was the priest busy in the back room?" He smiled.

Julio clenched his fists. "Gimme to do, already," he said; and, all at once, he thought of his father, Papa Velasquez. Papa would be working late right now, in the pharmacy, mixing sodas and prescriptions. Business was very good, with the new housing project and all the new trade.

Julio was going to be a pharmacist—everybody knew that, though no one believed it. No one but Father Laurent: he talked to Julio many times, softly, understandingly. And there were many times when Julio wanted to tell the priest what he had done—about the motorcycle or the time he helped the guys push tea—but he could never seem to get the words out.

He waited, hands tight together, listening to the breathing, and thinking: I could go right to the drugstore now, if I wanted. It was only a mile away . . .

He cleared his throat. Albert Dominguin was staring at him.

And now Danny Arriaga was getting sore, too: Julio could tell.

"You want to know, huh? Guys—think I should tell him?"

"Tell him already," Danny snapped, rising to his feet. He looked a lot bigger than Paco, suddenly. "Now."

"Who asked for your mouth?" Paco said, glaring. He looked quickly away. "All right, Julio. But first you got to see this."

Paco reached in his pocket and took out a large bone-handled knife. Julio didn't move.

"Ever use one, kid?"

"Yeah."

"Hey, no shit? What do you think, guys—Julio's an expert!" Paco pressed a button on the knife with his thumb. A long silver blade flashed out, glittering in the greenish light of the boathouse.

"So?"

"So you're going to use it tonight, Julio," Paco said, grinning broadly and rocking in the chair. The others crouched and held their cigarettes in their mouths.

Danny seemed about to speak up, but he held himself in check.

"On what?" Julio said.

"No, kid—not on *what*, on *who*." Paco flipped the knife toward Julio's foot, but it landed handle-down and slid to a corner. Julio picked it up, pressed the button, folded back the blade and put the knife in his pocket.

"All right, who. On who?"

He remembered what the Kats had done to the old woman over on Pregunta. For eighty-three cents.

"A dirty son of a bitch that's got it coming," Paco said. He waited. "Hey, kid, what's wrong? You look sick."

"What are you talking, for Chrissakes? What do you want I should do?"

"Carry out a very important mission for our group, that's what. You're a very important man, Julio Velasquez. Know that?"

Near Cuernavaca, by the caverns of Cacahuamilpa, Grandfather had seen a man lying still in the bushes. The man was dead. But not only that—he had been dead for a long time. Grandfather used to sit after the coffee and tell about it; and it was always terrifying because Grandfather had a quiet way of talking, without emphasis, without excitement.

—*¿Quien fué el hombre, Papá?*

—*¿Quien¡ Un hombre muy importante en el pueblo!*

Always; then the slow description, unrolling like one of Mama's stringballs. The man had been a rich one of the village, influential and well liked, owner of a beautiful hacienda, over two thousand acres of land. Then one night he didn't come back when he should have, and the next night it was the same, and the next night, and after the searches, he was forgotten. It was Grandfather who found him. But the flies and the vultures had found him first.

—*¿Comó murió el hombre?* He had been murdered. The knife was still between his ribs and the flesh had softened and decayed around the knife.

Death . . .

Julio always thought of death as the rich man from Cuernavaca.

"What'd he do?" Julio asked. "This guy."

"He got to *do* something?" Paco said, laughing. Then: "Plenty. You know when we all went to the Orpheum the other night and you had to stay home on account of your old man or something?"

"Yeah. Sure."

"Okay. They got Billy Daniels and a picture that's supposed to be good, y'know? Okay, we start to pay when the chick at the window picks up the phone and says, 'Wait a minute.' Pretty soon the brass comes out and starts to look us over, real cool, see, like he had a bug up or something. I talk to him and it's all right—we go in. Five goddam dollars. So—the show stinks, the movie: it's cornball, and we go to get our loot back. Guy at the window now, no broad. He says 'Nooo.' I ask to see the manager, but he's gone. They won't give us back our loot. What do we do? What would *you* do, Julio?"

"Raise a stink."

"You bet your sweet ass. That's what we do, what happens? Big Jew punk comes barrelin' down the aisle, says he's the assistant manager. We got to blow, see. But no loot, no, man. Then he took Albert by the hair and kicked him. Right, Albert?"

Albert nodded.

"So naturally this isn't for The Aces. I didn't say nothing after that, except I let the schmuck know he'd get his, later on. So we just casually walked out. And here's the thing—" Paco's eyes narrowed dramatically. "That louse is still walking around, Julio, like he never done a thing to anybody, like he never insulted all of us. Know what he said? Know what he called us, Julio?"

"What'd he call you?"

"Pachooks. Wetbacks. Dirty Mex bastards. Crapped his mouth off like that in front of everybody in the show."

"So you want him cut up?"

Paco rocked and smiled. "No, not just cut up. I want that liddle-Yiddle dead, where he can't crap off any more. That's your assignment, Julio. Bring back his ears."

Julio glanced at Danny, who was not smiling. The others were very quiet. They all looked at him.

"When's he get off?" Julio asked, finally.

"Ten-thirty. He walks down Los Angeles street, then he hits Third, down Third till he's around the junction. It's a break, Julio. We followed him for three nights, and there's never anybody around the junction. Get him when he's passing the boon docks over to Alameda. Nobody'll ever see you."

"How will I know him?"

"Fat slob. Big nose, big ears, curly brown hair. Carries something, maybe his lunch-pail—you might bring that back with you. Albert'll go along and point him out, in case he wants to try to give you trouble. He's big, but you can take him."

Julio felt the knife in his pocket. He nodded.

"All right, so this is it. You and Albert, take off in half an hour, wait and hang around the loading docks, but make sure nobody sees you. Then check the time and grab a spot behind the track next to Merchant Truck—you know where it is. He'll pass there around eleven. All right?"

Julio reached for the pill box and controlled his fingers as they removed the last cigarette. Paco grinned.

"So in the meantime, let's have our meeting. Whoever got what, lay it out on the floor."

The boys began reaching into the bags and parcels, and into their pockets, and taking out watches and rings and handfuls of money. These items they spread on the floor.

The rich man, Julio thought, lying still in the bushes, with his fat dead face, waiting for the flies, waiting, while a little Mexican boy with red wet hands runs away, fast, fast . . .

* * *

The grating sound of heavy machinery being pushed across cement came muffled through the wooden doors of the freight dock. There were a few indistinct voices, and the distant hum of other machines that never stopped working.

The night was still airless. Julio and Albert Dominguin walked along the vacant land by the boxcar, clinging to the shadows and speaking little.

Finally Julio said, "This guy really do all that Paco said?"

"He got smart," Albert said.

"Kick you?"

"You could call it that. Just as good."

"So what kind of stink you guys raise to cause all that?"

"Nothing."

"Nothing my ass."

"Aah, you know Paco. He got p-o'ed at the picture and started to horse around. Dropped a beer bottle off of the balcony or something, I don't know."

"Then this guy booted you guys out?"

"Yeah."

"Did Paco give him a fight?"

"No," Albert said, thoughtfully. They climbed up the side of a car and jumped from the top to the ground. "He's too smart for that. They would of called the cops and all that kind of crap. This way's better."

"Yeah."

"Nervous?"

"Yeah, real nervous. I'm dying to death, I'm so frigging nervous. Listen—when I get through tonight, Paco and all the rest of you guys better lay off me."

"Don't worry."

"So what is it?"

"Twenty-of. This is the place—he went by right over there."

Julio wondered if Albert could hear his heart. And if Albert could read his thoughts . . .

He felt the greasy knife handle slip in his hands, so he took it out and wiped it on his trousers and tested it. He pushed the point of the blade into the soft wood of a car, pretending it was the Jewish boy's neck.

He pulled the knife and didn't do that any more.

They sat on the cindery ground beside a huge iron wheel.

"Really a rat, huh?" Julio said.

"The most," Albert said.

"How old?"

"Who knows—twenty-five, thirty. You can't tell with them."

"You don't suppose he—I mean this guy—you don't think he's got a family or anything like that, do you?"

"What the hell kind of thing is that to say? Christ, no! Who'd marry a greaseball slob like that?" Albert laughed softly, and took from his leather jacket pocket a red-handled knife that had to be operated manually. He opened it and began to clean his fingernails. Every two or three seconds he glanced up toward the dark unpaved street.

"So nobody's going to miss *him*, right?" Julio said.

"No. We're going to all break down and cry. What's the matter, you chickening out? If you are, I ain't going to sit here on my can all—"

Julio clutched Albert's shirt-front and gathered it in his fist. "Shut up. You hear? Shut your goddam face about that stuff or I'll break it for you."

"Shhh, quiet down . . . we'll talk later. Let go. If you want to screw everything, just keep shooting your mouth."

Julio felt perspiration course down his legs.

He tried to stop the shudder.

"Okay," he said.

On tracks a mile distant a string of freight cars lumbered clumsily out of a siding, punching with heavy sounds at the night. There were tiny human noises, too, like small birds high out of sight. Otherwise, there was only his own breathing.

"I want to hear 'mackerel snapper' when this is over," Julio said.

"You ain't done nothing yet," Albert said, looking away quickly.

"Screw you," Julio said. But his voice started to crack, so he forced a yawn and stretched out his legs. "So when the hell we going to get a goddam sickle?" he said.

Albert didn't answer.

"Kind of a gang is this, anyway, we don't have any goddam sickles?"

"Five-of. He ought to be along pretty quick now."

Julio grinned, closed the knife, reopened it with a swift soft click, closed it again. His hands were moist and the knife handle was coated with a grimy sweat which made it slippery. He wiped it carefully along the sides of his jeans.

"The Kats have got sickles. Five, for Chrissakes."

"Kats, schmats," Albert said. "Knock it off, will you?"

"What's the matter, Albert? Don't tell me you're scared!"

Albert drew back his fist and hit Julio's shoulder, then quickly put a finger to his lips. *"Shhh!"*

They listened.

It was nothing.

"Hey, little boy, hey A*l*bert, know what?" Julio combed his hair. "Know what I know? Paco, he don't think I'll do it. He wants you and I to come back so he can give with the big-man routine. He don't think I'll do it."

Albert looked interested.

"He's real sharp. Having a great big ball right now. Where it's going to put him when we get back with the Jewboy's ears?" Julio laughed.

In the stillness, footsteps rang sharply on the ground,

but ponderously as gravel was crunched and stones were sent snapping.

The footsteps grew louder.

Albert listened, then he rose slowly and brushed the dirt from his jeans. He opened his knife, looked at Julio and Julio got up. They hunched close by the shadow of the boxcar.

The steps were irregular, and for a moment Julio thought it sounded like a woman. For another moment he heard Grandfather's words and saw the carrion in the bushes.

The images scattered and disappeared.

"Dumb jerk don't know what he walking into, right?" Julio whispered. The words frightened him. Albert wasn't moving. "Wetbacks. Greasers. Mex—right? Okay. Okay, Albert? Okay." The blade sprang out of the handle.

"Shut up," Albert whispered. "There he is. See him?"

There were no streetlamps, so the figure was indistinct. In the darkness it could be determined that the figure was that of a man: heavy set, not old, walking slowly, almost as if he were afraid of something.

"That's him," Albert said, letting out a stream of breath.

Julio's throat was dry. It pained him when he tried to swallow. "Okay," he said.

Albert said, "Okay, look. Go up and pretend you want a handout, y'know? Make it good. Then let him have it, right away."

"I thought I saw something," Julio said.

"What's that supposed to mean?"

"I thought I saw something, I thought I saw something. You mind?"

"Where?"

"I couldn't make out."

"Who you bulling? You want to go back?"

"All right, so I was wrong."

The figure had passed the boxcar and disappeared into the shadows, but the footsteps were still clear.

"You ready?" Albert said.

Julio paused, then he nodded.

"The hell," Albert said. "You're scared green. You'll probably louse it all up. Let's go back."

Julio thought of going back. Of what would be said, of all the eyes turned on him like ominous spotlights. The laughter he heard was what he hated most.

Albert looked anxious; the footsteps were dying away.

"Screw you," Julio said. "You coming with, or not?" He put the knife up his sleeve and held it there with his palm cupped underneath.

Albert rubbed his hands along his shirt. "All right, I'll follow you—about a minute. Sixty seconds."

Julio listened. Suddenly he didn't tremble any more, though his throat was still dry. There was no more pictures in his mind.

He waited, counting.

Then he smiled at Albert and started to walk.

It will take only a few minutes, he thought. No one will see. No one will give Julio Valasquez the old crap about chicken after this. No one . . .

Up ahead, he could see the man. No one else: just the man who was a louse and who didn't deserve to live.

And the long shadows.

He looked over his shoulder once, but the darkness seemed alive, so he jerked his head around and walked faster, with less care.

At last he caught up with the man.

"Hey, mister," Julio said.

THE HUNGER

Introduction by
Richard Christian Matheson

I was young and saw him rarely.

But when he was around, I always watched him secretly; entranced.

As if he were lined with silk.

He wasn't feeling well by then and seemed like a weary Merlin. Grey; half-voiced. But incantation phosphored in his tired eyes.

Wizards are strong.

For years he'd alchemized words into sublime ideas. Those into haunting tales of charm and tragedy. Mystic. Despairing. Beautiful.

Magically, he even turned too few years into a stunning lifetime. And when he disappeared for the final time, not in a puff of smoke, but quiet sleep, he left us a few secrets; maps to his miracles. This one is called The Hunger.

Water to wine. Brilliance and poetry from paper and ink. He could do anything.

Except live forever.

Farewell great magician.

Now, with the sun almost gone, the sky looked wounded—as if a gigantic razor had been drawn across it, slicing deep. It bled richly. And the wind, which came down from High Mountain, cool as rain, sounded a little like children crying: a soft, unhappy kind of sound, rising and falling.

Afraid, somehow, it seemed to Julia. Terribly afraid.

She quickened her step. I'm an idiot, she thought, looking away from the sky. A complete idiot. That's why I'm frightened now; and if anything happens—which it won't, and can't—then I'll have no one to blame but myself.

She shifted the bag of groceries to her other arm and turned, slightly. There was no one in sight, except old Mr. Hannaford, pulling in his newspaper stands, preparing to close up the drug-store, and Jake Spiker, barely moving across to the Blue Haven for a glass of beer: no one else. The rippling red brick streets were silent.

But even if she got nearly all the way home, she could scream and someone would hear her. Who would be fool enough to try anything right out in the open? Not even a lunatic. Besides, it wasn't dark yet, not technically, anyway.

Still, as she passed the vacant lots, all shoulder-high in wild grass, Julia could not help thinking, He might be hiding there, right now. It was possible. Hiding there, all crouched up, waiting. And he'd only have to grab her, and—she wouldn't scream. She knew that suddenly, and the thought terrified her. Sometimes you *can't* scream . . .

If only she'd not bothered to get that spool of yellow thread over at Younger's, it would be bright daylight now, bright clear daylight. And—

Nonsense! This was the middle of the town. She was surrounded by houses full of people. People all around. Everywhere.

(*He was a hunger; a need; a force. Dark emptiness filled him. He moved, when he moved, like a leaf caught in some*

dark and secret river, rushing. But mostly he slept now, an
animal, always ready to wake and leap and be gone . . .)

The shadows came to life, dancing where Julia walked.
Now the sky was ugly and festered, and the wind had become stronger, colder. She clicked along the sidewalk, looking straight ahead, wondering, Why, why am I so infernally
stupid? What's the matter with me?

Then she was home, and it was all over. The trip had
taken not more than half an hour. And here was Maud,
running. Julia felt her sister's arms fly around her, hugging.
"God, my God."

And Louise's voice: "We were just about to call Mick to
go after you."

Julia pulled free and went into the kitchen and put down
the bag of groceries.

"Where in the world have you been?" Maud demanded.

"I had to get something at Younger's." Julia took off
her coat. "They had to go look for it, and—I didn't keep
track of the time."

Maud shook her head. "Well, I don't know," she said
wearily. "You're just lucky you're alive, that's all."

"Now—"

"You listen! He's out there somewhere. Don't you understand that? It's a fact. They haven't even come close to
catching him yet."

"They will," Julia said, not knowing why: she wasn't
entirely convinced of it.

"Of course they will. Meantime, how many more is he
going to murder? Can you answer me that?"

"I'm going to put my coat away." Julia brushed past her
sister. Then she turned and said, "I'm sorry you were worried. It won't happen again." She went to the closet, feeling strangely upset. They would talk about it tonight. All
night. Analyzing, hinting, questioning. They would talk of
nothing else, as from the very first. And they would not be
able to conceal their delight.

"Wasn't it awful about poor Eva Schillings?"

No, Julia had thought: from her sister's point of view it was not awful at all. It was wonderful. It was priceless.

It was news.

Julia's sisters . . . Sometimes she thought of them as mice. Giant gray mice, in high white collars: groaning a little, panting a little, working about the house. Endlessly, untiringly: they would squint at pictures, knock them crooked, then straighten them again; they swept invisible dust from clean carpets and took the invisible dust outside in shining pans and dumped it carefully into spotless apple-baskets; they stood by beds whose sheets shone gleaming white and tight, and clucked in soft disgust, and replaced the sheets with others. All day, every day, from six in the morning until most definite dusk. Never questioning, never doubting that the work had to be done.

They ran like arteries through the old house, keeping it alive. For it had become now a part of them, and they a part of it—like the handcrank mahogany Victrola in the hall, or the lion-pelted sofa, or the Boutelle piano (ten years silent, its keys yellowed and decayed and ferocious, like the teeth of an aged mule).

Nights, they spoke of sin. Also of other times and better days: Maud and Louise—sitting there in the bellying heat of the obsolete but streadfast stove, hooking rugs, crocheting doilies, sewing linen, chatting, chatting.

Occasionally Julia listened, because she was there and there was nothing else to do; but mostly she didn't. It had become a simple thing to rock and nod and think of nothing at all, while *they* traded dreams and dead husbands, constantly relishing their mutual widowhood—relishing it!—pitching these fragile ghosts into moral combat. "Ernie, God rest him, was an honorable man." (So were they all, Julia would think, all honorable men; but we are here to praise Caesar, not to bury him . . .) "Jack would be alive today if it hadn't been for the trunk lid slamming down on his head: that's what started it all." Poor Ernie! Poor Jack!

(*He walked along the railroad tracks, blending with the night. He could have been young, or old: an age-hiding beard dirtied his face and throat. He wore a blue sweater, ripped in a dozen places. On the front of the sweater was sewn a large felt letter: E. Also sewn there was a small design showing a football and calipers. His gray trousers were dark with a stain where he had fouled them. He walked along the tracks, seeing and not seeing the pulse of light far ahead; thinking and not thinking, Perhaps I'll find it there, Perhaps they won't catch me, Perhaps I won't be hungry any more . . .*)

"You forgot the margarine," Louise said, holding the large sack upside down.

"Did I? I'm sorry." Julia took her place at the table. The food immediately began to make her ill: the sight of it, the smell of it. Great bowls of beans, crisp-skinned chunks of turkey, mashed potatoes. She put some on her plate, and watched her sisters. They ate earnestly; and now, for no reason, this, too, was upsetting.

She looked away. What was it? What was wrong?

"Mick says that fellow didn't die," Maud announced. "Julia—"

"What fellow?"

"At the asylum, that got choked. He's going to be all right."

"That's good."

Louise broke a square of toast. She addressed Maud: "What else did he say, when you talked to him? Are they making any progress?"

"Some. I understand there's a bunch of police coming down from Seattle. If they don't get him in a few days, they'll bring in some bloodhounds from out-of-state. Of course, you can imagine how much Mick likes *that*!"

"Well, it's his own fault. If he was any kind of a sheriff, he'd of caught that fellow a long time before this. I mean, after all, Burlington just isn't that big." Louise dismembered a turkey leg, ripped little shreds of the meat off, put them into her mouth.

Maud shook her head. "I don't know. Mick claims it isn't like catching an ordinary criminal. With this one, you never can guess what he's going to do, or where he'll be. Nobody has figured out how he stays alive, for instance.

"Probably," Louise said, "he eats bugs and things."

Julia folded her napkin quickly and pressed it onto the table.

Maud said, "No. Most likely he finds stray dogs and cats."

They finished the meal in silence. Not, Julia knew, because there was any lull in thought: merely so the rest could be savored in the living room, next to the fire. A proper place for everything.

They moved out of the kitchen. Louise insisted on doing the dishes, while Maud settled at the radio and tried to find a local news broadcast. Finally she snapped the radio off, angrily. "You'd think they'd at least keep us informed! Isn't that the least they could do?"

Louise materialized in her favorite chair. The kitchen was dark. The stove warmed noisily, its metal sides undulating.

And it was time.

"Where do you suppose he is right now?" Maud asked.

Louise shrugged. "Out there somewhere. If they'd got him, Mick would of called us. He's out there somewhere."

"Yes. Laughing at all of us, too, I'll wager. Trying to figure out who'll be next."

Julia sat in the rocker and tried not to listen. Outside, there was a wind. A cold wind, biting; the kind that slips right through window putty, that you can feel on the glass. Was there ever such a cold wind? she wondered.

Then Louise's words started to echo. "He's out there somewhere . . ."

Julia looked away from the window, and attempted to take an interest in the lace-work in her lap.

Louise was talking. Her fingers flashed long silver needles. ". . . spoke to Mrs. Schillings today."

"I don't want to hear about it." Maud's eyes flashed like the needles.

"God love her heart, she's about crazy. Could barely talk."

"God, God."

"I tried to comfort her, of course, but it didn't do any good."

Julia was glad she had been spared that conversation. It sent a shudder across her, even to think about it. Mrs. Schillings was Eva's mother, and Eva—only seventeen . . . The thoughts she vowed not to think, came back. She remembered Mick's description of the body, and his words: ". . . she'd got through with work over at the telephone office around nine. Carl Jasperson offered to see her home, but he says she said not to bother, it was only a few blocks. Our boy must have been hiding around the other side of the cannery. Just as Eva passed, he jumped. Raped her and then strangled her. I figure he's a pretty man-sized bugger. Thumbs like to went clean through the throat . . ."

In two weeks, three women had died. First, Charlotte Adams, the librarian. She had been taking her usual short-cut across the school playground, about 9:15 P.M. They found her by the slide, her clothes ripped from her body, her throat raw and bruised.

Julia tried very hard not to think of it, but when her mind would clear, there were her sisters' voices, droning, pulling her back, deeper.

She remembered how the town had reacted. It was the first murder Burlington had had in fifteen years. It was the very first mystery. Who was the sex-crazed killer? Who could have done this terrible thing to Charlotte Adams?

One of her gentleman friends, perhaps. Or a hobo, from one of the nearby jungles. Or . . .

Mick Daniels and his tiny force of deputies had swung into action immediately. Everyone in town took up the topic, chewed it, talked it, chewed it, until it lost its shape completely. The air became electrically charged. And a grim gaiety swept Burlington, reminding Julia of a circus where everyone is forbidden to smile.

Days passed, uneventfully. Vagrants were pulled in and released. People were questioned. A few were booked, temporarily.

Then, when the hum of it had begun to die, it happened again. Mrs. Dovie Samuelson, member of the local P.T.A., mother of two, moderately attractive and moderately young, was found in her garden, sprawled across a rhododendron bush, dead. She was naked, and it was established that she had been attacked. Of the killer, once again, there was no trace.

Then the State Hospital for the Criminally Insane released the information that one of its inmates—a Robert Oakes—had escaped. Mick, and many others, had known this all along. Oakes had originally been placed in the asylum on a charge of raping and murdering his cousin, a girl named Patsy Blair.

After he had broken into his former home and stolen some old school clothes, he had disappeared, totally.

Now he was loose.

Burlington, population 3,000, went into a state of ecstasy: delicious fear gripped the town. The men foraged out at night with torches and weapons; the women squeaked and looked under their beds and . . . chatted.

But still no progress was made. The maniac eluded hundreds of searchers. They knew he was near, perhaps at times only a few feet away, hidden; but always they returned home, defeated.

They looked in the forests and in the fields and along

the river banks. They covered High Mountain—a miniature hill at the south end of town—like ants, poking at
every clump of brush, investigating every abandoned tunnel and water tank. They broke into deserted houses,
searched barns, silos, haystacks, treetops. They looked everywhere, everywhere. And found nothing.

When they decided for sure that their killer had gone
far away, that he couldn't conceivably be within fifty miles
of Burlington, a third crime was committed. Young Eva
Schillings' body had been found, less than a hundred yards
from her home.

And that was three days ago . . .

". . . they get him." Louise was saying, "they ought to
kill him by little pieces, for what he's done."

Maud nodded. "Yes; but they won't."

"Of course they—"

"No! You wait. They'll shake his hand and lead him
back to the bughouse and wait on him hand and foot—till
he gets a notion to bust out again."

"Well, I'm of a mind the people will have something to
say about that."

"Anyway," Maud continued, never lifting her eyes from
her knitting, "what makes you so sure they *will* catch him?
Supposing he just drops out of sight for six months, and—"

"You stop that! They'll get him. Even if he *is* a maniac,
he's still human."

"I really doubt that. I doubt that a human could have
done these awful things." Maud sniffed. Suddenly, like
small rivers, tears began to course down her snowbound
cheeks, cutting and melting the hard white-packed powder,
revealing flesh underneath even paler. Her hair was shot
with gray, and her dress was the color of rocks and moths;
yet, she did not succeed in looking either old or frail. There
was nothing whatever frail about Maud.

"He's a man," she said. Her lips seemed to curl at the
word. Louise nodded, and they were quiet.

(His ragged tennis shoes padded softly on the gravel bed. Now his heart was trying to tear loose from his chest. The men, the men . . . They had almost stepped on him, they were that close. But he had been silent. They had gone past him, and away. He could see their flares back in the distance. And far ahead, the pulsing light. Also a square building: the depot, yes. He must be careful. He must walk in the shadows. He must be very still.

The fury burned him, and he fought it.

Soon.

It would be all right, soon . . .)

". . . think about it, this here maniac is only doing what every man would *like* to do but can't."

"Maud!"

"I mean it. It's a man's natural instinct—it's all they ever think about." Maud smiled. She looked up. "Julia, you're feeling sick. Don't tell me you're not."

"I'm all right," Julia said, tightening her grip on the chairarms slightly. She thought, they've been married! They talk this way about men, as they always have, and yet soft words have been spoken to them, and strong arms placed around their shoulders . . .

Maud made tiny circles with her fingers. "Well, I can't force you to take care of yourself. Except, when you land in the hospital again, I suppose you know who'll be doing the worrying and staying up nights—as per usual."

"I'll . . . go on to bed in a minute." But, why was she hesitating? Didn't she want to be alone?

Why didn't she want to be alone?

Louise was testing the door. She rattled the knob vigorously, and returned to her chair.

"What would he want, anyway," Maud said, "with two old biddies like us?"

"We're not so old," Louise said, saying, actually: "That's true; we're old."

But it wasn't true, not at all. Looking at them, studying them, it suddenly occurred to Julia that her sisters were ashamed of their essential attractiveness. Beneath the 'twenties hair-dos, the ill-used cosmetics, the ancient dresses (which did not quite succeed in concealing their still voluptuous physiques), Maud and Louise were youthfully full and pretty. They were. Not even the birch-twig toothbrushes and traditional snuff could hide it.

Yet, Julia thought, they envy me.

They envy my plainness.

"What kind of man would do such heinous things?" Louise said, pronouncing the word, carefully, heen-ious.

And Julia, without calling or forming the thought, discovered an answer grown in her mind: an impression, a feeling.

What kind of a man?

A lonely man.

It came upon her like a chill. She rose from the pillowed chair, lightly. "I think," she said, "I'll go on to my room."

"Are your windows good and locked?"

"Yes."

"You'd better make sure. All he'd have to do is climb up the drainpipe." Maud's expression was peculiar. Was she really saying, "This is only to comfort you, dear. Of the three of us, it's unlikely he'd pick on you."

"I'll make sure." Julia walked to the hallway. "Good night."

"Try to get some sleep." Louise smiled. "And don't think about him, hear? We're perfectly safe. He couldn't possibly get in, even if he tried. Besides," she said, "I'll be awake."

(*He stopped and leaned against a pole and looked up at the deaf and swollen sky. It was a movement of dark shapes, a hurrying, a running.*

He closed his eyes.

> "The moon is the shepherd,
>   The clouds are his sheep . . ."

He tried to hold the words, tried very hard, but they scattered and were gone.

"No."

He pushed away from the pole, turned, and walked back to the gravel bed.

The hunger grew: with every step it grew. He thought that it had died, that he had killed it at last and now he could rest, but it had not died. It sat inside him, inside his mind, gnawing, calling, howling to be released. Stronger than ever before.

> "The moon is the shepherd . . ."

A cold wind raced across the surrounding fields of wild grass, turning the land into a heaving dark-green ocean. It sighed up through the branches of cherry trees and rattled the thick leaves. Sometimes a cherry would break loose, tumble in the gale, fall and split, filling the night with its fragrance. The air was iron and loam and growth.

He walked and tried to pull these things into his lungs, the silence and coolness of them.

But someone was screaming, deep inside him. Someone was talking.

"What are you going to do—"

He balled his fingers into fists.

"Get away from me! Get away!"

"Don't—"

The scream faded.

The girl's face remained. Her lips and her smooth white skin and her eyes, her eyes . . .

He shook the vision away.

The hunger continued to grow. It wrapped his body in sheets of living fire. It got inside his mind and bubbled in hot acids, filling and filling him.

He stumbled, fell, plunged his hands deep into the gravel, withdrew fists full of the grit and sharp stones and squeezed them until blood trailed down his wrists.

He groaned, softly.

Ahead, the light glowed and pulsed and whispered, Here, Here, Here, Here, Here.

He dropped the stones and opened his mouth to the wind and walked on . . .)

Julia closed the door and slipped the lock noiselessly. She could no longer hear the drone of voices: it was quiet, still, but for the sighing breeze.

What kind of a man . . .

She did not move, waiting for her heart to stop throbbing. But it would not stop.

She went to the bed and sat down. Her eyes travelled to the window, held there.

"He's out there somewhere . . ."

Julia felt her hands move along her dress. It was an old dress, once purple, now gray with faded gray flowers. The cloth was tissue-thin. Her fingers touched it and moved upward to her throat. Then undid the top button.

For some reason, her body trembled. The chill had turned to heat, tiny needles of heat, puncturing her all over.

She threw the dress over a chair and removed the underclothing. Then she walked to the bureau and took from the top drawer a flannel nightdress, and turned.

What she saw in the tall mirror caused her to stop and make a small sound.

Julia Landon stared back at her from the polished glass.

Julia Landon, thirty-eight, neither young nor old, attractive nor unattractive, a woman so plain she was almost invisible. All angles and sharpnesses, and flesh that would once have been called "milky" but was now only white, pale white. A little too tall. A little too thin. And faded.

Only the eyes had softness. Only the eyes burned with life and youth and—

Julia moved away from the mirror. She snapped off the light. She touched the window shade, pulled it slightly, guided it soundlessly upward.

Then she unfastened the window latch.

Night came into the room and filled it. Outside, giant clouds roved across the moon, osbcuring it, revealing it, obscuring it again.

It was cold. Soon there would be rain.

Julia looked out beyond the yard, in the direction of the depot, dark and silent now, and the tracks and the jungles beyond the tracks where lost people lived.

"I wonder if he can see me."

She thought of the man who had brought terror and excitement to the town. She thought of him openly, for the first time, trying to imagine his features.

He was probably miles away.

Or, perhaps he was nearby. Behind the tree, there, or under the hedge . . .

"I'm afraid of you, Robert Oakes," she whispered to the night. "You're insane, and a killer. You would frighten the wits out of me."

The fresh smell swept into Julia's mind. She wished she were surrounded by it, in it, just for a little while.

Just for a few minutes.

A walk. A short walk in the evening.

She felt the urge strengthening.

"You're dirty, young man. And heartless—ask Mick, if you don't believe me. You want to love so badly you must kill for it—but nevertheless, you're heartless. Understand? And you're not terribly bright, either, they say. Have you read Shakespeare's Sonnets? Herrick? How about Shelley, then? There, you see! I'd detest you on sight. Just look at your fingernails!"

She said these things silently, but as she said them she moved toward her clothes.

She paused, went to the closet.

The green dress. It was warmer.

A warm dress and a short walk—that will clear my head. Then I'll come back and sleep.

It's perfectly safe.

She started for the door, stopped, returned to the window. Maud and Louise would still be up, talking.

She slid one leg over the sill; then the other leg.

Softly she dropped to the frosted lawn.

The gate did not creak.

She walked into the darkness.

Better! So much better. Good clean air that you can breathe!

The town was a silence. A few lights gleamed in distant houses, up ahead; behind, there was only blackness. And the wind.

In the heavy green frock, which was still too light to keep out the cold—though she felt no cold; only the needled heat—she walked away from the house and toward the depot.

It was a small structure, unchanged by passing years, like the Landon home and most of the homes in Burlington. There were tracks on either side of it.

Now it was deserted. Perhaps Mr. Gaffey was inside, making insect sounds on the wireless. Perhaps he was not.

Julia stepped over the first track, and stood, wondering what had happened and why she was here. Vaguely she understood something. Something about the yellow thread that had made her late and forced her to return home through the gathering dusk. And this dress—had she chosen it because it was warmer than the others . . . or because it was prettier?

Beyond this point there was wilderness, for miles. Marshes and fields overgrown with weeds and thick foliage.

The hobo jungles: some tents, dead campfires, empty tins of canned meat.

She stepped over the second rail, and began to follow the gravel bed. Heat consumed her. She could not keep her hands still.

In a dim way, she realized—with a tiny part of her—why she had come out tonight.

She was looking for someone.

The words formed in her mind, unwilled: "Robert Oakes, listen, listen to me. You're not the only one who is lonely. But you can't steal what we're lonely for, you can't take it by force. Don't you know that? Haven't you learned that yet?"

I'll talk to him, she thought, and he'll go along with me and give himself up . . .

No.

That isn't why you're out tonight. You don't care whether he gives himself up or not. You . . . only want him to know that you understand. Isn't that it?

You couldn't have any other reason.

It isn't possible that you're seeking out a lunatic for any other reason.

Certainly you don't want him to touch you.

Assuredly you don't want him to put his arms around you and kiss you, because no man has ever done that—assuredly, assuredly.

It isn't you he wants. It isn't love. He wouldn't be taking Julia Landon . . .

"But what if he doesn't!" The words spilled out in a small choked cry. "What if he sees me and runs away! Or I don't find him. Others have been looking. What makes me think I'll—"

Now the air swelled with signs of life: frogs and birds and locusts, moving; the wind, running across the trees and reeds and foliage at immense speed, whining, sighing.

Everywhere there was this loudness, and a dark like none

Julia had ever known. The moon was gone entirely. Sha-
dowless, the surrounding fields were great pools of liquid
black, stretching infinitely, without horizon.

Fear came up in her chest, clutching.

She tried to scream.

She stood paralyzed, moveless, a pale terror dying into
her throat and into her heart.

Then, from far away, indistinctly, there came a sound.
A sound like footsteps on gravel.

Julia listened, and tried to pierce the darkness. The
sounds grew louder. And louder. Someone was on the
tracks. Coming closer.

She waited. Years passed, slowly. Her breath turned into
a ball of expanding ice in her lungs.

Now she could see, just a bit.

It was a man. A black man-form. Perhaps—the thought
increased her fear—a hobo. It mustn't be one of the hobos.

No. It was a young man. Mick! Mick, come to tell her,
"Well, we got the bastard!" and to ask, narrowly, "What
the devil you doing out here, Julia?" Was it?

She saw the sweater. The ball of ice in her lungs began
to melt, a little. A sweater. And shoes that seemed almost
white.

Not a hobo. Not Mick. Not anyone she knew.

She waited an instant longer. Then, at once, she knew
without question who the young man was.

And she knew that he had seen her.

The fear went away. She moved to the center of the
tracks.

"I've been looking for you," she said, soundlessly.
"Every night I've thought of you. I have." She walked
toward the man. "Don't be afraid, Mr. Oakes. Please don't
be afraid. I'm not."

The young man stopped. He seemed to freeze, like an
animal, prepared for flight.

He did not move, for several seconds.

Then he began to walk toward Julia, lightly, hesitantly, rubbing his hands along his trousers.

When Julia was close enough to see his eyes, she relaxed, and smiled.

Perhaps, she thought, feeling the first drops of rain upon her face, perhaps if I don't scream he'll let me live.

That would be nice.

BLACK COUNTRY

Introduction by Ray Russell

The irony seared my mind like acid, and inwardly I winced as I helped carry Charles Beaumont's coffin that morning early in 1967. Suddenly I had realized, as I and my fellow pallbearers approached the open grave, that my introduction to Beaumont, years before, had involved another cemetery, another funeral: the burial of Spoof Collins in Beaumont's novella, "Black Country." The fictive funeral and the all-too-real one merged in my thoughts, temporarily becoming the same. Even now, I have a little trouble keeping them apart. That's why I find it difficult to be objective about the story.

But I'll try . . .

Words are not music, but I know of no other way to define "Black Country" than to say it is musical. I don't mean merely that the subject matter is musicians and their music. I mean that the writing itself has cadence, rhythm, a beat, a sound. It seems to have been "composed" rather than written, and composed at white heat, without interruption, from first word to last, in a fever of creativity.

The vibrancy, this musicality was the first thing that impressed me when I began to read the story in typescript in 1954, Playboy's first year. As I read on, I found other things to admire— such as the author's command of character, idiom, structure and suspense. I was also swept along by the passion and energy of the prose—but these two qualities are not rare in a young, talented writer. What is rare in a wordsmith only a couple of dozen years old is a firm grasp of technique, and this sizable piece displayed a control of craft and form usually found only in older, more experienced professionals. I read it all the way through at one sitting, put it down stunned and breathless, and immediately recommended it for purchase.

The story required no editing. It went to the printer unscathed by my pencil. At press time, a column space emergency necessitated the cutting of two short words, but even this was dictated by purely mechanical, not literary, needs. Everything about the story was right—even the title, with its strong, symbolic simplicity, echoing a song title (of Beaumont's own invention) and representing not only the dark "country" of Death but also the black race of Spoof Collins and most of the other characters.

Today, it might be easy to forget that the love between white Sonny Holmes and black Rose-Ann was still a "daring" theme in the early Fifties when this story was written—"miscegenation," no less!—requiring courage on the part of Beaumont as writer and Playboy as the story's first medium of publication. Many popular magazines of that time, wary of offending the bigots among their readers, probably would have suppressed that aspect of the story, diminishing its total impact.

"Black Country," the first of many Beaumont writings Playboy was to accept, appeared in our September 1954 issue. In the decades since that first appearance, my opinion of the story has not changed. It remains a fresh, vital work; powerful; a masterpiece among American short stories. "Though not a horror story in any of the usual senses," I later wrote, in the year of Beaumont's death, "it tells of a special kind of demonic possession, thoroughly contemporary and compellingly believable; and its infectious, finger-popping tempo propels the tale irresistibly toward a most unsuspected and macabre finale."

I wouldn't change a word of that description. To me, "Black Country" is the brightest and best of Beaumont's achievements.

SPOOF COLLINS BLEW his brains out, all right—right on out through the top of his head. But I don't mean with a gun. I mean with a horn. Every night: slow and easy, eight to one. And that's how he died. Climbing, with that horn, climbing up high. For what? *"Hey, man, Spoof—listen, you picked the tree, now come on down!"* But he couldn't come down, he didn't know how. He just kept climbing, higher and higher. And then he fell. Or jumped. Anyhow, *that's* the way he died.

The bullet didn't kill anything. I'm talking about the one that tore up the top of his mouth. It didn't kill anything that wasn't dead already. Spoof just put in an extra note, that's all.

We planted him out about four miles from town—home is where you drop: residential district, all wood construction. Rain? You know it. Bible type: sky like a month-old bedsheet, wind like a stepped-on cat, cold and dark, those Forty Days, those Forty Nights! But nice and quiet most of the time. Like Spoof: nice and quiet, with a lot underneath that you didn't like to think about.

We planted him and watched and put what was his down into the ground with him. His horn, battered, dented, nicked—right there in his hands, but not just there; I mean in position, so if he wanted to do some more climbing, all right, he could. And his music. We planted that too, because leaving it out would have been like leaving out Spoof's arms or his heart or his guts.

Lux started things off with a chord from his guitar, no particular notes, only a feeling, a sound. A Spoof Collins kind of sound. Jimmy Fritch picked it up with his stick and they talked a while—Lux got a real piano out of that gitbox. Then when Jimmy stopped talking and stood there, waiting, Sonny Holmes stepped up and wiped his mouth and took the melody on his shiny new trumpet. It wasn't Spoof, but it came close; and it was still *The Jimjam Man*, the way Spoof wrote it back when he used to write things down. Sonny got off with a high-squealing blast, and no eyes came up—we knew, we remembered. The kid always had it collared. He just never talked about it. And listen to him now! He stood there over Spoof's grave, giving it all back to The Ol' Masshuh, giving it back right—*"Broom off, white child, you got four sides!"* "I want to learn from you, Mr. Collins. I want to play jazz and you can teach me." *"I got things to do, I can't waste no time on a half-hipped young 'un."* "Please, Mr. Collins." *"You got to stop that, you got to stop callin' me 'Mr. Collins,' hear?"* "Yes sir, yes sir."— He put out real sound, like he didn't remember a thing. Like he wasn't playing for that pile of darkmeat in the ground, not at all; but for the great Spoof Collins, for the man Who Knew and the man Who Did, who gave jazz spats and dressed up the blues, who did things with a trumpet that a trumpet couldn't do, and more; for the man who could blow down the walls or make a chicken cry, without halftrying—for the mighty Spoof, who'd once walked in music like a boy in river mud, loving it, breathing it, living it.

Then Sonny quit. He wiped his mouth again and stepped back and Mr. "T" took it on his trombone while I beat up the tubs.

Pretty soon we had *The Jimjam Man* rocking the way it used to rock. A little slow, maybe: it needed Bud Meunier on bass and a few trips on the piano. But it moved.

We went through *Take It From Me* and *Night in the Blues* and *Big Gig* and *Only Us Chickens* and *Forty G's*—Sonny's insides came out through the horn on that one, I could tell— and *Slice City Stomp*—you remember: sharp and clean, like sliding down a razor—and *What the Cats Dragged In*—the longs, the shorts, all the great Spoof Collins numbers. We wrapped them up and put them down there with him.

Then it got dark.

And it was time for the last one, the greatest one . . . Rose-Ann shivered and cleared her throat; the rest of us looked around, for the first time, at all those rows of split-wood grave markers, shining in the rain, and the trees and the coffin, dark, wet. Out by the fence, a couple of farmers stood watching. Just watching.

One—Rose-Ann opens her coat, puts her hands on her hips, wets her lips;

Two—Freddie gets the spit out of his stick, rolls his eyes;

Three—Sonny puts the trumpet to his mouth;

Four—

And we played Spoof's song, his last one, the one he wrote a long way ago, before the music dried out his head, before he turned mean and started climbing: *Black Country*. The song that said just a little of what Spoof wanted to say, and couldn't.

You remember. Spider-slow chords crawling down, soft, easy, and then bottom and silence and, suddenly, the cry of the horn, screaming in one note all the hate and sadness and loneliness, all the want and got-to-have; and then the note dying, quick, and Rose-Ann's voice, a whisper, a groan, a sigh . . .

> "*Black Country is somewhere, Lord,*
> *That I don't want to go.*
> *Black Country is somewhere*
> *That I never want to go.*
> *Rain-water drippin'*
> *On the bed and on the floor,*
> *Rain-water drippin'*
> *From the ground and through the door . . .*"

We all heard the piano, even though it wasn't there. Fingers moving down those minor chords, those black keys, that black country . . .

> "Well, in that old Black Country
> If you ain't feelin' good,
> They let you have an overcoat
> That's carved right out of wood.
> But way down there
> It gets so dark
> You never see a friend—
> Black Country may not be the Most,
> But, Lord! it's sure the End . . ."

Bitter little laughing words, piling up, now mad, now sad; and then, an ugly blast from the horn and Rose-Ann's voice screaming, crying:

> "I never want to go there, Lord!
> I never want to be,
> I never want to lay down
> In that Black Country!"

And quiet, quiet, just the rain, and the wind.

"Let's go, man," Freddie said.

So we turned around and left Spoof there under the ground.

Or, at least, that's what I thought we did.

Sonny took over without saying a word. He didn't have to: just who was about to fuss? He was white, but he didn't play white, not these days; and he learned the hard way— by unlearning. Now he could play gutbucket and he could play blues, stomp and slide, name it, Sonny could play it. Funny as hell to hear, too, because he looked like everything else but a musician. Short and skinny, glasses, nose

like a melted candle, head clean as the one-ball, and white?
Next to old Hushup, that café sunburn glowed like a flashlight.

"Man, who skinned you?"

"Who dropped you in the flour barrel?"

But he got closer to Spoof than any of the rest of us did.
He knew what to do, and why. Just like a school teacher
all the time: "That's good, Lux, that's awful good—now
let's play some music." "Get off it, C.T.—what's Lenox
Avenue doing in the middle of Lexington?" "Come on,
boys, hang on to the sound, hang on to it!" Always using
words like "flavor" and "authentic" and "blood," peering
over those glasses, pounding his feet right through the floor:
STOMP! STOMP! "That's it, we've got it now—oh, listen! It's true, it's clean!" STOMP! STOMP!

Not the easiest to dig him. Nobody broke all the way
through.

"How come, boy? What for?" and every time the same
answer:

"I want to play jazz."

Like he'd joined the Church and didn't want to argue
about it.

Spoof was still Spoof when Sonny started coming around.
Not a lot of people with us then, but a few, enough—the
longhairs and critics and connoisseurs—and some real ears
too—enough to fill a club every night, and who needs more?
It was COLLINS AND HIS CREW, tight and neat, never
a performance, always a session. Lot of music, lot of fun.
And a line-up that some won't forget: Jimmy Fritch on
clarinet, Honker Reese on alto-sax, Charles di Lusso on
tenor, Spoof on trumpet, Henry Walker on piano, Lux Anderson on banjo and myself—Hushup Paige—on drums.
Newmown hay, all right, I know—I remember, I've heard
the records we cut—but, the Road was there.

Sonny used to hang around the old Continental Club on
State Street in Chicago, every night, listening. Eight o'clock

roll 'round, and there he'd be—a little different: younger,
skinnier—listening hard, over in a corner all to himself,
eyes closed like he was asleep. Once in a while he put in a
request—*Darktown Strutter's Ball* was one he liked, and
some of Jelly Roll's numbers—but mostly he just sat there,
taking it all in. For real.

And it kept up like this for two or three weeks, regular
as 2/4.

Now Spoof was mean in those days—don't think he
wasn't—but not blood-mean. Even so, the white boy in
the corner bugged Ol' Massuh after a while and he got to
making dirty cracks with his horn: *WAAAAA! Git your ass
out of here. WAAAAA! You only think you're with it!
WAAAAA! There's a little white child sittin' in a chair there's
a little white child losin' all his hair . . .*

It got to the kid, too, every bit of it. And that made
Spoof even madder. But what can you do?

Came Honker's trip to Slice City along about then: our
saxman got a neck all full of the sharpest kind of steel. So
we were out one horn. And you could tell: we played a little bit too rough, and the head-arrangements Collins and His
Crew grew up to, they needed Honker's grease in the worst
way. But we'd been together for five years or more, and a
new man just didn't play somehow. We were this one solid
thing, like a unit, and somebody had cut off a piece of us and
we couldn't grow the piece back so we just tried to get along
anyway, bleeding every night, bleeding from that wound.

Then one night it busts. We'd gone through some slow
walking stuff, some tricky stuff and some loud stuff—still
covering up—when this kid, this white boy, got up from
his chair and ankled over and tapped Spoof on the shoulder. It was break-time and Spoof was brought down about
Honker, about how bad we were sounding, sitting there
sweating, those pounds of man, black as coaldust soaked in
oil—he was the *blackest* man!—and those eyes, beady white
and small as agates.

"Excuse me, Mr. Collins, I wonder if I might have a word with you?" He wondered if he might have a word with Mr. Collins!

Spoof swiveled in his chair and clapped a look around the kid. "Hnff?"

"I noticed that you don't have a sax man any more."

"You don't mean to tell me?"

"Yes sir. I thought—I mean, I was wondering if—"

"Talk up, boy. I can't hear you."

The kid looked scared. Lord, he looked scared—and he was white to begin with.

"Well sir, I was just wondering if—if you needed a saxophone."

"You know somebody plays sax?"

"Yes sir, I do."

"And who might that be?"

"Me."

"You."

"Yes sir."

Spoof smiled a quick one. Then he shrugged. "Broom off, son," he said. "Broom 'way off."

The kid turned red. He all of sudden didn't look scared any more. Just mad. Mad as hell. But he didn't say anything. He went on back to his table and then it was end of the ten.

We swung into *Basin Street*, smooth as Charley's tenor could make it, with Lux Anderson talking it out: *Basin Street, man, it is the street, Where the elite, well, they gather 'round to eat a little* . . . And we fooled around with the slow stuff for a while. Then Spoof lifted his horn and climbed up two-and-a-half and let out his trademark, that short high screech that sounded like something dying that wasn't too happy about it. And we rocked some, Henry taking it, Jimmy kanoodling the great headword that only Jimmy knows how to do, me slamming the skins—and it was nowhere. Without Honker to keep us all on the ground, we were just making noise. Good noise, all right, but not music. And Spoof knew it. He broke his mouth blowing—to prove it.

And we cussed the cat that sliced our man.

Then, right away—nobody could remember when it came in—suddenly, we had us an alto-sax. Smooth and sure and snaky, that sound put a knot on each of us and said: Bust loose now, boys, I'll pull you back down. Like sweet-smelling glue, like oil in a machine, like—Honker.

We looked around and there was the kid, still sore, blowing like a madman, and making fine fine music.

Spoof didn't do much. Most of all, he didn't stop the number. He just let that horn play, listening—and when we slid over all the rough spots and found us backed up neat as could be, the Ol' Massuh let out a grin and a nod and a "Keep blowin', young 'un!" and we knew that we were going to be all right.

After it was over, Spoof walked up to the kid. They looked at each other, sizing it up, taking it in.

Spoof says: "You did good."

And the kid—he was still burned—says: "You mean I did *damn* good."

And Spoof shakes his head. "No, that ain't what I mean."

And in a second one was laughing while the other one blushed. Spoof had known all along that the kid was faking, that he'd just been lucky enough to know our style on *Basin Street* up-down-and-across.

The Ol' Massuh waited for the kid to turn and start to slink off, then he said: "Boy you want to go to work?"

Sonny learned so fast it scared you. Spoof never held back; he turned it all over, everything it had taken us our whole lives to find out.

And—we had some good years. Charley di Lusso dropped out, we took on Bud Meunier—the greatest bass man of them all—and Lux threw away his banjo for an AC-DC git-

bot and old C.T. Mr. "T" Green and his trombone joined the Crew. And we kept growing and getting stronger—no million-copies platter sales or stands at the Paramount—too "special"—but we never ate too far down on the hog, either.

In a few years Sonny Holmes was making that sax stand on its hind legs and jump through hoops that Honker never dreamed about. Spoof let him strictly alone. When he got mad it wasn't ever because Sonny had white skin—Spoof always was too busy to notice things like that—but only because The Ol' Massuh had to get T'd off at each one of us every now and then. He figured it kept us on our toes.

In fact, except right at first, there never was any real blood between Spoof and Sonny until Rose-Ann came along.

Spoof didn't want a vocalist with the band. But the coonshouting days were gone alas, except for Satchmo and Calloway—who had style: none of us had style, man, we just hollered—so when push came to shove, we had to put out the net.

And chickens aplenty came to crow and plenty moved on fast and we were about to give up when a dusky doll of 20-ought stepped up and let loose a hunk of *The Man I Love* and that's all, brothers, end of the search.

Rose-Ann McHugh was a little like Sonny: where she came from, she didn't know a ball of cotton from a piece of popcorn. She's studied piano for a flock of years with a Pennsylvania longhair, read music whipfast and had been pointed toward the Big Steinway and the O.M.'s, Chopin and Bach and all that jazz. And good—I mean, she could pull some very fancy noise out of those keys. But it wasn't the Road. She'd heard a few records of Muggsy Spanier's, a couple of Jelly Roll's—*New Orleans Bump, Shreveport Stomp*, old *Wolverine Blues*—and she just got took hold of. Like it happens, all the time. She knew.

Spoof hired her after the first song. And we could see

things in her eyes for The Ol'Massuh right away, fast. Bad
to watch: I mean to say, she was chicken dinner, but what
made it ugly was, you could tell she hadn't been in the
oven very long.

Anyway, most of us could tell. Sonny, for instance.

But Spoof played tough to begin. He gave her the treat-
ment, all the way. To see if she'd hold up. Because, above
everything else, there was the Crew, the Unit, the Group.
It was right, it had to stay right.

*"Gal, forget your hands—that's for the cats out front. Leave
'em alone. And pay attention to the music, hear?"*

*"You ain't got a 'voice,' you got an instrument. And you
ain't ever started to learn how to play on it. Get some sound,
bring it on out."*

*"Stop that throat stuff—you' singin' with the Crew now.
From the belly, gal, from the belly. That's where music comes
from, hear?"*

And she loved it, like Sonny did. She was with The Ol'
Massuh, she knew what he was talking about.

Pretty soon she fit just fine. And when she did, and
everybody knew she did, Spoof eased up and waited and
watched the old machine click right along, one-two, one-
two.

That's when he began to change. Right then, with the
Crew growed up in long pants at last. Like we didn't need
him any more to wash our face and comb our hair and
switch our behinds for being bad.

Spoof began to change. He beat out time and blew his
riffs, but things were different and there wasn't anybody
who didn't know that for a fact.

In a hurry, all at once, he wrote down all his great arrangements, quick as he could. One right after the other.
And we wondered why—we'd played them a million times.

Then he grabbed up Sonny. *White Boy, listen. You want
to learn how to play trumpet?"*

And the blood started between them. Spoof rode on

Sonny's back twenty-four hours, showing him lip, showing him breath. *"This ain't a saxphone, boy, it's a trumpet, a music-horn. Get it right—do it again—that's lousy—do it again—that was nowhere—do it again—do it again!"* All the time.

Sonny worked hard. Anybody else, they would have told The Ol'Massuh where he could put that little old horn. But the kid knew something was being given to him—he didn't know why, nobody did, but for a reason—something that Spoof wouldn't have given anybody else. And he was grateful. So he worked. And he didn't ask any how-comes, either.

Pretty soon he started to handle things rights. 'Way down the road from great but coming along. The sax had given him a hard set of lips and he had plenty of wind; most of all, he had the spirit—the thing that you can beat up your chops about it for two weeks straight and never say what it is, but if it isn't there, buddy-ghee, you may get to be President but you'll never play music.

Lord, Lord, Spoof worked that boy like a two-ton jockey on a ten-ounce horse. *"Do it again—that ain't right— goddamn it, do it again! Now one more time!"*

When Sonny knew enough to sit in with the horn on a few easy ones, Ol' Massuh would tense up and follow the kid with his eyes—I mean it got real crawly. What for? Why was he pushing it like that?

Then it quit. Spoof didn't say anything. He just grunted and quit all of a sudden, like he'd done with us, and Sonny went back on sax and that was that.

Which is when the real blood started.

The Lord says every man has got to love something, sometimes, somewhere. First choice is a chick, but there's other choices. Spoof's was a horn. He was married to a piece of brass, just as married as a man can get. Got up with it in the morning, talked with it all day long, loved it at night like no chick I ever heard of got loved. And I

don't mean one-two-three: I mean the slow-building kind.
He'd kiss it and hold it and watch out for it. Once a cat
full of tea tried to put the snatch on Spoof's horn, for
laughs: when Spoof caught up with him, that cat gave up
laughing for life.

Sonny knew this. It's why he never blew his stack at all
the riding. Spoof's teaching him to play trumpet—*the*
trumpet—was like as if The Ol' Massuh had said: *"You
want to take my wife for a few nights? You do? Then here,
let me show you how to do it right. She likes it done right."*

For Rose-Ann, though, it was the worst. Every day she
got that deeper in, and in a while we turned around and,
man! *Where* is little Rosie? She was gone. That young half-
fried chicken had flew the roost. And in her place was a
doll that wasn't dead, a big bunch of curves and skin like
a brand-new penny. Overnight, almost. Sonny noticed.
Freddie and Lux and even old Mr. "T" noticed. *I* had eyes
in my head. But Spoof didn't notice. He was already in
love, there wasn't any more room.

Rose-Ann kept snapping the whip, but Ol' Massuh, he
wasn't *about* to make the trip. He'd started climbing, then,
and he didn't treat her any different than he treated us.

*"Get away, gal, broom on off—can't you see I'm busy?
Wiggle it elsewhere, hear? Elsewhere. Shoo!"*

And she just loved him more for it. Everytime he kicked
her, she loved him more. Tried to find him and see him
and, sometimes, when he'd stop for breath, she'd try to
help, because she knew something had crawled inside
Spoof, something that was eating from the inside out, that
maybe he couldn't get rid of alone.

Finally, one night, at a two-weeker in Dallas, it tumbled.

We'd gone through *Georgia Brown* for the tourists and
things were kind of dull, when Spoof started sweating. His
eyes began to roll. And he stood up, like a great big animal—like an ape or a bear, big and powerful and mean-
looking—and he gave us the two-finger signal.

Sky-High. 'Way before it was due, before either the audience or any of us had got wound up.

Freddie frowned. "You think it's time, Top?"

"Listen," Spoof said, "goddammit, who says when it's time—you, or me?"

We went into it, cold, but things warmed up pretty fast. The dancers grumbled and moved off the floor and the place filled up with talk.

I took my solo and beat hell out of the skins. The Spoof swiped at his mouth and let go with a blast and moved it up into that squeal and stopped and started playing. It was all headwork. All new to us.

New to anybody.

I saw Sonny get a look on his face, and we sat still and listened while Spoof made love to that horn.

Now like a scream, now like a laugh—now we're swinging in the trees, now the white men are coming, now we're in the boat and chains are hanging from our ankles and we're rowing, rowing—*Spoof, what is it?*—now we're sawing wood and picking cotton and serving up those cool cool drinks to the Colonel in his chair—*Well, blow, man!*—now we're free, and we're struttin' down Lenox Avenue and State & Madison and Pirate's Alley, laughing, crying—*Who said free?*—and we want to go back and we don't want to go back—*Play it, Spoof? God, God, tell us all about it! Talk to us!*—and we're sitting in a cellar with a comb wrapped up in paper, with a skin-barrel and a tinklebox—*Don't stop, Spoof? Oh Lord, please don't stop!*—and we're making something, something, what is it? Is it jazz? Why, yes, Lord, it's jazz. Thank you, sir, and thank you, sir, we finally got it, something that is *ours*, something great that belongs to us and to us alone, that we made and *that's* why it's important, and *that's* what it's all about and—*Spoof! Spoof you can't stop now*—

But it was over, middle of the trip. And there was Spoof standing there facing us and tears streaming out of those eyes and down over that coaldust face, and his body shaking and shaking. It's the first we ever saw that. It's the first we ever heard him cough, too—like a shotgun going off every two seconds, big raking sounds that tore up from the bottom of his belly and spilled out wet and loud.

The way it tumbled was this. Rose-Ann went over to him and tried to get him to sit down. "Spoof, honey, what's wrong? Come on and sit down. Honey, don't just stand there."

Spoof stopped coughing and jerked his head around. He looked at Rose-Ann for a while and whatever there was in his face, it didn't have a name. The whole room was just as quiet as it could be.

Rose-Ann took his arm. "Come on, honey, Mr. Collins—"

He let out one more cough, then, and drew back his hand—that black-topped, pink-palmed ham of a hand—and laid it, sharp across the girl's cheek. It sent her staggering. "Git off my back, hear? Damn it, git off! Stay 'way from me!"

She got up crying. Then, you know what she did? She waltzed on back and took his arm and said: "Please."

Spoof was just a lot of crazy-mad on two legs. He shouted out some words and pulled back his hands again. "Can't you never learn? What I got to do, goddamn little—"

Then—Sonny moved. All-the-time quiet and soft and gentle Sonny. He moved quick across the floor and stood in front of Spoof.

"Keep your black hands off her," he said.

Ol' Massuh pushed Rose-Ann aside and planted his legs, his breath rattling fast and loose, like a bull's. And he towered over the kid, Goliath and David, legs far apart on the boards and fingers curled up, bowling balls at the ends of his sleeves.

"You talkin' to me, boy?"

Sonny's face was red, like I hadn't seen it since that first

time at the Continental Club, years back. "You've got ears,
Collins. Touch her again and I'll kill you."

I don't know exactly what we expected, but I know what
we were afraid of. We were afraid Spoof would let go; and
if he did . . . well, put another bed in the hospital, men.
He stood there, breathing, and Sonny give it right back—
for hours, days and nights, for a month, toe to toe.

Then Spoof relaxed. He pulled back those fat lips, that
didn't look like lips any more, they were so tough and
leathery, and showed a mouthful of white and gold, and
grunted, and turned, and walked away.

We swung into *Twelfth Street Rag* in *such* a hurry!

And it got kicked under the sofa.

But we found out something, then, that nobody even
suspected.

Sonny had it for Rose-Ann. He had it bad.

And that ain't good.

Spoof fell to pieces after that. He played day and night,
when we were working, when we weren't working. Climbing. Trying to get it said, all of it.

"Listen, you can't hit Heaven with a slingshot, Daddy-O!"

"What you want to do, man—blow Judgement?"

He never let up. If he ate anything, you tell me when.
Sometimes he tied on, straight stuff, quick, medicine type
of drinking. But only after he'd been climbing and started
to blow flat and ended up in those coughing fits.

And it got worse. Nothing helped, either: foam or booze
or tea or even Indoor Sports, and he tried them all. And
got worse.

*"Get fixed up, Mr. C, you hear? See a bone-man; you in
bad shape . . ."*

"Get away from me, get on away!" Hawk! and a big red
spot in the handkerchief. *"Broom off! Shoo!"*

And gradually the old horn went sour, ugly and bitter
sounding, like Spoof himself. Hoo Lord, the way he rode

Sonny then: *How you like the dark stuff, boy? You like it pretty good? Hey there, don't hold back. Rosie's fine talent— I know. Want me to tell you about it, pave the way, show you how? I taught you everything else, didn't I?* And Sonny always clamming up, his eyes doing the talking: "*You were a great musician, Collins, and you still are, but that doesn't mean I've got to like you—you won't let me. And you're damn right I'm in love with Rose-Ann! That's the biggest reason why I'm still here—just to be close to her. Otherwise, you wouldn't see me for the dust. But you're too dumb to realize she's in love with you, too dumb and stupid and mean and wrapped up with that lousy horn!*"

What *Sonny* was too dumb to know was, Rose-Ann had cut Spoof out. She was now Public Domain.

Anyway, Spoof got to be the meanest, dirtiest, craziest, low-talkin'est man in the world. And nobody could come in: he had signs out all the time . . .

The night that he couldn't even get a squeak out of his trumpet and went back to the hotel—alone, always alone— and put the gun in his mouth and pulled the trigger, we found something out.

We found out what it was that had been eating at The Ol' Massuh.

Cancer.

Rose-Ann took it the hardest. She had the dry-weeps for a long time, saying it over and over: "Why didn't he let us know? Why didn't he tell us?"

But, you get over things. Even women do, especially when they've got something to take its place.

We reorganized a little. Sonny cut out the sax—saxes were getting cornball anyway—and took over on trumpet. And we decided against keeping Spoof's name. It was now SONNY HOLMES AND HIS CREW.

And we kept on eating high up. Nobody seemed to miss Spoof—not the cats in front, as least—because Sonny blew as great a horn as anybody could want, smooth and sure, full of excitement and clean as a gnat's behind.

We played across the States and back, and they loved us—thanks to the kid. Called us an "institution" and the disc-jockeys began to pick up our stuff. We were "real," they said—the only authentic jazz left, and who am I to push it? Maybe they were right.

Sonny kept things in low. And then, when he was sure—damn that slow way: it had been a cinch since back when—he started to pay attention to Rose-Ann. She played it cool, the way she knew he wanted it, and let it build up right. Of course, who didn't know she would've married him this minute, now, just say the word? But Sonny was a very conscientious cat indeed.

We did a few stands in France about that time—Listen to them holler!—and a couple in England and Sweden—getting better, too—and after a breather, we cut out across the States again.

It didn't happen fast, but it happened sure. Something was sounding flat all of a sudden like—wrong, in a way.

During an engagement in El Paso we had *What the Cats Dragged In* lined up. You all know *Cats*—the rhythm section still, with the horns yelling for a hundred bars, then that fast and solid beat, that high trip and trumpet solo? Sonny had the ups on a wild riff and was coming on down, when he stopped. Stood still, with the horn to his lips; and we waited.

"Come on, wrap it up—you want a drum now? What's the story, Sonny?"

Then he started to blow. The notes came out the same almost, but not quite the same. They danced out of the horn strop-razor sharp and sliced up high and blasted low and the cats all fell out. "Do it! Go! Go, man! Oooo, I'm out of the boat, don't pull me back! Sing out, man!"

The solo lasted almost seven minutes. When it was time for us to wind it up, we just about forgot.

The crowd went wild. They stomped and screamed and whistled. But they couldn't get Sonny to play any more. He pulled the horn away from his mouth—I mean that's the way it looked, as if he was yanking it away with all his strength—and for a second he looked surprised, like he'd been goosed. Then his lips pulled back into a smile.

It was the *damndest* smile.

Freddie went over to him at the break. "Man, that was the craziest. How many tongues you got?"

But Sonny didn't answer him.

Things went along all right for a little. We played a few dances in the cities, some radio stuff, cut a few platters. Easy walking style.

Sonny played Sonny—plenty great enough. And we forget about what happened in El Paso. So what? So he cuts loose once—can't a man do that if he feels the urge? Every jazz man brings that kind of light at least once.

We worked through the sticks and were finally set for a New York opening when Sonny came in and gave us the news.

It was a gasser. Lux got sore. Mr. "T" shook his head.

"Why? How come, Top?"

He had us booked for the corn-belt. The old-time route, exactly, even the old places, back when we were playing razzmatazz and feeling our way.

"You trust me?" Sonny asked. "You trust my judgement?"

"Come off it, Top; you know we do. Just tell us how come. Man, New York's what we been working for—"

"That's just it," Sonny said. "We aren't ready."

That brought us down. How did *we* know—we hadn't even thought about it.

"We need to get back to the real material. When we play in New York, it's not anything anybody's liable to forget in a hurry. And that's why I think we ought to take a refresher course. About five weeks. All right?"

Well, we fussed some and fumed some, but not much, and in the end we agreed to it. Sonny knew his stuff, that's what we figured.

"Then it's settled."

And we lit out.

Played mostly the old stuff dressed up—*Big Gig, Only Us Chickens* and the rest—or head-arrangements with a lot of trumpet. Illinois, Indiana, Kentucky . . .

When we hit Louisiana for a two-nighter at the Tropics, the same thing happened that did back in Texas, Sonny blew wild for eight minutes on a solo that broke the glasses and cracked the ceiling and cleared the dance-floor like a tornado. Nothing off the stem, either—but like it was practice, sort of, or exercise. A solo out of nothing, that didn't even try to hang on to a shred of the melody.

"Man, it's great, but let us know when it's gonna happen, hear!"

About then Sonny turned down the flame on Rose-Ann. He was polite enough and a stranger wouldn't have noticed, but we did, and Rose-Ann did—and it was tough for her to keep it all down under, hidden. All those questions, all those memories and fears.

He stopped going out and took to hanging around his rooms a lot. Once in a while he'd start playing: one time we listened to that horn all night.

Finally—it was still somewhere in Louisiana—when Sonny was reaching with his trumpet so high he didn't get any more sound out of it than a dog-whistle, and the front cats were laughing up a storm, I went over and put it to him flatfooted.

His eyes were big and he looked like he was trying to say something and couldn't. He looked scared.

"Sonny . . . look, boy, what are you after? Tell a friend, man, don't lock it up."

But he didn't answer me. He couldn't.

He was coughing too hard.

Here's the way we doped it: Sonny had worshipped Spoof, like a god or something. Now some of Spoof was rubbing off, and he didn't know it.

Freddie was elected. Freddie talks pretty good most of the time.

"Get off the train, Jack. Ol' Massuh's gone now, dead and buried. Mean, what he was after ain't to be had. Mean, he wanted it all and then some—and all is all, there isn't any more. You play the greatest, Sonny—go on, ask anybody. Just fine. So get off the train . . ."

And Sonny laughed, and agreed and promised. I mean in words. His eyes played another number, though.

Sometimes he snapped out of it, it looked like, and he was fine then—tired and hungry, but with it. And we'd think, He's okay. Then it would happen all over again—only worse. Every time, worse.

And it got so Sonny even talked like Spoof half the time: "Broom off, man, leave me alone, will you? Can't you see I'm busy, got things to do? Get away!" And walked like Spoof—that slow walk-in-your-sleep shuffle. And did little things—like scratching his belly and leaving his shoes unlaced and rehearsing in his undershirt.

He started to smoke weeds in Alabama.

In Tennessee he took the first drink anybody ever saw him take.

And always with that horn—cussing it, yelling at it, getting sore because it wouldn't do what he wanted it to.

We had to leave him alone, finally. "I'll handle it . . . I—understand, I think . . . Just go away, it'll be all right . . ."

Nobody could help him. Nobody at all.

Especially not Rose-Ann.

* * *

End of the corn-belt route, the way Sonny had it booked was the Copper Club. We hadn't been back there since the night we planted Spoof—and we didn't feel very good about it.

But a contract isn't anything else.

So we took rooms at the only hotel there ever was in the town. You make a guess which room Sonny took. And we played some cards and bruised our chops and tried to sleep and couldn't. We tossed around in the beds, listening, waiting for the horn to begin. But it didn't. All night long, it didn't.

We found out why, oh yes . . .

Next day we all walked around just about everywhere except in the direction of the cemetery. Why kick up misery? Why make it any harder?

Sonny stayed in his room until ten before opening, and we began to worry, but he got in under the wire.

The Copper Club was packed. Yokels and farmers and high school stuff, a jazz "connoisseur" here and there—to the beams. Freddie had set up the stands with the music notes all in order, and in a few minutes we had our positions.

Sonny came out wired for sound. He looked—powerful; and that's a hard way for a five-foot four-inch baldheaded white man to look. At any time. Rose-Ann threw me a glance and I threw it back, and collected it from the rest. Something bad. Something real bad. Soon.

Sonny didn't look any which way. He waited for the applause to die down, then he did a quick One-Two-Three-Four and we swung into *The Jimjam Man*, our theme.

I mean to say, that crowd was with us all the way—they smelled something.

Sonny did the thumb-and-little-finger signal and we started *Only Us Chickens*. Bud Meunier did the intro on his bass, then Henry took over on the piano. He played one hand racing the other. The front cats hollered "Go! Go!" and Henry went. His left hand crawled on down over

the keys and scrambled and didn't fuzz once or slip once
and then walked away, cocky and proud, like a mouse full
of cheese from an unsprung trap.

"Hooo-boy! Play, Henry, play!"

Sonny watched and smiled. "Bring it out," he said, gentle, quiet, pleased. "Keep bringin' it out."

Henry did that counterpoint business that you're not
supposed to be able to do unless you have two right arms
and four extra fingers, and he got that boiler puffing, and
he got it shaking, and he screamed his Henry Walker
"WoooooOOOOO!" and he finished. I came in on the
tubs and beat them up till I couldn't see for the sweat, hit
the cymbal and waited.

Mr. "T," Lux and Jimmy fiddlefaddled like a coop and
capons talking about their operation for a while. Rose-Ann
chanted: "Only us chickens in the hen-house, Daddy, Only
us chickens here, Only us chickens in the hen-house,
Daddy, Ooo-bab-a-roo, Ooo-bob-a-roo . . ."

Then it was horn time. Time for the big solo.

Sonny lifted the trumpet—One! Two!—He got it into
sight—Three!

We all stopped dead. I mean we stopped.

That wasn't Sonny's horn. This one was dented-in and
beat-up and the tip-end was nicked. It didn't shine, not a
bit.

Lux leaned over—you could have fit a coffee cup into
his mouth, "Jesus God," he said. "Am I seeing right?"

I looked close and said: "Man, I hope not."

But why kid? We'd seen that trumpet a million times.

It was Spoof's.

Rose-Ann was trembling. Just like me, she remembered
how we'd buried the horn with Spoof. And she remembered how quiet it had been in Sonny's room last night . . .

I started to think real hophead thoughts, like—where
did Sonny get hold of a shovel that late? and how could he

expect a horn to play that's been under ground for two years? and—

That blast got into our ears like long knives.

Spoof's own trademark!

Sonny looked caught, like he didn't know what to do at first, like he was hypnotized, scared, almighty scared. But as the sound came out, rolling out, sharp and clean—new-trumpet sound—his expression changed. His eyes changed: they danced a little and opened wide.

Then he closed them, and blew that horn. Lord God of the Fishes, how he blew it! How he loved it and caressed it and pushed it up, higher and higher and higher. High C? Bottom of the barrel. He took off, and he walked all over the rules and stamped them flat.

The melody got lost, first off. Everything got lost, then, while that horn flew. It wasn't only jazz; it was the heart of jazz, and the insides, pulled out with the roots and held up for everybody to see; it was blues that told the story of all the lonely cats and all the ugly whores who ever lived, blues that spoke up for the loser lamping sunshine out of iron-gray bars and every hophead hooked and gone, for the bindlestiffs and the city slicers, for the country boys in Georgia shacks and the High Yellow hipsters in Chicago slums and the bootblacks on the corners and the fruits in New Orleans, a blues that spoke for all the lonely, sad and anxious downers who could never speak themselves . . .

And then, when it had said all this, it stopped and there was a quiet so quiet that Sonny could have shouted:

"It's okay, Spoof. It's all right now. You'll get it said, all of it—I'll help you. God, Spoof, you showed me how, you planned it—I'll do my best!"

And he laid back his head and fastened the horn and pulled in air and blew some more. Not sad, now, not blues—but not anything else you could call by a name. Except . . . jazz. It was jazz.

Hate blew out of that horn, then. Hate and fury and

mad and fight, like screams and snarls, like little razors shooting at you, millions of them, cutting, cutting deep . . .

And Sonny only stopping to wipe his lip and whisper in the silent room full of people: "You're saying it, Spoof! You are!"

God Almighty Himself must have heard that trumpet, then; slapping and hitting and hurting with notes that don't exist and never existed. Man! Life took a real beating! Life got groined and sliced and belly-punched and the horn, it didn't stop until everything had all spilled out, every bit of the hate and mad that's built up in a man's heart.

Rose-Ann walked over to me and dug her nails into my hand as she listened to Sonny . . .

"Come on now, Spoof! Come on! We can do it! Let's play the rest and play it right. You know it's got to be said, you know it does. Come on, you and me together!"

And the horn took off with a big yellow blast and started to laugh. I mean it laughed! Hooted and hollered and jumped around, dancing, singing, strutting through those notes that never were there. Happy music? Joyful music? It was chicken dinner and an empty stomach; it was big-butted women and big white beds; it was country walking and windy days and fresh-born crying and—Oh, there just doesn't happen to be any happiness that didn't come out of that horn.

Sonny hit the last high note—the Spoof blast—but so high you could just barely hear it.

Then Sonny dropped the horn. It fell onto the floor and bounced and lay still.

And nobody breathed. For a long, long time.

Rose-Ann let go of my hand, at last. She walked across the platform, slowly, and picked up the trumpet and handed it to Sonny.

He knew what she meant.

We all did. It was over now, over and done . . .

Lux plucked out the intro. Jimmy Fritch picked it up and kept the melody.

Then we all joined in, slow and quiet as we could. With Sonny—I'm talking about *Sonny*—putting out the kind of sound he'd always wanted to.

And Rose-Ann sang it, clear as a mountain wind—not just from her heart, but from her belly and her guts and every living part of her.

For The Ol' Massuh, just for him. Spoof's own song: *Black Country*.

Gentlemen, Be Seated
Introduction by
Frank M. Robinson

There was a time, not too long ago, when people talked about short stories and television shows—that is, the individual stories on television shows—with as much enthusiasm as they do today about movies or the latest novel by Stephen King or, for that matter, the most recent Batman or Superman universe.

They really did.

"Did you read that story by Bradbury in the Saturday Evening Post? The one about the dinosaur and the foghorn?"

"Did you catch Harlan Ellison in the recent Rogue? The girl who only carries folding money and doesn't have a dime for an emergency phone call?"

"Did you watch Twilight Zone last night? Where the old lady tries to escape Mr. Death?"

It was during the fifties and the late sixties and short stories were one of the major pillars of popular culture. We talked about them, we told the plots to one another, we waited for the magazines when they hit the newsstand and, of course, we never missed Twilight Zone. That was a period when the men's magazines were a little racy and a lot of fun (before they traded in a casual wink and a chuckle for short courses in gynecology and exercises in "personal journalism") and the last mass market for short fiction.

There were giants in those days and their names were Ray Bradbury and Richard Matheson and Charles Beaumont and Rod Serling . . .

Then Twilight Zone died in 1965 and Charles Beaumont died in 1967 and when they were gone, an era started to die. Night Gallery, Serling's last anthology series, died in 1972 and about the same time, fiction as a mainstay of the mass market men's magazines also began to vanish. (Everybody knew the magazines sold because of the stapled-in-the-navel nudes and the latest exhaustive interview with some transient VIP. Fiction was given the old heave-ho. None of the publishers noticed that when you took out the works, the old watch might look the same but it no longer kept time very well. By the mid-80's, circulation had plummeted. Readers turned on by soft-core porno were renting the real thing to watch on their VCR's.)

Of all the disasters to hit the short fiction market, one of the saddest was the decline and death of Charles Beaumont. A mainstay of Twilight Zone, he was also a mainstay of Playboy and Rogue.

He was a prolific talent and a unique one. Every writer reaches into himself for his characters, mines his own childhood for dramatic nuggets that he can adapt for his latest story.

Charlie's talent was broader than that. He could reach beyond his own life—he could reach into the hearts of the friends he knew and the people he met and construct his characters and stories from the living tissue of the everyday life around him.

Some musicians are credited with "soul," which is a very personal, internal thing. Charlie had that but he also had empathy, which is external. If you were hurting, he knew it. More importantly than that, he knew why—without you ever saying a word. It was this quality that gave his characters life, a quality that enabled his characters to engage the reader in a way those of few other writers could. In the science-fiction and fantasy field, dominated by mechanical plots and senseless action with cardboard cut outs going through the motions, stories by Charlie Beaumont stood out in vivid contrast.

It's with a great deal of bitter personal regret that I have to admit that both soul and empathy were not the sort of qualities that two-fifteen-year-olds in Chicago would notice in one another. I had to wait until my 30s to discover them in Charlie.

Harlan Ellison was largely responsible for Charles Beaumont appearing as "C.B. Lovehill" in the old Rogue. We loved his stories and we bought every one he submitted (Playboy had first pick—they paid more—and we took the leavings. But Beaumont was so consistently good that purchase by Playboy reflected editorial taste more than innate quality).

Of all the stories we published, I especially loved, "Gentlemen, Be Seated." Dated only slightly, it deals with the death of humor and the Society for the Preservation of Laughter and could serve more as a metaphor for the late 1980s than for the early 1960s, when it was written.

A clever idea . . .

But far more than that, it's the pathetic story of man who finally Got It (like most of us)—one day too late.

OF COURSE, KINKAID'S first thought was: I'm going to be sacked. A vision of disgrace, endless wandering, and inevitable death by starvation floated before his mind. Then, to his surprise, he relaxed. The terror vanished, and he found himself thinking: Well, at least I won't have to look at his stupid face any more. That's something. And I won't have to say yes to him when I mean no, hell no, you're as wrong as it's possible to get, you miserable fathead!

He pushed away from his desk and walked down the long aisle of drafting tables to a little gray door marked, simply: William A. Biddle—District Manager. He stood there a moment, wondering how he had sinned, not doubting that he had, for why else would he have been summoned? Then, swallowing, he knocked.

"Come in."

Kinkaid turned the plain metal knob and walked inside. The room, Model 17-B, "Regional Executive," was scientifically-designed for comfort and efficiency, but Kinkaid did not feel either comfortable or efficient. The Mov-E-Mural, depicting a wind-rippled mountain lake, the scent of rain and forests (#8124—"Huntsman"); the Day-Lite; and the distant strains of music *(La Gioconda)*—all chosen to keep the mind undeflected from its ordained course— served only to upset him further. He walked across the Earth 'n-Loam floor to the desk.

It was a perfectly ordinary desk, uncluttered by items of memorabilia, solid as a butcher's block, functional as the State. Yet it frightened Kinkaid. Perhaps because of the way it seemed to be not in the room but of it, perhaps because of the way it seemed to grow vertically from the floor and horizontally from the paunch of William A. Biddle.

"Sit down."

Kinkaid perched on the edge of the Relax-O-Kushion and met the gaze of his superior. Biddle drum-rolled his fingers on the Teletalk and frowned. Presently he spoke, in the unlubricated voice Kinkaid had come to despise: "I suppose you're wondering why I asked you to come in."

"Yes, sir."

Biddle opened a drawer and withdrew a sheaf of papers. "I have here," he said, "a dossier. It contains a full report on your life to date." He flipped through the light-green pages. "I see that you were born in 1952, that you are unmarried, and that you have been employed at Spears' Research Laboratories for seven years. At no time have you arrived at the office late or left early. You are a member of Rotary, and attend the Young Men's Political Forum every other Tuesday. Outside interests and hobbies; none. Is this correct?''

"Yes, sir."

"You are, in short, the perfect employee."

"I do what I can, sir."

"Precisely. No more and no less. One could scarcely tell you from a billion other laborers. Yet I believe there *is* a difference." Biddle continued to frown. "You may recall that on the way to my office yesterday morning, I tripped."

"Yes, sir."

"What was your reaction?"

"Regret, sir."

"Indeed?" Very slowly, Biddle removed a cigar from his breast pocket. He skinned off the cellophane wrapping and moistened the tip. "It's a serious world we live in," he said, "and that is why we are serious people." He touched a spring on his silver lighter and sucked flame into the cigar. "Don't you agree?"

Kinkaid nodded. "Definitely, sir."

"Definitely," said William Agnew Biddle, whereupon the cigar in his mouth exploded.

Kinkaid leapt to his feet.

He stared at his superior, whose face was now covered with the splayed ends of the demolished cigar, and then felt a curious constriction in his chest and a peculiar, uncontrollable force which caused the corners of his mouth to stretch upward.

"What are you doing?" asked Biddle, suddenly.

Kinkaid's hands twitched in a futile gesture. The more Kinkaid looked at his superior, the greater and more uncontrollable the constriction, the higher the corners of the mouth. It was a frightening sensation. "I don't know," he said.

"Then I'll tell you," said Biddle, scraping the tobacco from his blackened face. "You're doing the same thing you did when I tripped. You're *grinning*."

"Sir, I assure you—"

"Kinkaid, I have eyes in my head, and I say you're *grinning*! Why?"

"I don't know, sir!"

Biddle took a step closer. "I do. You're amused, Kinkaid. That's why. An incident has just occurred which might have caused blindness or permanent injury to my face. I ask you, is there anything funny in that?"

"No, sir."

"And yet you grinned."

"It was involuntary."

"That hardly matters, Kinkaid. The point is, you *did* grin. I knew it!"

"Sir?"

"How did it feel?"

Kinkaid shifted on the Relax-O-Kushion. "I'm afraid I don't understand," he said.

"Did it feel . . . strange?"

"Yes."

"But not unpleasant?"

Kinkaid shook his head.

"Good! Splendid!" Biddle wiped the remaining patches of soot from his face. "Kinkaid," he said, "what are you doing tonight?"

"Nothing in particular."

"Would you care to spend an evening with me?"

"That would be fine, sir. But—"

"No buts! Meet me at Kelly's, Ninth and Spring, at eight o'clock. Your questions will be answered then. In the meantime, say nothing of this episode—to anyone. Is that clear?"

"Yes, sir." Kinkaid rose.

"Kinkaid."

"Yes, sir?"

"Why do firemen wear red suspenders?"

"I don't know, sir."

"Poor boy," said Biddle. "You will."

Kelly's was unlike any restaurant Kinkaid had ever seen; except, of course, in the historicals. Entering, he felt peculiarly suspect. Instead of the usual bright light, there was darkness. Instead of the normal cataract of voices, silence. Instead of the endless rows of tables, emphasizing Togetherness, a few booths by the wall. At the last booth, he stopped. William Agnew Biddle was seated before a glass which contained a colorless fluid.

"James, I'm so glad you decided to come. Thought I saw you changing your mind by the door."

Kinkaid sat down across from his superior. Somehow Biddle was different. His voice was no longer dry and mechanical. His eyes seemed to have little lights in them.

"Ever been to a real restaurant?"

"Like this? No."

"Pity. I can't say the food is particularly health-giving—but once you've tried it, you can't go back to the lab stuff. Care to try?"

"I'm not very hungry, sir, to tell the truth."

"Oh. Well, you won't mind if I go ahead." Biddle drained the glass, then snapped his fingers. A man in a red jacket appeared out of the shadows. "A nice porterhouse, Sam. Salad, with roquefort. My usual."

"Yes, sir," the man said, and vanished.

"Being waited on is agreeable, too," said Biddle. "Now. I suppose at this point you're thinking: Poor old boy, he's flunked his mentals."

"Oh, no, sir. It's just that I'm a little—"

"Confused. Yes. And with good reason. First it appears you're going to be fired, then it appears you're being subjected to some sort of test. As it happens, neither is the case."

Kinkaid said, "Oh."

"You see, James, I've had my eyes on you for quite a

while. Not that there was ever anything overt, anything one could put one's finger on . . . But I *sensed* something about you."

The man in the red jacket reappeared, bearing trays. He set many dishes in front of Biddle. Then he vanished again.

Biddle began to eat. "They'll tell you there's no such thing as intuition," he said, between bites, "but they're wrong. I knew, somehow, that you'd grin when the cigar exploded. Of course, I'd *hoped* for a laugh, but we can't have everything can we? *How* did I know about the grin?" He shrugged, cocking his sparse-haired, pink-fleshed head to one side. "For a long time I've felt your hatred. Highly unscientific! But I've felt it nonetheless. The way you say 'good morning,' for instance. It's not a greeting, it's a curse. What you *mean* is: 'I hate you, Mr. Biddle. I hate everything about you.' Am I right?"

"Well . . ."

"Of *course* I'm right!" Biddle chewed lustily. "The district manager of Spear's Research is, by and large, a horse's ass. He is pompous and rude and officious and cold. But he is also highly competent, and therefore above suspicion. The authorities would believe him, no matter what they were told. No matter *what*. Remember that."

"All right," said Kinkaid.

Biddle glanced at his watch, then snapped his fingers again, loudly. The man in the red jacket materialized.

"Check, Sam," said Biddle. Then, rising: "Come along, James. It's just about that time."

They rode the moving belts to the dark north end of the city, then they walked. Soon Kinkaid's legs began to hurt. He wanted to stop and rest, but pride prevented him. Biddle, who was over seventy, appeared to be totally unaffected by the exertion.

After a while, the district manager said: "Been out this way before?"

Kinkaid shook his head.

"It's called No Man's Land. They'll have it torn down in a few years, torn down, swept away, forgotten." Biddle sighed. "All these lovely, impractical buildings . . ." He pointed to a huge, dark, sightless structure, untenanted for decades, poised, it seemed, on the fine edge of collapse. "A lot of unhappiness there, James. But a lot of happiness, too. Stop a moment. Close your eyes. Can't you almost hear the crying and the laughter?"

Kinkaid closed his eyes. He heard nothing but the hum of the city.

"It will come. Don't force it." Biddle reached into his pocket. "Now I'll have to ask you to cooperate." He withdrew a pair of glasses, opened them, and hooked them on Kinkaid's ears. "Can you see?"

"No."

"Good."

Kinkaid felt himself being revolved. Dizziness set in immediately.

"It's necessary the first time," said Biddle. "In case you're rejected."

Feeling slightly ill, Kinkaid walked what he considered a terrible distance, turning innumerable corners, doubling back, climbing steps. After perhaps an hour of this, Biddle said: "Take 'em off."

They were in an alcove of some sort. Biddle winked, walked to the paint-peeling door and knocked three times. There was a pause. Then a panel slid open and a face appeared.

"Why does a chicken cross the road?" inquired a voice.

"To get to the other side," said Biddle.

The door opened.

Kinkaid followed his superior into a plush-hung hallway. Standing in the hallway, blocking a second door, was a tall man in a peppermint-striped suit. His face was glistening black, except for the mouth, which was broadly outlined in white. His hair was short and kinky. He held a circular, bangled instrument which Kinkaid recognized as an ancient *tambourine*.

"Good evening, Mister Bones," said Biddle.

"Good evenin'," said the man with the black face.

"Is he in?"

"Yassuh."

"Tell him member seven-oh-nine is here, with the recruit."

"Yassuh, boss!" said the man. He tapped the *tambourine*, turned and walked out the doorway.

Within moments he was back.

"Dis yere way."

Kinkaid and Biddle accompanied the man up a long, narrow flight of stairs to a small red door and there they stopped. The man with the black face pressed a button.

From an overhead speaker a voice called: "Why does the fireman wear red suspenders?"

"To keep his pants up," said the *tambourine* man, flipping a toggle.

"So make the scene."

There was a sharp buzzing sound. The door swung open. Kinkaid and Biddle followed their guide in.

Instinctively, Kinkaid gasped and clutched at Biddle for support. His first impression had been that the room was upside down. He closed his eyes. Slowly, he opened them. The impression remained.

Biddle made a peculiar noise in his throat. "Don't be alarmed," he said. "This is known as a gag."

"A gag?" Kinkaid stared up at what could only be the floor. He saw a couch, a chair, a table, and even a small sleeping dog.

"Exactly. It will be explained." Biddle marched across the ceiling, from which sprouted a long chain topped by an antique light bulb. "Come along."

Taking care to look straight ahead, Kinkaid made his

way forward. His employer pressed a second button and a
panel slid back, exposing a second room.

It was hardly a comfort.

Here there were mirrors, stationed along the four walls.
As Kinkaid passed them, he saw himself turn fat, slim, big-
headed, pin-headed, three-faced, and invisible.

"Deposit the can titherwards, ofay," said the man known
as Mister Bones, gesturing.

"How's that?" Kinkaid looked at the chair which had
been pulled up. "Oh." He sat down. As he sank into the
frayed brown cushion, there was a loud, embarrassing noise.

"Yak, yak!" said Mister Bones.

Kinkaid rose, unsteadily. "I think," he said, "that I'd
better go."

"Too late," said Biddle.

"Boo!"

Kinkaid jumped backward, colliding with a large desk.
When equilibrium returned, he found himself staring at a
figure alongside which the man with the black face seemed
absolutely humdrum. This figure reflected a hundred times
throughout the room, wore a golden mask and a skin-tight
suit of many colors, each color in the shape of a diamond,
each diamond a different hue from the other. The figure
approached, and as it did so, the tiny bells attached to its
ankles and to its wrists and to its high-peaked cap tinkled
wildly.

"What goes up the chimney down but not down the
chimney up?"

"I don't understand the question," said Kinkaid.
"Would you repeat it?"

"No," said the belled figure. Pointing the stick at Biddle: "Tell him."

"An umbrella," said Biddle.

The man with the black face slapped his knees. Peculiar
noises issued from his throat. They were, Kinkaid thought,

like the noises of the Laff-Tracks on TV; but also not like them.

"Mister Bones," said the belled figure, "it's toodle-oosville, *s'il vous plaît*."

The man with the black face tapped his *tambourine*, turned and walked headlong into the wall. Again Kinkaid felt the strange constriction in his chest. The ends of his mouth curled upwards as the man crashed to the floor, rolled, picked himself up and staggered through the doorway.

"I don't know, Biddle," said the harlequin figure. Kinkaid could feel hot eyes staring upon him from behind the golden mask. "I'm very dubious."

"He smiled," said Biddle, frowning.

"Yes, but that was a yok. We've got to be *so* careful."

"Of course. I know that. That's why I waited to be sure." Biddle put his arm around Kinkaid's shoulder. "Understand, he's a beginner. And he *was* amused by the trick cigar."

The bells tinkled. "*Was* he?"

"He very nearly laughed."

"Well!" Silence. Then, once more, the bells; louder; much louder. The figure reached across the desk. "Good to meet up with ya, podnuh!"

Hesitantly, Kinkaid accepted the hand. There was a loud buzz, followed by a painful tickling sensation on his palm. He jerked away.

The Laff-Track noise again, from Biddle's throat. Listening, Kinkaid was hardly aware of the lava-hot ball gathering and expanding inside him. When it burst, he was as surprised as the others. "That's it!" he shouted, slamming his fist down on the desk. "I don't know what the hell all of this is about, but I know one thing—I don't want any part of it. You hear? You people—you're psycho! You know that? Psycho!"

He strode angrily to the door.

It was locked.

"You see!" said Biddle. "Emotion."

"Yes," said the belled figure. "That's encouraging, though far from conclusive." He gestured. "Mister Kinkaid, please calm yourself. This is all quite necessary."

"For what?"

"Membership. Do sit down, but take care to remove the Whoopee-Cushion. Now. I gather Mister Biddle has told you nothing."

"That's right," said Kinkaid, still annoyed.

"Then I'll explain. You are in the headquarters of the S.P.O.L.—the Society for the Preservation of Laughter. We're a secret organization, running counter to established law. Most of what we do is either frowned upon or strictly forbidden. We are, in short, outlaws."

Kinkaid glanced at Biddle, then struck a cigarette, nervously.

"I," said the belled figure, "am known as the Grand Jester. Mister Biddle, here, is one of our Interlocutors. Should you be accepted, you would start as a Schlock. It is no disgrace: we were all Schlocks, once. After six months, however, you would be entitled to apply for a raise in status. Assuming a positive vote, you would then ascend to the Second Degree, that of Hipster. And so forth. Am I making myself clear?"

"Not exactly," said Kinkaid.

"Well, then, skipping the parliamentary jazz for the mo," said the Grand Jester, "it should be enough to say that our title explains our purpose. The world has forgotten how to laugh, Mister Kinkaid. Some of us regret that fact. Unlike the authorities we feel that laughter is sufficiently important to be preserved, despite the grave psychological risk. You dig?"

"I didn't know there was any psychological risk in laughter."

"Then you have not been with it, friend-o. Most humor,

you see, had its roots in cruelty. In stamping out cruelty, we have automatically stamped out humor. Therefore, there ain't much to laugh at no more.

"This is the story," continued the man in the golden mask. "Once upon a time, the world was a basically bad scene. We had disease and war and oppression and prejudice, and all that scam. The worst! How did the people endure it? By laughing. They worked out all their beefs with boffs, so to speak. Then the psychologists and the censors came on. We got sophisticated. Conditions improved. And humor vanished." With his jeweled stick he pressed a number of buttons on the desk. "It's a fragile thing, humor. Analysis can kill it. But we are an analytical people now, so you'll have everything explained to you— once—to eliminate psychological after-blast. Now. I trust you understand the trick cigar episode?"

Before Kinkaid could answer, Biddle said: "I thought it best to wait." He turned. "James, it was simply that a figure of authority was momentarily rendered ridiculous. Sort of a consummation."

The Grand Jester shook his head, causing the bells to ring. "Leave him alone," he said. "Mister Kinkaid, what about the man who walked into the wall?"

Kinkaid thought a while. "What about him?"

"He was painted to represent a Negro. Negroes constitute a minority race. Somewhere deep inside you, you are prejudiced against minority races. You wish them ill. When ill befalls them, you laugh."

"That's absurd," said Kinkaid.

"Yes," said the Jester, "but partially true. If your mother had walked into the wall, you would not have grinned. Ergo and thus. How else do you account for the disappearance of Negro humor? Of all racial humor, for that matter? It's basically prejudicial, cruel."

"The upside-down room is another example," said Biddle.

"Precisely," said the Jester. "I have a peep-hole through which I observe visitors. As they stumble about in discomfort, or panic, I laugh. You, Mister Kinkaid, made me laugh quite heartily. It was endsville."

"The peculiar words," said Biddle, "amuse because they are an expression of individuality. They may be interpreted as a form of rebellion against organized society."

The Jester reached into his desk, withdrew four oranges and began to juggle them. "I don't think he gets it."

"Give him time!"

"All right." The oranges fell to the floor. "My own costume harks back to a figure of great pathos, the Court Jester. He was usually a dwarf or a cripple. Fu*neee*!"

A buzzer sounded. The man in the golden mask picked up a microphone. "What has four wheels and flies?" he shouted.

"A garbage truck!" returned a chorus of voices.

"Make it!"

The door opened. Five figures entered the room. The first was clad in a billowing polka-dot suit, the second in dark rags, the third in long underwear, the fourth in a toga, while the fifth and last was mother naked. The figures lined up in front of Kinkaid and regarded him speculatively.

"First degree interlocutors," said Biddle. "Your judges."

The naked man stepped forward. "Have you heard the one about the little moron who tried to look through a screen and strained his eyes?"

Kinkaid said, "No."

There was a pause. The naked man stepped back.

The ragged man took his place. In a high-pitched sing-song voice, he said: "Roses are red, daisies chartreuse. If you will bend over, I'll give you a start."

"What?"

The polka-dot man reached into his pocket and took out a large paper, which he unrolled. It was a lined drawing of two bearded men imbedded to their chests in jungle slime. A quotation at the bottom of the picture read: "Quicksand or not, I've half a mind to struggle."

The man in long underwear leaned on a cane, which snapped in two. From the floor he said: "There were these real wild hopheads sitting on a curb. They're smoking away. Along comes this fire engine going about a hundred miles an hour, with the bells and the siren, screaming along. It screams right by them. Wait a minute, I forgot to say they were high. Y'know? Anyway, the first hophead turns to the other hophead and says, 'Like man. I thought they'd *never* leave.' "

The man in the toga raised his hand. "There was a young man from Saint Bee's, who was stung on the hand by a wasp. Said he, with a grin, as he something-something, 'I'm sure glad it wasn't a hornet.' "

The five figures then began to run about the room, singing:

"*He thought he saw a Banker's Clerk Descending from the bus:*

He looked again, and found it was A Hippopotamus:

'If this should stay to dine,' he said, 'There won't be much for us!' "

"Won't be much for us!" cried Biddle. "Won't be much for us!"

Abruptly the song stopped. The figures ceased their running. They peered at Kinkaid, who had sat frozen for the past several minutes; then they scampered, howling, from the room.

The Grand Jester balanced the jeweled stick on his nose and said: "They'll vote tonight."

"What do you think?" asked Biddle.

"Hard to say."

"I know, but what do you think?"

"Won't tell," said the Jester.

Biddle sighed. "All right," he said, and took Kinkaid's

arm. "Nothing to do now but wait. Let's go downstairs. Maybe we can catch an orgy."

They sat in heavy leather chairs, Biddle wiping his forehead with a handkerchief, Kinkaid merely sitting, waiting for the nausea to pass.

A man in a white jacket paused and put glasses in their hands.

"Absinthe," said Biddle. "It'll rot out your eyes if you make a habit of it. Like most sins, though, it's harmless in moderation."

The thickish liquid tasted bad to Kinkaid, but appeared to settle his stomach.

Biddle was mumbling.

"What?"

"I said, I may have made a mistake." The district manager swallowed all the liquid in his glass and belched. "No point being pessimistic, though." He rose from the chair. "Come along, it's almost show time. There are a few things I want you to see."

Kinkaid followed his superior across a deep red carpet to a room. The walls of the room were lined with books.

Biddle handed Kinkaid a gilt-edged book weighing at least ten pounds. Opening at random, Kinkaid found a drawing which depicted communal breeding.

"The Germans were great hands at pornography," Biddle said, chuckling. "They almost made an art of it. So did the Japanese. Here—this is our collection of *graffiti*." He reached down an impressive leather-bound volume. "You're probably not familiar with the word. It refers mainly to the scrawls one used to find on the walls of public restrooms." He flipped through the pages. "Some wonderful stuff, really. Completely uninhibited. Take this: 'Here I sit, brokenhearted—' "

"Mr. Biddle," said Kinkaid. "I'm not feeling very well."

"Oh? That's too bad. Well, next time. In case you're

alone: this section contains essays and short works of fiction; this section is devoted entirely to cartoons; that's the film vault over there. All the Chaplin pictures, Buster Keaton, W.C. Fields, Laurel and Hardy, the Marx Brothers, et al. Also a rather interesting selection of stag reels. When you decide to look at those, by the way, have one of the interlocutors help you. Personally I would recommend 'Bathroom Frolics,' though 'A Night at the Zoo' is also first rate."

There was an ugly bleating sound.

"The Bronx cheer," said Biddle. "That means showtime. Here go."

They hurried out of the book-filled room, across the crowded bar, through a curtained doorway, to a small amphitheatre.

They sat down. The lights dimmed. The curtains parted. A small man in a checkered suit walked to the center of the stage.

"Anybody wanna buy a duck?"

The people in the amphitheatre roared. A large man with white hair jabbed his elbow into Kinkaid's ribs. "Too much!" the man said. "Too much!"

The footlights became dimmer. A man in patched clothes shuffled across the stage. A spotlight came on. The man took a short-handled broom from his pocket and tried to sweep away the spotlight.

Again the roar.

Two men with black faces and white gloves shambled across the stage.

The tall one said: "Crony, my boy, where has you been? I ain't seen you in a long time!"

The short one said: "I been in de jailhouse."

"Whuffo?" asked the tall one.

"Well," said the short one, "lemme ax you sumfin'. What would you do if you come home and found yo wife in bed wid anudder man?"

"I would simply cut my wife's acquaintance."

"Dat's all I did. An' believe me, I cut him deep!"

"Yak! Yak!"

"Negroes," said Biddle, "were thought to be morally lax. The humor here derives from the odd speech patterns, the misunderstanding of a common phrase, and the casual attitude toward murder. But forget that. Take it for what it is. Try!"

Kinkaid tried, but he did not understand any of the things that passed before his eyes. Biddle's voice was a distant hum. The lights danced inside his mind.

When they returned to the lounge, Biddle ordered drinks.

They took a corner booth.

"Look at it this way," Biddle said. "Humor is an escape valve for the emotions. Everybody has emotions, even to-day. They're building up, all over the world. Getting ready to explode.

"James, listen to me," Biddle said. "This is the way it was. When television was born, censors started cracking down. Any humor that might offend—that's to say, all real humor—was banished. A new humor sprang up. It didn't offend anyone, but it didn't amuse anyone either. Nobody liked it, but that didn't matter. Vaudeville died. Burlesque died. Circuses died. The wonderful jokes that used to spread like wildfire . . ." Biddle sighed and peered at his glass. "It was phenomenal. You're too young to remember, James. We had jokes about everything under the sun, about insanity and disease, about sex and God and crime and marriage and—oh, nothing was sacred. And the wonder is, a lot of these jokes were good. Still are! I'm afraid it's a lost art. Everything's lost. Drink up, my boy. You're what's left."

Kinkaid threw down the remains of his drink and ordered another. There was a curious loss of control in his motor muscles. He looked at all the people, listened to the roar of their voices, and returned to the booth.

A naked woman sat in his lap.

"Coo, ducks," she said. "Have you heard the one about the married couple and the chimpanzee?"

"No," said Kinkaid. His mind was whirling now. The girl became two, then three. The voices faded.

". . . got into bed and here was this ape . . ."

He blinked furiously. Now there was a girl in Biddle's lap, and they were making those barking, Laff-Track noises.

"Get it?" said a voice.

Kinkaid felt a sudden hot rush of tears on his face. "No!" he cried, pressing his hot wet face between the girl's breasts. "No, I don't get it. *I don't get it!*"

A hand reached into his mind, then, and turned it off.

The morning light was cold and harsh. Kinkaid lay on the bed unmoving for a long time. When he did move, it was an agony. His head throbbed and his stomach felt as though someone had been punching it, hard, for hours.

It was not until after his shower that he remembered the previous night.

Excited, he dressed, breakfasted, and took the hi-speed belt to work.

"You are seven minutes, twenty seconds late," said the Time Box.

"Up yours," said Kinkaid, happily.

He ran the gauntlet of eyes to his desk, took out his papers and sat down. A red bulb flashed.

Kinkaid walked down the aisle toward the door marked: *William A. Biddle.* Biddle was seated behind his desk.

"Hi," said Kinkaid.

"You are late."

"I know. That absinthe must have got to me."

"Absinthe?"

"Maybe I didn't tell you, but I hadn't even tasted the

stuff before last night. I'm sorry about what happened. Who took me home?"

"Kinkaid, I don't know what you're talking about."

"About last night. S.P.O.L." The corners of Kinkaid's lips curled upward. "Anybody wanna buy a duck?"

Biddle's expression was grim.

"I'll be happy to give you a goose instead," said Kinkaid. "There, how's that? That's a joke, isn't it?"

"I couldn't say."

"Come on, Mister Biddle. I know I was a disappointment to you, but it was all so new. I didn't understand. I wanted to, I tried . . . I'm willing to learn."

Biddle said nothing.

"They're not going to hold it against me because I didn't laugh, are they?" Kinkaid found that his heart had begun to beat rapidly. "I didn't know how. But I do now. Listen. Ha! Ha-ha! *Ha-ha-ha*—"

"Kinkaid!"

"Yes, sir?"

"You're fired."

"What?" Kinkaid's mouth went dry. He stared at the stern man behind the desk and tried to remember how he looked with his tie loose and a naked woman in his lap. "Mister Biddle, I know the vote was against me. I know that. And I don't blame them. But, you can fix it, can't you?"

"Get out."

"Please! All I want is a second chance. Is that so much to ask? You people *lived* through the time, I didn't. I've got to learn."

"I don't know what you're babbling about, Kinkaid. But I warn you. If you repeat any of it to the authorities, they'll put you away."

Kinkaid stood there a moment, tense; then he sighed, turned around and walked quickly out of the building.

That night, and almost every night thereafter until the

final demolition, he rode the belts to No Man's Land. He walked to where the ugly sightless buildings were, and he searched, but he could never find the building he wanted.

Sometimes he would stand perfectly still on the crumbling sidewalks, and listen. And once in a while it almost seemed that he could hear the distant laughter.

It was a lovely, desperate sound.

THE JUNGLE

SUDDENLY IT WAS there. On foxfeet, invisibly, it had crept, past all the fences and traps he had laid, past all the barriers. And now it sat inside his mind, a part of him, like his pulse, like the steady beat of his heart.

Richard Austin became rigid in the chair. He closed his eyes and strained the muscles in his body until they were silent and unmoving as granite; and he listened to the thing that had come again, taking him by surprise even while he had been waiting. He listened to grow—it *seemed* to grow; he couldn't be sure: perhaps he was merely bringing it into sharper focus by filtering out the other constant sounds: the winds that whispered through the foliage of balloon-topped trees the murmurous insect-drone of all the machines that produced this wind and pumped blood through the city from their stations far beneath the night-heavy streets. Or, perhaps, it was because he was searching, trying to lay hands on it that the thing seemed to be different tonight, stronger, surer. Or—what did it matter?

He sat in the darkened room and listened to the drum; to the even, steady throb that really neither rose nor diminished, but held to that slow dignified tempo with which he'd become so familiar.

Then, quickly he rose from the chair and shook his head. The sounds died and became an indistinguishable part of the silence. It was only concentration, he thought, and the desire to hear them gave them life . . .

Richard Austin released a jagged breath from his swollen lungs, painfully. He walked to the bar and poured some whiskey into a glass and drank most of it in a single swallow: it went down his dry throat like knives, forcing the salivary glands back into action.

He shook his head again, turned and walked back across the living room to the far door. It swung out noiselessly as his hand touched the ornamented circle of hammered brass.

The figure of his wife lay perfectly still under the black light, still and pale, as she had lain three hours before. He walked toward her, feeling his nostrils dilate at the acrid medicine smells, harshly bitter and new to his senses. He blinked away the hot tears that had rushed, stinging, to his eyes; and stood for a time, quietly, trying not to think of the drums.

Then he whispered: "Mag . . . Mag, don't die tonight!"

Imbecile words! He clenched his fists and stared down at the face that was so full of pain, so twisted with defeat, that now you could not believe it had once been different, a young face, full of laughter and innocence and courage.

The color had gone completely. From the burning splotchy scarlet of last week to this stiff white mask, lifeless, brittle as dry paste. And covered over with perspiration that glistened above her mouth in cold wet buttons and over her face like oil on white stone. The bedding under and around her was drenched gray.

Austin looked at the bandage that covered his wife's head, and forced away the memory, brutally. The memory of her long silver hair and how it had fallen away in clumps in his hands within a week after she had been stricken . . .

But the thoughts danced out of control, and he found

himself remembering all the terrible steps in this nightmare.

The scientists had thought it malaria, judging from the symptoms, which were identical. But that was difficult to accept, for malaria had been effectively conquered— powerful new discoveries in vaccines having been administered first, and then the primary cause of the disease itself—the Anopheles mosquitoe—destroyed completely. And the liquid alloys which formed the foundations for this new city eliminated all the likely breeding places, the bogs and marshlands and rivers. No instance of reoccurrence of the disease had been reported for half a century. Yet— malarial parasites were discovered in the bloodstreams of those first victims, unmistakable parasites that multiplied at a swift rate and worked their destruction of the red corpuscles. And the chemists immediately had to go about the business of mixing medicines from now ancient prescriptions, frantically working against time. A disquieting, even a frightening thing; but without terror for the builders of the new city; not sufficient to make them abandon their work or to spark mass evacuations. Panic was by now so forgotten by most that it had become a new emotion, to be learned all over again.

It had not taken very long to relearn, Austin recalled. Terror had come soon enough. The stricken—some thirty husky workmen, engineers, planners—had rallied under the drugs and seemed to be out of critical condition when, one night, they had all suffered relapses, fallen into fevered comas and proceeded to alternate between unconsciousness and delirium. The scientists were baffled. They tried frenziedly to arrest the parasites, but without success. Their medicines were useless, their drugs and radium treatments and inoculations—all, useless. Finally, they could only look on as the disease took new turns, developed strange characteristics, changed altogether from what they had taken to be malaria to something utterly foreign. It began to as-

sume a horrible regular pattern: from prolonged delirium
to catatonia, whereby the victim's respiratory system and
heartbeat diminished to a condition only barely distinguish-
able from death. And then, the most hideous part: the swift
decomposition of the body cells, the destruction of the tis-
sues . . .

Richard Austin carefully controlled a shudder as he
thought of those weeks that had been the beginning. He
fingered out a cigarette from his pocket, started to strike
it, then broke the cylinder and ground its bright red flakes
into his palms.

No other real hint had been given then: only the disease.
Someone had nicknamed it "Jungle Rot"—cruel, but apt.
The victims *were* rotting alive, the flesh falling from them
like rain-soaked rags; and they did not die wholly, ever,
until they had been transformed into almost unrecognizable
mounds of putrescence . . .

He put out a hand and laid it gently against his wife's
cheek. The perspiration was chill and greasy to his touch,
like the stagnant water of slew banks. Instinctively his fingers recoiled and balled back into fists. He forced them
open again and stared at the tiny dottles of flesh that clung
to them.

"Mag!" It had started already! Wildly, he touched her
arm, applying very slight pressure. The outer skin crumbled
away, leaving a small wet gray patch. Austin's heart raced;
an involuntary movement caused his fingers to pinch his
own wrists, hard. A wrinkled spot appeared and disappeared, a small, fading red line.

She's dying, he thought. Very surely, very slowly, she's
begun to die—Mag. Soon her body will turn gray and then
it will come loose; the weight of the sheet will be enough
to tear big strips of it away . . . She'll begin to rot, and her
brain will know it—they had discovered that much: the
victims were never completely comatose, could not be ad-

equately drugged—she will know that she is mouldering
even while she lives and thinks . . .

And why? His head ached, throbbed. *Why?*

The years, these past months, the room with its stink of
decay—everything rushed up, suddenly, filling Austin's
mind.

If I had agreed to leave with the rest, he thought, to run
away, then Mag would be well and full of life. But—I didn't
agree . . .

He had stayed on to fight. And Mag would would not
leave without him. Now she was dying and that was the
end of it.

Or—he turned slowly—was it? He walked out to the
balcony. The forced air was soft and cool; it moved in little
patches through the streets of the city. Mbarara, *his city*;
the one he'd dreamed about and then planned and designed
and pushed into existence; the place built to pamper five
hundred thousand people.

Empty now, and deserted as a gigantic churchyard . . .

Dimly he recognized the sound of the drums with their
slow muffled rhythm, directionless as always, seeming to
come from everywhere and from nowhere. Speaking to him.
Whispering.

Austin lit a cigarette and sucked the calming smoke into
his lungs. He remained motionless until the cigarette was
down to the cork.

Then he walked back into the bedroom, opened a cabinet and took a heavy silver pistol.

He loaded it carefully.

Mag was still; almost, it seemed to Austin, expectant,
waiting, so very still and pale.

He pointed the barrel of the pistol at his wife's forehead
and curled his finger around the trigger. Another slight
pressure and it would be over. Her suffering would be over.
Just a slight pressure!

The drums droned louder until they were exploding in the quiet room.

Austin tensed and fought the trembling, gripped the pistol with his other hand to steady it.

But his finger refused to move on the curved trigger.

After a long moment, he lowered his arm and dropped the gun into his pocket.

"No." He said it quietly, undramatically. The word hit a barrier of mucus and came out high-pitched and childlike.

He coughed.

That was what they wanted him to do—he could tell, from the drums. That's what so many of the others had done. Panicked.

"No."

He walked quickly out of the room, through the hall, to the elevator. It lowered instantly but he did not wait for it to reach bottom before he leapt off and ran across the floor to the barricaded front door.

He tore at the locks. Then the door swung open and he was outside; for the first time in three weeks—outside, alone, in the city.

He paused, fascinated by the strangeness of it. Impossible to believe that he was the only white man left in the entire city.

He strode to a high-speed walkway, halted it and stepped on. Setting the power at half with his pass key, he pressed the control button and sagged against the rail as the belt whispered into movement.

He knew where he was going. Perhaps he even knew why. But he didn't think about that; instead, he looked at the buildings that slid by silently, the vast rolling spheres and columns of colored stone, the balanced shapes that existed now and that had once existed only in his mind. And he listened to the drums, wondering why the sound of them seemed natural and his buildings suddenly so unnatural, so strange and disjointed.

Like green balloons on yellow stocks, the cultured Grant Wood trees slipped by, uniform and straight, arranged in aesthetically pleasing designs on the stone islands between belts. Austin smiled: The touch of nature. Toy trees, ruffling in artificial winds . . . It all looked, now, like the model he had presented to the Senators. About as real and lifelike.

Austin moved like a carefully carved and painted figurine, incredibly small and lonely-looking on the empty walkway. He thought about the years of preparation; the endless red tape and paper work that had preceded the actual job. Then of the natives, how they had protested and petitioned to influence the Five-Power governments and how that had slowed them down. The problem of money, whipped only by pounding at the point of overpopulation, again and again, never letting up for a moment. The problems, problems . . .

He could not recall when the work itself had actually begun—it was all so joined. Laying the first railroad could certainly not have been a particle as beset with difficulty. Because the tribes of the Kenya territory numbered into the millions; and they were all filled with hatred and fury, opposing the city at every turn.

No explanation had satisfied them. They saw it as the destruction of their world and so they fought. With guns and spears and arrows and darts, with every resource at their disposal, refusing to capitulate, hunting like an army of mad ants scattered over the land.

And, since they could not be controlled, they had to be destroyed. Like their forests and rivers and mountains, destroyed, to make room for the city.

Though not, Austin remembered grimly, without loss. The white men had fine weapons, but none more fatal than machetes biting deep into neck flesh or sharp wooden shafts coated with strange poisons. And they did not all escape. Some would wander too far, unused to this green world where a white man could become hopelessly lost within three minutes. Others would forget their weapons. And a few were too brave.

Austin thought of Joseph Fava, the engineer, who had been reported missing. And of how Fava had come running back to the camp after two days, running and screaming, a bright crimson nearly dead creature out of the worst dreams. He had been cleanly stripped of all his skin, except for the face, hands, and feet . . .

But, the city had grown, implacably, spreading its concrete and alloy fingers wider every day over the dark and feral country. Nothing could stop it. Mountains were stamped flat. Rivers were damned off or drained or put elsewhere. The marshes were filled. The animals shot from the trees and then the trees cut down. And the big gray machines moved forward, gobbling up the jungle with their iron teeth, chewing it clean of its life and all its living things.

Until it was no more.

Leveled, smoothed as a highway is smoothed, its centuries choked beneath millions and millions of tons of hardened stone.

The birth of a city . . . It had become the death of a world.

And Richard Austin was its murderer.

As he traveled, he thought of the shaman, the half-naked toothless Bantu medicine man who had spoken for most of the tribes. *"You have killed us, and we could not stop you. So now we will wait, until you have made our city and others come to live here. Then YOU will know what it is to die."* Bokawah, who lived in superstition and fear, whom civilization had passed, along with the rest of his people. Who never spoke again after those words, and allowed himself to be moved to the wide iron plateau that had been built for the surviving natives.

Bokawah, the ignorant shaman, with his eternal smile . . . How distinct that smile was now!

The walkway shuddered, suddenly, and jarred to a noisy grinding stop. Austin pitched forward and grasped the railing in order to break his fall.

Awareness of the silence came first. The eerie dead silence that hung like a pall. It meant that the central machines had ceased functioning. They had been designed to operate automatically and perpetually; it was unthinkable that these power sources could break down!

As unthinkable as the drums that murmured to life again beyond the stainless towers, so loud now in the silence, so real.

Austin gripped his pistol tightly and shook away the panic that had bubbled up like acid in his chest. It was merely that the power had gone off. Strike out impossible, insert improbable. Improbabilities happen. The evil spirits do not summon them, they *happen*. Like strange diseases.

I am fighting, he thought, *a statistical paradox. That's all. A storage pike of coincidences. If I wait*—he walked close to the sides of the buildings—*and fight, the graph will change. The curve will* . . .

The drums roared out a wave of scattered sound, stopped, began again . . .

He thought a bit further of charts; then the picture of Mag materialized, blocking out the thick ink lines, ascending and descending on their giant graphs.

Thinking wasn't going to help . . .

He walked on.

Presently, at the end of a curve in the city maze, the "village" came into view, suspended overhead like a gigantic jeweled spider. It thrust out cold light. It was silent.

Austin breathed deeply. By belt, his destination was only minutes away. But the minutes grew as he walked through the city, and when he had reached the lift, hot pains wrenched at his muscles. He stood by the crystal platform, working action back into numbed limbs.

Then he remembered the silence, the dead machines. If they were not functioning, then the elevator—

His finger touched a button, experimentally.

A glass door slid open with a pneumatic hiss.

He walked inside, and tried not to think as the door closed and the bullet-shaped lift began to rise.

Below, Mbarara grew small. The treated metals glowed in a dimming lace of light. And the city looked even more like the little clay model he had built with his hands.

At last, movement ceased. Austin waited for the door to slide open again, then he strode out onto the smooth floor.

It was very dark. The artificial torches did not even smolder; their stubs, he noticed, were blackened and cold.

But the gates to the village lay open.

He looked past the entrance into the frozen shadows.

He heard the drums, throbbing from within, loud and distinct. But—ordinary drums, whose sound-waves would dissipate before ever reaching the city below.

He walked into the village.

The huts like glass blisters on smooth flesh, sat silent. Somehow, they were obscene in the dark, to Austin. Built to incorporate the feel and the atmosphere of their originals and yet to include the civilized conveniences; planned from an artistic as well as a scientific standpoint—they were suddenly obscene.

Perhaps, Austin thought, as he walked, perhaps there was something to what Barney had been saying . . . No— these people had elected to stay of their own free will. It would have been impossible to duplicate *exactly* the monstrous conditions under which they had lived. If not impossible, certainly wrong.

Let them wallow in their backward filth? In their disease and corruption, let them die—merely because their culture had failed to absorb scientific progress? No. You do not permit a man to leap off the top of a hundred-story building just because he has been trained to believe it is the only way to get to the ground floor—even though you insult him and blaspheme against his gods through your intervention. You restrain him, at any cost. Then, much later, you show him the elevator. And because he is a man, with a brain no smaller than yours, he will understand. He will understand that a crushed superstition is better than a crushed head. And he will thank you, eventually.

That is logic.

Austin walked, letting these thoughts form a thick crust. He felt the slap of the pistol against his thigh and this, also, was comforting.

Where were they now? Inside the huts, asleep? All of them? Or had they, too, contracted the disease and begun to die of it? . . .

Far ahead, at the clearing which represented the tip of the design, a glow of light appeared. As he approached, the drums grew louder, and other sounds—voices. How many voices? The air was at once murmurous and alive.

He stopped before the clearing and leaned on the darkness and watched.

Nearby a young woman was dancing. Her eyes were closed, tightly, and her arms were straight at her sides like black roots. She was in a state of possession, dancing in rhythm to the nearest drum. Her feet moved so fast they had become a blur, and her naked body wore a slick coat of perspiration.

Beyond the dancing woman, Austin could see the crowd, squatted and standing, swaying; over a thousand of them—surely every native in the village!

A clot of brown skin and bright white paint and brilliant feathers, hunched in the firelight.

An inner line of men sat over drums and hollow logs, beating these with their palms and with short sticks of

wood. The sounds blended strangely into one—the one
Austin had been hearing, it seemed, all his life.

He watched, fascinated, even though he had witnessed
Bantu ceremonies countless times in the past, even though
he was perfectly familiar with the symbols. The little leather
bags of hex-magic: nail-filings, photographs, specks of flesh;
the rubbing boards stained with fruit-skins; the piles of
bones at the feet of the men—old bones, very brittle and
dry and old.

Then he looked beyond the natives to the sensible clean
crystal walls that rose majestically, cupping the area, giving
it form.

It sent a chill over him.

He walked into the open.

The throng quieted, instantly, like a scream cut off. The
dancers caught their balance, blinked, drew in breath. The
others lifted their heads, stared.

All were turned to dark, unmoving wax.

Austin went past the gauntlet of eyes, to one of the painted
men.

"Where is Bokawah?" he said loudly, in precise Swahili.
His voice regained its accustomed authority. "Bokawah.
Take me to him."

No one moved. Hands lay on the air inches above drums,
petrified.

"I have come to talk!"

From the corner of his eyes, Austin felt the slight dis-
turbance. He waited a moment, then turned.

A figure crouched beside him. A man, unbelievably old
and tiny, sharp little bones jutting into loose flesh like pins,
skin cross-hatched with a pattern of white paint, chalky as
the substance some widows of the tribes wore for a year
after the death of their mates. His mouth was pulled into
a shape not quite a smile, but resembling a smile. It revealed hardened toothless gums.

The old man laughed, suddenly. The amulet around his chicken-neck bobbled. Then he stopped laughing and stared at Austin.

"We have been waiting," he said, softly. Austin started at the perfect English. He had not heard English for a long time; and now, coming from the little man . . . Perhaps Bokawah had learned it. Why not? "Walk with me, Mr. Austin."

He followed the ancient shaman, dumbly, not having the slightest idea why he was doing so, to a square of moist soil. It was surrounded by natives.

Bokawah looked once at Austin, then reached down and dipped his hands into the soil. The horny fingers scratched away the top-dirt, burrowed in like thin, nervous animals, and emerged, finally, holding something.

Austin gasped. It was a doll.

It was Mag.

He wanted to laugh, but it caught in his throat. He knew how primitives would try to inflict evil upon an enemy by burying his effigy. As the effigy rotted symbolically, so would . . .

He snatched the doll away from the old man. It crumbled in his hands.

"Mr. Austin," Bokawah said, "I'm very sorry you did not come for this talk long ago." The old man's lips did not move. The voice was his and yet not his.

Austin knew, suddenly, that he had not come to this place of his own accord. He had been summoned.

The old man held a hyena's tail in his right hand. He waved this and a slight wind seemed to come up, throwing the flames of the fire into a neurotic dance.

"You are not convinced, even now, Mr. Austin. Aiii. You have seen suffering and death, but you are not convinced." Bokawah sighed. "I will try one last time." He squatted on the smooth floor. "When you first came to our country, and spoke your plans, I told you—even then—

what must happen. I told you that this city must not be. I told you that my people would fight, as *your* people would fight if *we* were to come to your land and build jungles. But you understood nothing of what I said." He did not accuse; the voice was expressionless. "Now Mbarara lies silent and dead beneath you and still you do not wish to understand. What must we do, Mr. Austin? How shall we go about proving to you that this Mbarara of yours will *always* be silent and dead, that your people will never walk through it?"

Austin thought of his old college friend Barney—and of what Barney had once told him. Staring at Bokawah, at this scrawny, painted savage, he saw the big Texan clearly and he remembered his wild undergraduate theories— exhuming the antique view of primitives and their religions, their magics.

"Go on, pal, laugh at their tabus," Barney, who was an anthropologist, used to be fond of saying, *"sneer, while you throw salt over your shoulder. Laugh at their manas, while you blab about our own 'geniuses'!"*

He had even gone beyond the point of believing that magic was important because it held together the fabric of culture among these natives, because it—and their religious superstitions—gave them a rule for behavior, therefore, in most cases, happiness. He had even come to believe that native magic was just another method of arriving at physical truths.

Of course, it was all semantic nonsense. It suggested that primitive magic could lift a ship into space or destroy disease or . . .

That had been the trouble with Barney. You could never tell when he was serious. Even a social anthropologist wouldn't go so far as to think there was more than one law of gravity.

"Mr. Austin, we have brought you here for a purpose. Do you know what that purpose is?"

"I don't know and I don't—"

"Have you wondered why you, alone, of all your people, have been spared? Then—listen to me, very carefully. Because if you do not, then what has happened in your new city is merely the beginning. The winds of death will blow over Mbarara and it will be far more awful than what has been." The medicine man stared down at the scattered piles of bones. Panther bones, Austin knew—a divination device. Their position on the ground told Bokawah much about the white people.

"Go back to your chiefs. Tell them that they must forget this city. Tell them that death walks here and that it will always walk, and that their magic is powerful but not powerful enough. It cannot stand against the spirits from time who have been summoned to fight. Go and talk to your chiefs and tell them these things. Make them believe you. *Force* them to understand that if they come to Mbarara, they will die, in ways they never dreamed, of sickness, in pain, slowly. Forever."

The old man's eyes were closed. His mouth did not move at all and the voice was mechanical.

"Tell them, Mr. Austin, that at first you thought it was a strange new disease that struck the workers. But then remind them that your greatest doctors were powerless against the contagion, that it spread and was not conquered. Say these things. And, perhaps, they will believe you. And be saved."

Bokawah studied the panther bones carefully, tracing their arrangement.

Austin's voice was mechanical, also. "You are forgetting something," he said. He refused to let the thoughts creep in. He refused to wonder about the voice that came through closed lips, about where the natives could have found soil or fresh panther bones or . . . "No one," he said to the old man, "has fought back—yet."

"But why would you do that, Mr. Austin, since you do

not believe in the existence of your enemy? Whom shall you fight?" Bokawah smiled.

The crowd of natives remained quiet, unmoving, in the dying firelight.

"The only fear you hold for us," Austin said, "is the fear that you may prove psychologically harmful." He looked at the crushed doll at his feet. The face was whole; otherwise, it lay hideously disfigured.

"Yes?"

"Right now, Bokawah, my government is sending men. They will arrive soon. When they do, they will study what has happened. If it is agreed that your rites—however harmless in themselves—cause currents of fear—are in *any way* responsible for the disease—you will be given the opportunity to go elsewhere or—"

"Or, Mr. Austin?"

"—you will be eliminated."

"Then people will come to Mbarara. Despite the warnings and the death, they will come?"

"Your magic sticks aren't going to scare away five hundred thousand men and women."

"Five hundred thousand . . ." The old man looked at the bones, sighed, nodded his head. "You know your people very well," he murmured.

Austin smiled. "Yes, I do."

"Then I think there is little left for us to talk about."

Austin wanted to say, No, you're wrong. We must talk about Mag! She's dying and I want to keep her from dying. But he knew what these words would mean. They would sketch his real feelings, his fears and doubts. And everything would be lost. He could not admit that the doll was anything more than a doll. He must not!

The old man picked up a calabash and ran water over his hands. "I am sorry," he said, "that you must learn the way you must."

A slow chant rose from the natives. It sounded to Austin

like Swahili, yet it was indistinct. He could recognize none of the words, except *gonga* and *bagana*. Medicine? The man with the medicine? It was a litany, not unlike the Gregorian chants he had once heard, full of overpowering melancholy. Calm and ethereal, and sad as only the human voice can be sad. It rode on the stale air, swelling, diminishing, cutting through the stench of decay and rot with profound dignity.

Austin felt the heaviness of his clothes. The broken machines had stopped pumping fresh breezes, so the air was like oil, opening the pores of his body, running coldly down his arms and legs.

Bokawah made a motion with his hand and sank back onto the smooth floor. He breathed wrackingly, and groaned as if in pain. Then he straightened and looked at Austin and hobbled quickly away.

The drums began. Movement eased back into the throng and soon the dancers were up, working themselves back into their possessed states.

Austin turned and walked quickly away from the ceremony. When he reached the shadows, he ran. He did not stop running until he had reached the lift, even while his muscles, long dormant, unaccustomed to the activity, turned to stone, numb and throbbing stone.

He stabbed the button and closed his eyes, while his heart pumped and roared sound into his ears and colored fire into his mind. The platform descended slowly, unemotional and calm as its parts.

Austin ran out and fell against a building, where he tried to push away the image of the black magic ceremony, and what he had felt there.

He swallowed needles of pain into his parched throat.

And the fear mounted and mounted, strangling him slowly . . .

* * *

The towers of Mbarara loomed, suddenly, to Austin, more unreal and anachronistic than the tribal rites from which he had just come. Stalagmites of crystal pushing up to the night sky that bent above them; little squares and diamonds and circles of metal and stone. Office buildings; apartments; housing units; hat stores and machine factories and restaurants; and, cobwebbing among them, all these blind and empty shells, the walkways, like colored ribbons, like infinitely long reptiles, sleeping now, dead, still.

Or, were they only waiting, as he wanted to believe?

Of course they're waiting, he thought. People who know the answers will come to Mbarara tomorrow. Clear-headed scientists who have not been terrorized by a tribe of beaten primitives. And the scientists will find out what killed the workers, correct it, and people will follow. Five hundred thousand people, from all over the closet-crowded world, happy to have air to breathe once more—air that hasn't had to travel down two-hundred feet—happy to know the Earth can yet sustain them. No more talk, then, of "population decreases"—murder was a better word—; no more government warnings screaming "depopulation" at you . . .

The dream would come true, Austin told himself. Because it must. Because he'd promised Mag, and they'd lived it all together, endless years, hoped and planned and fought for the city. With Mbarara, it would begin: the dark age of a sardine can world would end, and life would begin. It would be many years before the worry would begin all over—for half the earth lay fallow, wasted. Australia, Greenland, Iceland, Africa, the Poles . . . And perhaps then the population graph would change, as it had always changed before. And men would come out of their caverns and rat-holes and live as men.

Yes. But only if Mbarara worked. If he could show them his success here . . .

Austin cursed the men who had gone back and screamed the story of what had happened to the other engineers.

God knew there were few enough available, few who had been odd enough to study a field for which there seemed little further use.

If they'd only kept still about the disease! Then others would have come and . . .

Died. The word came out instantly, uncalled, and vanished.

Austin passed the Emperor, the playhouse he had thought of that night with Mag, ten years before. As he passed, he tried to visualize the foyer jammed with people in soup-and-fish and jeweled gowns, talking of whether the play had meat or not. Now, its marbled front putting out yellow glow, it looked foolish and pathetic. The placard case shone through newly gathered dust, empty.

Austin tried to think of what had been on this spot originally. Thick jungle growth alone. Or had there been a native village—with monkeys climbing the trees and swinging on vines and white widows mourning under straw roofs?

Now playing: JULIUS CAESAR. Admission: Three coconuts.

Be still. You've stayed together all this time, he thought, you can hold out until tomorrow. Tcheletchew will be here, sputtering under his beard, and they'll fly Mag to a hospital and make her well and clear up this nonsense in a hurry.

Just get home. Don't think and get home, and it will be all right.

The city was actually without formal streets. Its plan did not include the antiquated groundcars that survived here and there in old families. Therefore, Mbarara was literally a maze. A very pretty maze. Like an English estate—Austin had admired these touches of vanished gentility—the areas were sometimes framed by green stone hedges, carved into functional shapes.

He had no difficulty finding his way. It was all too fresh, even now, the hours of planning every small curve and design, carefully leaving no artistic 'holes' or useless places. He could have walked it blindfolded.

But when he passed the food dispensary and turned the corner, he found that it did not lead to the 'copter-park, as it should have. There were buildings there, but they were not the ones they ought to have been.

Or else he'd turned the wrong—He retraced his steps to the point where he had gone left. The food dispensary was nowhere in sight. Instead he found himself looking at the general chemistry building.

Austin paused and wiped his forehead. The excitement of course. It had clouded his mind for a moment, making him lose his way.

He began walking. Warm perspiration coursed across his body, turning his suit dark-wet, staining his jacket.

He passed the food dispensary.

Austin clenched his fists. It was impossible that he could have made a complete circle. He had built this city, he knew it intimately. He had walked through it without even thinking of direction, in the half-stages of construction, and never taken a wrong step.

How could he be lost?

Nerves. Nothing strange in it. Certainly enough had happened to jar loose his sense of direction.

Calmly, now. Calmly.

The air hung fetid and heavy. He had to pull it into his lungs, push it out. Of course, he could go below and open the valves—at least *they* could be operated by hand. He could, but why? It would mean hunching down in a dark shaft—damn, should have made that shaft larger! And, there were, after all, enough openings in the sealing-bubble to keep a breathable flow of oxygen in circulation. If the air was heavy and still outside the bubble, he could scarcely expect it to be different within . . .

He looked up at the half-minaretted tower that was one

of the 'copter repair centers. It was located in exactly the
opposite direction to the one he thought he'd taken.

Austin sank onto a stone bench. Images floated through
his mind. He was lost; precisely as lost as if he had wandered into the jungle that had stood here before the building of Mbarara, and then tried to find his way back.

He closed his eyes and saw a picture, startling clear, of
himself, running through the matted growths of dark green
foliage, stumbling across roots, bumping trees, face grotesque with fear, and screaming . . .

He opened his eyes quickly, shook away the vision. His
brain was tired; that was why he saw such a picture. He
must keep his eyes open.

The city was unchanged. The park, designed for house-
wives who might wish to pause and rest or chat, perhaps
feed squirrels, surrounded him.

Across the boating lake was the university.

Behind the university was home.

Austin rose, weakly, and made his way down the grassy
slope to the edge of the artificial lake. Cultured city trees
dotted the banks: the lake threw back a geometrically perfect reflection.

He knelt and splashed water onto his face. Then he
gulped some of it down and paused until the ripples spread
to the center of the lake.

He studied his image in the water carefully. White skin,
smooth cheeks, iron-colored hair. Good clothes. A dolicho-
cephalic head, evenly spaced, the head of a twenty-second
century civilized . . .

Above his reflection, Austin detected movement. He
froze and blinked his eyes. As the water smoothed, the
image of an animal appeared on the surface, wavering
slightly. A small animal, something like a monkey. Like a
monkey hanging from the branches of a tree.

Austin whirled around.

There was only the darkness, the golfing-green lawn, the cultured trees—smooth-barked, empty.

He passed a hand through his hair. It was a trick of the lights. His subconscious fear, the shimmering water . . .

He walked quickly to the darkened boathouse, across its floor, his footsteps ringing against the stone, echoing loudly.

At the end of the miniature pier, he untied a small battery boat and jumped into it. He pulled a switch at the side, waited, forced himself to look back at the deserted bank.

The boat moved slowly, with only a whisper of sound, through the water.

Hurry, Austin thought. *Hurry—Oh God, why are they so slow!*

The boat, whose tin flag proclaimed its name to be Lucy, sliced the calm lake with its toy prow, and, after many minutes, reached the center.

The glow was insufficient to make the approaching bank distinct. It lay wrapped in darkness, a darkness that hid even the buildings.

Austin narrowed his eyes and stared. He blinked. It was the fuzziness of the luminescence, of course, that gave movement to the bank. That made it seem to seethe with unseen life.

It was only that his position to the shadows kept changing that made them turn into dark and feral shapes; trees, where buildings surely were, dense growth . . .

It was the milky phosphorescence of the metals that rose like marsh-steam from the nearing water . . .

He closed his eyes and gripped the sides of the boat.

There was a scraping. Austin felt the cement guard, sighed, switched off the battery and leapt from the little boat.

There was no jungle. Only the lime-colored city trees and the smooth lawn.

The university sat ahead like a string of dropped pearls; blister-shaped, connected by elevated tunnels, twisting, delicate strands of metal and alloy.

Austin scrambled up the embankment. It must be very late now. Perhaps nearly morning. In a few hours, the others would arrive. And—

He halted, every muscle straining.

He listened.

There were the drums. But not only the drums, now.

Other sounds.

He closed his eyes. The airless night pressed against him. He heard a rustling noise. Like something traveling through dense brush. He heard, far away, tiny sounds, whistlings, chitterings. Like monkeys and birds.

He tore open his eyes. Only the park, the city.

He went on. Now his feet were on stone and the park was behind him. He walked through the canyons of the city again, the high buildings, metal and crystal and alloy and stone.

The rustling noises did not cease, however. They were behind him, growing nearer. Bodies, moving through leaves and tall grass.

Austin suddenly remembered where he'd heard the sound before. Years ago, when he'd first visited this land. They had taken him on a hunting expedition, deep into the wild country. They were going to bag something—he forgot exactly what. Something strange. Yes; it was a wild pig. They had walked all day, searching, through the high tan grass, and then they had heard the rustling sounds.

Exactly like the sound he heard now.

Austin recalled the unbelievable fury of the boar, how it had disemboweled two dogs with a couple of swipes of those razor-sharp fangs. He recalled clearly the angry black snout, curled over yellow teeth.

He turned and stared into the darkness. The noises grew

steadily louder, and were broken by yet another sound. Deep and guttural, like a cough.

As the sound behind him came closer, he ran, stumbled and fell, pulled himself from the stone, and ran until he had reached a flight of steps.

The coughing noise was a fast, high-pitched scream now, grunting, snorting, a rush of tiny feet galloping across tamped earth, through dry grass. Austin stared blindly, covered his face with his arms and sank back until the sound was almost upon him.

His nostrils quivered at the animal smell.

His breath stopped.

He waited.

It was gone. Fading in the distance, the rustling, the coughing, and then there was the silence of the drums again.

Austin pressed the bones of his wrist into his throbbing skull to quiet the ache.

The panic drained off slowly. He rose, climbed the steps and walked through the shadowed courtyard onto the campus.

It was a vast green plain, smooth and grassy.

Across from it, in sight, was Austin's home.

He gathered his reason about him like a shield, and decided against taking the other routes. If he had gotten lost before, it could happen again. Certainly now, with his imagination running wild.

He must cross the campus.

Then it would be all right.

He began treading, timorously at first, listening with every square inch of his body.

The shaman's voice slithered into his mind. Chanting ". . . *you were destroying us against our will, Mr. Austin. Our world, our life. And such is your mind, and the mind of so-called 'civilized' men, that you could not see this was wrong. You have developed a culture and a social structure that pleased you, you were convinced that it was right; therefore, you could-*

not understand the existence of any that differed. You saw us as ignorant savages—most of you did—and you were anxious to 'civilize' us. Not once did it occur to you that we, too, had our culture and our social structure; that we knew right and wrong; that, perhaps, we might look upon you as backward and uncivilized . . ."

The sound of birds came to Austin; birds calling in high trees, circling impossibly in the night sky.

". . . we have clung to our 'magic,' as you call it, and our 'superstitions' for longer than you have clung to yours. Because—as with your own—they have worked for us. Whether magic can be explained in Roman numerals or not, what is the difference, so long as it works? Mr. Austin, there is not only one path to the Golden City—there are many. Your people are on one path—"

He heard the chatter of monkeys, some close, some far away, the sound of them swinging on vines, scolding, dropping to mounds of foliage, scrambling up other trees.

"—my people are on another. There is room in this world for both ways. But your failure to grasp this simple fact has killed many of us and it will kill many more of you. For we have been on our path longer. We are closer to the Golden City . . ."

Austin clapped his hands to his ears. But he did not stop walking.

From the smooth stone streets, from the direction of the physics department, came the insane trumpeting of elephants, their immense bulks crashing against brittle bark, their huge feet crunching fallen limbs and branches . . .

The shaman's voice became the voice of Barney Chadfield . . . He spoke again of his theory that if one could only discover the unwritten bases of black magic and apply formulae to them, we could find that they were merely another form of science . . . perhaps less advanced, perhaps more.

The sounds picked up, and the feelings, and the sensa-

tions. Eyes firmly open, Austin thought of Mag and felt
needled leaves slap invisibly against his legs; he smelled the
rot and the life, the heavy, wild air of the jungle, like animal steam; the odors of fresh blood and wet fur and decaying plants; the short rasping breath of a million different
animals—the movement, all around him, the approaches,
the retreats, the frenzied unseen . . .

Eyes open he felt and smelled and heard all these things;
and saw only the city.

A pain shot through his right arm. He tried to move it:
it would not move. He thought of an old man. The old
man had a doll. The old man was crushing the doll's arm,
and laughing . . . He thought of reflexes and the reaction
of reflexes to emotional stimuli.

He walked, ignoring the pain, not thinking about the
arm at all.

". . . tell them, Mr. Austin. Make them believe. Make them
believe . . . Do not kill all these people . . ."

When he passed the Law College, he felt a pain wrench
at his leg. He heard another dry-grass rustle. But not behind him: in front. Going forward.

Going toward his apartment.

Austin broke into a run, without knowing exactly why.

There was a pounding, a panting at his heels: vaguely he
was aware of this. He knew only that he must get inside,
quickly, to the sanity of his home. Jaws snapped, clacked.
Austin stumbled on a vine, his fingers pulled at air, he leapt
away and heard the sound of something landing where he
had just been, something that screamed and hissed.

He ran on. At the steps, his foot pressed onto something
soft. It recoiled madly. He slipped and fell again, and the
feel of moist beaded skin whipped about his legs. The thunder was almost directly above. He reached out, clawed loose
the thing around his leg and pulled him forward.

There was a swarming over his hands. He held them in-front of his eyes, tried to see the ants that had to be there, slapped the invisible creatures loose.

The apartment door was only a few feet away now. Austin remembered his pistol, drew it out and fired it into the night until there were no more bullets left.

He pulled himself into the lobby of the unit.

The door hissed closed.

He touched the lock, heard it spring together.

And then the noises ceased. The drums and the animals, all the wild nightmare things—ceased to be. There was his breathing, and the pain that laced through his arm and leg.

He waited, trembling, trying to pull breath in.

Finally he rose and limped to the elevator. He did not even think about the broken machines. He knew it would work.

It did. The glass doors whirred apart at his floor, and he went into the hall.

It was soundless.

He stood by the door, listening to his heart rattle crazily in his chest.

He opened the door.

The apartment was calm, silent. The walls glowed around the framed Mirós and Mondrians and Picassos. The furniture sat functionally on the silky white rug, black thin-legged chairs and tables . . .

Austin started to laugh, carefully checked himself. He knew he probably would not be able to stop.

He thought strongly about Tcheletchew, and the men who would come to Mbarara in the morning. He thought of the city teeming with life. Of the daylight screaming onto the streets of people, the shops, the churches, the schools. His work. His dream . . .

He walked across the rug to the bedroom door.

It was slightly ajar.

He pushed it, went inside, closed it softly.

"Mag," he whispered. "Mag—"

There was a noise. A low, throaty rumble. Not of anger; of warning.

Richard Austin came close to the bed, adjusted his eyes to the black light.

Then he screamed.

It was the first time he had ever watched a lion feeding.

THE NEW PEOPLE

Introduction by Saul David

It was when I was re-reading the story that it came back to me. Not the story itself—I remembered that in a vague way as soon as the title was suggested—but Chuck's barely suppressed snicker when I reacted to the name of one of the main characters, Matt Dystal. Dystel, Oscar Dystel, was the name of the then new president of Bantam Books. The businessmen who head publishing companies often don't have editorial backgrounds and they're sometimes suspicious of the artistic airs and graces of editors and the lunatics who actually write the damn books. Publishers would often say, not quite joking, "This would be a good business if it wasn't for editors and writers." And since Dystel had inherited me along with a lot of editors and writers, he looked hard at every lifted eyebrow.

"Don't you think he should feel honored?" asked Chuck. I said "He may never read it. But if he does, he'll be sure it's an inside joke."

"Okay—you want to change the name?"

If I said yes, Chuck would have something funny to tell the guys who met in his cellar to swap ideas. I had my own image to keep up. So I said, "forget it."

"Tell you what," Chuck said magnanimously, "spell it different."

That's why it's spelled with an "a" where the other man is spelled with an "e".

One of the things I remember best is that playfulness. As a tribe, sci-fi and fantasy writers tend toward solemnity—at least in public. Probably it comes from reading all those deep-dish critical pieces about far-sightedness and prophecy. When someone tells you that your stories have deep significance and look forward down the corridors of time, it's hard to deny. Look at Ron Hubbard. But Chuck was not that kind of True Believer. He played with ideas and enjoyed the play. That accounts for the sparkle you find in the grimmest of them.

In publishing jargon, these stories—all sci-fi, fantasy, etc. were called "category fiction" and, in literary status, sat below the salt. To escape from his caste was not easy for a writer. He had to break an invisible quality barrier—out of the category ghetto and into hard covers and slick magazines; into the company of Roald Dahl and John Cheever and Saki. Chuck used to speculate about that barrier—was it really literary quality?

The results of his musings are evident in the stories. In most of them there's an effort to add a bit of dimension to the people— very difficult in the kind of story in which the idea, the event, the surprise ending is what makes the sale and the memory. In "The New People," Prentice casts a shadow, he is almost real enough to make the reader wonder if he could have escaped—gotten off the story's rails. Could he have done so? Of course not—but it's a measure of the writer's reach that the question comes up at all. Chuck died tragically young with his reach still far beyond his grasp—a great loss.

IF ONLY HE had told her right at the beginning that he didn't like the house, everything would have been fine. He could have manufactured some plausible story about bad plumbing or poor construction—something; anything!—and she'd have gone along with him. Not without a fight, maybe: he could remember the way her face had looked when they stopped the car. But he could have talked her out of it. Now, of course, it was too late.

For what? he wondered, trying not to think of the party and all the noise that it would mean. Too late for what? It's a good house, well built, well kept up, roomy. Except for that blood stain, cheerful. Anyone in his right mind . . .

"Dear, aren't you going to shave?"

He lowered the newspaper gently and said, "Sure." But Ann was looking at him in that hurt, accusing way, and he knew that it was hopeless.

Hank-what's-wrong, he thought, starting toward the bathroom.

"Hank," she said.

He stopped but did not turn. "Uh-huh?"

"What's wrong?"

"Nothing," he said.

"Honey. Please."

He faced her. The pink chiffon dress clung to her body, which had the firmness of youth; her face was unblemished, the lipstick and powder incredibly perfect; her hair, cut long, was soft on her white shoulders: in seven years Ann hadn't changed.

Resentfully, Prentice glanced away. And was ashamed. You'd think that in this time I'd get accustomed to it, he thought. *She* is. Damn it!

"Tell me," Ann said.

"Tell you what? Everything is okay," he said.

She came to him and he could smell the perfume, he could see the tiny freckles that dotted her chest. He wondered what it would be like to sleep with her. Probably it would be very nice.

"It's about Davey, isn't it?" she said, dropping her voice

to a whisper. They were standing only a few feet from their son's room.

"No," Prentice said; but it was true—Davey was part of it. For a week now Prentice had ridden on the hope that getting the locomotive repaired would change things. A kid without a train, he'd told himself, is bound to act peculiar. But he'd had the locomotive repaired and brought it home and Davey hadn't even bothered to set up the track.

"He appreciated it, dear," Ann said. "Didn't he thank you?"

"Sure, he thanked me."

"Well?" she said. "Honey, I've *told* you: Davey is going through a period, that's all. Children do. Really."

"I know."

"And school's been out for almost a month."

"I know," Prentice said, and thought: *Moving to a neighborhood where there isn't another kid in the whole damn block for him to play with, that might have something to do with it, too!*

"Then," Ann said, "it's me."

"No, no, no." He tried to smile. There wasn't any sense in arguing: they'd been through it a dozen times, and she had an answer for everything. He could recall the finality in her voice . . . "I love the house, Hank. And I love the neighborhood. It's what I've dreamed of all my life, and I think I deserve it. Don't you?" (It was the first time she'd ever consciously reminded him). "The trouble is, you've lived in dingy little apartments so long you've come to *like* them. You can't adjust to a really *decent* place—and Davey's no different. You're two of a kind: little old men who can't stand a change, even for the better! Well, I can. I don't care if *fifty* people committed suicide here, I'm happy. You understand, Hank? Happy."

Prentice had understood, and had resolved to make a real effort to like the new place. If he couldn't do that, at least he could keep his feelings from Anne—for they were, he knew, foolish. Damned foolish. Everything she said was true, and he ought to be grateful.

Yet, somehow, he could not stop dreaming of the old man who had picked up a razor one night and cut his throat wide open . . .

Ann was staring at him.

"Maybe," he said, "I'm going through a period, too." He kissed her forehead, lightly. "Come on, now; the people are going to arrive any second, and you look like Lady Macbeth."

She held his arm for a moment. "You are getting settled in the house, aren't you?" she said. "I mean, it's becoming more like home to you, isn't it?"

"Sure," Prentice said.

His wife paused another moment, then smiled. "Okay, get the whiskers off. Rhoda is under the impression you're a handsome man."

He walked into the bathroom and plugged in the electric shaver. Rhoda, he thought. First names already and we haven't been here three weeks.

"Dad?"

He looked down at Davey, who had slipped in with nine-year-old stealth. "Yo." According to ritual, he ran the shaver across his son's chin.

Davey did not respond. He stepped back and said, "Dad, is Mr. Ames coming over tonight?"

Prentice nodded. "I guess so."

"And Mr. Chambers?"

"Uh-huh. Why?"

Davey did not answer.

"What do you want to know for?"

"Gee." Davey's eyes were red and wide. "Is it okay if I stay in my room?"

"Why? You sick?"

"No. Kind of."

"Stomach? Head?"

"Just sick," Davey said. He pulled at a thread in his shirt and fell silent again.

Prentice frowned. "I thought maybe you'd like to show them your train," he said.

"Please," Davey said. His voice had risen slightly and Prentice could see tears gathering. "Dad, please don't make me come out. Leave me stay in my room. I won't make any noise, I promise, and I'll go to sleep on time."

"Okay, okay. Don't make such a big deal out of it!" Prentice ran the cool metal over his face. Anger came and went, swiftly. Stupid to get mad. "Davey, what'd you do, ride your bike on their lawn or something? Break a window?"

"No."

"Then why don't you want to see them?"

"I just don't."

"Mr. Ames likes you. He told me so yesterday. He thinks you're a fine boy, so does Mr. Chambers. They—"

"*Please*, Dad!" Davey's face was pale; he began to cry. "Please, please, please. Don't let them get me!"

"What are you talking about? Davey, cut it out. Now!"

"I saw what they were doing there in the garage. And they know I saw them, too. They know. And—"

"Davey!" Ann's voice was sharp and loud and resounding in the tile-lined bathroom. The boy stopped crying immediately. He looked up, hesitated, then ran out. His door slammed.

Prentice took a step.

"No, Hank. Leave him alone."

"He's upset."

"Let him be upset." She shot an angry glance toward the bedroom. "I suppose he told you that filthy story about the garage?"

"No," Prentice said, "he didn't. What's it all about?"

"Nothing. Absolutely nothing. Honestly, I'd like to meet Davey's parents!"

"We're his parents," Prentice said, firmly.

"All right, all right. But he got that imagination of his from *somebody*, and it wasn't from us. You're going to have to speak to him, Hank. I mean it. Really."

"About what?"

"These wild stories. What if they got back to Mr. Ames? I'd—well, I'd die. After he's gone out of his way to be nice to Davey, too."

"I haven't heard the stories," Prentice said.

"Oh, you will," Ann undid her apron and folded it, furiously. "Honestly! Sometimes I think the two of you are trying to make things just as miserable as they can be for me."

The doorbell rang, stridently.

"Now make an effort to be pleasant, will you? This is a *house*warming, after all. And do hurry."

She closed the door. He heard her call, "Hi!" and heard Ben Roth's baritone booming: "Hi!"

Ridiculous, he told himself, plugging the razor in again. Utterly goddam ridiculous. No one complained louder than I did when we were tripping over ourselves in that little upstairs coffin on Friar. *I'm* the one who kept moaning for a house, not Ann.

So now we've got one.

He glanced at the tiny brownish blood stain that wouldn't wash out of the wallpaper, and sighed.

Now we've got one.

"Hank!"

"Coming!" He straightened his tie and went into the living room.

The Roths, of course, were there. Ben and Rhoda. Get it right, he thought, because we're all going to be pals. "Hi, Ben."

"Thought you'd deserted us, boy," said the large, pink man, laughing.

"No. Wouldn't do that."

"Hank," Ann signaled. "You've met Beth Cummings, haven't you?"

The tall, smartly dressed woman giggled and extended her hand. "We've seen each other," she said. "Hello."

Her husband, a pale man with white hair, crushed Prentice's fingers. "Fun and games," he said, tightening his grip and wheezing with amusement. "Yes, sir."

Trying not to wince, Prentice retrieved his hand. It was instantly snatched up by a square, bald man in a double-breasted brown suit. "Reiker," the man said. "Call me Bud. Everyone does. Don't know why; my name is Oscar."

"*That's* why," a woman said, stepping up. "Ann introduced us but you probably don't remember, if I know men. I'm Edna."

"Sure," Prentice said. "How are you?"

"Fine. But then, I'm a woman: I *like* parties!"

"How's that?"

"Hank!"

Prentice excused himself and walked quickly into the kitchen. Ann was holding up a package.

"Honey, look what Rhoda gave us!"

He dutifully handled the salt and pepper shakers and set them down again. "That's real nice."

"You turn the rooster's head," Mrs. Roth said, "and it grinds your pepper."

"Wonderful," Prentice said.

"And Beth gave us this lovely salad bowl, see? And we've needed *this* for *cen*turies!" She held out a gray tablecloth with gold bordering. "Plastic!"

"Wonderful," Prentice said. Again, the doorbell rang. He glanced at Mrs. Roth, who had been staring thoughtfully at him, and returned to the living room.

"How you be, Hank?" Lucian Ames walked in, rubbing his hands together briskly. "Well! The gang's all here, I see. But where's that boy of yours?"

"Davey? Oh," Prentice said, "he's sick."

"Nonsense! Boys that age are never sick. Never!"

Ann laughed nervously from the kitchen. "Just something he ate!"

"Not the candy we sent over, I hope."

"Oh, no."

"Well, tell him his Uncle Lucian said hello."

A tan elf of man, with sparkling eyes and an ill fitting mustache, Ames reminded Prentice somewhat of those clerks who used to sit silently on high wooden stools, posting infinitesimal figures in immense yellow ledgers. He was, however, the head of a nationally famous advertising agency.

His wife Charlotte provided a remarkable contrast. She seemed to belong to the era of the twenties, with her porcelain face, her thin, delicately angular body, her air of fragility.

Nice, Prentice told himself.

He removed coats and hung them in closets. He shook hands and smiled until his face began to ache. He looked at presents and thanked the women and told them they shouldn't have. He carried out sandwiches. He mixed drinks.

By eight-thirty, everyone in the block had arrived. The Johnsons, the Ameses, the Roths, the Reikers, the Klementaskis, the Chamberses; four or five others whose names Prentice could not remember, although Ann had taken care to introduce them.

What it is, he decided, looking at the people, at the gifts they had brought, remembering their many kindnesses and how, already, Ann had made more friends than she'd ever had before, is, I'm just an antisocial bastard.

After the third round of whiskeys and martinis, someone turned on the FM and someone else suggested dancing. Prentice had always supposed that one danced only at New Year's Eve parties, but he said the hell with it, finally, and tried to relax.

"Shall we?" Mrs. Ames said.

He wanted to say no, but Ann was watching. So he said, "Sure, if you've got strong toes," instead.

Almost at once he began to perspire. The smoke, the drinks, the heat of the crowded room, caused his head to ache; and, as usual, he was acutely embarrassed at having to hold a strange woman so closely.

But, he continued to smile.

Mrs. Ames danced well, she followed him with unerring instinct; and within moments she was babbling freely into his ear. She told him about old Mr. Thomas, the man who had lived here before, and how surprised everyone had been at what had happened; she told him how curious they'd all been about The New People and how relieved they were to find him and Ann so very nice; she told him he had strong arms. Ann was being twirled about by Herb Johnson. She was smiling.

An endless, slow three-step came on, then, and Mrs. Ames put her cheek next to Prentice's. In the midst of a rambling sentence, she said, suddenly, in a whisper: "You know, I think it was awfully brave of you to adopt little Davey. I mean considering."

"Considering what?"

She pulled away and looked at him. "Nothing," she said. "I'm awfully sorry."

Blushing with fury, Prentice turned and strode into the kitchen. He fought his anger, thinking, God, God, is she telling strangers about it now? Is it a topic for backfence gossip? *My husband is impotent, you know. Is yours?*

He poured whiskey into a glass and drank it, fast. It made his eyes water, and when he opened them, he saw a figure standing next to him.

It was—who? Dystal. Matthew Dystal; bachelor; movie writer or something; lives down the block. Call him Matt.

"Miserable, isn't it?" the man said, taking the bottle from Prentice's hand.

"What do you mean?"

"Everything," the man said. He filled his glass and drained it smartly. "Them. Out there." He filled the glass again.

"Nice people," Prentice forced himself to say.

"You think so?"

The man was drunk. Clearly, very drunk. And it was only nine-thirty.

"You think so?" he repeated.

"Sure. Don't you?"

"Of course. I'm one of them, aren't I?"

Prentice peered at his guest closely, then moved toward the living room.

Dystal took his arm. "Wait," he said. "Listen. You're a good guy. I don't know you very well, but I like you, Hank Prentice. So I'm going to give you some advice." His voice dropped to a whisper. "Get out of here," he said.

"What?"

"Just what I said. Move away, move away to another city."

Prentice felt a quick ripple of annoyance, checked it. "Why?" he asked, smiling.

"Never mind that," Dystal said. "Just do it. Tonight. Will you?" His face was livid, clammy with perspiration; his eyes were wide.

"Well, I mean, Matt, that's a heck of a thing to say. I thought you said you liked us. Now you want to get rid of us."

"Don't joke," Dystal said. He pointed at the window. "Can't you see the moon? You bloody idiot, can't you—"

"Hey, hey! Unfair!"

At the sound of the voice, Dystal froze. He closed his eyes for a moment and opened them, slowly. But he did not move.

Lucian Ames walked into the kitchen. "What's the story

here," he said, putting his arm on Dystal's shoulder, "you trying to monopolize our host all night?"

Dystal did not answer.

"How about a refill, Hank?" Ames said, removing his hand.

Prentice said, "Sure," and prepared the drink. From the corner of his eye, he saw Dystal turn and walk stiffly out of the room. He heard the front door open and close.

Ames was chuckling. "Poor old Matt," he said. "He'll be hung over tomorrow. It seems kind of a shame, doesn't it? I mean, you know, of all people, you'd think a big Hollywood writer would be able to hold his liquor. But not Matt. He gets loaded just by staring at labels."

Prentice said, "Huh."

"Was he giving you one of his screwball nightmares?"

"What? No—we were just sort of talking. About things."

Ames dropped an ice cube into his drink. "Things?" he said.

"Yeah."

Ames took a sip of the whiskey and walked to the window, looking lithe, somehow, as well as small. After what seemed a long time, he said, "Well, it's a fine night, isn't it. Nice and clear, nice fine moon." He turned and tapped a cigarette out of a red package, lighted the cigarette. "Hank," he said, letting the gray smoke gush from the corners of his mouth, "tell me something. What do you do for excitement?"

Prentice shrugged. It was an odd question, but then, everything seemed odd to him tonight. "I don't know," he said. "Go to a movie once in a while. Watch TV. The usual."

Ames cocked his head. "But—don't you get bored?" he asked.

"Sure, I guess. Every so often. Being a C.P.A. you know, that isn't exactly the world's most fascinating job."

Ames laughed sympathetically. "It's awful, isn't it?"

"Being a C.P.A.?"

"No. Being bored. It's about the worst thing in the world, don't you agree? Someone once remarked they thought it was the only real sin a human could commit."

"I hope not," Prentice said.

"Why?"

"Well, I mean—everybody gets bored, don't they?"

"Not," Ames said, "if they're careful."

Prentice found himself becoming increasingly irritated at the conversation. "I suppose it helps," he said, "if you're the head of an advertising agency."

"No, not really. It's like any other job: interesting at first, but then you get used to it. It becomes routine. So you go fishing for other diversions."

"Like what?"

"Oh . . . anything. Everything." Ames slapped Prentice's arm good naturedly. "You're all right, Hank," he said.

"Thanks."

"I mean it. Can't tell you how happy we all are that you moved here."

"No more than we are!" Ann walked unsteadily to the sink with a number of empty glasses. "I want to apologize for Davey again, Lucian. I was telling Charlotte, he's been a perfect beast lately. He should have thanked you for fixing the seat on his bike."

"Forget it," Ames said, cheerfully. "The boy's just upset because he doesn't have any playmates." He looked at Prentice. "Some of us elders have kids, Hank, but they're all practically grown. You probably know that our daughter, Ginnie, is away at college. And Chris and Beth's boy lives in New York. But, you know, I wouldn't worry. As soon as school starts, Davey'll straighten out. You watch."

Ann smiled. "I'm sure you're right, Lucian. But I apologize, anyway."

"Nuts." Ames returned to the living room and began to dance with Beth Cummings.

Prentice thought then of asking Ann what the devil she meant by blabbing about their personal life to strangers, but decided not to. This was not the time. He was too angry, too confused.

The party lasted another hour. Then Ben Roth said, "Better let these folks get some sleep!" and, slowly, the people left.

Ann closed the door. She seemed to glow with contentment, looking younger and prettier than she had for several years. "Home," she said, softly, and began picking up ash trays and glasses and plates. "Let's get all this out of the way so we won't have to look at it in the morning," she said.

Prentice said, "All right," in a neutral tone. He was about to move the coffee table back into place when the telephone rang.

"Yes?"

The voice that answered was a harsh whisper, like a rush of wind through leaves. "Prentice, are they gone?"

"Who is this?"

"Matt Dystal. Are they gone?"

"Yes."

"All of them? Ames? Is he gone?"

"Yes. What do you want, Dystal? It's late."

"Later than you might think, Prentice. He told you I was drunk, but he lied. I'm not drunk. I'm—"

"Look, what is it you want?"

"I've got to talk with you," the voice said. "Now. To-night. Can you come over?"

"At eleven o'clock?"

"Yes. Prentice, listen to me. I'm not drunk and I'm not kidding. This is a matter of life and death. Yours. Do you understand what I'm saying?"

Prentice hesitated, confused.

"You know where my place is—fourth house from the corner, right-hand side. Come over now. But listen, carefully: go out the back door. The back door, Prentice, are you listening?"

"Yes," Prentice said.

"My light will be off. Go around to the rear. Don't bother to knock, just walk in—but be quiet about it. They mustn't see you."

Prentice heard a click, then silence. He stared at the receiver for a while before replacing it.

"Well?" Ann said. "Man talk?"

"Not exactly." Prentice wiped his palms on his trousers. "That fellow Matt Dystal, he's apparently sick. Wants me to come over."

"Now?"

"Yeah. I think I better; he sounded pretty bad. You go on to sleep, I'll be back in a little while."

"Okay, honey. I hope it isn't anything serious. But, it *is* nice to be doing something for *them* for a change, isn't it?"

Prentice kissed his wife, waited until the bathroom door had closed; then he went outside, into the cold night.

He walked along the grass verge of the alleyway, across the small lawns, up the steps to Dystal's rear door.

He deliberated with himself for a moment, then walked in.

"Prentice?" a voice hissed.

"Yes. Where are you?"

A hand touched his arm in the darkness and he jumped, nervously. "Come into the bedroom."

A dim lamp went on. Prentice saw that the windows were covered by heavy tan drapes. It was chilly in the room, chilly and moist.

"Well?" Prentice said, irritably.

Matthew Dystal ran a hand through his rope-colored hair. "I know what you're thinking," he said. "And I don't blame you. But it was necessary, Prentice. It was necessary.

Ames has told you about my 'wild nightmares' and that's going to stick with you, I realize; but get this straight." His hand became a fist. "Everything I'm about to say is true. No matter how outlandish it may sound, it's *true*— and I have proof. All you'll need. So keep still, Prentice, and listen to me. It may mean your life: yours and your wife's and your boy's. And, maybe, mine . . ." His voice trailed off; then, suddenly, he said, "You want a drink?"

"No."

"You ought to have one. You're only on the outskirts of confusion, my friend. But, there are worse things than confusion. Believe me." Dystal walked to a bookcase and stood there for almost a full minute. When he turned, his features were slightly more composed. "What do you know," he asked, "about the house you're living in?"

Prentice shifted uncomfortably. "I know that a man killed himself in it, if that's what you mean."

"But do you know why?"

"No."

"Because he lost," Dystal said, giggling. "He drew the short one. How's that for motivation?"

"I think I'd better go," Prentice said.

"Wait." Dystal took a handkerchief from his pocket and tapped his forehead. "I didn't mean to begin that way. It's just that I've never told this to anyone, and it's difficult. You'll see why. Please, Prentice, promise you won't leave until I've finished!"

Prentice looked at the wiry, nervous little man and cursed the weakness that had allowed him to get himself into this miserably uncomfortable situation. He wanted to go home. But he knew he could not leave now.

"All right," he said. "Go on."

Dystal sighed. Then, staring at the window, he began to talk. "I built this house," he said, "because I thought I was going to get married. By the time I found out I was wrong, the work was all done. I should have sold it, I know,

I see that, but I was feeling too lousy to go through the paper work. Besides, I'd already given up my apartment. So I moved in." He coughed. "Be patient with me, Prentice: this is the only way to tell it, from the beginning. Where was I?"

"You moved in."

"Yes! Everyone was very nice. They invited me to their homes for dinner, they dropped by, they did little favors for me; and it helped, it really did. I thought, you know, what a hell of a great bunch of neighbors. Regular. *Real.* That was it: they were real. Ames, an advertising man; Thomas, a lawyer; Johnson, paint company; Chambers, insurance; Reiker and Cummings, engineers—I mean, how average can you get?" Dystal paused; an ugly grin appeared on his face, disappeared. "I liked them," he said. "And I was really delighted with things. But, of course, you know how it is when a woman gives you the business. I was still licking my wounds. And I guess it showed, because Ames came over one evening. Just dropped by, in a neighborly way. We had some drinks. We talked about the ways of the female. Then, bang, out of nowhere, he asked me the question. Was I bored?"

Prentice stiffened.

"Well, when you lose your girl, you lose a lot of your ambition. I told him yes, I was plenty bored. And he said, 'I used to be'. I remember his exact words. 'I used to be,' he said. 'The long haul to success, the fight, the midnight oil: it was over. I'd made it', he said. 'Dough in the bank. Partnership in a top agency. Daughter grown and away to school. I was ready to be put out to pasture, Matt. But the thing was, I was only fifty-two! I had maybe another twenty years left. And almost everybody else in the block was the same way—Ed and Ben and Oscar, all the same. You know: they fooled around with their jobs, but they weren't interested any more—not really. Because the jobs didn't *need* them any more. They were bored.' " Dystal walked to the nightstand and poured himself a drink. "That was five years ago," he murmured. "Ames, he pussy-footed around the thing for a while—feeling me out, testing me; then he told me that he had decided to do something about it. About being bored. He'd organized everyone in the block. Once a week, he explained, they played games. It was real Group Activity. Community effort. It began with charades, but they got tired of that in a while. Then they tried cards. To make it interesting they bet high. Everybody had his turn at losing. Then, Ames said, someone suggested making the game even *more* interesting, because it was getting to be a drag. So they experimented with strip poker one night. Just for fun, you understand. Rhoda lost. Next time it was Charlotte. And it went that way for a while, until, finally, Beth lost. Everyone had been waiting for it. Things became anticlimactic after that, though, so the stakes changed again. Each paired off with another's wife; lowest scoring team had to—" Dystal tipped the bottle. "Sure you won't have a bracer?"

Prentice accepted the drink without argument. It tasted bitter and powerful, but it helped.

"Well," Dystal went on. "I had one hell of a time believing all that. I mean, you know: *Ames*, after all—a little bookkeeper type with gray hair and glasses ... Still, the way he talked, I knew—somehow, I *knew*—it was the truth. Maybe because I didn't feel that a guy like Ames could make it all up! Anyway: when they'd tried all the possible combinations, things got dull again. A few of the women wanted to stop, but, of course, they were in too deep already. During one particular Fun Night, Ames had taken photographs. So, they had to keep going. Every week, it was something new. Something different. Swapsies occupied them for a while, Ames told me: Chambers took a two week vacation with Jacqueline, Ben and Beth went to Acapulco, and that sort of thing. And that is where I came into the picture." Dystal raised his hand. "I know, you don't need to tell me, I should have pulled out. But I was younger then. I was a big writer, man of the world. Training in Hollywood. I couldn't tell him I was shocked: it would have been betraying my craft. And he figured it that way, too: that's why he told me. Besides, he knew I'd be bound to find out eventually. They could hide it from just about everybody, but not someone right in the block. So, I played along. I accepted his invitation to join the next Group Activity—which is what he calls them.

"Next morning, I thought I'd dreamed the whole visit, I really did. But on Saturday, sure enough, the phone rings and Ames says, 'We begin at eight, sharp.' When I got to his house, I found it packed. Everybody in the neighborhood. Looking absolutely the same as always, too. Drinks; dancing; the whole bit. After a while, I started to wonder if the whole thing wasn't an elaborate gag. But at ten, Ames told us about the evening's surprise." Dystal gave way to a shudder. "It was a surprise, all right," he said. "I told them I wanted nothing to do with it, but Ames had done something to my drink. I didn't seem to have any control. They led me into the bedroom, and . . ."

Prentice waited, but Dystal did not complete his sentence. His eyes were dancing now.

"Never mind," he said. "Never mind what happened! The point is, I was drunk, and—well, I went through with it. I *had* to. You can see that, can't you?"

Prentice said that he could see that.

"Ames pointed out to me that the only sin, the *only* one, was being bored. That was his justification, that was his incentive. He simply didn't want to sin, that was all. So the Group Activities went on. And they got worse. Much worse. One thing, they actually plotted a crime and carried it off: the Union Bank robbery, maybe you read about it: 1953. I drove the car for them. Another time, they decided it would ward off ennui by setting fire to a warehouse down by the docks. The fire spread. Prentice—do you happen to remember that DC-7 that went down between here and Detroit?"

Prentice said, "Yes, I remember."

"Their work," Dystal said. "Ames planned it. In a way, I think he's a genius. I could spend all night telling you the things we did, but there isn't time. I've got to skip." He placed his fingers over his eyes. "Joan of Arc," he said, "was the turning point. Ames had decided that it would be diverting to re-enact famous scenes from literature. So he and Bud went down to Main Street, I think it was, and found a beat doll who thought the whole thing would be fun. They gave her twenty-five dollars, but she never got a chance to spend it. I remember that she laughed right to the point where Ames lit the pile of oil-soaked rags . . . Afterwards, they re-enacted other scenes. The execution of Marie Antoinette. The murder of Hamlet's father. You know *The Man in the Iron Mask*? They did that one. And a lot more. It lasted quite a while, too, but Ames began to get restless." Dystal held out his hands suddenly and stared at them. "The next game was a form of Russian roulette. We drew straws. Whoever got the short one had to commit suicide—in his own way. It was understood that if he failed, it would mean something much worse—and Ames had developed some damned interesting techniques. Like the nerve clamps, for instance. Thomas lost the game, anyway. They gave him twelve hours to get it over with."

Prentice felt a cold film of perspiration over his flesh. He tried to speak, but found that it was impossible. The man, of course, was crazy. Completely insane. But—he had to hear the end of the story. "Go on." he said.

Dystal ran his tongue across his lower lip, poured another drink and continued. "Cummings and Chambers got scared then," he said. "They argued that some stranger would move into the house and then there'd be all sorts of trouble. We had a meeting at Reiker's, and Chris came out with the idea of us all chipping in and buying the place.

But Ames didn't go for it. 'Let's not be so darned exclusive,' he said. 'After all, the new people might be bored, too. Lord knows we could use some fresh blood in the Group'. Cummings was pessimistic. He said, 'What if you're wrong? What if they don't want to join us?' Ames laughed it off, 'I hope,' he said 'that you don't think we're the only ones. Why, every city has its neighborhood just like ours. We're really not that unique.' And then he went on to say that if the new people didn't work out, he would take care of the situation. He didn't say how."

Dystal looked out the window again.

"I can see that he's almost ready to give you an invitation, Prentice. Once that happens, you're finished. It's join them or accept the only alternative."

Suddenly the room was very quiet.

"You don't believe me, do you?"

Prentice opened his mouth.

"No, of course you don't. It's a madman's ravings. Well, I'm going to prove it to you, Prentice." He started for the door. "Come on. Follow me; but don't make any noise."

Dystal walked out the back door, closed it, moved soundlessly across the soft, black grass.

"They're on a mystic kick right now," he whispered to Prentice. "Ames is trying to summon the devil. Last week we slaughtered a dog and read the Commandments backward; the week before, we did some chants out of an old book that Ben found in the library; before that it was orgies—" He shook his head. "It isn't working out, though. God knows why. You'd think the devil would be so delighted with Ames that he'd sign him up for the team."

Prentice followed his neighbor across the yards, walking carefully, and wondering why. He thought of his neat little office on Harmon Street, old Mrs. Gleason, the clean, well-lighted restaurant where he had his lunch and read newspaper headlines; and they seemed terribly far away.

Why, he asked himself, am I creeping around backyards with a lunatic at midnight?

Why?

"The moon is full tonight, Prentice. That means they'll be trying again."

Silently, without the slightest sound, Matthew Dystal moved across the lawns, keeping always to the shadows. A minute later he raised his hand and stopped.

They were at the rear of the Ameses' house.

It was dark inside.

"Come on," Dystal whispered.

"Wait a minute." Somehow, the sight of his own living room, still blazing with light, reassured Prentice. "I think I've had enough for this evening."

"Enough?" Dystal's face twisted grotesquely. He bunched the sleeve of Prentice's jacket in his fist. "Listen," he hissed, "listen, you idiot. I'm risking my life to help you. Don't you understand yet? If they find out I've talked . . ." He released the sleeve. "Prentice, *please*. You have a chance now, a chance to clear out of this whole stinking mess; but you won't have it long—Believe me!"

Prentice sighed. "What do you want me to do?" he said.

"Nothing. Just come with me, quietly. They're in the basement."

Breathing hard now, Dystal tiptoed around to the side of the house. He stopped at a small, earth-level window.

It was closed.

"Prentice. *Softly*. Bend down and keep out of view."

In invisible, slow movements, Dystal reached out and pushed the window. It opened a half inch. He pushed it again. It opened another half inch.

Prentice saw yellow light stream out of the crack. Instantly his throat felt very dry, very painful.

There was a noise. A low, murmurous sound, a susurrus, like distant humming.

"What's that?"

Dystal put a finger to his lips and motioned: "Here."

Prentice knelt down at the window and looked into the light.

At first he could not believe what his eyes saw.

It was a basement, like other basements in old houses, with a large iron furnace and a cement floor and heavy beams. This much he could recognize and understand. The rest, he could not.

In the center of the floor was a design; obviously drawn in colored chalks. It looked a bit, to Prentice, like a Star of David, although there were other designs around and within it. They were not particularly artistic, but they were intricate. In the middle was a large cup, similar to a salad bowl, vaguely familiar, empty.

"There," whispered Dystal, withdrawing.

Slightly to the left were drawn a circle and a pentagram, its five points touching the circumference equally.

Prentice blinked and turned his attention to the people.

Standing on a block of wood, surrounded by men and women, was a figure in a black robe and a serpent-shaped crown.

It was Ames.

His wife, Charlotte, dressed in a white gown, stood next to him. She held a brass lamp.

Also in robes and gowns were Ben and Rhoda Roth, Bud Reiker and his wife, the Cummingses, the Chamberses, the Johnsons—

Prentice shook away his sudden dizziness and shaded his eyes.

To the right, near the furnace, was a table with a white sheet draped across it. And two feet away, an odd, six-sided structure with black candles burning from a dozen apertures.

"Listen," Dystal said.

Ames' eyes were closed. Softly, he was chanting:

All degradation, all sheer infamy,
    Thou shalt endure. Thy head beneath the mire.
    And drug of worthless women shall desire
As in some hateful dream, at last to lie;
    Woman must trample thee thou respire
        That deadliest fume;
The vilest worms must crawl, the loathliest vampires
    gloom . . .

"The Great Beast," chuckled Dystal.

"I," said Ames, "am Ipsissimus," and the others chanted, "He is Ipsissimus."

"I have read the books, dark Lord. *The Book of Sacred Magic of Abra-Melin the Mage* I have read, and I reject it!"

"We reject it!" murmured the Roths.

"The power of Good shall be served by the power of Darkness, always."

He raised his hands. "In Thy altar is the stele of Ankf-f-n-Khonsu; there, also, *The Book of the Dead* and *The Book of the Law*, six candles to each side, my Lord, Bell, Burin, Lamen, Sword, Cup, and the Cakes of Life . . ."

Prentice looked at the people he had seen only a few hours ago in his living room, and shuddered. He felt very weak.

"We, your servants," said Ames, signing the words, "beseech your presence, Lord of Night and of Life Eternal, Ruler of the Souls of men in all Thy vast dominion . . ."

Prentice started to rise, but Dystal grasped his jacket. "No," he said. "Wait. Wait another minute. This is something you ought to see."

". . . we live to serve you, grant us . . ."

"He's begging the devil to appear," whispered Dystal.

". . . tonight, and offer the greatest and most treasured gift. Accept our offering!"

"Accept it!" cried the others.

"What the hell is this, anyway?" Prentice demanded, feverishly.

Then Ames stopped talking, and the rest were silent. Ames raised his left hand and lowered it. Chris Cummings and Bud Reiker bowed and walked backwards into the shadows where Prentice could not see them.

Charlotte Ames walked to the six-sided structure with the candles and picked up a long, thin object.

She returned and handed this to her husband.

It was a knife.

"*Killnotshaltthou!*" screamed Ed Chambers, and he stepped across the pentagram to the sheet-shrouded table.

Prentice rubbed his eyes.

"Shhh."

Bud Reiker and Chris Cummings returned to the center of light then. They were carrying a bundle. It was wrapped in blankets.

The bundle thrashed and made peculiar muffled noises. The men lifted it onto the table and held it.

Ames nodded and stepped down from the block of wood. He walked to the table and halted, the long-bladed butcher knife glittering in the glow of the candles.

"To Thee, O Lord of the Underground, we made this offering! To Thee, the rarest gift of all!"

"What is it?" Prentice asked. "What is this gift?"

Dystal's voice was ready and eager. "A virgin," he said. Then they removed the blanket.

Prentice felt his eyes bursting from their sockets, felt his heart charging the walls of his chest.

"Ann," he said, in a choked whisper. "Ann!"

The knife went up.

Prentice scrambled to his feet and fought the dizziness. "Dystal," he cried. "Dystal, for God's sake, what are they doing? Stop them. You hear me? Stop them!"

"I can't," said Matthew Dystal, sadly. "It's too late. I'm afraid your wife said a few things she shouldn't have, Prentice. You see—we've been looking for a real one for such a long time . . ."

Prentice tried to lunge, but the effort lost him his balance. He fell to the ground. His arms and legs were growing numb, and he remembered, suddenly, the bitter taste of the drink he'd had.

"It really couldn't have been avoided, though," Dystal said. "I mean, the boy knew, and he'd have told you eventually. And you'd have begun investigating, and—oh, you understand. I told Lucian we should have bought the place, but he's so obstinate; thinks he knows *every*thing! Now, of course, we'll have to burn it, and that does seem a terrible waste." He shook his head from side to side. "But don't you worry," he said. "You'll be asleep by then and, I promise, you won't feel a thing. Really."

Prentice turned his eyes from the window and screamed silently for a long time.

PERCHANCE TO DREAM

"PLEASE SIT DOWN," the psychiatrist said, indicating a somewhat worn leather couch.

Automatically, Hall sat down. Instinctively, he leaned back. Dizziness flooded through him, his eyelids fell like sashweights, the blackness came. He jumped up quickly and slapped his right cheek, then he slapped his left cheek, hard.

"I'm sorry, Doctor," he said.

The psychiatrist, who was tall and young and not in the least Viennese nodded. "You prefer to stand?" he asked, gently.

"Prefer?" Hall threw his head back and laughed. "That's good," he said. *"Prefer!"*

"I'm afraid I don't quite understand."

"Neither do I, Doctor." He pinched the flesh of his left hand until it hurt. "No, no: that isn't true. I do understand. That's the whole trouble. I do."

"You—want to tell me about it?"

"Yes. No." It's silly, he thought. You can't help me. No one can. I'm alone! "Forget it," he said and started for the door.

The psychiatrist said, "Wait a minute." His voice was

friendly, concerned; but not patronizing. "Running away won't do you much good, will it?"

Hall hesitated.

"Forgive the cliché. Actually, running away is often the best answer. But I don't know yet that yours is that sort of problem."

"Did Dr. Jackson tell you about me?"

"No. Jim said he was sending you over, but he thought you'd do a better job on the details. I only know that your name is Philip Hall, you're thirty-one, and you haven't been able to sleep for a long time."

"Yes. A long time . . ." To be exact, seventy-two hours, Hall thought, glancing at the clock. Seventy-two horrible hours . . .

The psychiatrist tapped out a cigarette. "Aren't you—" he began.

"Tired? God yes. I'm the tiredest man on Earth! I could sleep forever. But that's just it, you see: I would. I'd never wake up."

"Please," the psychiatrist said.

Hall bit his lip. There wasn't, he supposed, much point to it. But, after all, what *else* was there for him to do? Where would he go? "You mind if I pace?"

"Stand on your head, if you like."

"Okay. I'll take one of your cigarettes." He drew the smoke into his lungs and walked over to the window. Fourteen floors below, the toy people and the toy cars moved. He watched them and thought, this guy's all right. Sharp. Intelligent. Nothing like what I expected. Who can say—*maybe* it'll do some good. "I'm not sure where to begin."

"It doesn't matter. The beginning might be easier for you."

Hall shook his head, violently. The beginning, he thought. Was there such a thing?

"Just take it easy."

After a lengthy pause, Hall said: "I first found out about
the power of the human mind when I was ten. Close to
that time, anyway. We had a tapestry in the bedroom. It
was a great big thing, the size of a rug, with fringe on the
edges. It showed a group of soldiers—Napoleonic soldiers—on horses. They were at the brink of some kind of
cliff, and the first horse was reared up. My mother told me
something. She told me that if I stared at the tapestry long
enough, the horses would start to move. They'd go right
over the cliff, she said. I tried it, but nothing happened.
She said, 'You've got to take time. You've got to *think*
about it.' So, every night, before I went to bed, I'd sit up
and stare at that damn tapestry. And, finally, it happened.
Over they went, all the horses, all the men, over the edge
of the cliff . . ." Hall stubbed out the cigarette and began
to pace. "Scared hell out of me," he said. "When I looked
again, they were all back. It got to be a game with me.
Later on, I tried it with pictures in magazines, and pretty
soon I was able to move locomotives and send balloons
flying and make dogs open their mouths: everything, anything I wanted."

He paused, ran a hand through his hair. "Not too unusual, you're thinking," he said. "Every kid does it. Like
standing in a closet and shining a flashlight through your
finger, or sewing up the heel of your palm . . . common
stuff?"

The psychiatrist shrugged.

"There was a difference," Hall said. "One day it got
out of control. I was looking at a coloring book. One of
the pictures showed a knight and a dragon fighting. For
fun I decided to make the knight drop his lance. He did.
The dragon started after him, breathing fire. In another
second the dragon's mouth was open and he was getting
ready to eat the knight. I blinked and shook my head,
like always, only—nothing happened. I mean, the picture
didn't go back. Not even when I closed the book and

opened it again. But I didn't think too much about it, even then."

He walked to the desk and took another cigarette. It slipped from his hands.

"You've been on Dexedrine," the psychiatrist said, watching as Hall tried to pick up the cigarette.

"Yes."

"How many grains a day?"

"Thirty, thirty-five, I don't know."

"Potent. Knocks out your co-ordination. I suppose Jim warned you?"

"Yes, he warned me."

"Well, let's get along. What happened then?"

"Nothing." Hall allowed the psychiatrist to light his cigarette. "For a while, I forgot about the 'game' almost completely. Then, when I turned thirteen, I got sick. Rheumatic heart—"

The psychiatrist leaned forward and frowned. "And Jim let you have thirty-five—"

"Don't interrupt!" He decided not to mention that he had gotten the drug from his aunt, that Dr. Jackson knew nothing about it. "I had to stay in bed a lot. No activity; might kill me. So I read books and listened to the radio. One night I heard a ghost story. 'Hermit's Cave' it was called. All about a man who gets drowned and comes back to haunt his wife. My parents were gone, at a movie. I was alone. And I kept thinking about that story, imagining the ghost. Maybe, I thought to myself, he's in that closet. I knew he wasn't; I knew there wasn't any such thing as a ghost, really. But there was a little part of my mind that kept saying, 'Look at the closet. Watch the door. He's in there, Philip, and he's going to come out.' I picked up a book and tried to read, but I couldn't help glancing at the closet door. It was open a crack. Everything dark behind it. Everything dark and quiet."

"And the door moved."

"That's right."

"You understand that there's nothing terribly unusual in anything you've said so far?"

"I know," Hall said. "It was my imagination. It *was*, and I realized it even then. But—I got just as scared. Just as scared as if a ghost actually *had* opened the door! And that's the whole point. The mind, Doctor. It's everything. If you *think* you have a pain in your arm and there's no physical reason for it, you don't hurt any less ... My mother died because she thought she had a fatal disease. The autopsy showed malnutrition, nothing else. But she died just the same!"

"I won't dispute the point."

"All right. I just don't want you to tell me it's all in my mind. I *know* it is."

"Go on."

"They told me I'd never really get well, I'd have to take it easy the rest of my life. Because of the heart. No strenuous exercises, no stairs, no long walks. No shocks. Shock produces excessive adrenalin, they said. Bad. So that's the way it was. When I got out of school, I grabbed a soft desk job. Unexciting: numbers, adding numbers, that's all. Things went okay for a few years. Then it started again. I read about where some woman got into her car at night and happened to check for something in the back seat and found a man hidden there. Waiting. It stuck with me; I started dreaming about it. So every night, when I got into my car, I automatically patted the rear seat and floorboards. It satisfied me for a while, until I started thinking, 'What if I forgot to check?' Or, 'What if there's something back there that isn't human?' I had to drive across Laurel Canyon to get home, and you know how twisty that stretch is. Thirty-fifty-foot drops, straight down. I'd get this feeling halfway across. 'There's someone ... something ... in the back of the car!' Hidden, in darkness. Fat and shiny. I'll look in the rear-view mirror and I'll see his hands ready to circle my throat . . . Again, Doctor: understand me. *I knew it was my imagination.* I had no doubt at all that the back seat was empty—hell, I kept the car locked and I double-checked! But, I told myself, you keep thinking this way, Hall, and you'll see those hands. It'll be a reflection, or somebody's headlights, or nothing at all—but you'll see them! Finally, one night, I did see them! The car lurched a couple of times and went down the embankment."

The psychiatrist said, "Wait a minute," rose, and switched the tape on a small machine.

"I knew how powerful the mind was, then," Hall continued. "I knew that ghosts and demons did exist, they did, if you only thought about them long enough and hard enough. After all, one of them almost killed me!" He pressed the lighted end of the cigarette against his flesh; the fog lifted instantly. "Dr. Jackson told me afterwards that one more serious shock like that would finish me. And that's when I started having the dream."

There was a silence in the room, compounded of distant automobile horns, the ticking of the ship's-wheel clock, the insectival tapping of the receptionist's typewriter. Hall's own tortured breathing.

"They say dreams last only a couple of seconds," he said. "I don't know whether that's true or not. It doesn't matter. They *seem* to last longer. Sometimes I've dreamed a whole lifetime; sometimes generations have passed. Once in a while, time stops completely; it's a frozen moment, lasting forever. When I was a kid I saw the Flash Gordon serials; you remember? I loved them, and when the last episode was over, I went home and started dreaming more. Each night, another episode. They were vivid, too, and I remembered them when I woke up. I even wrote them down, to make sure I wouldn't forget. Crazy?"

"No," said the psychiatrist.

"I did, anyway. The same thing happened with the Oz

books and the Burroughs books. I'd keep them going. But after the age of fifteen, or so, I didn't dream much. Only once in a while. Then, a week ago—" Hall stopped talking. He asked the location of the bathroom and went there and splashed cold water on his face. Then he returned and stood by the window.

"A week ago?" the psychiatrist said, flipping the tape machine back on.

"I went to bed around eleven-thirty. I wasn't too tired, but I needed the rest, on account of my heart. Right away the dream started. I was walking along Venice Pier. It was close to midnight. The place was crowded, people everywhere; you know the kind they used to get there. Sailors, dumpy looking dames, kids in leather jackets. The pitchmen were going through their routines. You could hear the roller coasters thundering along the tracks, the people inside the roller coasters, screaming; you could hear the bells and the guns cracking and the crazy songs they play on calliopes. And, far away, the ocean, moving. Everything was bright and gaudy and cheap. I walked for a while, stepping on gum and candy apples, wondering why I was there." Hall's eyes closed. He opened them quickly and rubbed them. "Halfway to the end, passing the penny arcade, I saw a girl. She was about twenty-two or -three. White dress, very thin and tight, and a funny white hat. Her legs were bare, nicely muscled and tan. She was alone. I stopped and watched her, and I remember thinking, "She *must* have a boy friend. He *must* be here, somewhere." But she didn't seem to be waiting for anyone, or looking. Unconsciously, I began to follow her. At a distance.

"She walked past a couple of concessions, then she stopped at one called 'The Whip' and strolled in and went for a ride. The air was hot. It caught her dress as she went around and sent it whirling. It didn't bother her at all. She just held onto the bar and closed her eyes, and—I don't know, a kind of ecstasy seemed to come over her. She began to laugh. A high-pitched, musical sound. I stood by the fence and watched her, wondering why such a beautiful girl should be laughing in a cheap carnival ride, in the middle of the night, all by herself. Then my hands froze on the fence, because suddenly I saw that she was looking at me. Every time the car would whip around, she'd be looking. And there was something that said, Don't go away, don't leave, don't move . . .

"The ride stopped and she got out and walked over to me. As naturally as if we'd known each other for years, she put her arm in mine, and said, 'We've been expecting you, Mr. Hall.' Her voice was deep and soft, and her face, close up, was even more beautiful than it had seemed. Full, rich lips, a little wet; dark, flashing eyes; a warm gleam to her flesh. I didn't answer. She laughed again and tugged at my sleeve. 'Come on, darling,' she said. 'We haven't much time.' And we walked, almost running, to The Silver Flash—a roller coaster, the highest on the pier. I knew I shouldn't go on it because of my heart condition, but she wouldn't listen. She said I had to, for her. So we bought our tickets and got into the first seat of the car . . ."

Hall held his breath for a moment, then let it out, slowly. As he relived the episode, he found that it was easier to stay awake. Much easier.

"That," he said, "was the end of the first dream. I woke up sweating and trembling, and thought about it most of the day, wondering where it had all come from. I'd only been to Venice Pier once in my life, with my mother. Years ago. But that night, just as it'd happened with the serials, the dream picked up exactly where it had left off. We were setting into the seat. Rough leather, cracked and peeling, I recall. The grab bar iron, painted black, the paint rubbed away in the center.

"I tried to get out, thinking. Now's the time to do it; do it now or you'll be too late! But the girl held me, and whispered to me. We'd be together, she said. Close together. If I'd do this one thing for her, she'd belong to me. 'Please! Please!' Then the car started. A little jerk; the kids beginning to yell and scream; the *clack-clack* of the chain pulling up; and up, slowly, too late now, too late for anything, up the steep wooden hill . . .

"A third of the way to the top, with her holding me, pressing herself against me, I woke up again. Next night, we went up a little farther. Foot by foot, slowly, up the hill. At the halfway point, the girl began kissing me. And laughing. 'Look down!' she told me. 'Look down, Philip!' And I did and saw little people and little cars and everything tiny and unreal.

"Finally we were within a few feet of the crest. The night was black and the wind was fast and cold now, and I was scared, so scared that I couldn't move. The girl laughed louder than ever, and a strange expression came into her eyes. I remembered then how no one else had noticed her. How the ticket-taker had taken the two stubs and looked around questioningly.

" 'Who are you?' I screamed. And she said, 'Don't you know?' And she stood up and pulled the grab-bar out of my hands. I leaned forward to get it.

"Then we reached the top. And I saw her face and I knew what she was going to do, instantly: I knew. I tried to get back in the seat, but I felt her hands on me then and I heard her voice, laughing, high, laughing and shrieking with delight, and—"

Hall smashed his fist against the wall, stopped and waited for calm to return.

When it did, he said, "That's the whole thing, Doctor. Now you know why I don't care to go to sleep. When I do—and I'll have to, eventually; I realize that!—the dream will go on. And my heart won't take it!"

The psychiatrist pressed a button on his desk.

"Whoever she is," Hall went on, "she'll push me. And

I'll fall. Hundreds of feet. I'll see the cement rushing up in a blur to meet me and I'll feel the first horrible pain of contact—"

There was a click.

The office door opened.

A girl walked in.

"Miss Thomas," the psychiatrist began, "I'd like you to—"

Philip Hall screamed. He stared at the girl in the white nurse's uniform and took a step backward. "Oh, Christ! No!"

"Mr. Hall, this is my receptionist, Miss Thomas."

"No," Hall cried. "It's her. It is. And I know who she is now, God save me! I know who she is!"

The girl in the white uniform took a tentative step into the room.

Hall screamed again, threw his hands over his face, turned and tried to run.

A voice called, "Stop him!"

Hall felt the sharp pain of the sill against his knee, realized in one hideous moment what was happening. Blindly he reached out, grasping. But it was too late. As if drawn by a giant force, he tumbled through the open window, out into the cold clean air.

"Hall!"

All the way down, all the long and endless way down past the thirteen floors to the gray, unyielding, hard concrete, his mind worked; and his eyes never closed . . .

"I'm afraid he's dead," the psychiatrist said, removing his fingers from Hall's wrist.

The girl in the white uniform made a little gasping sound. "But," she said, "only a minute ago, I saw him and he was—"

"I know. It's funny; when he came in, I told him to sit

down. He did. And in less than two seconds he was asleep. Then he gave that yell you heard and . . ."

"Heart attack?"

"Yes." The psychiatrist rubbed his cheek thoughtfully. "Well," he said. "I guess there are worse ways to go. At least he died peacefully."

THE CROOKED MAN

Introduction by Robert Bloch

It's difficult for me to write objectively about a colleague who was also my friend. In order to do so I would need the skill, the intelligence and the perceptive insight of someone who ranks as a major talent.

Someone like Charles Beaumont.

Fortunately, there's no need for me to establish his creative credentials. The stories in this collection are proof of his professional prowess, along with his outstanding achievements in television and films.

Let me confine myself instead to our personal relationship. I was never privileged to count myself a close companion of this remarkable man, but during the latter years of his life our paths crossed constantly, and for this I am truly grateful.

When I came out to Hollywood, late in 1959, I was a lowly apprentice as a scriptwriter, while Chuck had already begun his spectacular rise. I'd met him casually on a few prior occasions and knew him as a highly-acclaimed contributor to Playboy. Now we found ourselves together on a social basis and I witnessed the soaring of his career. Soon he was enjoying well-earned eminence for his work on Twilight Zone and his filmwriting future appeared assured. One of his screenplays, The Intruder,

seemed destined to become a major production with a top director, big-name stars and high-budget promotion.

Then, as so often happens in such circumstances, problems
arose and high hopes fell. But eventually the film was made—on
a shoe-string budget, a curtailed production-schedule—the stuff of
which bad dreams are made. Bad dreams, and B pictures.

So when I was invited, along with Chuck's friends and the
usual studio functionaries, to a screening at Twentieth Century-
Fox, I had qualms and misgivings about what to expect from the
evening's entertainment.

To my surprise and delight, The Intruder proved to be just
that—a surprise and a delight. Shot on location, in black-and-
white, it is arguably Roger Corman's best directorial effort. The
then virtually-unknown leading player, one William Shatner, con-
tributed a remarkable performance. So did his supporting cast—
including none other than Charles Beaumont himself, in a small
part as a high school principal. Two other writer friends of his,
George Clayton Johnson and Bill Nolan, had a hoot playing a
pair of redneck racists. But the film, a powerful drama of bigotry
and rabble-rousing in a southern setting, was truly ahead of its
time; apparently the general public was not yet ready to respond
to the social issues which the script so realistically raised.

The film failed, but Chuck succeeded. He went on to other
assignments on top productions, and though these too were apt
to furnish frustrations, Beaumont's talent was recognized. Almost
twenty years later, when I found myself working with George Pal
on his last projects before his sudden death, he told me how
highly he esteemed Chuck's work on The Seven Faces of Dr.
Lao and The Wonderful World of the Brothers Grimm. It was
still a matter of his major regret that studio executives forced
changes in the shooting scripts which Pal had wanted to keep
inviolate. And the portions of these films which were not tam-
pered with clearly demonstrate Beaumontian brilliance in comedy
concepts.

Chuck's life, however, had lost any claim to comic elements.
As success increased, the toll on his health escalated.

Attending the World Science Fiction Convention in Chicago, in 1962, I was surprised to encounter Chuck—a tired, driven man who, by his own account, was in the process of fleeing Hollywood for good. He was finishing an assignment for Playboy, heading for New York, and after that he meant to hole up and get to work on what he hoped would be a major novel.

All this I learned when we'd repaired to the bar. As he confided his plans over drinks I asked him just where he intended to do his actual writing on the book.

"I'm going to Rome," he said.

His statement astonished me. Rome, in 1962, was a major motion picture production center, with its Cinecitta; a hotbed of international stars and director-producers who moved from one hot bed to another.

"Don't do it," I advised. "Can't you see you're moving out of the frying-pan into the fire? You won't get away from movies if you go to Rome."

Chuck seemed startled; he hadn't consciously realized the implications of his decision. Whether or not I influenced him I don't know, but he didn't go to Rome. Instead he ended up by returning to Hollywood, and the novel was never completed.

Illness and death ended his brilliant career within a few short years, but his work lives on. Now, after a period of comparative neglect, a rightful resurrection has begun.

The story I've selected for this volume—"The Crooked Man"— is an example of his genius in a genre he helped elevate to high literary levels. While its basic concept is less startling today, it was daring and innovative at the time of first publication. And it illustrates perfectly why the name of Charles Beaumont will be recognized and honored by generations yet to come.

*"Professing themselves to be wise, they became fools
. . . who changed the truth of God into a lie . . . for
even their women did change the natural use into that
which is against nature: and likewise also the men,
leaving the natural use of the women, burned in their
lust one toward another; men with men working that
which is unseemly . . ."*

—St. Paul: Romans, I

HE SLIPPED INTO a corner booth away from the dancing
men, where it was quietest, where the odors of musk and
frangipani hung less heavy on the air. A slender lamp
glowed softly in the booth. He turned it down: down to
where only the club's blue overheads filtered through the
beaded curtain, diffusing, blurring the image thrown back
by the mirrored walls of his light, thin-boned handsome-
ness.

"Yes sir?" The barboy stepped through the beads and
stood smiling. Clad in gold-sequined trunks, his greased
muscles seemed to roll in independent motion, like fat
snakes beneath his naked skin.

"Whiskey," Jesse said. He caught the insouciant grin,
the broad white-tooth crescent that formed on the young
man's face. Jesse looked away, tried to control the flow of
blood to his cheeks.

"Yes sir," the barboy said, running his thick tanned fingers over his solar plexus, tapping the fingers, making them
hop in a sinuous dance. He hesitated, still smiling, this time
questioningly, hopefully, a smile drenched in admiration
and desire. The Finger Dance, the accepted symbol,
stopped: the pudgy brown digits curled into angry fists.
"Right away, sir."

Jesse watched him turn; before the beads had tinkled
together he watched the handsome athlete make his way
imperiously through the crowds, shaking off the tentative

hands of single men at the tables, ignoring the many desire symbols directed toward him.

That shouldn't have happened. Now the fellow's feelings were hurt. If hurt enough, he would start thinking, wondering—and that would ruin everything. No. It must be put right.

Jesse thought of Mina, of the beautiful Mina—It was such a rotten chance. It *had* to go right!

"Your whiskey, sir," the young man said. His face looked like a dog's face, large, sad; his lips were a pouting bloat of line.

Jesse reached into his pocket for some change. He started to say something, something nice.

"It's been paid for," the barboy said. He scowled and laid a card on the table and left.

The card carried the name E.J. TWO HOBART, embossed, in lavender ink. Jesse heard the curtains tinkle.

"Well, hello. I hope you don't mind my barging in like this, but—you didn't seem to be with anyone . . ."

The man was small, chubby, bald; his face had a dirty growth of beard and he looked out of tiny eyes encased in bulging contacts. He was bare to the waist. His white hairless chest dropped and turned in folds at the stomach. Softly, more subtly than the barboy had done, he put his porky stubs of fingers into a suggestive rhythm.

Jesse smiled. "Thanks for the drink," he said. "But I really am expecting someone."

"Oh?" the man said. "Someone—special?"

"Pretty special," Jesse said smoothly, now that the words had become automatic. "He's my fiancée."

"I see." The man frowned momentarily and then brightened. "Well, I thought to myself, I said: E.J., a beauty like that couldn't very well be unattached. But—well, it was certainly worth a try. Sorry."

"Perfectly all right," Jesse said. The predatory little eyes

were rolling, the fingers dancing in one last-ditch attempt.
"Good evening, Mr. Hobart."

Bluey veins showed under the whiteness of the man's
nearly female mammae. Jesse felt slightly amused this time:
it was the other kind, the intent ones, the humorless ones
like—like the barboy—that repulsed him, turned him ill,
made him want to take a knife and carve unspeakable ug-
liness into his own smooth ascetic face.

The man turned and waddled away crabwise. The club
was becoming more crowded. It was getting later and heads
full of liquor shook away the inhibitions of the earlier hours.
Jesse tried not to watch, but he had long ago given up
trying to rid himself of his fascination. So he watched the
men together. The pair over in the far corner, pressed close
together, dancing with their bodies, never moving their
feet, swaying in slow lissome movements to the music, their
tongues twisting in the air, jerking, like pink snakes, con-
tracting to points and curling invitingly, barely making
touch, then snapping back. The Tongue Dance . . . The
couple seated by the bar. One a Beast, the other a Hunter,
the Beast old, his cheeks caked hard and cracking with
powder and liniments, the perfume rising from his body
like steam; the Hunter, young but unhandsome, the fury
evident in his eyes, the hurt anger at having to make do
with a Beast—from time to time he would look around,
wetting his lips in shame . . . And those two just coming
in, dressed in Mother's uniforms, tanned, mustached, proud
of their station . . .

Jesse held the beads apart, *Mina must come soon*. He
wanted to run from this place, out into the air, into the
darkness and silence.

No. He just wanted Mina. To see her, touch her, listen
to the music of her voice . . .

Two women came in, arm in arm, Beast and Hunter,
drunk. They were stopped at the door. Angrily, shrilly, told
to leave. The manager swept by Jesse's booth, muttering

about them, asking why they should want to come dirtying up The Phallus with their presence when they had their own section, their own clubs—

Jesse pulled his head back inside. He'd gotten used to the light by now, so he closed his eyes against his multiplied image. The disorganized sounds of love got louder, the singsong syrup of voices: deep, throaty, baritone, falsetto. It was crowded now. The Orgies would begin before long and the couples would pair off for the cubicles. He hated the place. But close to Orgy-time you didn't get noticed here—and where else was there to go? Outside, where every inch of pavement was patrolled electronically, every word of conversation, every movement recorded, catalogued, filed?

Damn Knudson! Damn the little man! Thanks to him, to the Senator, Jesse was now a criminal. Before, it wasn't so bad—not this bad, anyway. You were laughed at and shunned and fired from your job, sometimes kids lobbed stones at you, but at least you weren't hunted. Now—it was a crime. A sickness.

He remembered when Knudson had taken over. It had been one of the little man's first telecasts; in fact, it was the platform that got him the majority vote:

"Vice is on the upswing in our city. In the dark corners of every Unit perversion blossoms like an evil flower. Our children are exposed to its stink, and they wonder—*our children wonder*—why nothing is done to put a halt to this disgrace. We have ignored it long enough! The time has come for *action*, not mere words. The perverts who infest our land must be fleshed out, eliminated *completely*, as a threat not only to public morals but to society at large. These sick people must be cured and made normal. The disease that throws men and women together in this dreadful abnormal

relationship and leads to acts of retrogression—
retrogression that will, unless it is stopped and
stopped fast, push us inevitably back to the status
of animals—this is to be considered as any other
disease. It must be conquered as heart trouble,
cancer, polio, schizophrenia, paranoia, all other
diseases have been conquered . . ."

The Women's Senator had taken Knudson's lead and
issued a similar pronounciamento and then the bill became
law and the law was carried out.

Jesse sipped at the whiskey, remembering the Hunts.
How the frenzied mobs had gone through the city at first,
chanting, yelling, bearing placards with slogans: WIPE
OUT THE HETEROS! KILL THE QUEERS! MAKE
OUR CITY CLEAN AGAIN! And how they'd lost interest finally after the passion had worn down and the novelty
had ended. But they had killed many and they had sent
many more to the hospitals . . .

He remembered the nights of running and hiding, choked
dry breath glued to his throat, heart rattling loose. He had
been lucky. He didn't look like a hetero. They said you
could tell one just by watching him walk—Jesse walked
correctly. He fooled them. He was lucky.

And he was a criminal. He, Jess Four Martin, no different from the rest, tube-born and machine-nursed, raised in
the Character Schools like everyone else—was terribly different from the rest.

It had happened—his awful suspicions had crystallized—
on his first formal date. The man had been a Rocketeer,
the best high quality, even out of the Hunter class. Mother
had arranged it carefully. There was the dance. And then
the ride in the spacesled. The big man had put an arm
about Jesse and—Jess knew. He knew for certain and it
made him very angry and very sad.

He remembered the days that came after the knowledge:

bad days, days fallen upon evil, black desires, deep-cored frustrations. He had tried to find a friend at the Crooked Clubs that flourished then, but it was no use. There was a sensationalism, a bravura to these people, that he could not love. The sight of men and women together, too, shocked the parts of him he could not change, and repulsed him. Then the vice squads had come and closed up the clubs and the heteros were forced underground and he never sought them out again or saw them. He was alone.

The beads tinkled.

"Jesse—" He looked up quickly, afraid. It was Mina. She wore a loose man's shirt, an old hat that hid her golden hair: her face was shadowed by the turned-up collar. Through the shirt the rise and fall of her breasts could be faintly detected. She smiled once, nervously.

Jesse looked out the curtain. Without speaking, he put his hands about her soft thin shoulders and held her like this for a long minute.

"Mina—" She looked away. He pulled her chin forward and ran a finger along her lips. Then he pressed her body to his, tightly, touching her neck, her back, kissing her forehead, her eyes, kissing her mouth. They sat down.

They sought for words. The curtain parted.

"Beer," Jesse said, winking at the barboy, who tried to come closer, to see the one loved by this thin handsome man.

"Yes sir."

The barboy looked at Mina very hard, but she had turned and he could see only the back. Jesse held his breath. The barboy smiled contemptuously then, a smile that said: You're insane—I was hired for my beauty. See my chest, look—a pectoral vision. My arms, strong; my lips—come, were there ever such sensuous ones? And you turn me down for this bag of bones . . .

Jesse winked again, shrugged suggestively and danced his

fingers: *Tomorrow, my friend, I'm stuck tonight. Can't help it. Tomorrow.*

The barboy grinned and left. In a few moments he returned with the beer. "On the house," he said, for Mina's benefit. She turned only when Jesse said, softly:

"It's all right. He's gone now."

Jesse looked at her. Then he reached over and took off the hat. Blond hair rushed out and over the rough shirt.

She grabbed for the hat. "We mustn't," she said. "Please—what if somebody should come in?"

"No one will come in. I told you that."

"But what if? I don't know—I don't like it here. That man at the door—he almost recognized me."

"But he didn't."

"Almost though. And then what?"

"Forget it. Mina, for God's sake. Let's not quarrel."

She calmed. "I'm sorry, Jesse. It's only that—this place makes me feel—"

"—what?"

"Dirty." She said it defiantly.

"You don't really believe that, do you?"

"No. I don't know. I just want to be alone with you."

Jesse took out a cigarette and started to use the lighter. Then he cursed and threw the vulgarly shaped object under the table and crushed the cigarette. "You know that's impossible," he said. The idea of separate Units for homes had disappeared, to be replaced by giant dormitories. There were no more parks, no country lanes. There was no place to hide at all now, thanks to Senator Knudson, to the little bald crest of this new sociological wave. "This is all we have," Jesse said, throwing a sardonic look around the booth, with its carved symbols and framed pictures of entertainment stars—all naked and leering.

They were silent for a time, hands interlocked on the table top. Then the girl began to cry. "I—I can't go on like this," she said.

"I know. It's hard. But what else can we do?" Jesse tried to keep the hopelessness out of his voice.

"Maybe," the girl said, "we ought to go underground with the rest."

"And hide there, like rats?" Jesse said.

"We're hiding here," Mina said, "like rats."

"Besides, Parker is getting ready to crack down. I know, Mina—I work at Centraldome, after all. In a little while there won't be any underground."

"I love you," the girl said, leaning forward, parting her lips for a kiss. "Jesse, I do." She closed her eyes. "Oh, why won't they leave us alone? Why? Just because we're que—"

"Mina! I've told you—don't ever use that word. It isn't true! *We're* not the queers. You've got to believe that. Years ago it was *normal* for men and women to love each other: they married and had children together; that's the way it was. Don't you remember anything of what I've told you?"

The girl sobbed. "Of course I do. But, darling, that was a long time ago."

"Not so long! Where I work—listen to me—they have books. You know, I told you about books? I've read them, Mina. I learned what the words meant from other books. It's only been since the use of artificial insemination—not even five hundred years ago."

"Yes dear," the girl said. "I'm sure, dear."

"Mina, stop that! We are not the unnatural ones, no matter what they say. I don't know exactly how it happened—maybe, maybe as women gradually became equal to men in every way—or maybe solely because of the way we're born—I don't know. But the point is, darling, the whole world was like us, once. Even now, look at the animals—"

"Jesse! Don't you dare talk as if we're like those horrid dogs and cats and things!"

Jesse sighed. He had tried so often to tell her, show her. But he knew, actually, what she thought. That she felt she was exactly what the authorities told her she was—God, maybe that's how they all thought, all the Crooked People, all the "unnormal" ones . . .

The girl's hands caressed his arms and the touch became suddenly repugnant to him. Unnatural. Terribly unnatural.

Jesse shook his head. Forget it, he thought. Never mind. She's a woman and you love her and there's nothing wrong nothing wrong nothing wrong in that . . . or am I the insane person of old days who was insane because he was so sure he wasn't insane because—

"Disgusting!"

It was the fat little man, the smiling masher, E.J. Two Hobart. But he wasn't smiling now.

Jesse got up quickly and stepped in front of Mina. "What do you want? I thought I told you—"

The man pulled a metal disk from his trunks. "Vice squad, friend," he said. "Better sit down." The disk was pointed at Jesse's belly.

The man's arm went out the curtain and two other men came in, holding disks.

"I've been watching you quite a while, mister," the man said. "Quite a while."

"Look," Jesse said, "I don't know what you're talking about. I work at Centraldome and I'm seeing Miss Smith here on some business."

"We know all about that kind of business," the man said.

"All right—I'll tell you the truth. I forced her to come here. I—"

"Mister—didn't you hear me? I said I've been watching you. All evening. Let's go."

One man took Mina's arm, roughly; the other two began

to propel Jesse out through the club. Heads turned. Tangled bodies moved embarrassedly.

"It's all right," the little fat man said, his white skin glistening with perspiration. "It's all right, folks. Go on back to whatever you were doing." He grinned and tightened his grasp on Jesse's arm.

Mina didn't struggle. There was something in her eyes— it took Jesse a long time to recognize it. Then he knew. He knew what she had come to tell him tonight: that even if they hadn't been caught—she would have submitted to the Cure voluntarily. No more worries then, no more guilt. No more meeting at midnight dives, feeling shame, feeling dirt . . .

Mina didn't meet Jesse's look as they took her out into the street.

"You'll be okay," the fat man was saying. He opened the wagon's doors. "They've got it down pat now—couple days in the ward, one short session with the doctors; take out a few glands, make a few injections, attach a few wires to your head, turn on a machine: presto! You'll be surprised."

The fat officer leaned close. His sausage fingers danced wildly near Jesse's face.

"It'll make a new man of you," he said.

Then they closed the doors and locked them.

BLOOD BROTHER

"NOW THEN," SAID the psychiatrist, looking up from his note pad, "when did you first discover that you were dead?"

"Not dead," said the pale man in the dark suit. "Undead."

"I'm sorry."

"Just try to keep it straight. If I were dead, I'd be in great shape. That's the trouble, though. I can't die."

"Why not?"

"Because I'm not alive."

"I see." The psychiatrist made a rapid notation. "Now, Mr. Smith, I'd like you to start at the beginning, and tell me the whole story."

The pale man shook his head. "At twenty-five dollars an hour," he said, "are you kidding? I can barely afford to have my cape cleaned once a month."

"I've been meaning to ask you about that. Why do you wear it?"

"You ever hear of a vampire without a cape? It's part of the whole schmear, that's all. *I* don't know why!"

"Calm yourself."

"Calm myself! I wish I could. I tell you, Doctor, I'm

going right straight out of my skull. Look at this!" The man who called himself Smith put out his hands. They were a tremblous blur of white. "And look at this!" He pulled down the flaps beneath his eyes, revealing an intricate red lacework of veins. "Believe me," he said, flinging himself upon the couch, "another few days of this and I'll be ready for the funny farm!"

The psychiatrist picked a mahogany letter opener off his desk and tapped his palm. "I would appreciate it," he said, "if you would make an effort to avoid those particular terms."

"All right," said the pale man. "But you try living on blood for a year, and see how polite you are. I mean—"

"The beginning, Mr. Smith."

"Well, I met this girl, Dorcas, and she bit me."

"Yes?"

"That's all. It doesn't take much, you know."

The psychiatrist removed his glasses and rubbed his eyes. "As I understand it," he said, "you think you're a vampire."

"No," said Smith. "I *think* I'm a human being, but I *am* a vampire. That's the hell of it. I can't seem to adjust."

"How do you mean?"

"Well, the hours for instance. I used to have very regular habits. Work from nine to five, home, a little TV, maybe, into bed by ten, up at six-thirty. Now—" He shook his head violently from side to side. "You know how it is with vampires."

"Let's pretend I don't," said the psychiatrist, soothingly. "Tell me. How is it?"

"Like I say, the hours. Everything's upside-down. That's why I made this appointment with you so late. See, you're supposed to sleep during the *day* and work at *night*."

"Why?"

"Boy, you've got me. I asked Dorcas, that's the girl bit

me, and she said she'd try and find out, but nobody seems to be real sure about it."

"Dorcas," said the psychiatrist, pursing his lips. "That's an unusual name."

"Dorcas Schultz is an unusual girl, I'll tell you. A real nut. She's on that late-late TV show, you know? The one that runs all those crummy old horror movies?" Smith scraped a stain from his coat with his fingernail. "Maybe you know her. She recommended you."

"It's possible. But let's get back to you. You were speaking of the hours."

Smith wrung his hands. "They're murdering me," he said. "Eight fly-by-night jobs I've had—eight!—and lost every one!"

"Would you care to explain that?"

"Nothing to explain. I just can't stay awake, that's all. I mean, every night—I mean every *day*—I toss and turn for hours and then when I finally *do* doze off, boom, it's nightfall and I've got to get out of the coffin."

"The coffin?"

"Yeah. That's another sweet wrinkle. The minute you go bat, you're supposed to give up beds and take a casket. Which is not only sick, but expensive as *hell*." Smith shook his head angrily. "First you got to buy the damn thing. Do you know the cost of the average casket?"

"Well—" began the psychiatrist.

"Astronomical! Completely out of proportion. I'm telling you, it's a racket! For anything even halfway decent you're going to drop five bills, easy. But that's just the initial outlay. Then there's the cartage and the cleaning bills."

"I don't—"

"Seventy-five to a hundred every month, month in, month out."

"I'm afraid I—"

"The grave dirt, man! Sacking out in a coffin isn't bad

enough, no, you've got to line it with *soil from the family plot.* I ask you, who's got a family plot these days? Have you?"

"No, but—"

"Right. So what do you do? You go out and buy one. Then you bring home a couple pounds of dirt and spread it around in the coffin. Wake up at night and you're *covered* with it." Smith clicked his tongue exasperatedly. "If you could just wear pajamas—but no, the rules say the full bit. Ever *hear* of anything so crazy? You can't even take off your *shoes*, for cry eye!" He began to pace. "Then there's the blood-stains."

The psychiatrist lowered his pad, replaced his glasses, and regarded his patient with a not incurious eye.

"I must go through twenty white shirts a month," continued Smith. "Even at two-fifty a shirt, that's a lot of dough. You're probably thinking, Why isn't he more careful? Well, listen, I try to be. But it isn't like eating a bowl of tomato soup, you know." A shudder, or something like a shudder, passed over the pale man. "That's another thing. The diet. I mean, I always used to like my steaks rare, but this is ridiculous! Blood for breakfast, blood for lunch, blood for dinner. Uch—just the thought of it makes me queasy to the stomach!" Smith flung himself back onto the couch and closed his eyes. "It's the monotony that gets you," he said, "although there's plenty else to complain about. You know what I mean?"

"Well," said the psychiatrist, clearing his throat, "I—"

"Filthy stuff! And the routines I have to go through to get it! What if you had to rob somebody every time you wanted a hamburger—I mean, just supposing. That's the way it is with me. I tried stocking up on plasma, but that's death warmed over. A few nights of it and you've got to go after the real thing, it doesn't matter *how* many promises you've made to yourself."

"The real thing?"

"I don't like to talk about it," said Smith, turning his head to the wall. "I'm actually a very sensitive person, know what I mean? Gentle. Kind. Never could stand violence, not even as a kid. Now . . ." He sobbed wrackingly, leaped to his feet, and resumed pacing. "Do you think I *enjoy* biting people? Do you think I don't *know* how disgusting it is? But, I tell you, *I can't help it*! Every few nights I get this terrible urge . . ."

"Yes?"

"You'll hate me."

"No, Mr. Smith."

"Yes you will. Everybody does. Everybody hates a vampire." The pale man withdrew a large silk handkerchief from his pocket and daubed at sudden tears. "It isn't fair," he choked. "After all, we didn't *ask* to become what we are, did we? Nobody ever thinks of that."

"You feel, then, that you are being persecuted?"

"Damn right," said Smith. "And you know why? I'll tell you why. Because I *am* being persecuted. That's why. Have you ever heard a nice thing said about a vampire? Ever in your whole life? No. Why? Because people hate us. But I'll tell you something even sillier. They *fear* us, too!" The pale man laughed a wild, mirthless laugh. "*Us*," he said. "The most helpless creatures on the face of the Earth! Why, it doesn't take *anything* to knock us over. If we don't cut our throats trying to shave—you know the mirror bit: no reflection—we stand a chance to land flat on our back because the neighbor downstairs is cooking garlic. Or bring us a little running water, see what happens. We flip our lids. Or silver bullets. *Daylight*, for crying out loud! If I'm not back in that stupid coffin by dawn, zow, I'm out like a light. So I'm out late, and time sorts of gets away from me, and I look at my watch and I've got ten minutes. What do I do? Any other vampire in his right mind, he changes into a bat and flies. Not me. You know why?"

The psychiatrist shook his head.

"Because I can't stand the ugly things. They make me sick just to look at, let alone *be*. And then there's all the hassle of taking off your clothes and all. So I grab a cab and just pray there isn't any traffic. Boy. Or take these." He smiled for the first time, revealing two large pointed incisors. "What do you imagine happens to us when our choppers start to go? I've had this one on the left filled it must be half a dozen times. The dentist says if I was smart I'd have 'em all yanked out and a nice denture put in. Sure. Can't you just see me trying to rip out somebody's throat with a pair of false teeth? Or take the routine with the wooden stake. It used to be that was kind of a secret. Now with all these lousy movies, the whole *world* is in on the gag. I ask you, Doctor, how are you supposed to be able to sleep when you know that everybody in the block is just itching to find you so they can drive a piece of wood into your heart? Huh? Man, you talk about *sick*! Those people are in *really* bad shape!" He shuddered again. "I'll tell you about the jazz with crosses, but frankly, even thinking about it makes me jumpy. You know what? I have to walk three blocks out of my way to avoid the church I used to go to every Sunday. But don't get the idea it's just churches. No; it's *anything*. Cross your fingers and I'll start sweating. Lay a fork over a knife and I'll probably jump right out the window. So then what happens? I splatter myself all over the sidewalk, right? But do I die? Oh, hell, no. Doc, listen! You've got to help me! If you don't, I'm going to go off my gourd, I know it!"

The psychiatrist folded his note pad and smiled. "Mr. Smith," he said, "you may be surprised to learn that yours is a relatively simple problem . . . with a relatively simple cure."

"Really?" asked the pale man.

"To be sure," said the psychiatrist. "Just lie down on the couch there. That's it. Close your eyes. Relax. Good." The psychiatrist rose from his chair and walked to his desk.

"While it is true that this syndrome is something of a rarity," he said, "I do not forsee any great difficulty." He picked something off the top of the desk and returned. "It is primarily a matter of adjustment and of right thinking. Are you quite relaxed?"

Smith said that he was.

"Good," said the psychiatrist. "Now we begin the cure." With which comment he raised his arm high in the air, held it there for a moment, then plunged it down, burying the mahogany letter opener to its hilt in Mr. Smith's heart.

Seconds later, he was dialing a telephone number.

"Is Dorcas there?" he said, idly scratching the two circular marks on his neck. "Tell her it's her fiancée."

A DEATH
IN THE COUNTRY

Introduction by William F. Nolan

For eight years, from the mid 1950s into the early 1960s, Chuck Beaumont and I shared a feverish passion for auto racing. I owned and raced British Austin-Healeys; he owned and raced German Porsches. We co-edited two fat books of motor racing material, Omnibus of Speed and When Engines Roar. We attended (and reported on) dozens of road races from Pebble Beach to Sebring to Nassau in the Bahamas. We watched James Dean race his white Porsche Speedster at Palm Springs and Steve McQueen power to victory in his silver Lotus at Santa Barbara. We flew to Europe in 1960, to glory in the Monaco Grand Prix— full-throttle Formula One machines blasting through the streets of Monte Carlo! We knew all the top drivers, drank with them, rapped with them, anguished over their losses, celebrated their victories. And we wrote numerous articles and stories about the sport we loved. Among these: "A Death In the Country."

Although Chuck and I were almost totally into sports car and Grand Prix racing, the "stockers" also fascinated us. "A Death in the Country" reflects that fascination. It's a study of true grit, and had Ernest Hemingway turned his attention to the racing stockers, this is the kind of tale he would have written.

Professional stock-car racing can be glamourous and financially rewarding. But there is a second, darker side to the coin.

On the small dirt ovals, in numerous "tank towns" scattered across country, the big stockers lose their shine. Here the crowds are impatient and bloodthirsty, the purses small, the duels hard-fought and bitter. In the choking Sunday afternoon dust of the fender-to-fender conflict, fair play is a seldom indulged luxury; victory does not always belong to the swift, but more often to the savage. In this brilliantly-etched character study, Beaumont tells us about Buck Larsen, a scarred track warrior of the old school, who could not afford to lose.

When I read this story I remember long afternoons of blazing sun, the smells of oil and hot metal, the snarling sound of un-muffled engines at full battle cry. I remember the tension, the heart-in-the-throat excitement as a downswept flag releases the pack, the sudden roar of the crowd ... and I remember Chuck Beaumont, the finest, dearest friend a man could ever have. My racing days are many years behind me. I miss them. But, most of all, I miss old Chuck, God bless him.

I miss him very much.

HE HAD BEEN driving for 11 hours and he was hungry and hot and tired, but he couldn't stop, he couldn't pull over to the side of the road and stop under one of those giant pines and rest a little while; no. Because, he thought, if you do that, you'll fall asleep. And you'll sleep all night, you know that, Buck, and you'll get into town late, maybe too late to race, and then what will you do?

So he kept on driving, holding a steady 70 down the long straights, and through the sweeping turns that cut through the fat green mountains. He could climb to 80 and stay there and shorten the agony, except that it had begun to rain; and it was the bad kind that is light, like mist, and puts a slick film on the road. At 80 he would have to work.

Besides, you have got to take it easy now. He thought, you
have got a pretty old mill under the hood, and she's cranky
and just about ready to sour out, but she'd better not sour
out tomorrow. If she does, you're in a hell of a shape. You
know that all right. So let her loaf.

Buck Larsen rolled the window down another three
inches and sucked the cool, sharp air into his lungs. It was
clean stuff, with a wet pine smell, and it killed the heat
some and cleared his head, but he hated it, because rain
made it that way. And rain was no good. Sure, it was OK
sometimes; it made things grow, and all that; and probably
people were saying, by God, that's wonderful, that's
great—rain! But they would feel different if they had to
race on it, by Christ. It would be another story then. All
of a sudden they would look up at the sky and see some
dark clouds and their hearts would start pounding then and
they'd be scared, you can bet your sweet ass; they'd start
praying to God to hold it off just a little while, just a few
hours, please. But it would come, anyway. It would come.
And that nice dirt track would turn to mush and maybe
you're lucky and you don't total your car out, and maybe
this is not one of your lucky days and the money is gone
and you don't have a goddamn thing except your car and
you make a bid, only the rain has softened the track and
somebody has dug a hole where there wasn't any hole a lap
ago, and you hit it, and the wheel whips out of your hands
and you try to hold it, but it's too late, way too late, you're
going over. You know that. And nothing can stop you,
either, not all the lousy prayers in the world, not all the
promises; so you hit the cellar fast and hope that the roll
bar will hold, hope the doors won't fly open, hope the
yoyos in back won't plow into you—only they will, they
always do. And when it's all over, and maybe you have a
broken arm or a cracked melon, then you begin to wonder
what's next, because the car is totaled, and they'll insure a

blind airplane pilot before they'll insure you. And you can't blame them much, either. You're not much of a risk.

He shook his head hard, and tried to relax. It was another 60 miles to Grange. Sixty little miles. Nothing. You can do it standing up, you have before; plenty of times. (But you were younger then, remember that. You're 48 now. You're an old bastard, and you're tired and scared of the rain. That's right. You're scared.)

The hell!

Buck Larsen looked up at the slate-colored sky and frowned; then he peered through the misted windshield. A bend was approaching. He planted his foot on the accelerator and entered the curve at 97 miles per hour. The back end of the car began to slide gently to the left. He eased off the throttle, straightened, and fed full power to the wheels. They stuck.

Yeah, he said.

The speedometer needle slipped back to 70 and did not move. It was fine, you're OK, he thought, and you'll put those country fair farmers in your back pocket. You'd better, anyway. Maybe not for a first, but a second; third at worst. Third money ought to be around three hundred. But, he thought, what if the rain spoils the gate? Never mind, it won't. These yokels are wild for blood. A little rain won't stop them.

A sign read: GRANGE—41 MILES.

Buck snapped on his headlights. Traffic was beginning to clutter up the road, and he was glad of it, in a way; you don't get so worried when there are people around you. He just wished they wouldn't look at him that way, like they'd come to the funeral too early. You sons of bitches, he thought. You don't know me, I'm a stranger to you, but you all want to see me get killed tomorrow. That's what you want, that's why you'll go to the race. Well, I'm sorry to disappoint you. I really am. That's why I ain't popular: I stayed alive too long. (And then he thought, no, that isn't why. The reason you're not popular is because you don't go very good. Come on, Larsen, admit it. Face it. You're old and you're getting slow. You're getting cautious. That's why you don't run in the big events no more, because in those you're a tail-ender; maybe not dead last, but back in the back. Nobody sees you. Nobody pays you. And you work just as hard. So you make the jumps out here, in the sticks, running with the local boys, because you used to be pretty good, you used to be, and you've got a hell of a lot of experience behind you, and you can count on finishing in the money. But you're losing it. The coordination's on the way out; you don't think fast any more, you don't move fast; you don't drive fast.)

A big Lincoln, dipping with the ruts, rolled by. The driver stared. I'm sorry, Buck told him. I'd like to die for you, Buddy, but I just ain't up to it; I been kind of sick, you know how it goes. But come to the track anyway; I mean you never can tell. Maybe I'll go on my head, maybe I'll fall out and the stinking car will roll over the top of me and they'll have to get me up with a rake. It could happen.

Buck steadied the wheel with his elbows and lit the stump of his cigar. It could happen, OK, he thought. But not to me. Not to Buck Larsen. He clamped his teeth down hard on the cigar, and thought, yeah, that's what Carl Beecham always said: you got to believe it'll never happen to you. Except, Carl was wrong; he found that out—what was it?— four years ago at Bonelli, when he hit the wall and bounced off and went over . . .

He tightened his thick, square fingers on the taped wheel. He pulled down the shutters, fast. Whenever he'd find himself thinking about Carl, or Sandy, or Chick Snyder, or Jim Lonnergan, or any of the others, he would just pull a cord and giant shutters would come down in his mind and he would stop thinking about them. They had all been friends of his. Now they were dead, or retired and in business for themselves, and he didn't have anyone to go out and have a beer with, or maybe play cards or just fool around; he was alone; and you don't want to make a thing like that worse, do you?

So I'm alone. Lots of people are alone. Lots of people don't even have jobs not even lousy ones like this.

He told himself that he was in plenty good shape, and did not wonder—as he had once wondered—why, since he hated it, he had ever become a race driver. It was no great mystery. There'd been a dirt track in the town where he grew up. He'd started hanging around the pits, because he liked to watch the cars and listen to the noise. And he was young, but he was a pretty good mechanic anyway so he helped the drivers work on their machines. Then, he couldn't recall who it was, somebody got sick and asked him to drive. It was a thrill, and he hadn't had many thrills before. So he tried it again.

And that was it. He'd been driving ever since; it was the only thing he knew how to do for Christ's sake. (No, that wasn't true, either. He could make a living as a mechanic.)

So why don't I? I will. I'll take a few firsts and salt the dough away and start a garage and let the other bastards risk their necks. The hell with it.

The rain grew suddenly fierce, and he rolled up the window angrily. For almost an hour he thought of nothing but the car, mentally checking each part and making sure it was right. God knew he was handicapped enough as it was with a two-year-old engine; it took his know-how to find those extra horses, and still he was short. The other boys would be in new jobs, most of them. More torque. More top end. He'd have to fight some.

Buck slowed to 45, then to 25, and pulled up in front of a gas station. He went to the bathroom, splashed cold water over his face, wiped away some of the grime.

He went to a restaurant and spent one of his remaining six dollars on supper.

Then he took the Chevy to a hotel called The Plantation

and locked it up. The rain gleamed on its wrinkled hide, wrinkled from the many battles it had waged, and made it look a little less ugly. But it was ugly, anyhow. It had a tough, weathered appearance, an appearance of great and disreputable age; and though it bore a certain resemblance to ordinary passenger cars, it was nothing of the kind. It was a stripped-down, tight-sprung, lowered, finely-tuned, balanced savage, a wild beast with a fighter's heart and a fighter's instincts. On the highway, it was a wolf among lambs; and it was only on the track that it felt free and happy and at home.

The Chevy was like Buck Larsen himself, and Buck sensed this. The two of them had been through a lot together. They had come too close too many times. But they were alive, somehow, both of them, now, and they were together, and maybe they were ugly and old and not as fast as the new jobs, but they knew some things, by God, they knew some tricks the hot-dogs would never find out.

Buck glanced at the tires, nodded, and went into the hotel. He left a call for 5:30. the old man at the desk said he wouldn't fail. Buck went to his room, which was small and hot but only cost him three dollars, and what can you expect for that?

He listened to the rain and told it, Look, I'll find second or third tomorrow, you can't stop me, I'm sorry. A man's got to eat.

He switched off the light and fell into a dark black sleep.

When he awoke, he went to the window and saw that the rain had stopped; but it had stopped within the hour, and so it didn't matter. He went out and found a place that was open and ate a light breakfast of toast and coffee.

Then he drove the Chevy the 13 miles out of town to the Soltan track. It sat in the middle of a field that would normally have been dusty but now was like a river bank, the surface slimy with black mud. The track itself was like most others: a fence of gray, rotting boards; a creaking round of hard, spintery benches; a heavy wooden crash wall; and a narrow oval of wet dirt. A big roller was busily tamping it down, but this would do no good. A few hot qualifying laps and the mud would loosen. One short heat and it would be a lake again.

Dawn had just broken, and the gray light washed over the sky. It was quiet, the roller making no sound on the dirt, the man behind the roller silent and tired. It was cold, too, but Buck stripped off his cloth jacket. He got his tools out of the trunk and laid them on the ground. He removed the car's muffler's first; then, methodically, jacked up the rear end, took off the back left tire and examined it. He checked it for pressure, fitted it back onto the wheel and did the same with the other tires. Then he checked the wheels. Then the brakes.

Soon more cars arrived, and in a while the pits were full. When Buck finished with the Chevy, when he was sure as he could ever be that it was right and ready to go, he wiped his big hands on an oily rag and took a look at the competition.

It was going to be rougher than he'd thought. There were two brand new super-charged Fords, a 1957 fuel-injection Chevrolet, three Dodge D-500s, and a hot-looking Plymouth Fury. The remaining automobiles were more standard, several of them crash jobs, almost jalopies, the sides and top pounded out crudely.

Nineteen, in all.

And I've got to beat at least 17 of them, Buck thought. He walked over to a new Pontiac and looked inside. It was a meek job, real meek. But you can't tell. He examined the name printed on the side of the car: Tommy Linden.

Nobody. Buck put the rag away, returned to the Chevy. Several hours had passed, and soon it would be 12 o'clock, qualifying time. He'd better get some rest.

He lay down on a canvas tarpaulin and was about to

close his eyes, when he saw a young man walking up to the
Pontiac. They apparently hadn't heard of the No Females
Allowed rule in Soltan, for a girl was with him. She was
young, too; maybe 21, 22. And not hard and mannish, like
most of them, but soft and light and clean. Some girls always stay clean, Buck thought. No matter what they do,
where they are. If Anna-Lee had been more that way (or
even a little) maybe he'd of stuck with her. But she was a
dog. Why the hell do you marry a damn sloppy broad like
that in the first place? God. He looked at the girl and
thought of his ex-wife, then focused on the kid. Twenty-
five. Handsome, brawny: he thinks he's got a lot, that one.
You can usually tell. Look at his eyes.

Buck half-dozed until a loudspeaker announced time for
qualifying; he sat up then and listened to the order of the
numbers. Twenty-two, first. Ninety-one, second, Seven,
third.

He was ninth.

People started running around in the pits; customers
drifted up into the grandstands; the speaker blared; then
number 22, a yellow Ford, rolled up to the line.

It roared away at the drop of the flag.

Others followed.

When he was called, Buck patted the Chevy, listened to
it, and grunted. The track was getting chewed up, but it
was still possible to get around quickest time. He eased off
the mark slowly as the flag dropped, got up some steam on
the backstretch and came thundering across the line with
his foot planted. He grazed the south wall slightly on his
second try, but it was nothing, only a scratch.

He went to the pits and removed his helmet in time to
hear the announcer's voice: "Car number six, driven by
Buck Larsen—26:15."

The crowd murmured approval. Buck decided it would
be a decent gate and settled down again. The Fury went
through at something over 26:15.

Then it was the Pontiac's turn.

"Car number 14, driven by Tommy Linden, up."

The gray car's pipes growled savagely as it rolled out. The track was bad, now. Really bad. Buck felt better: he had second starting position sewed up. No one could drop a hell of a lot off of 26:15 in this soup.

The Pontiac accelerated so hard at take-off that the rear almost slewed around. Easy, 14, Buck thought. Easy. It'll impress the little girl but your ass'll be at the end of the pack.

Number 14 came through the last turn almost sideways, straightened, and screamed across the line. It stuck high on the track, near the wall, at every curve. Buck saw the kid's face as he went by. It was unsmiling. The eyes were fixed straight ahead.

Then it was over, and the loudspeaker roared: "Tommy Linden, number 14, turns it in 26:13!"

Buck frowned. The other supercharged Ford would probably make it under 26. Sure it would, with that torque.

The kid crawled out of the Pontiac but before he could get his helmet off, the girl in the pink dress jumped from the stack of tires and began to pull awkwardly at the strap. The kid grinned. "Come on, leave it go," he said, and pushed the girl gently aside. Already his face was dirty, no longer quite so young. He looked at his tires and walked over to Buck. "Hey," he said, "I had somebody fooling with my hat, I didn't get the time. You remember what I turned?"

"26:13," Buck said.

"Not too bad, huh?" the kid said, happily. Then, he spit out his gum. "What'd you turn?"

"26:15."

The kid appraised Buck, looked at his age and the worry in his face. "That's all right," he said, "hell, nothing wrong with that. You been around Soltan before?"

"Not for a while," Buck said.

"Well, like, sometimes I steal a little practice; you know?" He paused. "I'm Tommy Linden, live over to Pinetop."

Buck did not put out his hand. "Larsen," he said.

The young man took another piece of gum from his pocket, unwrapped it, folded it, put it into his mouth. "I'll tell you something," he said. "See, like I told you, I practice here once in a while. I got Andy Gammon's garage backing me—they're in Pinetop?—see, and the thing is, I'm kind of after 36. You know? The blown Ford?"

"Yeah."

"So, what I mean is, if you can pass me, what the hell, go on, know what I mean? But, uh—if you can't, I'd appreciate it if you'd stay out of my way." The kid's eyes looked hard and angry. "I mean I really want me that Ford."

Buck lit his cigar, carefully. "I'll do what I can," he said.

"Thanks a lot," the kid said. Then he winked. "I got the chick along, see. She thinks I'm pretty good. I don't want to let her down; you know?" He slapped Buck's arm and walked back to his own car, walked lightly, on the balls of his feet. His jeans were tight and low on his waist and the bottoms were stuffed into a pair of dark boots. He doesn't have a worry, Buck thought. He may be a little scared, but he's not worried. It's better that way.

The sun began to throb and the heat soaked into Buck's clothes and he began to feel the old impatience, the agony of waiting. Why the hell did they always take so damn long? he wondered. No reason for it.

He started to walk across the track, but the plate in his leg was acting up—it did that whenever it rained—and he sat down instead. His face was wet; dirt caked into the shiny scar tissue behind his ear, and perspiration beaded the tips of the black hairs that protruded from his nostrils. He looked over and saw Tommy Linden and the girl in the pink dress. She was whispering something into the kid's ear; he was laughing.

Damn the heat! He wiped his face, turned from Tommy Linden and the girl and rechecked his tires. Then he checked them again. Then it was time for the first race, a five-lap trophy dash. It didn't count for anything.

The race started; the two Fords shot ahead at once, Buck gunned the Chevy and took after them. Number 14 spent too much time spinning its wheels and had to drop behind. But it stayed there, weaving to the right, then to the left, pushing hard. Buck knew he could hold his position—anyone could in a five lapper—but he decided not to take any chances; it didn't mean a goddamn. So he swung wide and let the Pontiac rush past on the inside. It fishtailed violently with the effort, but remained on the track.

Within a couple of minutes it was over, and Buck's Chevy was the only car that had been passed: he'd had no trouble holding off the Mercs, and they kept daylight between themselves and the Fury.

But of course it meant nothing. The short heats were just to fill up time for the crowd; nobody took them seriously.

A bunch of motorcycles went around for 10 laps, softening up the dirt even more; there were two more dashes; and then it was time for the big one—for the 150 lap Main Event.

Once again Buck pulled into line; it was to be an inverted start. Fast cars to the rear, slow cars in front.

He slipped carefully into the shoulder harness, cinched the safety belt tight across his lap, checked the doors, and put on his helmet. It was hot, but he might as well get used to it; he'd have the damn thing on for a long time.

Number 14 skidded slightly beside him, its engine howling. Tommy Linden fitted his helmet on and stretched theatrically. His eyes met Buck's and held.

"You know what?" Linden yelled. "I don't think them two Fords is exactly stock, you know what I mean?"

Buck smiled. The kid's OK, he thought. A pretty nice kid. "Well, are *you*?" he shouted.

"Hell, no!" Linden roared with amusement.

"Me either."

"What?"

The loudspeaker crackled. "Red Norris will now introduce the drivers!"

Up ahead, the track was like a rained-on mountain trail; great clots of mud and sticky pools of black surfaced it all the way around; there wasn't a clear hard spot anywhere.

Buck glanced over at number 14 and saw Tommy Linden waving up at the grandstand. A middle-aged man waved back. Buck turned away.

"Gonna let me get him?" The kid was pointing at number 36.

"Don't ask me! Ask him!"

"Yeah, why don't I do that!"

After the introductions, the official starter walked up with a green flag, furled. The drivers all buckled their helmets. The silence lasted a moment, then was torn by the successive explosions that trembled out of the 19 racing stock cars.

Buck stopped smiling; he stopped thinking of Tommy Linden, of any other human being. He thought only of the moments to come. I'll follow 36 he decided, let it break trail; then I'll hang on. That's all I have to do. Just don't get too damn close to the wall. You don't want to spend time pounding out a door. Be smooth. Hang on to 36 and you're in hardward.

The cars roared like wounded lions for almost a full minute, and some sounded healthy while others coughed enough to show that they were not so healthy; then the man with the flag waved them off, in a bunch, for the rolling start. Buck could see the Pontiac straining at the leash, inching forward, and he kept level. They circulated slowly around, the starter judged them, he judged they were all right, and gave them the flag.

It was a race.

Buck immediately cut his wheel for a quick nip inside the Pontiac, but the kid was quicker; he'd anticipated the move and edged to the right to hold Buck off. At the first turn, number 14 threw its rear around viciously, and Buck knew he'd have to kiss the wall and bull through or drop back. He dropped back. There was plenty of time.

He followed the Pontiac closely, but he found that it was not so easy after all. The car cowboyed through every turn, scaring off the tail-enders, and it was everything he could do to hang on. Ahead, the Fords were threading their way through traffic with great ease, leaving a wake of thick mud.

He relaxed some and allowed the long years of his experience to guide the car. Gradually the Pontiac was picking off the stragglers; within 15 minutes it had passed the sixth place Mercury, and was drawing up on five.

You better not try it, Buck said. Those boys aren't working too hard. They can go a lot faster. I hope you know that.

But the Pontiac didn't settle down, it didn't slacken its pace any, and Buck knew that he would have to revise his strategy. He'd planned to wait for number 14 to realize that it couldn't hope for better than a third; then he was going to bluff him. You can bluff them when the fever's passed, when they're not all out and driving hard.

But he could see that he wasn't going to be able to bluff the Pontiac.

He could only outdrive him, nerf him a little, maybe, shake him up, cause him to bobble that one time, and then streak by.

Once the decision was made, Buck moved well back in the seat. They were about halfway through now. Give it seven more laps; then make the bid.

He swung past a beat-up Dodge on the north turn and
was about to correct when the driver lost it. The Dodge
went into a frenzied spin, skimmed across the muddy track
and bounded off the wall. Buck yanked his tape-covered
wheel violently to the left, then to the right, and managed
to avoid the car. Damn! Now number 14 was four up and
going like the wind. Well. Buck put his bumper next to the
Merc in front of him and stabbed the accelerator. The Merc
wavered, moved; Buck went by. It worked on the second
car, too; and he was in position to catch 14 as it was passing
a Ford on the short straight.

He waited another three laps, until they were out of the
traffic somewhat, and began to ride the Pontiac's tail. They
both hit a deep rut and both fishtailed, but no more than
three inches of daylight showed between them.

Buck tried to pass on the west turn by swinging left and
going in a little deeper, but the Pontiac saw him and went
just as deep; both missed the wall by less than a foot.

Perspiration began to course down Buck's forehead, and
when he tried nerfing 14, and found that it wouldn't work,
that 14 wasn't going to scare, the thought suddenly brushed
his mind that perhaps he would not finish third after all.
But if he didn't then he wouldn't be able to pay for gas to
the next town or for a hotel, even, or anything.

His shoulders hunched forward, and Buck Larsen began
to drive; not the way he had been driving for the past two
years, but as he used to, when he was young and worried
about very little, when he had friends and women.

You want to impress your girlfriend, he said to the Pontiac.

I just want to go on eating.

He made five more passes during the following six laps,
and twice he almost made it, but the track was just a little
too short, a little too narrow, and he was forced to drop
behind each time.

When he was almost certain that the race was nearing

its finish, he realized that other tactics would have to be used. He clung to 14's bumper through traffic on the straight; then, as they dived into the south turn, he hung back for a fraction of a second—long enough to put a bit of space between them. Then he pulled down onto the inside and pushed the accelerator flat. The Chevy jumped forward; in a moment it was nearly even with the Pontiac.

Buck considered nothing whatever except keeping his car in control; he knew that the two of them were at that spot, right there, where one would have to give, but he didn't consider any of this.

The two cars entered the turn together, and the crowd screamed and some of the people got to their feet and some closed their eyes. Because neither car was letting off.

Neither car was slowing.

Buck did not move his foot on the pedal; he did not look at the driver to his right; he plunged deeper, and deeper, up to the point where he knew that he would lose control, even under the best of conditions; the edge, the final thin edge of destruction.

He stared straight ahead and fought the wheel through the turn, whipping it back and forth, correcting, correcting.

Then, it was all over.

He was through the turn; and he was through first.

He didn't see much of the accident: only a glimpse, in his rear view mirror, a brief flash of the Pontiac swerving to miss the wall, losing control, going up high on its nose and teetering there . . .

A flag stopped the race. The other cars had crashed into the Pontiac, and number 14 was on fire. It wasn't really a bad fire, but the automobile had landed on its right side, and the left side was bolted and there were bars on the window, so they had to get it cooled off before they could pull the driver out.

He hadn't broken any bones. But something had happened to the fuel line and the hood had snapped open and the windshield had collapsed and some gasoline had splashed onto Tommy Linden's shirt. The fumes had caught and he'd burned long enough.

He was dead before they got him into the ambulance.

Buck Larsen looked at the girl in the pink dress and tried to think of something to say, but there wasn't anything to say, there never was.

He collected his money for third place—it amounted to $350—and put the mufflers back on the Chevy and drove away from the race track, out onto the long highway.

The wind was hot on his face, and soon he was tired and hungry again; but he didn't stop, because if he stopped he'd sleep, and he didn't want to sleep, not yet. He thought one time of number 14, then he lowered the shutters and didn't think any more.

He drove at a steady 70 miles per hour and listened to the whine of the engine. She would be all right for another couple of runs, he could tell, but then he would have to tear her down.

Maybe not, though.

Maybe not.

THE MUSIC OF
THE YELLOW BRASS

EVEN NOW HE could not believe it, so quickly had it happened, so unexpectedly, and after so many years. How many? Juanito tried to remember. Three. No; four. Four years of sleeping in filthy boxcars, on park benches, on the ground with only his dirt-stiffened cape for protection against the angry winds; of stealing, and, when he could not, begging; of running in the path of Impresarios (*"Next year!"*)—and all the long nights, dreaming. And now. *Now!*

"How do I look?" he asked.

"All right," said Enrique Córdoba, shrugging.

"Just all right? Just that?"

The older man said, "Look, Juanito, look. You're skinny. A scarecrow."

"So?" The boy smiled. "In the *traje de luces* it will be different. No belly for the horn. Huh?"

"Right."

"Are you annoyed with me, Enrique?"

"No."

"You act that way."

"And you act like a fool!"

"Because I'm happy? Because I show it?"

They walked in silence.

"I know. You're afraid I'll put on a bad show; that's it. You've worked for me and got me a fight at the Plaza and you're thinking. Maybe he won't do well—"

"Shut up."

For another two blocks they walked, not speaking. Then Juanito saw the big white sign, saw the glass doors of the hotel and, beyond, the rich wine-colored rug and the crystal chandeliers, and his heart beat faster.

"Relax," whispered Enrique.

They went into the hotel. At a thick ivory door, the older man seemed to hesitate. Then, in solid motions, he rapped his horny knuckles against the wood, once, twice.

"Enter!"

The door opened to a vast, luxurious room hung in bright tapestries and decorated with *puntillas* and capes and swords of antique silver, and, over the bar, the head of a bull.

Juanito tried to swallow, but could not. He looked once at the people, who were talking loudly and moving, then directed his blurred gaze toward Enrique.

A voice said: *"Hola!"*

Enrique did not smile. Instead, he nodded and touched his brow. "I hope that we're not late, Don Alfredo."

Juanito felt the approach of the giant Impresario. A heavy hand touched his shoulder. *"Hola,* Matador. Are you afraid to look at us?"

"No, Señor."

Don Alfredo, Alfredo Camara, who had stepped around him as though he were a cockroach yesterday, was grinning widely. His face was shiny with sweat and there were sacks beneath his large wet eyes. He learned forward. "How is it, then? Are you in shape?" he asked. "All ready for to-morrow?"

"Yes, Señor."

The hand thumped Juanito's back. "Good!" Then Don Alfredo turned and cried, in a high, squeaking voice: "Attention! Attention!"

The people in the room stopped talking. Juanito recognized some of them: Francesco Perez, who only last week cut both ears and the tail; Manolo Lombardini, the idol of the season; the great Garcia, who never smiled and never left a ring without a smear of blood across his thighs . . .

"You've heard me talk of my new discovery," said Don Alfredo. "Well, here he is. Juan Galvez!"

There was applause; the first applause that Juanito had ever heard. A sweet, exciting sound!

"So, at last you see him. But you do not truly see him, as I have, facing the horns. Then he is most fearsome, most beautiful. Eh, Señor Córdoba?"

Enrique nodded again.

"So close, my friends! It is a marvel. I know. Would I allow him in the Plaza otherwise?"

Some of the men laughed. Others did not.

Don Alfredo pointed to a girl in a black dress and snapped his fingers. She poured tequila into two glasses and gave the glasses to Enrique and Juanito.

"The other is his manager, also his *mozo de espada*: Enrique Córdoba. He came to me a month ago, to plead for his boy. 'We are filled up!' I told him; and, you know, 'Come again next year—' "

Garcia chuckled and shook his head.

"But wait, this fellow is persistent. Most persistent. 'Don Alfredo,' he says, 'I ask only that you watch my boy work out. In the Plaza. Watch and you will see that he is a star.' What they all say, huh? But, as it happened, Perez was going to be there—to work off a hangover, isn't that so, Francesquito?"

The great Matador made a motion with his hands. "No." he said, "that isn't so. You're a liar and a bandit."

"Unkind!"

As Juanito listened to the exchange, standing there with the fat hand clamped upon him, his eyes wandered past Perez to the corner of the room.

A woman was there, a young woman, in a bright red dress of velvet which showed off her smooth skin and her high, large breasts.

She was staring.

"Like all *toreros*!" roared Don Alfredo. "An eye for beauty. Hey!"

The woman walked toward them, slowly, her hips moving beneath the velvet dress.

"This," said the Impresario, "is Andrée. I think she has noticed you, Galvez!"

With a grunt, Enrique moved away.

"Well, young fellow, don't you want to make the lady's acquaintance?"

The woman smiled. Again, Juanito could not swallow. He touched her outstretched hand.

The Impresario's high voice shrieked: "A shy *torero*! God deliver me!"

The woman came closer. "I am happy to meet you at last Señor Galvez," she said.

"Yes, but you will be happier tomorrow night! For then he'll be the talk of Mexico!"

Juanito imitated her motions with the glass. The tequila was like fire in his throat. It made his eyes water.

"He weeps at the thought," cried Garcia solemnly.

"It shows he is sensitive," answered the Impresario. "Listen, everybody: I'm not through with the introduction! Where was I?"

"Robbing a blind grandmother," said Pérez. "You were forced to kick her senseless—"

"Quiet! Now listen; we had access to a novillo. Small, but dangerous. Right, Francesquito?"

"Always," said Pérez.

"When you were through, remember? I saw this Córdoba. How he got through the guards, I could not guess. Anyway: 'Let my boy show you!' he said; 'Only watch him for a few minutes!' I demurred. 'Suicide!' I told him. But,

like I said, he is persistent. To shut him off, I granted his
wish." Camara turned to the woman. "Andrée, do you
know what happened then?"

"No. Tell me."

"This boy, Juan Galvez, sprang into the ring with the
dirtiest *capote* I have ever seen, and right off—right off,
with an experienced bull!—he made a *perfect Chicuelina*!"

"No."

"Yes! Then another, then a half-veronica—God, how
excited he made me! Like a spectator. My mouth was
open."

The girl next to Lombardini giggled.

"Silence. For *ten minutes* he worked this *novillo*;
then—"

"Then?"

"He was tossed. Of course." Don Alfredo shrugged.
"But it was not his fault: the bull by this time knew man
from cape. However, do you think he was fazed by it,
this Galvez? He was *not* fazed by it! Up again and some of
the finest passes I have witnessed since the time of El
Gallo!"

The woman in the velvet dress turned. "Olé," she said,
softly.

"So, well, you can see, all of you, why I did not *hesitate*
to put him on the same bill with Pérez and Lombardini."
The large man snorted. "And if you two charlots are not
careful, the little boy will steal all the glory, too!"

Juanito's body tingled. Even to be in the same room with
these men whom he had seen before only as gods in gold
thread, that was enough; but to hear these words . . .

"Great caution, Galvez," said Garcia, wagging his finger, "or the ears I cut will be yours."

Everyone laughed. Then the Impresario released his grip.
"I tell you what," he said. "You and Andrée get ac-
quainted. Enjoy yourselves."

"Yes, Señor."

"Good." Camara slapped Juanito's arm, hard, and wandered back to the crowd of people. Surprisingly, Enrique was drinking. In long swallows. Drinking, then filling up, and drinking more.

"What shall I call you?" asked the woman whose name was Andrée.

"Whatever you like."

"Juanito?"

"If you wish."

A fast tune began to play on the phonograph; couples began to dance.

"Don Alfredo tells me you have style."

"I try. You—follow the bulls?"

"Oh yes," she said. "It's a passion."

They looked at one another, silently, for a moment; then Juanito said, "Excuse me, please," and walked to the other side of the room.

"Enrique, let's go home," he said.

"What? Why?"

"I'm tired."

Enrique shook his head. "It would be an insult to Don Alfredo," he said. "Do you want to offend the man who's giving you your big break?"

"No, of course not. But—"

"Then, relax. It's early: only nine. Drink a little, talk to the woman."

"You said women were bad for me."

"Only the bunis. This one is all right. She's got class. Don't you like her?"

Juanito knew that she was staring at him. "Yes," he said. "She is very beautiful."

"Then what?"

"I don't know."

"Aah! Take your sad face away from here, then, so I can enjoy myself!"

Juanito stepped back. So long he had known this man,

so well; but never had he seen this mood upon Enrique. Perhaps, he thought, it is his way of being excited. Certainly; yes!

"Care to dance?"

The woman, Andrée, was moving slightly in time to the music. Young, Juanito decided. Not so young as his own nineteen years, maybe. But not much over. The flesh was firm everywhere, and everywhere smooth: incredibly smooth!

"If you don't," she said. "I'll tell Don Alfredo and he'll be angry. Now, take my arms."

"I'm sorry, but I—"

"No, no! You're doing fine. Just twirl me a little, this way; now back, so. Wonderful!"

The music grew louder and faster and soon Juanito was remembering the steps that whore from Tijuana had taught him. He was beginning to like the nearness of the woman, though it still frightened him, and he particularly liked it when she clapped her hands and threw her head back and then touched her hips to his.

"Well done!" cried a voice, Don Alfredo's.

"Yes!" said Andrée. "He is light on my feet!"

Juanito got the joke and laughed. From the corner of his eye, he watched the other men, the great Matadors, and saw that they were dancing, also, with their women.

I am one of them, he thought, remembering the endless dream.

They accept me, I am one of them!

Andrée was perspiring now. Her rich black hair, like tiny slender strips of dark metal, hung about her face; her eyes were ponds in which the lights were swimming; and her lips, to Juanito, were the softest and fullest in all the world, half-open always, revealing the whitest and straightest of teeth, the most quickly darting tongue that ever hid in the warm night of a girl's mouth . . .

"More tequila, *torero*?"

He started to say no, no more, but in a flash the woman was gone, and in a flash, back again.

"To us," she said.

Juanito drank. Then, as his limbs were losing all their weight, the music slowed, and the woman pressed her body close to his and put her face next to his.

"Andrée," he said.

She made a catlike sound in her throat.

"Andrée, who are you with?"

She pulled her head back lazily. "With you," she murmured.

"No. That isn't what I mean. Whose . . . woman are you?"

Only the deep sound again, from her throat.

"Garcia's?"

"Don't worry," she said. "You didn't steal me."

"Perez's?"

"I'm here as Don Alfredo's guest. He is a relative."

"Oh."

" 'Oh' ? You sound disappointed, Señor Galvez. Tell me, does the fruit always taste better when it's stolen?"

Juanito blushed hotly. "No," he said, "No, no."

"Then why are you so afraid to take a bite?"

Her flesh burned against his, then, and his mind began to swirl. He saw the bull's head, dead eyes staring blindly down . . . "Forgive me," he said, and made for the corner where Enrique had been drinking. As he walked he saw that most of the other guests had departed. Of the Matadors, only Lombardini remained, asleep on the floor.

A clock read ten minutes until midnight.

"Hey, *torero*! Are you lost?"

Don Alfredo thrust out a pudgy hand. He came close, smelling of liquor and colognes.

"I didn't know it was so late," said Juanito, looking away from the fat, glistening face. "Have you seen Enrique?"

"Your manager? The ugly one?"

"Enrique, my *mozo*."

"He is gone," said Don Alfredo Camara, grinning. "Too much tequila."

Juanito felt a tightening in his chest. On this night of all nights, for Enrique to desert him! To go without a word! "When did he leave?"

"An hour ago. Two hours. Why?"

Once more, Juanito could not find the words.

"He was going to take you with him," said the large man, lighting a fresh cigarette from the one he had been smoking, "but I pointed out, how unfair! I told him we'd take care of you. And . . . have we?"

"Yes, Señor."

"So, then, everything is okay." The fingers dug into Juanito's arm. "Take it from one who knows, you must be calm, relaxed, the night before the big fight. So important. Believe me."

"Yes, Señor."

"The going home early is an old wive's tale, a fantasy. It doesn't work. You try to sleep, but instead you dream about the next afternoon. It grows real in your mind. So real. You hear the crowd screaming and you see the toril gate opening . . . so? No sleep at all. Next day you're a wreck. Logical, Juan Galvez? Reasonable?"

Juanito nodded. It went against everything he'd ever heard, against Enrique's advice, but it sounded right, somehow. Certainly it was true that he would dream . . .

"I apologize, Don Alfredo."

"For what? Go, now, back and have some fun. Get yourself exhausted. Then sleep soundly!"

Juanito watched as the Impresario turned and weaved his way back to the couch and sprawled, giggling, over the woman in the black dress.

"Your keeper is missing?"

The words were mocking. He wheeled. Andrée was smiling at him, her body still moving to the music.

"Enrique is not my keeper," he said, in a slow, even voice.

"No? Who then?"

He took a step toward her. "No one." He pulled her quickly to him and pressed with all his strength. "No one," he repeated, angrily. "No one. You understand?"

Her eyes were big. When she tried to slip from his grasp, Juanito pressed harder. "Yes," she said, finally. His hands moved up to her hair; slowly he forced her lips to his, then, feeling a river of strange new sensations sweeping over him, he released the woman.

She stared at him, a difference in her eyes. Then she walked to the ivory closet door and returned.

"Help me," she said.

He held the dark fur jacket.

"Have you a car?"

"No," he said.

"I do." She put her arm through his. "Come on."

Juanito cast a glance back at the room. Don Alfredo was peering behind a gray curtain of smoke; there was no expression on his face, no expression at all.

The door closed.

In another room, in another part of the city, another door closed.

"Pour us a drink," the woman said, pointing to the nightstand next to the large yellow bed.

Juanito took a curved silver flask from the drawer, unscrewed the top and let it dangle by this tiny steel necklace. His heart was pumping fast, the way it used to when he would steal into the big ranches at night and work the bulls by starlight and shadow. He was afraid. And that was why he knew he must not run, must not take a backward step.

He tilted his head and let the liquid fire sear down his throat; then he carried the flask to the woman.

She drank. He saw the muscles of her neck moving.

Together, in minutes, they emptied the silver flask.

Then the woman took off her coat, flinging it into a corner. In the dim light of the single shell-shaded lamp, her red dress burned into Juanito's eyes.

He moved toward her. Quickly, she stepped aside, twisting her body and laughing.

He shook his head. Again he reached for her, again she was not there.

"Heiiiiiii! *Toro!*" the woman said, softly.

Juanito lunged, missed, slammed against the wall.

"Toro! Toro!"

Then he felt the velvet in his hands. Soft as light, hot as a wound! So hot!

"Wait, Señor Galvez!"

He took his hands away, fingers spread, and watched as Andrée removed first the slender black ribbon from her throat, then the dress, the shoes, the silk stockings . . .

"Now, my torero," she whispered, coming toward him, "let us see some of this style Don Alfredo talks about!"

In his mind there was not the blackness of true sleep, but, instead, bright afternoon sun, the colors of the crowd, the sand against is slippers, wind, and the toril gate, opening, and from it thundering—Andrée . . .

"No!"

He felt the firm, familiar grip around his arms.

"Not yet, Enrique. I'm tired. I've got to sleep some more!"

"Like hell!" Enrique's voice was loud. "Up!"

Juanito leaped when the water struck his face. The sudden movement made him aware of the ache in his head, in his muscles, of the empty throb in his stomach.

"What a filthy mess you are!"

He opened his eyes, carefully, and closed them. He tried to remember. "What time is it?"

"Late."

"I—Enrique, Enrique, get me a glass of water."

"Get it yourself!"

Painfully, he moved to the sink and drank until he could drink no more. Then he turned and said, "I'm sorry."

The older man grunted. He walked to the window and stood there for a time. Finally, after many minutes, he said, "Forget it."

"You're not angry?"

"No,"said Enrique Córdoba. His face took on a new expression: an expression of kindness, gentleness. "These things, they happen," he said. "You're young. I guess that once won't hurt you. How do you feel?"

"Fine," Juanito lied.

His manager lighted a cigar and puffed on it. "You never had one with class before," he said. "How did you like it?"

Juanito smiled. The ache in his stomach was great, but his relief to know that Enrique was not angry was greater. "You shouldn't have left me, poppa," he said.

Enrique's face darkened. "Don't call me that," he said.

"Just a joke."

"This is not the time for jokes, stupid. This is a time for thought."

"I've never been much good at it. You're my brains—"

"No! I am not your brains! I am not your poppa! I am only Enrique, only that, understand?"

"Sure!" Juanito said, holding back his anger and his confusion. "Sure, all right." He tried to whistle a miriachi tune, then stopped because it sounded bad. "You—want to take a trip down to the pens?" he asked. "I'd like to see my *novillo*."

"No, bad luck on the first one. I've seen him, he's nothing special. Just a big ox with horns."

"Big, you say?"

Enrique shrugged. "Nothing," he repeated. "You'll have no trouble."

"I still can't believe it," Juanito said, rubbing water into his hair. "Yesterday we were starving. That guy in Villa de Nombre de Dios—you remember?—Diaz; he wouldn't even let me touch his precious seed bull. And now, today—"

Enrique slapped his hands together. "No time for mooning," he said. "There are newspapermen coming. We'll have to rake out this corral."

Two hours later the men came. One, a thin fellow with a mustache kept smiling; but that, Juanito understood, was because he did not expect much of a *novillero*. *Novilleros* almost always fell on their faces the first time out.

But not I, he thought.

And thought this until an hour and a half before the time of the event, with the people already filling the stands, seating themselves, discussing prospects. Then Enrique laid out the expensive suit of lights.

Slowly, as though modeling an exotic statue, he dressed Juanito. Starting first with the *talequilla*, the pants, skintight; and then, the tassels on the knees; the shirt, the jacket, the vest, and the slim red four-in-hand tie.

"So, diestro," he said, moving back.

Juanito looked at his image in the mirror. It was the first *traje de luces* he had ever worn, and he felt great excitement and pride. "*Diestro*," he murmured, rolling the word over and over in his mind. "Enrique, it feels right, Enrique. Such a brave outfit. Who could be afraid and dressed like this?"

The manager picked up his cigar and relighted it. "Nice fit," was all he said.

"Maybe," said Juanito, grinning, "we should leave me home and send the suit to fight, huh?"

Enrique did not laugh; he picked up the moña, the pigtail, and clipped it to Juanito's head.

"Come on," he said.

They went out to the waiting car and rode in silence through the crowded streets to the Plaza.

When the car stopped, Enrique said: "How do you feel? I mean, *really*?"

"Fine, fine."

"Liar!"

Juanito shook his head. "No," he said. "It's true. How else could I feel on the greatest day of my life? The day we dreamed about and talked about, Enrique, all those years! Remember? Think of them."

The manager started out of the automobile. He was perspiring heavily, and his fingers trembled. The sounds of the crowd could be heard, then suddenly, the music. He fell back against the seat and closed his eyes.

"Christ in His pain!" he said.

"What is it?" Juanito asked. "You sick?"

"Yes," said Enrique Córdoba. "Yes! Sick!" He covered his face with his hands. "Juan," he said, in a muffled voice, "listen to me. Listen to me. I'm a fool and more stupid than the most stupid ox and I'm putting a knife into my own throat to tell you this—" He removed his hands from his face. His eyes were berry-black and cold now; moving. "I am not a killer!" he said.

"I don't understand what you're saying."

"Then *listen*, I tell you! If you were not so dumb, so stupid, you'd have guessed it yourself! This deal—it's fake, all if it. Fake, Juanito! Engineered. You comprehend?"

"No."

"Why do you think Don Alfredo took you on?"

"Because he saw me fight, because he liked my style!"

"Your style! My mother. You have none, Juanito; none at all! This will hurt, very deep, but we're through, anyway, all through, so I'm going to give it to you straight." The older man paused, then went on, his words rushing together: "You're no good. You never were. I have seen *espontaneos* a hundred times better. But I stuck with you because you knew how to steal, anyway, and I did not like to be alone. It's true that for a while I thought I could teach you a little—but I couldn't; no one could. You were hopeless. Guts; nothing else." Another pause. "One night, when we were starving, here in the city, I went to the Cafe de los Niños. To see if I could borrow some money. I ran into a boy named Pepete, who worked for Don Alfredo. He told me something. Maybe it would interest me—"

"Go on, Enrique."

"I will! The boy told me that business was getting bad at the Plaza. No torero, he said, had been killed for a long time. Too long. The people were losing enthusiasm. They were getting bored."

Juanito's fingers rubbed hard against the gold lamé of his suit.

"I got drunk," continued Enrique, "and this Pepete, he took me to the hotel of the Impresario. One thousand pesos that fat slug offered me, Juanito. One thousand! To a man who had not eaten in a week!"

"What did he offer you the one thousand pesos for, Enrique?"

"Use your head! It's simple. For the sum I would guarantee an unskilled *torero*. Camara watched you in that pitiful spectacle with Perez's bull a few days later, to make sure. And the deal was settled. You see?"

Juanito sat very still for several minutes, listening to the music and the people. Unable to believe it yet, he said: "You did not think I could stand up to a *novillo*?"

"Novillo!" Enrique wiped his forehead with a handkerchief. "Listen, the bull they have got for you knows Latin. He has fought before, on the ranch; many times. He's twice as smart as any torero could ever be."

"And—the girl, Andrée, last night?"

"Of course! To be absolutely certain. The girl, the drinks!"

"Everything."

"Everything." Enrique lowered his voice. "Let's go," he said. "I have a third of the money, it will take us a few miles, then we can hide for a month or so . . ."

Juanito checked the hot rush of tears. Thoughts were leaping in his brain. He turned to the window, and saw the gaudy poster that had been pasted to the wall of the Plaza.

GRANDIOSA CORRIDA! GRANDIOSA CORRIDA!
3 MAGNIFICAS RESES 3!
FRANCESCO PEREZ—MONOLO LOMBARDINI
JUAN GALVEZ . . .

"No," Juanito said, turning back.

The older man stopped wiping his face. "Are you crazy?" he said.

"Maybe I am."

"Juanito, believe me, please: I have been in the business for twenty years. You don't have a chance. It's all against you. Three minutes you'll last, not a second more."

Grandiosa Corrida . . . Juan Galvez . . . Juanito opened the door. *Galvez . . .*

"Don't be a fool! I'm telling you the truth!"

"I know. I don't doubt you."

"Then what are you doing? Come on, now, while we have time!"

"Time? For what? For starving again, for stealing and running away? Time for that, Enrique?"

"It's better than having your guts slashed out by a filthy animal."

"Is it?" Juanito looked at the man who was his friend. "Let's go," he said. "It's getting late. Don Alfredo must be worried about his investment."

Enrique Córdoba hesitated. "You think you'll be lucky," he said. "Sure. You think you'll go into the ring and fight like Manolete, huh! Cut both ears and the tail, and spit in Don Alfredo's eye. Juanito, I betrayed you. I admit it. But you *must* believe what I say now. Only in stories does it happen the way you think. The truth is that you are a dead man the moment you walk away from the burladero. One pass, two, maybe even three—you will have confidence. So, a little closer this time. Perhaps a Chicuelina; why not? But the animal ignors the cape. Suddenly you see that he's coming toward *you*. You want to run, but no, that would be cowardly. Better to suck it in and pray. But God does not hear you, Juanito. And now it's too late. Too late! The horn goes in like a razor, deep, and starts up, through your belly—"

"You have the tools?" Juanito asked.

Enrique Córdoba stared; then he sighed. "I have them." he said.

"Get them ready."

Invisibly, the older man straightened. Something was in his eyes; something entirely new. "Yes," he said in a quiet voice.

Juanito walked into the Plaza. Children screamed at him. He listened to the screams. He collected them. The screams, the soft smell of old wood and the sharp smell of the cattle, crowds above, the men who looked at him with sadness, love, respect; these things he forced inside him, forcing past and future out, for now, the golden now.

Within the Chapel, he touched the white lace, knelt and made the sign of the cross, as all toreros did.

Then, when it was time, he joined the *puerta de cuadrillas*, standing on the left of Francesco Perez, who saluted him; and, to the music of the yellow brass, marched out into the ring.

The moments filled him. Standing quite still in the afternoon sun, he watched Perez dispatch his bull; then, Lombardini, who was awarded one ear.

"There is an *alternativa*," whispered Enrique Córdoba. "You can pull out now."

But Juanito did not hear the words.

Waiting, he searched the faces along the shady side of the *barrera*; and found her.

"*Va por ti*, Andrée," he said. "I dedicate the death to you."

And then he heard the swell of sound, the trumpets; and he turned his head.

The toril gate began to open slowly.

Slowly, from the center of darkness, came a shape.

Juanito Galvez smiled. Stepping out onto the warm and welcoming sand, he wondered what he had ever done to deserve such good fortune.

NIGHT RIDE

HE WAS A scrawny white kid with junkie eyes and no place for his hands, but he had the look. The way he ankled past the tables, all alone by himself; the way he yanked the stool out, then, and sat there doing nothing: you could tell. He wasn't going to the music. The music had to come to him. And he could wait.

Max said, "High?"

I shook my head. You get that way off a fresh needle, but then you're on the nod: everything's upbeat. "Goofers, maybe," I said, but I didn't think so.

"Put a nickel in him, Deek," Max said, softly. "Turn him on."

I didn't have to. The kid's hands crawled up and settled on the keys. They started to walk, slow and easy, taking their time. No intro. No chords. Just, all of a sudden, music. It was there all the while, Poppa-san, how come you didn't notice?

I couldn't hear a hell of a lot through all the lip-riffs in that trap, but a little was plenty. It was real sound, sure enough, and no accident. The Deacon had been dead right. Blues, first off: the tune put down and then brushed and a lot of improvising on every note; then finally, all of them pulled into the melody again, and all fitting. It was gut-stuff, but the boy had brains and he wasn't ashamed of them.

Max didn't say anything. He kept his eyes closed and his ears open, and I knew he was hooked. I only hoped it wouldn't be the same old noise again. We'd gone through half a dozen box men in a year.

Not like this one, though.

The kid swung into some chestnuts, like "St. James Infirmary" and "Bill Bailey," but what he did to them was vicious. St. James came out a place full of spiders and snakes and screaming broads, and Bailey was a dirty bastard who left his woman when she needed him most. He played "Stardust" like a Boy Scout helping a cripple across the street. And you want to know something about "Sweet Georgia Brown"? Just another seedy hustler too tired to turn a trick, that's all.

Of course, nobody knew what he was doing. To the customers, those smears and slides and minor notes were only mistakes; or maybe the ears didn't even notice.

"What's his name?" Max said.

"David Green."

"Ask him to come over when he's through."

I sliced my way past the crowd, tapped the kid's shoulder, told him who I was. His eyes got a little life in them. Not much.

"Max Dailey's here," I said. "He wants some words."

Eight notes and you wouldn't touch "Laura" with a ten-foot pole. "Okay," the kid said.

I went back. He dropped the knife for a while and played "Who," straight, or pretty straight. The way I'd heard it the night before, anyway, when it was too hot to sleep and I'd gone out for that walk. Funny thing about a box: a million guys can hammer it, they can play fast and hit all the notes and transpose from here to Wednesday. But out of that million, you'll find maybe one who gets it across.

And like as not he can't play fast and won't budge out of
C. Davy Green wasn't what you'd call a virtuoso, exactly.
He didn't hit all the notes. Only the right ones.

After a while he came over and sat down.

Max grabbed his paw. "Mr. Green," he said, "you are
a mess of fingers."

The kid nodded; it *could* have been "Thanks."

"You don't do a whole lot, but it's mostly good. The
Deacon likes it." He took off his sunglasses and folded
them real slow. "I'm a tight man with a compliment, Mr.
Green," he said. "Rebop with the mouth, that passes the
time of day, but I'm here for other reasons."

A chick in a green sarong popped out of the smoke. She
had a little here and a little there. "Gents?"

"Bushmill's and soda," Max said, "and if you don't carry
it, Bushmill's and nothing. Mr. Green?"

"Same, whatever it is," he said.

My cue: I got up and killed the rest of my Martini. Max
always liked to business solo. "Gotta make a phone call,
boss," I said. "Meet you outside."

"Good enough."

I told the kid maybe we'd see him around and he said,
sure, maybe, and I took a fade.

Outside it was hot and wet, the way it gets in N.O. I
wandered up one side of Bourbon, down the other, lamping
the broads. Tried a joint, but the booze was watered and
the dancer didn't know. A pint-sized you-all with a nervous
tic and rosy cheeks. She came on like a pencil sharpener. I
blew the place.

Jazz might have been born in New Orleans, but it left
home a long time ago.

Max was waiting in front of the Gotcha Club: he wasn't
smiling, he wasn't frowning. We walked some blocks. Then,
in that whispery-soft voice of his, he said: "Deek, I think
maybe we have us a box."

I felt proud, oh yes; that's how I felt. "Cuckoo."

"Got to be handled right, though. The kid has troubles. Great troubles."

He grinned. It was the kind of a grin a hangman might flash at a caught killer, but I didn't know that. I didn't even know there'd been a crime. All I thought was, the Band of Angels has got ten new fingers.

We broke at the pad, but the train didn't leave till eight the next p.m., so I had a party by myself. It didn't help. I dreamed all night about that little girl, and I kept hitting her with the car and backing up and hitting her and watching her bleed.

Funny part was, once it wasn't me in the car, it was Max, and the little girl was David Green . . .

The kid hooked up with us in Memphis. No suitcase, same clothes, same eyes. We were doing a five-nighter at the Peacock Room, going pretty good but nothing to frame on the wall. Davey eared a set and tapped Max's bass. "So I'm here," he said. "Want me to sit it?"

Max said no. "You listen. After the bit, then we'll talk."

Kid shrugged. Either he didn't give a damn or he was elsewhere. "Hello, Mr. Jones," he said.

"Hello, Mr. Green," I said. Brilliant stuff. He slumped into a chair, stuck his head on his arms and that was it.

Nobody was hot, so we played some standard dance tunes and faked a jam session and sort of piddled around until two. Then we packed up and headed for the hotel.

"This is the Band of Angels," Max said, but he didn't say it before we were at attention, all present and accounted for. "Deacon Jones you already know. He is a trumpet, also a cornet and sometimes, when we're in California, a flute. I'm bass; you know that, too. The tall, ugly fellow over there is Bud Parker, guitar. Rollo Vigon and Parnelli Moss, sax and valve trombone. Hughie Wilson, clarinet. Sig Shulman, our drummer, the quiet, thoughtful guy to my right. All together, the very best in the world—

when they want to be. Gentlemen, our new piano: David Green."

The kid looked scared. He passed a limp hand around, as if he wished he was in Peoria. He almost jumped when Max put the usual to him. Who wouldn't?

"We're a jazz band, Green. Do you know what jazz is?"

Davey threw me a glance and ran his hand over his hair. "You tell me."

"I can't. No one can. It was a stupid question." Max was pleased: if the kid had tried an answer, that would've been bad. "But I'll tell you *one* of the things it is. It's vocabulary. A way of saying something. You can have a small vocabulary or a large one. We have a large one, because we have a lot on our minds. If you want to make it with the Angels, you've got to remember that."

Sig began to tap out some rhythm on a table, impatiently.

"Another thing. You've got to forget about categories. Some bands play Storyville, some play Lighthouse; head music and gut music—always one or the other. Well, we don't work that way. Jazz is jazz. Sometimes we'll spend a week kanoodling on the traditional, flip over and take up where Chico Hamilton leaves off. Whichever says what we have to say best. It's all in how we fell at the time. You dig?"

Davey said he dug. Whenever Max got the fever like this and started the sermon, you didn't plan to argue. Because he meant it; and he knew what he was talking about. Maybe it was the twentieth time most of us heard the routine, but it made sense. Practically everybody thinks of jazz in steps: from this to that. And there aren't any steps. Which is more "advanced"—Stravinsky or Mozart?

Davey didn't know how important it was for him to say the right thing, but he managed fine. For a few minutes he'd laid his troubles down. "I never thought of it just that way," he said. "It's quite a theory."

"Take it in, Green. Think hard about it. What you've been doing is high up, but one way. I believe you can be all ways. I believe it because I have faith in you."

He stuck his hand on Davey's shoulder, almost the same way he'd done with each of us over the years, and I could see that it hit the kid just as hard.

"I'll try, Mr. Dailey," he said.

"Make it Max. Doesn't take as long, and it's friendlier."

Then it was all over. Max closed the Bible and broke out Catto's scotch, which is a drink he does not generally like to share; then he got the kid into a corner, by themselves.

I should have felt great, and in a way I did, but something was spoiling it. I went over to the window for some fresh: the sidewalks had been hosed down and they put up a nice clean smell, next best to summer rain.

"Nice kid." I looked over; it was Parnelli Moss. He still had the shakes, but not so bad as sometimes. Hard to see how a man could hit the bottle the way Parnelli did and still finger a horn. Hard to see how he could stay alive.

He was wound. And I wasn't in any mood for it. "Yeah."

"Nice fine kid." He held the ice-water near his forehead. Cold turkey, on and off. "Max hummin' up a new crutch."

I ignored it: maybe it'd go away.

It didn't. "Good?" Parnelli said.

"Good."

"Poor Mr. Green. Deek, you listen—he'll stay good, but he won't stay nice. Hey, look out with that hoe, there, Max!"

"Parnelli," I said, just as cool as I could, "you're a fair horn but that's all I can say for you."

"That's what I mean," he said, and grinned. I suddenly wanted to pitch him out of the window. Or jump, myself. I couldn't tell why.

He rolled the glass across his forehead. "Give us this day," he said, singsong, "our Dailey bread—"

"Shut up." I kept it in whispers, so no one else would hear. Moss was loaded; he had to be. "Parnelli, listen, you want a hook in Max. That's okay, that's fine by me. Stick it in and wiggle it. But keep it away from me—I don't want to hear about it."

"What's the matter, Deek—afraid?"

"No. See, the way I look at it, Max picked you up when your own mother wouldn't have done it, even with rubber gloves. You were O, Parnelli. Zero. Now you're eating. You ought to be on your goddamn knees to him!"

"Father," Parnelli said, with a real amazed look, "I am. I *am*!"

"He's been a nurse to you," I said, wondering why I was so sore and why I wanted to hurt the guy this much. "Nobody else would have bothered."

"For a fact, Deek."

"They'd have let you kick off in Bellevue."

"For a fact."

I wanted to slug him then, but I couldn't. I knew he hated Max Dailey. For the life of me, I couldn't figure out why. It was like hating your best friend.

"You like the kid, Deek? Green, I mean?"

"Yeah," I said. It was true. I felt—maybe that was it—responsible.

"Tell him to cut out, then. For the love of Christ, tell him that."

"Go to hell!" I swung across to the other room: it was like busting out of a snake house. Davey Green was there, all to himself, sitting. Only he was different. Those hard, bitter-type lines were gone. Now he just looked—sad.

"How you makin' it?"

The kid looked up. "The hard way," he said. "I've been talking to Mr. Dailey. He's—quite a guy."

I pulled up a chair. My back was sweating. Cold sweat. "How you mean?"

"I don't know, exactly. I never met anyone like him

before. The way he has of, well, of knowing what's wrong and how it's wrong, and pulling it out of you—"

"You got troubles, kid?" The sweat was getting colder.

He smiled. He was damned young, maybe only twenty-five; handsome, in a Krupa kind of way. It wasn't junk. It wasn't booze. "Tell the Deacon."

"No troubles," he said. "Just a dead wife."

I sat there, getting scared and sick and wondering why. "How far back?"

"A year," he said, like he still didn't believe it. "Funny thing, too. I never used to be able to talk about it. But Mr. Dailey seemed to understand. I told him everything. How Sal and I met, when we got married and went to live in the development, and—" He shoved his face against the wall quick.

"If you talk about it, kid, you get rid of it," I said.

"That's what Mr. Dailey told me."

"Yeah." I know. It was exactly what Mr. Dailey had told me, six years ago, after the accident.

Except, I was still dreaming about that little girl, as if it had happened yesterday . . .

"You think I'll fit in, Deek?" the kid asked.

I looked at him and remembered what Parnelli had said; and I remembered Max, his voice, low, always low; and it got too much.

"Cinch," I said, and blew back to my room on the second floor.

I don't bug easy, never did, but I had a crawly kind of a thing inside me and it wouldn't move. They have a word for it: premonition.

"*. . . tell him to cut out, Deek. For the love of Christ, tell him that . . .*"

Next night the kid showed up on time in one of Rollo's extra suits. He looked very hip but also very skunked, and you could see that he hadn't had much sack time.

Max gave him a little introduction to the crowd and he sat down at the box.

Things were pretty tense. A one. A two.

We did "Night Ride," our trademark and the kid did everything he was supposed to. Very fine backing, but nothing spectacular, which was good. Then we broke and he got the nod from Max and started in on some sad little dancing on "Jada." It isn't easy to make that tune sad. He did it.

And the crowd loved it.

He minored "Lady Be Good," and then threw a whole lot of sparks over "The A Train;" and the Peacock Room began to jam. I mean, we were always able to get them to listen, and all that foot-stomping routine, but this was finally *it*.

Davey Green wasn't good. He was great. He Brubecked the hell out of "Sentimental Lady"—keeping to Max's arrangement enough so we could tag along, but putting in five minutes more—and it was real reflective, indeed. Then, with everything cool and brainy, he turned right around and there was Jelly Roll, up from the dead, doing "Wolverine" the way it hadn't been done.

And all the hearing aids were turned to "loud" when he rode out a solo marked Personal. Almighty sad stuff; bluesy; you knew—I knew—what he was thinking about. Him and his wife in bed on a hot morning, with the sun screaming in, them half-awake, and the air bright and everything new. Red ice. Warm blues.

Max listened with his eyes tight shut. He was saying: Don't touch a thing, boys; don't make a move. You might break it. Leave the kid alone.

Davey stopped, suddenly. Ten beat pause. And we thought it was over, but it wasn't. He was remembering something else now, and I knew that that first was just the beginning.

He started a melody, no life in it, no feeling: Just the

notes: "If You Were the Only Girl in the World"—Then
he smeared his fist down the keys and began to improvise.
It was wicked. It was brilliant. And the cats all swallowed
their ties.

But I got his message. It came into me like private needles:

> There's a girl in a box,
> Deacon Jones, Deacon Jones,
> And that girl in a box
> Is nothin' but bones . . .

Which girl you talking about? I wondered. But there
wasn't any time to figure it out, because he was all done.
The Peacock Room was exploding and Davey Green was
sitting there, sitting there, looking at his hands.

"A one. A two," softly from Max.

We all took off on "St. Louis Blues," every one of us
throwing in something of his own, and I blew my horn and
it was break time.

Max put on his blinkers and went over to the kid. I could
barely hear him. "Very clean, Mr. Green." The kid was
still with it, though: he didn't seem to be listening. Max
whispered a few things and came on down off the stand.
He was ten feet tall.

"We've got it, Deek," he said. There was a light in back
of his forehead. "It's ours now."

I knocked the spit out of my trumpet and tried a grin.
It was a falsie.

Max put a hand on my shoulder. "Deek," he said, "that
was a sanitary solo you blew, but I'm worried. You've been
thinking about the accident. Right?"

"No."

"I don't blame you a lot. But we're *complete* now, you
dig, and we're going high. So forget about the goddamn

thing—or talk it over with me after the show. I'm available." He smiled. "You know that, don't you, Deek?"

I'd been praying to God he wouldn't say it. Now it was said. "Sure, Max," I told him. "Thanks."

"Nothing," he said, and went over to Bud Parker. Bud was hooked and Max kept him supplied. It always seemed okay because otherwise he'd be out stealing, or maybe killing, for the stuff.

Now I wasn't so sure. Parnelli leaned over and blew a sour note out of his valve bone. "Nice kid," he said. "I think Max'll want to keep him."

So right. With ten hot fingers, we started doing business in a great big way. I don't know why. Why did Woody Herman die for weeks in a Chicago pad and then move two blocks away and hit like a mother bomb? It just happens.

We got out of the Corn Belt fast, got booked into the Haig in L.A. and out-pulled everything since Mulligan. Quartets and trios were all the bit then, and that made us a ricky-tick Big Band, but nobody cared. In a month the word got around and they were coming down from Frisco to give a listen.

I didn't have much to do with either Max or Davey: they were buddy-buddy now. Max almost never let him out of sight—not that he neglected us. Every couple of p.m.'s he'd show, just like always, ready with the jaw. He was available. "Got to take care of my boys . . ." But Davey was the star of the show, and he didn't circulate much. It was enough just to see him, anyway. His piano was getting better, but he was getting worse. Every night he told the story about him and Sally, how happy they were, how much he loved her, and how she got whatever she got and died. Every mood they might have had, he pulled it out of the box. And always ended up in Weep City. Used to be he'd get mad as hell at the son of a bitch that took her breath out of her body and put her under ground; now he was mostly just sad, lonely, brought down.

And the Band of Angels couldn't do anything wrong. Before, we were a bunch of smart musicians; we could give you Dixieland or we could give you Modern; hot or cold; and nothing you could call a style. With Davey's fingers, we had a style. We were just as smart, could play all the different jazz, but we were blues men. We played mostly for the dame at the end of the bar, all alone, with too much paint or too much fat. Or for the little guy who won't dance so they think he hates women, only he's crazy about women, but he's scared of what will happen when he's up that close. We played for little chicks with thick glasses, thick chicks with little asses, and that drunk loser who kissed it all good-bye.

Blues men.

A paid ad said it: "The Max Dailey band plays to that piece of everybody that got hurt and won't heal up."

Blues men.

The Haig would have kept us six months more, forever maybe, but we had to spread the Gospel. Max's Gospel. What was wrong with Birdland?

Not a thing. Max had been sniffing around The Apple for years, but who were we then?

Day we hit, he tiptoed in church-style. Spoke ever lower, to Davey.

"Kid, this layout is all for the Bird."

Common knowledge.

"Big troubles that spade had, yes, indeed," he said. "Big talent."

We crept out; later on we came back and ripped that church apart at the seams. Davey was going like never before, but you couldn't get at him: he was lower than a snake's kidney. Once after a show I asked him did he want to go out and have a beer with the Deacon, and he allowed that was all right, but Max came along and I wasn't about to break through.

And that's the way it went. *Downbeat* tagged us as "the

most individual group in action today" and we cut a flock of albums—*Blue Mondays; Moanin' Low; Deep Shores*—and it was gravy and champagne for breakfast.

Then, I can't remember what night it was, Max came up to my place and he didn't look gleeful. First time I'd seen him alone since Rollo got picked up for molesting. He made it real casual.

"Deek, you seen Davey around?"

Something jumped up my throat. "Not for quite a while," I said.

He did a shrug.

"You worried?" I asked.

"Why should I be worried? He's of age."

He powdered; then, the next night, it went and blew itself to pieces. I'd finished my bit with the horn—Saturday p.m.—when Parnelli tapped me and said, "Look out there." I saw people. "Look out there again," he said.

I saw a chick. She was eyeballing Davey.

"Max's going to *love* that," Parnelli said. "He's just going to eat that all up, oh yes."

When it was over, the kid ankled down and gave the doll a full set of teeth. She gave them back. And they went over to a dark corner and sat down.

"Oo-weee. Mr. Green has got himself a something. I do declare. And won't you kindly lamp Big M?"

Max was looking at them, all right. You couldn't tell exactly what he was thinking, because none of it showed in his face. He turned the knobs on his bass, slow, and looked. That's all.

After a while Davey and the girl got up and headed for the stand.

"Max, I'd like you to meet Miss Schmidt. Lorraine."

Hughie Wilson's eyes fell out, Bud Parker said "Yeah" and even Rollo picked up—and Rollo doesn't go the girl route. Because this chick was hollerin': little-girl style, pink dress and apple cheeks and a build that said, I'm all here, don't fret about that, just take my word for it.

"She's been coming to hear us every night," Davey said.

"I know," Max said. "I've seen you around, Miss Schmidt."

She smiled some pure sunshine. "You have a fine band, Mr. Dailey."

"That's right."

"I particularly loved 'Deep Shores' tonight. It was—"

"Great, Miss Schmidt. One of Davey's originals. I guess you knew that."

She turned to the kid. "No, I didn't. Davey—Mr. Green didn't tell me."

Our little box-man grinned: first I'd seen him do it for real. You wouldn't have recognized him.

And that's all she wrote. It was plain and simple: Davey was going upstairs with this baby and she was liking it; and let no cat put these two asunder.

She showed up on the dot every p.m., always solo. Listen out the sets and afterward, she and the kid would cut out. He looked plenty beat of a morning, but the change was there for all to see. No question: David Green was beginning to pick up some of the marbles he had lost.

And Max never said a word about it, either. Pretended he didn't gave a hoot one way or the other; nice as hell to both of them. But Parnelli wouldn't wipe that look off his face.

"Playing out the line," he'd say. "Max is a smart fella, Deek. Anybody else, he'd put it on the table. Say: 'We're taking a European tour' or something like that. Not our bossman. Smart piece of goods . . ."

It got thicker between Davey and his doll, and pretty soon, if you listened hard, you could hear bells. You could hear more. I didn't know why, you couldn't finger the difference: but it was there, okay. We were playing music. Like a lot of guys play music. But we'd lost something.

But Max wasn't upset—and he was a tuning fork on two legs—so I figured it must be me. The dreams again, maybe. They were coming all the time, no matter how much I talked about them . . .

It wasn't me, though. We were beginning to sound lousy and it kept up that way, night after night, and I was afraid I knew why, finally.

Three days after Davey had announced his engagement to Lorraine, the dam cracked. Like:

We'd all gathered on the stand and Max had one-twoed for "Tiger Rag" and we started to play. And *suddenly* it was all fine again. The sound was there, only a lot richer than it had ever been. Davey's piano was throttled up and spitting out sadness again, throwing that iron frame around all of us. Keeping us level.

Parnelli tapped me and I went cold. I looked at Davey— he was gone; out of it—and I looked into the audience, and the chick was gone too. I mean she wasn't there. And Max was picking those strings, eyes squinched, happy as a pig in September.

We swung into "Deep Shores" and I think—I'm not sure, but I think—that's when it all got clear to me. After six years.

I played it out, though. Then I started for Davey, but Max stopped me.

"Better leave the kid alone," he whispered. "He's had a rough one."

"What do you mean?"

"The chick was n.g., Deek."

"I don't believe it."

"She was n.g. I knew it right along, but I didn't want to say anything. But—listen, I've been around. She would have counted the kid out."

"What'd you do?" I asked.

"I proved it," he said. His voice was dripping with sympathy. "Chicks are all the same, Deek. Hard lesson to learn." He shrugged his shoulders. "So leave the kid alone. He'll tell you all about it—with his hands. You've just been bothered with those dreams of yours. Why don't you drop by tonight and—"

"What'd you do, Max?"

"I laid her, Deek. And it was easy."

I jerked my shoulder away and started up the stairs, but the box was empty. Davey was gone.

"Where does the doll hang out?" I said.

Max gave with the hands. "Forget it, will you? It's all over now. The kid was *grateful* to me!"

"At 45 Gardens Road," a voice said. "Apartment Five." It was Parnelli.

"You want some, too, Deek?" Max asked. He laughed: it was the nastiest sound I'd ever heard.

"Coo," Parnelli said. "The cold touch of the master."

I studied the man I'd loved for six years. He said, "She doesn't deny it," and I thought, this is the ax between the eyes for Davey. He'll never get up now. Never.

I grabbed Max's arm. He smiled. "I know how you like the kid," he said, "and believe me, I do, too. But it's better he found out now than later, isn't it? Don't you see—I had to do it, for his sake."

Some of the crowd was inching up to get a hear. I didn't care. "Dailey," I said, "listen good. I got an idea in me. If it turns out right, if it turns out that idea is right, I'm going to come back here and kill you. Dig?"

He was big, but I had wings. I shoved him out of the way, hard, ran outside and grabbed a taxi.

I sat in the back, praying to God she was home, wishing I had a horn to blow—*something*!

I skipped the elevator, took the stairs by three.

I knocked on Apartment Five. No answer. I felt the ice on my hide and pounded again.

The chick opened up. Her eyes were red. "Hello, Deacon."

I kicked the door shut and stood there, trying to find the right words. Everything seemed urgent. Everything was right now. "I want the truth," I said. "I'm talking about the truth. If you lie, I'll know it." I took a breath. "Did you sleep with Max Dailey?"

She nodded yes. I grabbed her, swung her around. "The truth, goddammit!" My voice surprised me: it was a man talking. I dug my fingers hard into her skin. "Think about Davey. Put him in your mind. Then tell me that you and Max slept together, tell me that you took off all your clothes and let Max Dailey lay you! Tell me that!"

She tried to get away; then she started to cry. "I didn't," she said, and I let go. "I didn't . . ."

"You love the kid?"

"Yes."

"Want to marry him?"

"Yes. But you don't understand. Mr. Dailey—"

"I'll understand in a hurry. There isn't any time now." I let the tears bubble up good and hot.

"Come on."

She hesitated a beat, but there wasn't any fooling around and she knew it. She got a coat on and we got back into the taxi.

Neither of us said a word the whole trip to Birdland.

By now it was closing time; the joint was empty, dark. Some slow blues were rolling out from the stand.

First guy I saw was Parnelli. He was blowing his trombone. The rest of the boys—all but two—were there, jamming.

Parnelli quit and came over. He was shaking good now.

"Where's Davey?" I asked.

He looked at me, then at Lorraine.

"Where is he?"

"You're too late," Parnelli said. "It looks like the Big M pushed a mite too far. Just a mite."

Lorraine started to tremble, I could feel her arm; and

somebody was slicing into my guts. The blues were still rolling "Deep Shores." The kid's tune.

Parnelli shook his head. "I went out after him the minute you left," he said."But I was too late, too."

"Where's Davey?" Lorraine said, like she was about to scream.

"In his room. Or maybe they've got him out by now—" Parnelli stared at me with those eyes. "He didn't have a gun so he used a razor. Good clean job. Fine job. Doubt if I'll be able to do any better myself . . ."

Lorraine didn't say a word. She took it in, then she turned around slow and walked out. Her heels hit the dance floor like daggers.

"You figured it out now?" Parnelli said.

I nodded. I was hollow for a second, but it was all getting filled up with hate now. "Where is he?"

"In his room, I guess."

"You want to come along?"

"I might just do that," he said. He blew a sour note and the session stopped. Bud Parker came down, so did Hughie and Rollo and Sig.

"They know?" I asked.

"Uh-huh. But, Deek, knowin' isn't enough sometimes. We've been waiting for you."

"Let's go then."

We went upstairs. Max's door was open. He was sitting in a chair, his collar loose, a bottle in his hand.

"Et tu, Deek?"

I grabbed a handful of shirt. "Davey's dead," I said.

He said, "I've been told." He lifted the bottle and I slapped the left side of his face, praying to God he'd want to fight. He didn't.

"You did it," I said.

"Yes."

I wanted to put my hands around his neck and squeeze

until his eyes ran down his face, I wanted to give him back the pain. But all of a sudden I couldn't. "Why?" I said.

Max tilted the bottle and let a lot of the stuff run down his throat. Then, very slowly, and in that soft voice, he said: "I wanted to make music. I wanted to make the best music that ever was."

"That's why you lied to Davey about the girl?"

"That's why," Max said.

Parnelli took away the bottle and killed it. He was shaking, scared. "See, Deek, you thought you were in a band," he said. "But you weren't. You were in a traveling morgue."

"Tell me more, Parnelli. Tell me how in the name of the sweet Lord this has anything to do with Davey and Lorraine."

"It had everything to do with it. Dailey went over to the chick's place and gave her one of his high-voltage snow jobs. Got her to go along with the lie and stay away from Green."

I tried to grab some light; it wouldn't come. My head was pounding. "Why?"

"Simple. She'd be taking the kid's talent and tossing it in the crud-heap. He'd be telling things to *her*, not to the box. And she didn't want to rob the world of a Great Genius, did she?"

Parnelli sucked a few more drops out of the bottle and tossed it in a corner.

"Here's the thing, Deek—our boss has quite a unique little approach to jazz. He believes you've got to be brought down before you can play. The worse off you are, and the longer you stay that way, the better the music is. Right, Max?"

Max had his face in his hands. He didn't answer.

"Look around you. You: ten years ago—it was ten, wasn't it, Deek?—you got drunk one night and got in a car and hit a little girl. Killed her. Rollo, over there—he's queer and doesn't like it. Hughie, what's your cross?"

Hughie stayed quiet.

"Oh, yeah: cancer. Hughie's gonna die one of these days soon. Bud Parker and Sig, poor babies: hooked. Main stream. And me—a bottle hound. Max picked me out of Bellevue. Shall I go on?"

"Go on," I said, I wanted to get it all straight.

"But for some reason Max couldn't find a real brought-down piano man. They pretended to be miserable, but hell, it turned out they only had a stomach ache or something. Then—he found David Green. Or you did, Deek. So we were complete, at last. Eight miserable bastards. See?" Parnelli patted Max's head, and hiccupped. "But you don't get bugged because you didn't catch on. Ol' Dailey's smart. You might have pulled out of your wing-ding years ago, only he kept the knife in. Every now and then he'd give it a twist—like winding us up, so we'd cry about it out loud, for the public."

Hughie Wilson said. "Bull. It's all bull. I can play just as good happy as—"

Max brought his hands down on the chair, and that was the last time he ever looked powerful and strong. "No," he said. He was trembling and red. "Look back, Deacon Jones. Who were the great pianos? I mean the great ones. I'll tell you. Jelly Roll—who they said belonged in a whore-house. Lingle—a hermit. Tatum—a blind man. Who blew the horns that got under your skin and into your bones and wouldn't let you be? I'll tell you that, too. A rum-dum boozie named Biederbecke and a lonely old man named Johnson. And Buddy Bolden—he went mad in the middle of a parade. Look back, I'm telling you, find the great ones. Show them to me. And I'll show you the loneliest, most miserable, beat and gone-to-hell bastards who ever lived. But they're remembered, Deacon Jones. They're remembered."

Max glared at us with those steady eyes of his.

"Davey Green was a nice kid," he said. "But the world is full of nice kids. I made him a great piano—and that's something the world *isn't* full of. He made music that reached in and touched you. He made music that only God could hear. And it took the trouble out of the hearts of everybody who heard him and everybody who will hear him—"

His hands were fists now. The sweat was pouring off him.

"There never was a great band," he said, "until this one. Never a bunch of musicians who could play anything under the goddamn sun and play it right and true. And there won't be another one. You were all great and I kept you great."

He got to his feet unsteadily. "Okay, it's all ripped now. It's over. I've screwed up every life in this room and made you prisoners and cheated and lied to you—okay. Who hits me first?"

Nobody moved.

"Come on," he said, only not in the soft voice. "Come on, you chicken-hearted sons of bitches! Let's go! I just murdered a fine clean kid, didn't I? What about you, Parnelli? You've been on to me for a long time. Why don't you start things off?"

Parnelli met his eyes for a while; then he turned and picked up his horn and went to the door.

Sig Shulman followed him. One by one the others left, nobody looking back.

And they were gone, and Max Dailey and I were alone.

"You told me something early tonight," he said. "You told me you were going to come back and kill me. What's holding you up?" He went over to the bureau, opened a drawer, took out an old .38. He handed it to me. "Go on," he said. "Kill me."

"I just did," I said, and laid the gun down on the table where he could get at it.

Max looked at me. "Blow out of here, Deek," he said, whispering. "Be free."

I went outside and it was pretty cool. I started walking. But there wasn't any place to go.

THE INTRUDER
(Chapter 10)

Introduction by Roger Corman

I first met Chuck Beaumont when I read his novel, The Intruder, and decided to make a picture of it. His novel concerned the integration of a school in a small southern town, and was critically hailed as a penetrating social study. I contacted Chuck and we discussed it, agreeing as to what we were trying to do. Chuck wanted to see his book brought to the screen exactly as he had written it: "No toning down of the events . . . no glossing over the basic attitudes of southern bigots, no whitewashing of the antipathetic Negro who calls himself 'nigger' . . ." A deal was signed and Chuck wrote the screenplay.

I had never believed in any picture as much as I believed in this one. We shot it on location and Chuck came along to help as production assistant and to play the part of the high school principal; he'd never acted before but was quite good.

The picture was done on a very low budget. I had enough money to shoot the film in three weeks on location in Missouri, in 1961, when the situation in the south was considerably different than what it is now, and the racial situation was still very explosive. We chose a town on what is called the "boot-heel" of Missouri, a place which dips down between Arkansas and Kentucky, a town that had a southern look. For the bit parts, I would get local citizens with southern accents but, being in Mis-

souri, the film crew would still be protected by the laws of a midwestern state. The schools in our chosen town had been integrated for six years—but it was token integration. In other schools in the area there was no integration at all and not likely to be any as long as it could be avoided.

Arrangements were quickly made with the superintendent of one local school for the rental of facilities, with no mention made of the subject matter of the film. It didn't work out. Some of the people were very friendly, but there was a great deal of opposition; during the climax of the film, when people started to catch on what the movie was really about, we began to have problems.

We were to shoot the climax for two days in front of a high school in East Prairie, Missouri. After the first day, the sheriff called us and said we weren't going to be allowed back. I told him we had a contract with the East Prairie school district. He said he didn't care anything about it, that we were communists and we were trying to promote equality between whites and blacks, and that was not going to be allowed in East Prairie; and if anybody came back, they would be immediately arrested. We then started shooting matching shots in a public park in Charleston, Missouri, but after a single morning, the chief of police told us to get out. We were in the middle of shooting one sequence and I said to my brother, Gene, who was working as co-producer, "Talk to him while I finish this sequence." I was shooting as fast as I could and Gene was saying, "Now officer, we don't really understand. Is there anything we can do? Can't we go to the mayor?" The officer was saying, "No. Get the hell out of here." Gene: "Well, there must be some way—" "Get outta here, or I'm running you all in!' And Gene was just talking. Making up conversation. He later told Chuck and me he didn't know what he was saying. He was just talking until I got the last shot—not the sequence, but of the pattern I had to finish.

Toward the end, we were getting threatening phone calls and letters; and so I had to hold a Klu Klux Klan parade until the last night of shooting. Then we left. We didn't even return to the hotel. We had it arranged to leave after shooting, because *the threats were very heavy, and we drove in the middle of the night up to St. Louis.*

Critically, the film was extremely successful; but it was not successful financially.

Chuck went on to write more scripts for me. He was intelligent and creative and very sensitive, and, at the same time, highly enthusiastic. He did not get blasé after a number of years in Hollywood, as it is easy for a writer to do. Had he lived, he probably would have become a very respected and established screenwriter, who would have written an occasional novel or short story.

It's hard to say.

WHEN THE BELL in the steeple ran to mark the half hour that had passed since six P.M., Caxton wore the same tired face that it always wore in the summer. The heat of the afternoon throbbed on. Cars moved up and down George Street like painted turtles, and the people moved slowly, too: all afraid of the motion that would send the perspiration coursing, the heart flying.

Adam Cramer sat in the far booth at Joan's Cafe, feeling grateful for the heat, trying to eat the soggy ham sandwich he had ordered. He knew the effect of heat on the emotions of people: Summer had a magic to it, a magic way of frying the nerve ends, boiling the blood, drying the brain. Perhaps it made no sense logically but it was true, nonetheless. Crimes of violence occurred with far greater frequency in hot climates than in cold. You would find more murders, more robberies, more kidnappings, more unrest in the summer than at any other time.

It was the season of mischief, the season of slow movements and sudden explosions, the season of violence.

Adam looked out at the street, then at the thermometer that hung behind the cash register. He could see the line of red reaching almost to the top.

How would The Man on Horseback have fared, he wondered, if it had been twenty below zero?

How would Gerald L.K. go over in Alaska?

He pulled his sweat-stained shirt away from his body and smiled. Even the weather was helping him!

He forced the last of the sandwich down, slid a quarter beneath the plate, and paid for his meal; then he went outside.

It was a furnace.

A dark, quiet furnace.

He started for the courthouse, regretting only that Max Blake could not be there. Seeing his old teacher in the crowd, those dark eyes snapping with angry pleasure, that cynical mouth twitching at the edges—damn!

Well, I'll write you about it, he thought. That'll be almost as good.

The picture of the man who had set his mind free blurred and vanished and Adam walked faster.

The Reverend Lorenzo Niesen was the first to arrive. His felt hat was sodden, the inner band caked with filth; his suspenders hung loosely over his two-dollar striped shirt; his trousers were shapeless—yet he was proud of his appearance, and it was a vicious, thrusting pride. Were someone to hand him a check for five thousand dollars, he would not alter any part of his attire. It was country-honest, as he himself was. Whoever despised dirt despised likewise the common people. God's favorites.

Was there soap in Bethlehem?

Did the Apostles have nail files and lotions?

He sat down on the grass, glared at the bright lights of the Reo motion picture theatre across the street, and began to fan himself with his hat. Little strands of silver hair lifted and fell, lifted and fell, as he fanned.

At six thirty-five, Bart Carey and Phillip Dongen appeared. They nodded at Lorenzo and sat down near him.

"Well, it's hot."

Others drifted into the area, some singly, some in groups.

"Hot!"

By six forty, over one hundred and fifty residents of Caxton were standing on the cement walk or sitting on the grass, waiting.

"You see 'em this morning?"

Fifty more showed up in the next ten minutes.

"Christ, yes."

At seven a bell was struck and a number of cars screeched, halted, discharging teenage children. They crowded at the steps of the courthouse.

It was quiet.

Ten minutes passed. Then, a young man in a dark suit walked across the empty street. He nodded at the people, made his way through the aisle that parted for him, and climbed to the top step. He stood there with his back to the courthouse door.

"That's him?" Phil Dongen whispered.

Bart Carey said, "Yeah."

Lorenzo Niesen was silent. He studied the young man, trying to decide whether or not he approved. Awful green, he thought. Too good of a clothes on him. Like as not a Northerner.

I don't know.

The crowd's voice rose to a murmuring, then fell again as the young man in the dark suit lifted his hands in the air.

"Folks," he said, in a soft, almost gentle voice, "my name is Adam Cramer. Some of you know me by now and you know what I'm here for. To those I haven't had a chance to talk with yet, let me say this: I'm from Washington, D.C., the Capital, and I'm in Caxton to help the people fight the trouble that's come up."

He smiled suddenly and took off his coat. "I wish one thing, though," he said. "I wish school started in January. I mean, it is *hot*. Aren't you hot?"

Hesitant, cautious laughter followed.

"Well," Adam Cramer said, dropping his smile, "it's going to get hotter, for a whole lot of people. I'll promise you that. This here little town is going to burn, what I mean; it's going to burn the conscience of the country, now, and put out a light that everyone and everybody will see and feel. This town, I'm talking about. Caxton!" He paused. "People, something happened today. You've all heard about it now. Some of you saw it with your own eyes. What happened was: Twelve Negroes went to the Caxton high school and sat with the white children there. Nobody stopped them, nobody turned them out. And, friends, listen; that makes today the most important day in the history of the South. Why? Because it marks the *real* beginning of integration. That's right. It's been tried other places, but you know what they're saying? They're saying, Well, if it works in Caxton, it'll work all over, *because Caxton is a typical Southern town*. If the people don't want integration, they'll do something about it! If they don't do something about it, that means they want it! Two plus two equals four!

"Except there's one thing wrong. They're saying you all don't give a darn whether the whites mix with the blacks because you haven't really got down to fighting; but I ask you, how can somebody fight what he doesn't see? They've kept the facts away from you; they've cheated and deceived every one of you, and filled your heads with filthy lies. It has all been a calculated campaign to keep you in the dark, so that when you finally do wake up, Why, we're sorry, it's just too late!

"All right; I'm associated with the Society of National

American Patriots, which is an organization dedicated to giving the people the truth about desegregation. We've been studying this situation here ever since January, when Judge Silver made his decision, and I'm going to give that situation to you. Of course, many present now are fully aware of it. Many have done what they consider their best to prevent it from happening. But there are quite a few who simply do not know the facts; who don't know either what led up to that black little parade into the school to-day, or what real significance it has for everyone in the country.

"I ask you to bear with me, folks, but I give you fair warning now. When you do know the truth, you're going to be faced with a decision. You don't think you've got one now, but you do, all right, and you'll see it. And it'll get inside your blood and make it boil and you won't be able to run away from it! Because I'm going to show you that the way this country is going to go depends entirely and wholly and completely on *you*!"

Tom McDaniel put away his note-pad and walked over to his friend, the lawyer James Wolfe. Wolfe, he noticed, was staring, strained and curious and expectant, like all the others. And, for some reason, this annoyed him. "Sound familiar?" he said.

Wolfe started. "Oh—Tom. Yes, he seems to be a pretty smart kid."

"But a phony," Tom said.

"Oh?"

"Absolutely. The accent's fake; I talked with him earlier. He thinks it's going to work!"

"What?"

"The plain-folks routine."

"And you don't?" Wolfe nodded toward the crowd. "I can't say I entirely agree."

"Do you think it's trouble, Jim?"

"No," Wolfe said, glancing away from Tom. "The time for trouble's over."

"Everything," Adam Cramer was saying, "has got to have a beginning. And the beginning to what you saw today was almost seventeen years ago. In 1940, a Negro woman named Charlotte Green, and her husband, let it be known that they didn't care much for the equal facilities that were being offered to their children. No sooner were the words out of their mouths but the NAACP swooped down. You all know about this organization, I imagine. The so-called National Association for the Advancement of Colored People is now and has always been nothing but a Communist front, headed by a Jew who hates America and doesn't make any bones about it, either. They've always operated on the 'martyr' system, which is: They pick out trouble spots or create them where they never existed, and start putting out publicity. Like take the Emmet Till case. A nigger tries to rape a white woman and tells her husband he'll keep on trying and nobody is going to stop him. The husband can't go to the police with just a threat, so he makes sure, like any of us would, that no nigger is going to rape his wife. Now those are the facts. But what happens? The NAACP moves in and says that the white man is a murderer! Yeah, for protecting his own wife! And you know the bitter tears was shed over that poor, mistreated little colored boy, poor Emmet Till whose only crime was being dark! Any of you read about it?" Adam Cramer shook his head in mock consternation. "The coon was made into a martyr, what they call, and things were rolling along real good, until somebody with some brains showed how Emmett Till's Hero Daddy—you remember how they said that's what he was, and he died in line of duty overseas?— was *hanged* and given a dishonorable discharge for, see if you can guess it: rape! Uh-huh! Of course, the jury wasn't hoodwinked and declared those men who taught the nigger boy a lesson (and it wasn't ever proved they'd done anything more!) innocent. But the old N-double-A-C-P almost had it knocked.

"Anyway, that's how those guys work. For all I know, they hired this Green woman (she lives on Simon's Hill) to stir things up in the first place. They put the pressure on between 1940 and 1949, pretending that all they wanted, you see, was really equal separate facilities. Farragut County said all right and helped the Negroes send their kids to an accredited school, Lincoln High, in Farragut. I visited this school, friends, and there isn't a thing wrong with it. It's a whole sight cleaner and neater than any place these nigger kids ever saw before, like as not; and that's for sure! But the Commie group tipped its hand right then and showed, for all to see, that it was after something different. Does September 1950 mean anything to you people? Well, it was the second big step toward today. In September 1950 a bunch of Negro boys tried to enroll in Caxton High! Remember?"

There was a murmuring from the crowd.

"Why?" Adam Cramer asked, modulating his voice to its original softness. "Do you think it was something they thought up by themselves? Would any Southern Negro have that much gall? No, sir. No. The NAACP engineered the whole operation, knowing in advance what would happen! The students were turned away; the county board of education refused to let them in—putting in on the line—and the usual arrangements were made for the Negroes to attend Lincoln. Then, three full months later, five of these kids—*with the full backing of the NAACP*—filed suit against the Farragut County School Board. And that's when the ball really got rolling. The Plaintiffs, these Negroes, claimed that the out-of-county arrangements didn't meet the county's obligation to furnish equal facilities. The District Court said they were crazy and ruled accordingly. All during 1952 and 1954 the case, which had been appealed, was held in abeyance, pending the United States Supreme Court's action in five school segregation cases under consideration at the same time.

"Well, the Commies didn't waste a second. They had most of the world, but America was a pocket of resistance to them. They couldn't attack from outside, so, they were attacking from *in*side. They knew only too well, friends, that the quickest way to cripple a country is to mongrelize it. So they poured all the millions of dollars the Jews could get for them into this one thing: desegregation.

"In August of 1955, the NAACP demanded a final judgment. Judge Silver, who is a Jew and is known to have leftist leanings—"

"Who says so?" a voice cried.

"The record says so," Adam Cramer said tightly. "Look it up. Abraham Silver belongs, for one thing, to the Quill and Pen Society, which receives its funds indirectly from Moscow."

Tom McDaniel grinned. He said to Wolfe, "He'll hang himself!"

"You think so?"

"Oh, hell, Jim—people love the judge around here. He's a public idol, and you know it. Everybody knows it wasn't his fault about the ruling!"

"I'm not so sure."

"Well, anyway; the Quill and Pen—that's really stretching it."

"I'm not so sure of that, either," James Wolfe said, in a rather grim voice. "Don't forget, Tom: 'You can fool some of the people all of the time . . .'"

". . . so what did the Judge do? He instructed the county school board to proceed with reasonable expedition to comply with the rule to desegregate. In spite of the complete disapproval of the PTA, in spite of the protests of the Far-

ragut County Society for Constitutional Government, in
spite of petitions presented by Verne Shipman, one of Caxton's leading citizens, and Thomas McDaniel, the editor of
the Caxton *Messenger*—Judge Abe Silver went right ahead
and *ordered* integration for Caxton High School, at a date
no later than fall, 1956.

"Mayor Harry Satterly could have stopped it, but he
didn't have the guts to, because he knew the powers that
were and are behind Silver. He knew how much his skin
was worth.

"The Governor could have stopped it in a *second*, but I
don't have to tell you about him; I hope I don't, anyway.

"And the principal of the high school, Harley Paton—
he could have brought the whole mess to a screaming halt.
But he's too lily-livered to do the right thing."

"That's a dirty lie!" A young man in a T-shirt and blue
jeans walked up to the lower step and glared at Adam Cramer. "The principal done everything he could!"

"Did he? Did he close down the school and refuse to
open it until the rights of the town were restored?"

"No, he didn't do that. But—"

"Did he bring the students together and tell them to stay
away?"

"Hell, he *couldn't* do that."

"No," Adam Cramer said, smiling condescendingly.
"No; he couldn't do that. It would take courage. It would
mean risking his fine job and that fat pay-check!"

The young man bunched his fists, reddened, and when
someone shouted, "Git on away, let 'im speak his piece,
kid!" walked back into the crowd.

"Just a moment," Adam Cramer said. "I know that Harley Paton has a lot of friends. And if I were here for any
other purpose than to bring the truth, I'd be smart enough
to leave him alone. Wouldn't I? Now I don't say that the
principal of Caxton High is necessarily a dishonest man. I
merely say, and the facts bring this out, that he is a weak

man. And weakness is no more to be tolerated than dis-
honesty—not when we have our children's future at stake,
leastwise! I warned you that the truth would be bitter. It
always is. But I ain't going to quit just because I've touched
a sore point. No, sir. There's a whole lot of sore points that
are going to be touched before I'm through!"

"Keep talking," Lorenzo Niesen called. "We're listening."

"All right. Now, you may think that the problem is simply whether or not we're going to allow twelve Negroes to
go to our school; but that's only a small, small part of it.
I'm in a position to know because I've been with an organization that's studied the *whole thing*. You don't see the
forest for the trees, my friends; believe me. The real problem, whether you like it or not, is whether you're going to
sit back and let desegregation spread throughout *the entire
South* . . ."

Verne Shipman stood on the sidewalk, hidden behind
the rusted lawn cannon, and listened to Adam Cramer. He
listened to the same speech he'd heard earlier, the same
statistics, and he observed that the people who comprised
the crowd were listening also. Intently. Which, of course,
they ought to do, for the words made sense.

However, there was yet no mention of money. No word
about the joining of this organization and the parting with
hard-earned funds.

I will listen, he thought, but that will be the test.

". . . and it's an indisputable fact," Adam Cramer spoke
on, "that there could be no other result. The Negroes will
literally, and I do mean *literally*, control the South. The
vote will be theirs. You'll have black mayors and black
policemen (like they do in New York and Chicago already)
and like as not, a black governor; and black doctors to
deliver your babies—if they find the time, that is—and

that's the way it'll be. Did you even stop to think about that when you let those twelve enter your white school? Did you?"

The miniscule festive note that had marked the beginning of the meeting was now instantly dissolved. Bart Carey and Phil Dongen wore deep frowns, and Rev. Lorenzo Niesen was shaking his head up and down, up and down, signifying rage.

"Some of us did!" Carey said, in a husky, thickly accented voice.

"I know," Adam Cramer granted. "The Farragut County Federation for Constitutional Government was a step in the right direction. But it didn't accomplish much because the liars have done their jobs well. They've made you think your hands are tied. You couldn't afford fancy lawyers, so you failed. But, Mr. Carey, I'm not talking specifically to you or to those like yourself who have worked to fight this thing. I'm talking to the people who are still confused, in the dark, who haven't fully realized or understood or grasped the meaning of this here ruling. To those, Mr. Carey, who have been soft and who have trusted the government to do right by them. It's a natural thing, you understand. We all love our country, and it's natural to believe that the people who run it are a hundred per cent square. But our great senator from Wisconsin showed us, I think, how wrong that view happens to be. He proved beyond a shadow of a doubt that there are skunks and rats and vermin in the government! Didn't he?"

"That's right!" shouted Lorenzo Niesen. "That's right. God bless the senator!"

"Yes," Adam Cramer said. "Amen to that, sir. We know now that there are men with fine titles and with great power, wonderful power, who are doing their level best to sell our country out to the Communists. And it's these men, folks, and nobody else, who're cramming integration down your throats. There isn't any question in the world about that."

Slowly Adam Cramer's voice was rising in pitch. Perspiration was running down his face, staining his collar, but he did not make any effort to wipe it away.

"Here's something," he said. "I'll bet you all don't know. In interpreting the school decisions of May 17, 1954 and May 31, 1955, by the United States Supreme Court, Judge John J. Parker of the Fourth Circuit Court of the United States, speaking in the case—" he removed a note from his breast pocket—"of Briggs *versus* Elliot, said: '. . . it is important that we point out exactly what the Supreme Court *has* decided and what it *has not* decided in this case. It has not decided that the Federal Courts are to take over and regulate the public schools of the states. It has not decided that the states *must* mix persons of different races in the schools *or must* require them to attend schools *or must deprive them of the right of choosing the schools they attend.* What it has decided, and all it has decided, is that a *state* may not deny to any person *on account of race* the right to attend any school *that it maintains.* This, under the decision of the Supreme Court, the *state* may not do directly or indirectly; *but if the schools which it maintains are open to children of all races, no violation of the Constitution is involved even though the children of different races voluntarily attend different schools, as they attend different churches.* Nothing in the Constitution or in the decision of the Supreme Court takes away from the *people freedom to choose the schools they attend. The Constitution, in other words, does not require integration . . .*'

"You get that, people? *'The Constitution does not require integration!'* That's an accurate record of a legal statement. A judge with a sense of justice and fairness said it. But I'm just a-wondering if Abraham Silver mentioned those little teeny things to you. Did he?

"We've got to follow the big law, the ruling and all that;

except, I'll say it again, loud and clear, and you listen, every one of you listen: The Constitution don't require integration!"

Adam Cramer stopped talking. His voice had risen sharply on the last five words; now angry silence filled the air above the courthouse lawn.

He continued, almost in a whisper: "Now I'll tell you what this whole long thing is about. It isn't about integration at all—in spite of what that would mean, and I've showed you, I hope, what it would mean. It isn't about the Negroes or having anything against them, either. I don't, any more than you people do. No: the real issue at stake here, friends, is the issue of States' rights. That's what it comes to. According to the Constitution, each state in the union is supposed to have local control of itself, isn't that so? That's supposed to be the *point* of a democratic government. Look at Article One, Section Eight, Paragraph Five, of the U.S. Constitution. Read over your government books in the library. States' rights is the whole meaning behind America—local control of purchasing power, local control of state and county politics, local control of schools. Okay! Now, you let the Federal Government step in and start to give orders—like they're doing now—and you may think it's just a step toward socialism, but that ain't so. It's a step toward Communism! The Soviet Union—Russia!—works just that way. A couple of the big boys decide that so much tax is to be levied in every town, or they decide the Siberians are going to share the schools with the whites—or whatever—and nobody can open their mouth. Why? Because in Communist Russia, no one single county *has* any rights of its own. It can't veto any judgments or stop any orders. It can't do anything but sit there and take it.

"You may think I'm getting off the point, or being a little far-fetched, but you're wrong! Friends, the eyes of the world are on Caxton. I've been in Washington, D.C.,

and I know that to be true. You all are the country's test
tube, the guinea pig! That's why I say you've got the future, not only of Caxton, but of *America* in your hands!''

Lucy Egan nudged Ella secretively and smiled. "Boy,"
she said, "he is really some talker. I mean, he honestly is."

Ella had been listening with a peculiar mixture of pride
and uneasiness, and the truth was, she did not know
whether to be pleased or displeased. Tom had not seen her
yet, for which she was, oddly, grateful (there being no reason to be grateful); he and Mr. Wolfe and some of the
others, a few, did not appear to be very happy with the
speech Adam Cramer was making, though most of the people were. You could see that.

"Sort of, if you squint, like Marlon Brando," Lucy Egan
said, squinting. "Like, mean. A little."

It made no particular sense to Ella, the speech. This dry
type of thing that her father and Gramp were always talking about, that was always in the newspapers these days,
mostly bored her, and she would have gone back home
(where, she supposed, she ought to be, anyway) except that
the speaker was Adam Cramer. And she knew, sensed, that
she would be seeing him again soon.

"He's really getting them worked up," Lucy Egan said.
"There hasn't been anything like this in Caxton in I don't
know how long. Don't you think he looks like Brando?"

"Kind of," Ella said.

"Did he kiss you good night?" Lucy Egan asked suddenly.

Ella hesitated, noting the anxiousness in her friend's
eyes. Then she said: "Sure."

"Boy, I don't guess there was anything else, like."

"Oh, Lucy, come on."

"There *was*?"

"No, no."

* * *

"A lot of what you say makes sense," James Wolfe said, stepping forward during a dramatic pause. "And certainly we all agree with you that this ruling was ill-considered. But it is a ruling, and can't be abrogated. I assure you we've tried everything."

"Who are you, sir?" Adam Cramer asked.

"My name is Wolfe, James Wolfe. I'm a lawyer. I spoke personally, you may be interested to know, with Judge Silver, and I'd like to correct you on at least one point. You're giving the impression that a district judge has authority to overrule a federal ruling. That's entirely wrong." James Wolfe turned toward the crowd. "The judge has absolutely no choice in the matter. As a matter off the record, he doesn't think any more of the decision than we do."

"Abraham Silver is a clever man, Mr. Wolfe. You'd have to have studied the situation and all of its ramifications to understand that, as we do. We—"

"Just a moment. Just a moment. As it happens, Mr. Cramer, I and a group of other qualified men *have* studied the situation. It's all very clear-cut. The Judge Parker quote that you take such stock in is ridiculous as applied to conditions in Caxton. Unless you propose to subrogate legal action with illegal action, I can't see that you've presented anything in the form of a positive idea."

Adam Cramer smiled tolerantly.

"As it happens, Mr. Wolfe," he said, "I do have ideas. And they're absolutely legal. They take courage and daring, now, I'll tell you all right off the bat. But they're legitimate."

"All right, then, let's have them."

"First, I want to get one thing clear." Adam Cramer spoke distinctly, addressing himself to the entire assemblage. "Do you people want nigras in your school? Answer yes or no!"

There was a roar from the crowd. "No!"

"No," Adam Cramer said, and smiled. "Fine. Now, are

you willing to fight this thing down to the last ditch and keep fighting until it's conquered?''

Another roar, like a giant wave: "Yes!"

"Yes. Fine!" Adam Cramer raised his hands, and the people were quiet. "Well, I'm willing to work with you. Maybe you want to know why. After all, I'm not a Southerner. I wasn't born in Caxton. But I *am* an American, friends, and I love my country—and I am ready to give up my life, if that be necessary, to see that my country stays free, white and American!"

Phillip Dongen, who had seldom been moved to such emotional heights, led off the applause. It was a frantic drum roll.

"Friends, listen to me for a minute." The young man's voice was soft again. It rose and fell, the words were soothing, or sharp as gunfire. "Please. Mr. Wolfe, over there, has mentioned something about keeping the attack legal. As far as I'm concerned, something is legal or illegal depending on whether it's right or wrong. If nine old crows in black robes tell me that breathing is against the law, I'm not going to feel like a criminal every time I take a breath. The way I see it, the *people* make the laws, hear? *The people!*"

The car, bearing an out-of-county license plate, swung slowly onto George Street from the highway. It was a 1939 Ford, caked with dust and rusty, loud with groans of dry metal. It had come a long way. The five people within were limp with the heat, silent and incurious. Only a small part of their minds, like icebergs, were above the conscious level of thought.

Ginger Beauchamp did not move the gear lever from high as they commenced the hill, nor was he concerned with the misfires and rattles that followed. His foot was numb on the accelerator pedal. He could think only of getting through the seventy miles that remained, of falling, exhausted, onto the cot. There was no damn sense to visiting his mother. She didn't appreciate it. If she was so anxious to see him, why didn't she ever try to be a little nice? he thought.

Well, she's old.

I say I ain't going to make this drive no more, but I am. And Harriet will want to come along and bring Willie and Shirley and Pete.

Now, damn. If I could go just myself, then maybe it wouldn't be so damn bad. But I can't. She just don't want to see me, she wants to see the kids. And—

Ginger Beauchamp saw the people gathered on the lawn in front of the courthouse and slowed down.

"What is it?" Harriet said. She opened her eyes, but did not move.

"Nothin'. Go back to sleep, get you plenty of sleep."

He glared at his wife and swore that next week he would make her learn to drive. That would take some of the strain off. Then he could sleep a little, too.

"What is it, Ginger?"

"Nothin', I said."

The car moved slowly, still coughing and gasping with its heavy load. The overhead traffic light turned red. Ginger pumped the brakes three times and put the gear lever in neutral.

Sure a lot of people.

He started to close his eyes, briefly, when out of the engine noise and murmur of the crowd, he heard a sharp, high voice.

"Hey-a, look!"

Then another voice, also high-pitched: "Git 'em, now. Come on!"

Ginger looked around and saw a group of young boys sprinting across the street toward his car. They were white boys.

What the hell, now, he thought.

"Ginger, it's green, Ginger."

He hesitated only a moment; then, when he saw the running people and heard what they were yelling, he put his foot down, hard, on the accelerator.

But he had forgotten to take the car out of gear. The engine roared, ineffectively.

"You niggers, hey. Wait a second, don't you run off, don't do that!"

Suddenly, the street in front of him was blocked with people. They surrounded the car in a cautious circle, only the young ones coming close.

"What's the trouble?" Ginger asked.

"No trouble," a boy in a T-shirt and levis answered. "You looking for trouble?"

"No, I ain't looking for no trouble," Ginger said. The exhaustion had left him. Harriet was staring, getting ready to cry. The children were asleep. "We just goin' on to Hollister."

"Oh, you jes' a-goin' on to Hollister? How do we know that?"

One of the boys put his hands on the window frame and began rocking the car.

"Don't do that now," Ginger said. He was a thin man; his bones poked into his dark black skin like tentpoles. But the muscles in his arms were hard; years of lifting heavy boxes had made them that way.

"Sweet Jesus," Harriet Beauchamp said. She had begun to tremble.

"Hush," Ginger said.

Another boy leaped on the opposite running board, and the rocking got worse.

"Cut it out, now, come on, you kids," Ginger said. "I don't want to spoil nobody's fun, but we got to get home."

"Who says you got to?"

The circle of people moved in, watching. Some of the

men peeled away and approached the car. Their throats were knotted. Their hands were clenched into fists.

A small white man with a crushed felt hat said, "Nobody gave you no permission to drive through Caxton, niggers. They's a highway to Hollister."

"Well, sure," Ginger said. "I know that. But—"

"But nothin'. How come you in our street, gettin' it all messed up?"

The two boys were rocking the car violently now. Pete Beauchamp, aged seven, woke up and began to cry.

Ginger looked at the small man in the crushed hat. "What's the matter with you folks?" he said. "We ain't done nothin'. We ain't done a thing."

"You got our street all dirty," the small man said.

Ginger felt his heart beating faster. Harriet was staring with wide eyes, shuddering.

"Awright," Ginger said. "We sorry. We won't come this way no more."

"That's what you say," another man said. "I figure you lying."

"I don't tell nobody lies, mister," Ginger said. He was trying very hard to hold the anger that was clawing up from his stomach. Dimly he heard a voice calling, *"Stop it. Stop all this, leave them alone!"* but it seemed distant and unreal. "You all just please get out the way, now, and we'll be gone."

"You *tellin'* us?" a boy shouted. "Hey, the coon's tellin' us what to do."

Two more young whites leaped onto the running boards. The Ford rocked violently, back and forth.

"State your business here," the small man said.

"I did," Ginger said. "I told you, we trying to get home."

"That's a crock of plain shit!"

Ginger Beauchamp felt it all explode inside him. He clashed the gear lever into first and said, "You all drunk or crazy, one. I'm driving through here. If you don't want to get yourself run over, move out the way!"

The boy in levis and T-shirt reached in suddenly and pulled the keys out of the ignition. Ginger grabbed him, but a fist shot into his neck. He gagged.

Young men with knives began to stab the tires of the Ford, then.

Others threw pebbles into the window. The sharp, hard little stones struck Ginger's face and Harriet's, and the children in the back seat were all awake now, shrilling.

"You crazy!" Ginger shouted. "Gimme back my keys!"

"Come and get it, black man!"

"Sure, come on out and get it!"

A stone glanced off Ginger's forehead. He felt a small trickle of warm blood. Now the circle had engulfed the car, the people were all shouting and yelling, and the Ford was lifted off its wheels.

"Maybe you learn now, maybe you learn we don't want you here!"

"Look at him, chicken!"

"Yah, chicken!"

Ginger forced the door open. The grinning boys jumped back, stared, waiting.

"Honey, don't, please don't!"

Ginger stood there, and a quiet came over the people. They stared at him, and he saw something in their faces that he had never seen before. He was thirty-eight years old, and he'd lived in the South all his life, and his mother had told him stories, but he had never seen anything like this or dreamed that it could happen.

It occurred, suddenly, to Ginger that he was going to die.

And standing there in the middle of the crowd of white people, he wondered why.

The word came out. "Why?"

The small man hawked and spat on the ground. "You ought t'know, nigger," he said.

There was no air. Only the heat and the smell of sweat and heavy breath.

The silence lasted another instant. Then the young men laughed, and ambled loosely over to the car. One of them supported himself on two others, lifted his feet and kicked the rear window. Glass exploded inward.

Ginger Beauchamp sprang, blind with fury. He pushed the two boys away and confronted the one who had kicked the glass. He was a gangling youth of no more than sixteen. His face was covered with blackheads and his hair hung matted over his forehead like strips of seaweed. He saw Ginger's rage and grinned widely.

"Don't you do it," Harriet cried. "Ginger, don't!"

The thin Negro knew what it would mean to strike a white man; but he also knew what it would mean if he did not fight to protect his family. All of this passed through his mind in a flash. As quickly, he decided.

He was about to smash his fist into the boy's face, when a voice cried, "Awright, now, break it up! Break it up!" and the people began to move.

"Nigger here come a-lookin' for trouble, Sheriff!"

"Which?"

"This one."

"Awright, Freddy, you go on home now. We'll take care of it."

"He like to run over me!"

"Go on home."

The circle of people gradually broke off, moved away, some standing and watching from the corner, others disappearing into the night.

Ginger Beauchamp stood next to his automobile, his hands still bunched solidly into fists, the cords tight in his neck and in his arms.

A large man in a gray suit said, "You better get along."

Ginger could see only the red faces and the angry eyes, and hear the words that had fallen on him like whiplashes.

"I think he's hurt, Sheriff."

"Naw, he ain't hurt. Are you, fella?"

Ginger couldn't answer. Someone was talking to him, the kids were crying, Harriet was looking at him—but he couldn't answer.

The large man in the gray suit nodded to a uniformed policeman. "Tony," he said, "get 'em out of here quick. Send one car along."

"Yes, sir."

"Don't waste any time."

The policeman walked over to Ginger Beauchamp and said, "Let's go."

Ginger nodded.

Suddenly he was very tired again.

"Tom, I know how you feel," the sheriff said, "but we don't want to go flying off the handle."

"Why not?" Tom McDaniel's heart was still hammering inside his chest, and the fury at what he had seen filled him. "Those people might have been killed if I hadn't dragged you out when I did."

"What people?"

"The Negroes in the car!"

Sheriff Parkhouse gave Tom a sidelong glance. He began to fill his pipe with tobacco, slowly, rocking in the cane-bottomed chair. "I been living here for thirty years," he said, "and in all that time, I ain't never seen a nigger get hurt. Have you?"

Tom found himself actively disliking the large man. He particularly disliked the easy, slow movements, the unruffled calm. A little tobacco, up and down, gently, with the silver tool, a little more tobacco . . . "That hasn't got anything to do with it." he said.

"Maybe not, maybe not. But answer the question, Tom. Have you ever seen a nigger get hurt in Caxton?"

"Yes," Tom said. "Tonight."

The sheriff sighed. His leathery, country flesh had begun to sag from the high cheekbones, and there was something incongruous about the crewcut that kept his white hair short and flat on his head. Here, Tom thought, in this jail, he's king. People fear him. People actually fear this ignorant man.

Parkhouse sucked fire into the scarred bowl of the pipe, released a cloud of thick, aromatic smoke. "Well," he said, smiling, "what you got in your mind for me to do?"

"Take action," Tom said. "Keep the peace. That's what you're getting paid for."

Parkhouse stopped smiling.

"That's right," Tom said angrily. "You're mighty quick to pick a drunk off the street, Rudy, some poor fella that doesn't care any what happens to him. But when it comes to real trouble, you just can't bring yourself to move off that seat."

The chair came forward with a crack. Parkhouse stared for a moment, and his eyes were hard and small. "That," he said slowly, "ain't very polite."

"Polite!" Tom walked to the window and turned. "Let me get this straight. A family was attacked in this town tonight. You know who did the attacking and so do I. Property was destroyed and people were injured. There was blood. And you don't intend to do a thing about it. Not a single goddamn thing. Is that correct?"

"Yeah, that's correct! Now listen, it's real easy for you to sit back and say 'Take action.' Yeah. But you don't even know what you're talking about. What *kind* of action?" The sheriff began to jab the air with his pipestem. "There was at least fifty people around that car. You want to arrest all of them?"

Tom opened his mouth to answer.

"Okay, let's say we do that. I arrest all of them fifty people. Charge 'em with disorderly conduct. Then what? This jail here was built in 1888, Tom. The doors are steel, but the walls are partly adobe: a thirteen-year-old could bust out in twenty minutes if he put his mind to it. Okay, fifty people. And they're hoppin' mad, too, don't think they ain't. I'd be. Now we got nine 18 by 18 cells and two runarounds, mostly filled as it is. You begin to get the drift?"

The sheriff brought his pipe to life again. "I like to see a real civic-minded citizen, Tom, I do. Somebody all the time thinking about the community. Shows real fine spirit. I just wish that you and your paper had of seen to it that we got us a decent jail before you come in here bellering for me to arrest half the town . . ."

Tom ran a hand through his hair. The sheriff's words stung, for it was true. He hadn't ever taken much interest in the condition of the jail. The man had a point, anyway.

"But let me tell you something else," Parkhouse went on dryly. The way he looked, sitting there, made it suddenly easy to understand why certain people feared him. "Even if we had a calaboose the size of San Quentin, I still wouldn't go out and start hauling everybody in. Tom, you don't seem to see. Half of those people were kids. School kids. Throwing them in jail would be like giving them a Christmas present."

"What do you mean?"

"I mean, every kid wants to get put in a cell for a night or so. It's a lark. Hell, they'd have so much fun they'd probably tear this old place down to the ground!"

"Maybe so, but—"

"And here's something else that I guess you ain't thought about. Who, exactly, do we arrest? The ones who was actually touching the car? The ones in the street, whether they did anything or not? Or, just to be on the safe side, should we arrest everybody who attended the meeting?"

Parkhouse chuckled. "That'd include you and your daughter. She was there, I heard."

"Who told you that?"

"Jimmy, or somebody. What's the difference? I'm just trying to show you why I can't 'take action.' And I wouldn't waste my time this way, either, if I didn't know you was a man with some sense."

Somewhere in the jail, somewhere upstairs, a voice was raised in song. It was not a particularly mournful or moving sound.

"But one thing still remains. A crime was committed and nobody's been punished. They got away with it, clean. So what's to stop them from doing the same thing tomorrow night?"

The sheriff took a bottle of pop from the refrigerator behind the desk and removed the cap.

"The people in this town are good," he said. "I ought to know that better than anyone else, ain't that so? They're good. But it's hot, and somebody just got them riled, that's all. Now it's out of their system. We—"

"That's right," Tom snapped. "Somebody got them riled. You might even say, somebody talked them into doing what they did."

Parkhouse nodded.

"You know what that's called, Rudy?"

"I don't get you."

"That's called 'inciting a riot.' It's a crime. If you don't believe me, look it up."

"I know what's a crime and what isn't," the sheriff said. "I don't have to look nothing up."

"Then why don't you throw Adam Cramer into jail?"

"Who?"

"Oh, for Christ's sake!" Tom slammed his palm down on the desk. "The kid who gave the speech! The kid who started the whole thing in the first place, who got the people all inflamed. Adam Cramer!"

"Oh." The sheriff emptied half of the bottle of Dr. Pepper down his throat and leaned back in his chair. "Well," he said, "I can't very well do that, either, Tom."

"You can't very well do that, either—*why not?*"

"Just take it easy, now, and I'll explain—just like I explained the other things. I can't arrest Cramer because he wasn't even around when the niggers drove up. To get him for sedition and inciting to riot, we'd have to catch him right there at the front of the mob, leading 'em on. As it was, he was in Joan's Cafe, having a cup of coffee with Verne Shipman, when it happened."

"With Verne?" The anger in Tom gave way suddenly to confusion, and fear.

"That's right," the sheriff said. "And you know, Tom, you can't put a man in jail for speaking his mind. If you don't believe me, look it up." He smiled. "Maybe you and me don't go along with that, now, but it's in the Constitution. If a man wants to, he can get out on a street corner and call the President of the United States a son of a bitch—and nobody can stop him. He can say America is no good and we ought to all be Communists—hell, he can say *anything*—and nobody's allowed to touch him. It's what's called Freedom of Speech. Besides, the way I heard it, this fella didn't say one solitary thing that everybody in town ain't been saying right along. What have you got against him, anyway?"

"Adam Cramer is a rabble-rouser," Tom said, in a hopeless voice.

"Well, hell, maybe we need a little rabble-rousing here!" The sheriff laughed good-naturedly. "But it could be I didn't get my facts straight. You were there. Did he tell those folks to stop the niggers in the car?"

"No."

"Did he tell them to do anything except maybe join this organization of his?"

"I—no. No, that's all he told them."

"Well, see, that ain't hardly grounds for arrest. Just good old Freedom of Speech in action, Tom!"

"Yes," Tom said.

"That's Democracy."

"Yes."

The sheriff slapped Tom's shoulder affably. "Don't get me wrong," he said. "I hate to see anybody get hurt in my town. I don't care whether he's white or black. But I personally think this particular nigra must of been one of those wise ones that are moving into the county from the north; I think he must of started shooting off his mouth: otherwise nothing like this would of happened, and you know it. They're good people here, but they won't put up with a smart-ass nigra. I can't blame them for that. Can you, Tom?"

"No, I can't blame them for that," Tom said and started out the door.

"Get some sleep," the sheriff called. "And don't worry. They got it all out of their system tonight!"

Got *what* out of their system? Tom thought.

The night air was moist and hot and windless, and the dark streets were empty now. Tom McDaniel walked to his car, got in and lit a cigarette.

The people I've lived with most of my life would have murdered that Negro, he thought, if I hadn't called Parkhouse. That's certain.

What is it that the people have to get out of their systems? What is it that stays so close to the surface that a few words from a Yankee stranger can send it flooding out?

Tonight, he thought, was the beginning.

A war is coming to my town; and I don't even know whose side I'm on.

MOURNING SONG

Introduction by Jerry Sohl

Those of us who knew Charles Beaumont well called him Chuck, when talking to him directly or referring to him with others, but looking back, the name doesn't fit. It doesn't fit because it makes him an ordinary guy, and Chuck was anything but ordinary.

It's hard to remember him as anything but the finished product, the hypnotic weaver of dreams, fright, awe, hungers and dreads, the man possessed of talents we all wished we had, in the telling, in the plotting, in the air of distinction and completeness that he brought to every piece he wrote. It is difficult to think that Charles Beaumont actually worked hard for many years to achieve his style, his effect, his discipline, yet we all know it wasn't easy and that he struggled to become the master storyteller he was.

That he fought against terrible odds can be seen in almost all his works, for he understood how it was for the dreamers, those who hunger after things or ideas or experiences or people because he had been there. He was able to bring to each tale a prismatic view of the world, a facet we are privileged to see and which we might never have seen if he hadn't written it.

"Mourning Song" is one of those stories that Beaumont was so good at, a tale of simple people simply told, about those who believe and one who does not. The blind singer of the "Mourning

Song," is Solomon, and to have him sing the mourning song for you means you're going to die. Solomon was whispered about and feared like the plague, but he was respected. That is, until Lonnie Younger doesn't believe it when the song is sung for him and he tries to fight the inevitable, and we see how Beaumont has gently led us where he has, to show us how Lonnie's disbelief only helps make Solomon's song come true in a startling, ironic twist that is Beaumont's hallmark.

HE HAD A raven on his shoulder and two empty holes where his eyes used to be, if he ever had eyes, and he carried a guitar. I saw him first when the snow was walking over the hills, turning them to white velvet. I felt good, I felt young, and, in the dead of winter, the spring wind was in my blood. It was a long time ago.

I remember I was out back helping my daddy chop up firewood. He had the ax up in the air, about to bring it down on the piece of soft bark I was holding on the block, when he stopped, with the ax in the air, and looked off in the direction of Hunter's Hill. I let go of the bark and looked off that way, too. And that's when I saw Solomon for the first time. But it wasn't the way he looked that scared me, he was too far away to see anything except that it was somebody walking in the snow. It was the way my daddy looked. My daddy was a good big man, as big as any I ever met or saw, and I hadn't ever seen him look afraid, but he looked afraid now. He put the ax down and stood there, not moving or saying anything, only standing there breathing out little puffs of cold and looking afraid.

Then, after a while, the man walking in the snow walked up to the road by our house, and I saw him close. Maybe I wouldn't have been scared if it hadn't been for the way my daddy was acting, but probably I would have been. I was little then and I hadn't ever in my whole life seen anybody without eyes in his head.

My daddy waited until he saw that the blind man wasn't coming to our house, then he grabbed me off the ground and hugged me so hard it hurt my chest. I asked him what the matter was, but he didn't answer. He started off down the road after the blind man. I went along with him, waiting for him to tell me to get on home, but he didn't. We walked for over two miles, and every time we came to somebody's house, the people who lived there would stand out in the yard or inside at the window, watching, the way my daddy did, and when we passed, they'd come out and join the parade.

Pretty soon there was us and Jack Overton and his wife and Peter Briley and old man Jaspers and the whole Randall family, and more I can't remember, trailing down along the road together, following the blind man.

I thought sure, somebody said.

So did I, my daddy said.

Who you suppose it's going to be? Mr. Briley said.

My daddy shook his head. Nobody knows, he said. Except him.

We walked another mile and a half, cutting across the Pritchetts' field where the snow was up to my knees, and nobody said anything more. I knew the only places there was in this direction, but it didn't mean anything to me because nobody had ever told me anything about Solomon. I know I wondered as we walked how you could see where you were going if you didn't have eyes, and I couldn't see how you could, but that old man knew just exactly where he was going. You knew that by looking at him and watching how he went around stumps and logs on the ground. Once I thought he was going to walk into the plow the Pritchetts left out to rust when they got their new one, but he didn't. He walked right around it, and I kept wondering how a thing like that could be. I closed my eyes and tried it but I couldn't keep them closed more than a couple of seconds. When I opened them, I saw that my daddy and all the rest of the people had stopped walking. All except the old blind man.

We were out by the Schreiber place. It looked warm and nice inside with all the lamps burning and gray smoke climbing straight up out of the chimney. Probably the Schreibers were having their breakfast.

Which one, I wonder, my daddy said to Mr. Randall.

The old one, Mr. Randall said.

He's going on eighty.

My daddy nodded his head and watched as the old blind man walked through the snow to the big pine tree that sat in the Schreiber's yard and lifted the guitar strap over his head.

Going on eighty, Mr. Randall said again.

Yes.

It's the old man, all right.

Everybody quieted down then. Everybody stood still in the snow, waiting, what for I didn't know. I wanted to pee. More than anything in the world I wanted to pee, right there in the snow, and watch it melt and steam in the air. But I couldn't any more than I could at church. In a way, this was like church.

Up ahead the old blind man leaned his face next to the guitar and touched the strings. I don't know how he thought he was going to play anything in this cold. It was cold enough to make your ears hurt. But he kept touching the strings, and the sound they made was just like the sound any guitar makes when you're trying to get it tuned, except maybe louder. I tried to look at his face, but I couldn't because of those holes where his eyes should have been. They made me sick. I wondered if they went all the way up into his head. And if they didn't where did they stop?

He began to play the Mourning Song then. I didn't know

that was the name of it, or what it meant, or anything, but I knew I didn't like it. It made me think of sad things, like when I went hunting by myself one time and this doe I shot fell down and got up again and started running around in circles and finally died right in front of me, looking at me. Or when I caught a bunch of catfish at the slew without bait. I carried them home and everything was fine until I saw that two of them were still alive. So I did what my daddy said was a crazy thing. I put those catfish in a pail of water and carried them back to the slew and dumped them in. I thought I'd see them swim away happy, but they didn't. They sank just like rocks.

That song made me think of things like that, and that was why I didn't like it then, even before I knew anything about it.

The old blind man started singing. You wouldn't expect anything but a croak to come out of that toothless old mouth, but if you could take away what he was singing, and the way he looked, you would have to admit he could really sing. He had a high, sweet voice, almost like a woman's, and you could understand every word.

Long valley, dark valley . . . hear the wind cry! . . . in darkness we're born and in darkness we die . . . all alone, alone, to the end of our days . . . to the end of our days, all alone . . .

Mr. Schreiber came outside in his shirtsleeves. He looked even more afraid than my daddy had looked. His face was white and you could see, even from where I stood, that he was shaking. His wife came out after a minute and started crying, then his father, old man Schreiber, and his boy Carl who was my age.

The old blind man went on singing for a long time, then he stopped and put the guitar back over his head and walked away. The Schreibers went back into their house. My daddy and I went back to our own house, not following the blind man this time but taking the long way.

We didn't talk about it till late that night. Then my daddy came into my room and sat down on my bed. He told me that the blind man's name was Solomon, at least that was what people called him because he was so old. Nobody knew how he lost his eyes or how he got around without them, but there were lots of things that Solomon could do that nobody understood.

Like what? I asked.

He scratched his cheek and waited a while before answering. He can smell death, he said, finally. He can smell it coming a hundred miles off. I don't know how. But he can.

I said I didn't believe it. My daddy just shrugged his shoulders and told me I was young. When I got older I'd see how Solomon was never wrong. Whenever Solomon walked up to you, he said, and unslung that guitar and started to sing Mourning Song, you might as well tell them to dig deep.

That was why he had looked so scared that morning. He thought Solomon was coming to our house.

But didn't nothing happen to the Schreibers, I said.

You wait, my daddy said. He'll keep on going there and then one day he'll quit.

I did wait, almost a week, but nothing happened, and I began to wonder if my daddy wasn't getting a little feeble, talking about people smelling death and all. Then on the eighth day, Mr. Randall came over.

The old man? my daddy asked.

Mr. Randall shook his head. Alex, he said, meaning Mr. Schreiber. Took sick last night.

My daddy turned to me and said. You believe it now?

And I said, No, I don't. I said I believed that an old blind man walked up to the Schreiber's house and sang a song and I believed that Mr. Alex Schreiber died a little over a week later but I didn't believe any man could know it was going to happen. Only God could know such a thing, I said.

Maybe Solomon is God, said my daddy.

That dirty old man without any eyes in his head?

Maybe. You know what God looks like?

No, but I know He ain't blind, I know He don't walk around with a bird on his shoulder, I know He don't sing songs.

How do you know that?

I just do.

Well and good, but take heed—if you see him coming, if you just happen to see him coming down from Hunter's Hill some morning, and he passes near you, don't you let him hear you talking like that.

What'll he do?

I don't know. If he can do what he can do, what can't he do?

He can't scare me, that's what—and he can't make me believe in him! You're crazy! I said to my daddy, and he hit me, but I went on saying it at the top of my voice until I fell asleep.

I saw Solomon again about six months later, or maybe a year, I don't remember. Looking the same, walking the same, and half the valley after him. I didn't go along. My daddy did, but I didn't. They all went to the Briley house that time. And Mrs. Briley died four days afterward. But I said I didn't believe it.

When Mr. Randall himself came running over one night saying he'd had a call from Solomon and him and my daddy got drunk on wine, and Mr. Randall died the next day, even then I didn't believe it.

How much proof you got to have, boy? my daddy said.

I couldn't make it clear then what it was that was tormenting me. I couldn't ask the right questions, because they weren't really questions, then, just feelings. Like this ain't the world here, this place. People die all over the world, millions of people, every day, every minute. You mean you think that old bastard is carting off all over the world? You think he goes to China in that outfit and plays the guitar? And what about the bird? Birds don't live long. What's he got, a dozen of 'em? And, I wanted to know, *why* does he do what he does? What the hell's the point of telling somebody they're going to die if they can't *do* something about it?

I couldn't believe in Solomon because I couldn't understand him. I did say that, and my daddy said, If you could understand him, he wouldn't be Solomon.

What's that mean?

Means he's mysterious.

So's fire, I said. But I wouldn't believe in it if it couldn't put out heat or burn anything.

You're young.

I was, too. Eleven.

By the time I was grown, I had the questions, and I had the answers. But I couldn't tell my daddy. On my eighteenth birthday, we were whooping it up, drinking liquor and singing, when somebody looked out the window. Everything stopped then. My daddy didn't even bother to look.

Could be for anybody here, somebody said.

No. I feel it. It's for me.

You don't know.

I know. Lonnie's a man now, it's time for me to move on.

I went to the window. Some of the people we hadn't invited were behind Solomon, gazing at our house. He had the guitar unslung, and he was strumming it.

The people finished up their drinking quietly and looked at my daddy and went back out. But they didn't go home, not until Solomon did.

I was drunk, and this made me drunker. I remember I laughed, but my daddy, he didn't and in a little while he went on up to bed. I never saw him look so tired, so worn out, never, and I saw him work in the field eighteen hours a day for months.

Nothing happened the first week. Nor the second. But he didn't get out of bed that whole time, and he didn't talk. He just waited.

The third week, it came. He started coughing. Next day he called for my mother, dead those eighteen years. Doc Garson came and looked him over. Pneumonia, he said.

That morning my daddy was still and cold.

I hated Solomon then, for the first time, and I hated the people in the valley. But I couldn't do anything about it. We didn't have any money, and nobody would ever want to buy the place. So I settled in, alone, and worked and tried to forget about the old blind man. He came to me at night, in my sleep, and I'd wake up, mad, sometimes, but I knew a dream couldn't hurt you, unless you let it. And I didn't plan to let it.

Etilla said I was right, and I think that's when I first saw her. I'd seen her every Sunday at church, with her ma, when my daddy and I went there together, but she was only a little thing then. I didn't even know who she was when I started buying grain from her at the store, and when she told me her name, I just couldn't believe it. I don't think there's been many prettier girls in the world. Her hair wasn't golden, it was kind of brown, her figure wasn't skinny like the pictures, but full and lush and she had freckles, but I knew, in a hurry, that she was the woman I wanted. I hadn't ever felt the way she made me feel. Excited and nervous and hot.

It's love, Bundy Matthews said. He was my best friend. You're in love.

How do you know?

I just do.

But what if she ain't in love with me?

You're a fool.

How can I find out?

You can't, not if you don't do anything except stand there and buy grain off of her.

It was the hardest thing I've ever done, asking her to walk with me, but I did it, and she said yes, and that's when I found out that Bundy was right. All the nervousness went away, but the excitement and heat, they stayed. I felt wonderful. Every time I touched her it made my whole life up to then nothing but getting ready, just twenty-four years of getting ready to touch Etilla.

Nothing she wouldn't talk about, that girl. Even Solomon, who never was talked about, ever, by anybody else, except when he was traveling.

Wonder where he lives, I'd say.

Oh, probably in some cave somewhere, she'd say.

Wonder *how* he lives.

I don't know what you mean.

I mean, where does he find anything to eat.

I never thought about it.

Stray dogs, probably.

And we'd laugh and then talk about something else. Then, after we'd courted six months, I asked Etilla to be my bride, and she said yes.

We set the date for the first of June, and I mean to tell you, I worked from dawn to dusk, every day, just to keep from thinking about it. I wanted so much to hold her in my arms and wake up to find her there beside me in the bed that it hurt, all over. It wasn't like any other hurt. It didn't go away, or ease. It just stayed inside me, growing, till I honestly thought I'd break open.

I was thinking about that one day, out in the field, when I heard the music. I let go of the plow and turned around, and there he was, maybe a hundred yards away. I hadn't laid eyes on him in six years, but he didn't look any different. Neither did the holes where his eyes used to be, or the raven. Or the people behind him.

Long valley, dark valley . . . hear the wind cry! . . . in darkness we're born and in darkness we die . . . all alone, alone, to the end of our days . . . to the end of our days, all alone . . .

I felt the old hate come up then, because seeing him made me see my daddy again, and the look on my daddy's face when he held the ax in the air that first time and when he died.

But the hate didn't last long, because there wasn't any part of me that was afraid, and that made me feel good. I waited for him to finish and when he did, I clapped applause for him, laughed, and turned back to my plowing. I didn't even bother to see when they all left.

Next night I went over to Etilla's, the way I did every Thursday night. Her mother opened the door, and looked at me and said, You can't come in, Lonnie.

Why not?

Why not? You know why not.

No, I don't. Is it about me and Etilla?

You might say. I'm sorry, boy.

What'd I do?

No answer.

I didn't do anything. I haven't done what you think. We said we'd wait.

She just looked at me.

You hear me? I promised we'd wait, and that's what we're going to do. Now let me in.

I could see Etilla standing back in the room, looking at me. She was crying. But her mother wouldn't open the door any farther.

Tell me!

He called on you, boy. Don't you know that?

Who?

Solomon.

So what? I don't believe in all that stuff, and neither

does Etilla. It's a lot of lies. He's just a crazy old blind man. Isn't that right, Etilla!

I got mad then, when she didn't answer, and I pushed the door open and went in. Etilla started to run. I grabbed her. It's lies, I said. We agreed on that!

I didn't think he'd call on you, Lonnie, she said.

Her mother came up. He never fails, she said. He's never been wrong in forty years.

I know, and I know why, too! I told her. Because everybody *believes* in him. They never ask questions, they never think, they just believe, and *that's* why he never fails! Well, I want you to know *I* don't believe and neither does Etilla and that's why this is *one* time he's going to fail!

I could have been talking to cordwood.

Etilla, tell your mother I'm right! Tell her we're going to be married, just like we planned, and we aren't going to let an old man with a guitar spoil our life.

I won't let her marry you, the old woman said. Not now. I like you, Lonnie Younger, you're a good, strong, hardworking boy, and you'd have made my girl a fine husband, but you're going to die soon and I don't want Etilla to be a widow. Do you?

No, you know I don't, but I keep trying to tell you, I'm *not* going to die. I'm healthy, and if you don't believe it, you go ask Doc Garson.

It wouldn't matter. Your daddy was healthy, remember, and so was Ed Kimball and Mrs. Jackson and little Petey Griffin, and it didn't matter. Solomon knows. He smells it.

The way Etilla looked at me, I could have been dead already.

I went home then and tried to get drunk, but it didn't work. Nothing worked. I kept thinking about that old man and how he took the one thing I had left, the one good, beautiful thing in my whole life, and tore it away from me.

He came every day, like always, followed by the people,

and I kept trying to see Etilla. But I felt like a ghost. Her mother wouldn't even come to the door.

I'm alive! I'd scream at them. Look at me. I'm alive.

But the door stayed barred.

Finally, one day, her mother yelled at me, Lonnie! You come here getting my Etilla upset one more time and I'll shoot you and then see how alive you'll be!

I drank a quart of wine that night, sitting by the window. The moon was bright. You could see like it was day, almost. For hours the field was empty, then they came, Solomon at their head.

His voice might not have been different, but it seemed that way, I don't know how. Softer, maybe, or higher. I sat there and listened and looked at them all, but when he sang those words, *All alone*, I threw the bottle down and ran outside.

I ran right up to him, closer then anyone ever had got, I guess, close enough to touch him.

God damn you, I said.

He went on singing.

Stop it!

He acted like I wasn't there.

You may be blind, you crazy old son of a bitch, but you're not deaf! I'm telling you—and all the rest of you—to get off my property, now! You hear me?

He didn't move. I don't know what happened inside me, then, except that all the hate and mad and sorrow I'd been feeling came back and bubbled over. I reached out first and grabbed that bird on his shoulder. I held it in my hands and squeezed it and kept on squeezing it till it stopped screaming. Then I threw it away.

The people started murmuring then, like they'd seen a dam burst, or an earthquake, but they didn't move.

Get out of here! I yelled. Go sing to somebody else, somebody who believes in you. I don't. Hear me? I don't!

I pulled his hands away from the strings. He put them back. I pulled them away again.

You got them all fooled, I said. But I know you can't smell death, or anything else, because you stink so bad yourself! I turned to the people. Come and take a sniff! I told them. Take a sniff of an old man who hasn't been near a cake of soap in all his life—see what it is you been afraid of!

They didn't move.

He's only a man! I yelled. Only a man!

I saw they didn't believe me, so I knew I had to show them, and I think it came to me that maybe this would be the way to get Etilla back. I should have thought of it before! If I could prove he wasn't anything but a man, they'd all have to see they were wrong, and that would save them because then they wouldn't just lie down and die, like dogs, whenever they looked out and saw Solomon and heard that damn song. Because they wouldn't *see* Solomon. He'd be gone.

I had my hands around his throat. It felt like wet leather. I pressed as hard as I could, and kept on pressing, with my thumbs digging into his gullet, deeper and deeper, and then I let him drop. He didn't move.

Look at him, I yelled holding up my hands. He's dead! Solomon is dead! God is dead! The man is dead! I killed him!

The people backed away.

Look at him! Touch him! You want to smell death, too? Go ahead, do it!

I laughed till I cried, then I ran all the way to Etilla's house. Her mother shot at me, just the way she said she would, but I knew she'd miss. It was an old gun, she was an old woman. I kicked the door open. I grabbed them both and practically dragged them back to my place. They had to see it with their own eyes. They had to see the old man sprawled out dead on the ground.

He was right where I dropped him.

Look at him, I said, and it was close to dawn now so they could see him even better. His face was blue and his tongue was sticking out of his mouth like a fat black snake.

I took loose the guitar while they were looking and stomped it to pieces.

They looked up at me, then, and started running.

I didn't bother to go after them, because it didn't matter any more.

It didn't matter, either, when Sheriff Crowder came to see me the next day.

You did murder, Lonnie, he said. Thirty people saw you.

I didn't argue.

He took me to the jail and told me I was in bad trouble, but I shouldn't worry too much, considering the facts. He never thought Solomon was anything but a lunatic, and he didn't think the judge would be too hard on me. Of course it could turn out either way and he wasn't promising anything, but probably it would go all right.

I *didn't* worry, either. Not until last night. I was lying on my cot, sleeping, when I had a dream. It had to be, because I heard Solomon. His voice was clear and high, and sadder than it had ever been. And I saw him, too, when I went to the window and looked out. It was him and no question, standing across the street under a big old elm tree, singing.

Long valley, dark valley . . . hear the wind cry! . . . in darkness we're born and in darkness we die . . . all alone, alone, to the end of our days . . . to the end of our days, all alone . . .

It scared me, all right, that dream, but I don't think it will scare me much longer. I mean I really don't.

Tomorrow's the trial. And when it's over, I'm going to take me a long trip. I am.

INTRODUCTION TO UNPUBLISHED STORIES

The following stories were left unpublished at the time of Beaumont's death. Three—"Appointment With Eddie," "The Man With the Crooked Nose" and "The Carnival"—were to have been included in a fourth Beaumont collection, A Touch of the Creature. The book, to have been released in 1964, was dropped after lengthy negotiations with Bantam Books fell through in late 1963.

"The Crime of Willie Washington" is an early work, and, according to one of Beaumont's letters, one for which he had a "great fondness." It reflects a young writer's obvious talents.

"To Hell with Claude" was to have been the last in a string of "Claude" stories ("The Last Word," "I, Claude," "The Guests of Chance;" "The Rest of Science Fiction") which Beaumont had written in collaboration with Chad Oliver. "The series," explains Oliver—which appeared in F&SF magazine—was the result of "a mutual dislike for all of the cliches that had crept into science fiction. We decided to just take all of them we could possibly cram into one story and just get rid of them. Forever. And, of course, we used an Adam and Eve frame, which was about as trite as you could possibly get . . ."

To Hell with Claude
Introduction by Chad Oliver

January 10, 1987

Dear Chuck:

A lot of years, as Claude might say. You'll remember. We roughed out this story in 1955, rolling around on the floor and howling like maniacs. You wrote your part and sent it to me in April, 1956. I wrote the rest and finished it up last night. Who knows, maybe we have set some kind of record for procrastination. In any event, what with one thing and another, it came out about half Beaumont and half Oliver, as usual. We'll leave it to the Claude scholars to figure out who wrote what.

There are probably a few things I forgot to tell you the last time we talked. You know how it is. Did I mention how much I treasured your friendship? Did I mention how much I admired your magic with words? Did I tell you how proud of you I was? I suppose we were always too busy having fun to speak what was in our hearts.

Writing this was pure joy for me. It brought you back for a few days. Chuck, I can hear you laughing, and that is as it should be. That's how I remember you.

If there is a sadness—a fly in the old ointment, so to speak— it is because there can never be another Claude story in this

*world. That's all she wrote Claude, dear Claude, whatever he
was, belonged to both of us. Where else could Tony Boucher,
who bought the first Claude stories, appear as a character in the
final epic? (Yes, and Mick McComas too, offstage but present in
spirit.)*

*I am a little older now. Beje and I think of you often. I have
looked a short distance down that last road you traveled. Not
far, and a different bug, but I understand what you faced. Cheers,
Chuck.*

*Hey, I'm not in any hurry. I'll hold the fort here for another
decade or two. But when I see you again, what think you?
Wouldn't it be great to do it all again, one last time?*

Old friend, Claude awaits. He won't let go of us.

*With love,
Chad*

THERE WAS A breeze, sun-warmed and gentle; the smell
of magnolia blossoms; and, from the work fields, happy
voices raised in song. To another, the day might have
spelled Peace. But to Claude Adams, thrice father of the
Earth's population, old now and tired, tired, but still possessed of a mind sharper than any razor, there was little to
cheer about. He fingered the bulky object in his lap for a
fleeting moment and then sent it hurtling across the room.

"Books!" he snorted.

"Now, Dad," his wife said.

"Books!" he repeated. "Confound it, Woola, it is not
fair. It is lacking in justice. I get a civilization ticking, tune
it finally to perfection, and what happens? The seeds of
decay are planted. The rumblings of revolution. By all the
Gods, woman, am I to have no rest?"

Woola wheeled herself to her husband's side and ran desiccated, though cool, fingers through his stone-white hair. "I know, I know," she wheezed in what she fondly imagined to be a soothing manner. "You've worked so hard. But isn't it possible that you're getting your dander up over nothing?"

"Be damned to dander!" Claude had his blood up. "Nothing? Do you call *those* nothing?" He gestured toward the stack of ill-bound volumes in the corner and trembled like a wind-whipped sapling.

Woola could not reply.

"Here's the thing," Claude said, aware that he had startled the old lady. "We've got a pretty neat little lifeway working now. Nothing fancy, mind you, but it clicks right along, one-two, one-two, and . . ."

Ah, but what was the use? The former Sarboomian princess had a doll's face and, he had to admit, a mind to match: how could he expect her to grasp the true complexities of the problem? Poor, frightened little bird, there was no way for her to understand that it was books of the imagination, not armies, not diseases, but *books*—these innocent-looking, silent volumes—that destroyed worlds . . .

"Go to your room," he commanded. "I must think. Wait!" He grasped her arm. "What are you hiding?"

Woola's eyes widened in terror. "Hiding?" she quavered. "Why, n-nothing. Claude, I implore you. You're hurting your Woola."

"No secrets, woman. Give it to me."

Woola went limp. Listlessly she reached into her literally voluminous bodice.

Claude reeled back as though struck by a crowbar. "What's this, what's this?" he cried.

"It's called," his wife said, softly, "*Alice in Wonderland.*"

"Under my own roof! My own wife . . ."

"Oh, Claude, I'm so sorry. But I didn't see where it

would do any harm. Just a little light reading before I went
to bed—"

Claude tossed the book onto the pile. "Depart," he said,
crisply.

Then, when the crash of crineline and tattoo of sobs had
diminished down the hall, he moved to the bell-cord and
gave it a stiff yank.

Everything, he mused dispiritedly, had been going so
well. He should have known. It was ever thus when the
serpent slithered into Eden.

Recalling the errors of advanced technological civiliza-
tions, Claude had built this new world along simple, almost
spartan lines. Medieval-Virginian, he had dubbed it, allowing the whimsical part of his nature some small leeway. It
combined the severe serious-mindedness of the Thirteenth
Century with the graceful *joie d'vivre* of the pre-bellum
Southern states. It worked so perfectly. Everyone had
slaves and yet were slaves themselves: an aristocratic bour-
geoisie, so to speak. And Claude, from whose remarkable
loins all these teeming millions had come, was alone the
government, the ministry, and The King; he ruled, be-
nignly, mercifully, but strictly, from Redolent Pines, the
grandest plantation of them all and Seat of World Government; and he was revered.

It was a happy, prosperous would. No television, no
motion pictures, in fact, no entertainment of any sort whatever: the people had plenty to do with their hands, and you
didn't find them slouching about imagining things or
dreaming. If they were inclined to be a trifle sluggish, well,
Claude reasoned, that was a small price to pay for harmony.

And now it was ending. He thought he had destroyed
the menace, fantasy, for good in the Forest of Darkness on
far Sarboom; but he had not. The growth still flourished,
and, if not checked, would cause another revolution, sure
as shooting.

"You rang, Colonel?"

Claude turned to face Ezra, his faithful retainer. Ezra seemed even paler than usual. In fact, Claude thought, the man looked like a ghost, much as Claude detested the expression.

"Ezra," he said, "the way I have doped it out, one man is responsible for these treasonable machinations. Knock him out and you have wiped out the trouble. Well?"

"You are probably right, Colonel."

Claude permitted himself a smile. He had a weakness for yes-men. "Dammit, I *know* I'm right," he advised, with some acerbity. "Oh, he's clever, I'll give him that. But I did not just fall off the turnip truck myself. I have, if I may say so, been around the barn a few times. I shall flush him out no matter what the cost!" He flipped his black string tie. "You know, of course, that the greatest concentration of fantasy books has been in Plainville in one of the states of the effete east. You are perhaps aware that the town has secretly changed its name to Arkham. You doubtless are cognizant of the fact that at Miskatonic University there is a veritable hotbed of fantasy activity."

"All news to me, Colonel. I didn't know."

"Well, Ezra, I make it my business to know. That is why I am Claude and you are Ezra. Between you and me and the old gatepost, I'd say our man is lurking in Plainville. But he is a shrewd firebrand or I miss my guess. If he thinks we're after him, he'll belt. So we must be foxy, eh? Ezra, summon the Royal Atom-Arranger: I believe the time has come for action!"

The retainer, ever faithful, bowed silently and shuffled away.

Claude's ancient brow furrowed as his plan took form. Devilish clever it was, but dangerous.

Very dangerous.

Still, he thought, thumbing down a goblet of damp shag and lighting his aged briar with a wooden stick match, this will not be the first tight squeak I've seen; and—one might as well confess it—there is a certain sameness to plantation life. Of all men, he knew that perfection had its flaws.

He stepped from his wheelchair and clapped his hands. Action! That was the ticket.

Ezra shambled back, not too fast. "You called, Colonel?"

"Yes," Claude snapped. "I will need a bit of equipment. Specifically, I want a mirror, a sprig of garlic, a wooden stake—no, make it two—a crossroads, seven silver bullets, and a stream of running water. Get on it, man!"

Ezra paled almost to transparency.

"And Ezra?"

"Yes, My Lord?"

"Tell the Royal Atom-Arranger to make it snappy!"

The hansom jounced and squealed and strained, uttering its weary song of the road. Claude held to the seat. From time to time he would turn his gaze to the passing countryside, and moan, gently: it was a long way to travel.

When at last he saw the sign marked PLAINVILLE, and the shadowed little twisting road, he put his discomfort aside and rapped sharply with his cane. "Turn off here, driver!"

The hansom shrilled to a halt, throwing up plumes of oddly-shaped dust. The driver pulled open the door, his seamed face a study in fear. "Sorry I be," he said, "but that there is a road I'll not be traveling, Lord and Master."

"But," observed Claude, "there is no other way to Plainville."

"*Plainville!*" The driver laughed mirthlessly, spat, shook his head, grimaced, blenched, and trembled. "Look here," he said, glancing nervously over his shoulder. "I'm not what you would call, now, a coward. But, say, there's no power on this Earth of yours that'd get me to go into that ancient, time-snubbed Abode of Evil!"

"You seem to have strong feelings on the subject."

"Indeed, Lord and Master." The driver climbed back up to the cab. He was shaking horribly. Somewhere, an owl laughed. "I beg you to reconsider. Why not give Harvard a try? There's a nice, friendly, respectable school."

Claude was about to answer, when the horse—which had been frantically pawing the ground and whinnying—rose, suddenly, eyes red as flame, flailed the fetid air with its hoofs, and galloped peremperterially away, the hansom clattering behind.

In moments, Claude was alone.

"Superstitious peasants," he muttered. Confound it, he had lost his equipment. He adjusted his beanie at a jaunty angle and set forth down the road. Precisely as planned, the touch of the beanie triggered a transformation that bordered on the awesome. To the untrained eye, Claude had become a typical college freshman, smooth of cheek and innocent of guile, a lad in his teens. The Royal Atom-Arranger had done his job well.

Yet, Claude knew, for all the plan's cunning, it was well not to count one's chickens before they were hatched. He was pleased with the turn of phrase.

He proceeded cautiously, noting that the sun had tucked itself behind a dreary clump of clouds, and that the trees were increasingly gnarled: naked reptilian shapes against the sulphurous sky. "Like fingers," Claude observed, admiring his simile.

He pressed on. The air turned into thick fog and the signposts now read: ARKHAM. Did the fools think that because they were a small village, off the beaten track as it were, they could escape notice?

A sound caused him to stop, abruptly. He listened: it came from the shrouded moor to his immediate left, the sinister side. It was a sing-song sort of chant:

Ia ia shub niggurath . . ."

Claude blinked. "Cthulhu," he sneezed. The fog was so heavy that he could hardly see the road. He walked carefully in the direction of the chanting.

The scene before him became momentarily clear.

In an unspeakable grave there were five nameless beings. All were reading the Bible backwards. Across the damp sward lay five couples engaged in abominations. There was a hideous stone idol, barnacled with age, infinitely evil, and a man dressed entirely in black. The man was doing something vile to a sheep.

Claude surmised instantly that he was on the right trail. But now was not the time for decisive action. Patience!

"I beg your pardon," he said, when the man had finished the act he had begun, "but I seem to have lost my way. Would you be so kind as to direct me to Arkham?"

"Ia, ia," the man said, advancing in what might be construed as an unfriendly manner.

"How's that?"

"Dia ad aghaidh's ad aodaun. Agus bas dunach ort! Ungl, ungl. Rrlh chchch . . ."

"Speak up, can't you? Don't mumble. My name is, ah, Smada, and I'm on my way to the University."

Ia, ia. Smerk ygdrsll yanter!"

"Oh, let it pass, let it pass." Claude snapped his fingers with disdain, turned from the black-robed figure, and found the road again. "Pesky Foreigners," he stated to nobody in particular.

At last the trail became cobbled, and topping a rise, Claude saw it.

The town was sunken in fog, of course, but one could discern gray chimneys, rotting towers, flickering gas lamps, scurrying figures, and time-lost streets.

Plainville? Claude shook his head, suffused with sadness. No, indeed.

Arkham. Why, he could *smell* the legends.

He stopped a hooded citizen whose face was deathly white, and inquired, in what he trusted was a callow fashion, "Where, pray tell, might I find Miskatonic U.?"

The creature pointed with a shaking finger to a wavering gray stone mansion, eaten by moss and consumed by years. It stank of decay. "Go half a mile down Providence Road, turn off at Lonely Yew Lane, go past Hangman's Corner, take thirteen steps and take a left at Sorcerer's Nook. You can't miss it."

"Clear as crystal," Claude said. "It is good to hear plain English again, and I offer my thanks."

The pale citizen pulled his hood across his face.

Claude shifted his satchel of school books, sighed with both excitement and resignation, and made his way down the cobble-stoned hill.

The game, he knew, was now afoot.

The Dean of Admissions was having trouble with his ice cream. The bats hanging in the rafters kept dropping ghastly pods into it. He stroked his lantern jaw and wiped his wig with a soiled cloth.

"Ah, Smada," he intoned. "No need for transcripts here. We rather pride ourselves on a certain informality."

Claude could hardly approve of that, but he held his tongue. Haste, as he had often observed, made waste.

The Dean picked up a quill pen, dipped it in some dark fluid, and scratched his initials on an official-looking parchment sheet: HPL. "Take this document to my assistant, whom you will find in the next chamber. He will be overjoyed to show you about. We receive few fresh students these cheerless days. Besides, it is his job."

Claude bowed. It would not do to push this informality craze too far. He made his exit.

It was then, in the ominous silence, that he first heard the Noise. It was a tap-tap-tapping, distant and vague. As of someone rapping? No, it was more of a clicking sound . . .

The man in the next room proved to be a bit of an enigma. He was as big as an ox, barrel-chested and wire-haired, and he had the massive leathery hands of a wrestler. However, his voice was astoundingly pleasant and cultured, enhanced by a slight lisp. "You are the Dean's assistant?" Claude asked.

The man nodded. "To be more exact," he said, conspiratorially, "I'm a good deal more than that. The old boy loves his craft, but he wouldn't be where he is today, in fact, without yours truly."

"You are Dr.—"

"Nameless," the man said, scanning the parchment. "A new student?" He grinned toothily. "Why, we haven't had one for over a year! Perhaps you would like to examine a course schedule?"

"I would," Claude said. One must play the role. "But first I would be grateful to learn about that Noise I hear. It seems to be coming from below."

The giant man frowned. "You mean a sort of tap-tap-tapping?"

"Yes, that's it."

"I hear nothing." Dr. Nameless picked Claude up by the shirt and held him a bare inch from his, Nameless's, face. "There is no Noise," he said, not without meaning.

"But," Claude swallowed. "But—well, come to think of it, you're right."

Dr. Nameless put Claude down. "Now, just you take a gander at the course schedule. Then I think we ought to visit the stadium." He winked. "I know about you lads. All is not dry scholarly book work here at Miskatonic U., you may be sure. We have our share of hearty outdoor activities."

"Hearty, eh?" Claude responded with feigned enthusiasm.

He studied the course schedule. It was not without a

certain fascination. It listed all of the courses offered at Miskatonic, and named all the department chairmen.

His keen eye was caught by the title of a biology class, Serological Genetics. It was taught by a count, no less. He was also intrigued by the copy concerning the Student Health Center. It read: "Dr. Jekyll, MWF. Mr. Hyde, TT."

And then there was Professor Monk Lewis, of the Department of Anthropology. A chap named Hodgson, Associate Professor of Marine Fungi. A mathematics class restricted to very young girls, taught by a Professor Carroll. A course in monstrous electrodes, of all things, offered by an assistant professor with the curious name of Dr. Frank N. Stein.

Claude's attention strayed. He had but scant interest in academics. "Onward to the stadium!" he cried with youthful vigor.

"Yes, indeed," said Dr. Nameless agreeably. "Boys will be boys, and all that. I believe that Cleve will join us about now. Can't get enough of it."

"Cleve?"

"You will share a room with Cleve. Lots of fun. Been with us several semesters, you know."

Sure enough, Cleve appeared on cue. Cleve was completely cloaked in a rather garish robe adorned with purple tassels. A sophomore, at least.

"Pleasedtameetcha," Cleve intoned.

"Likewise, I'm sure," Claude said.

Cleve? The diminutive of Cleveland, no doubt. Well, no matter.

They strolled to a large, though rickety, grandstand at the far end of the weed-choked campus. It was jammed with students, most of them bearing waxen expressions.

Claude could no longer hear the tap-tap-tapping. Somehow, he was glad.

"Nice turnout," he ventured, slapping at a low-flying bat with his beanie. "I confess that I like school spirit."

"We have them," Cleve said.

Claude edged along a slat and sat down next to a sallow youth who was munching candy skulls.

On the greensward there were four spindle-shanked men, all well advanced in years. They held olive branches. Otherwise, the gridiron was deserted.

"Are we early," Claude asked of his increasingly taciturn guides, "or are we late?"

"Neither," said Dr. Nameless. He was slowly crushing a cloth effigy with his thumbs. "The game is about to begin."

"Yay," said Cleve. "Hoo, boy."

There was a surging wail from the assembled multitude.

"The mascots!" Dr. Nameles screamed.

From a manger at one end of the field an immense number of kids appeared. They were led by a maternal looking nanny.

"Don't tell me," Claude sighed. "The Goat with a Thousand Young."

"Ygdrsll! Ia, ia, ia!" cried Dr. Nameless, losing control. "Now look!"

Claude looked. A cloud of diaphanous girls drifted out and took their stations. They gyrated.

"Virgins," Dr. Nameless hissed. "We require them for our matriculation ceremonies."

"Cheerleaders," Cleve explained.

"Watch!" yelled the giant Dr. Nameless. He shook Claude until his, Claude's, teeth rattled. Really, the man was positively beside himself.

Claude watched. The four old men clutched one another, fanning the air with their olive branches. Then, through an arch at one end of the stadium, four more figures charged onto the field.

They were dressed all in black. They had hoods. They also had battle-axes in their hands.

A red fire truck roared across the arena, bells clanging.

"What's that?" Claude whispered.

Dr. Nameless put a sausage finger to his lips. "It's symbolic," he said.

The figures in black overwhelmed the old men, trampling the olive branches.

The goats bleated.

The virgins ripped off their gowns and grabbed megaphones.

"Now!" shrilled Dr. Nameless. He was hysterical with school pride.

"Give 'em the ax," the megaphones implored.

The crowd took up the chant. "Give 'em the ax, the ax, the ax! Give 'em the ax, the ax, the ax!"

Claude closed his eyes. He had never been what you might call the queasy type, but—

The figures in black had given the old men the ax.

"I do believe," Claude said to his escorts, "that I would like to be shown to my room."

While the candle flames fluttered and the dank wind banged against the shutters, Claude abandoned his pose of innocence. He assumed Command.

"Cleve," he snapped, "there will be no sleep this night. Do you hear the tap-tap-tapping? Do you hear the Noise?"

Cleve twirled the tassels on the robe. "What Noise, Smada? Many are the freshmen who have imagined what you call a tap-tap-tapping. From the basement vaults, so the tale is told . . ."

Claude had no time to waste. He boxed Cleve one on the ear. "Now do you hear it?"

"I hear it, I hear it!" Cleve admitted. "But I like it where we are, in our cozy room. Observe the elegant chamber pots—"

"Thunder mugs be damned!" Claude barked. "Fire the tapers, unleash the hounds!"

"We have no pigs," Cleve quavered. "We have no dogs."

"Not tapirs, tapers! Torches! Don't they teach you anything in this place?"

"I know much," Cleve insisted. "You will see."

"Come, then! To the catacombs!"

Down the winding, moss-covered steps they went. Their shadows danced behind them, mournful arabesques . . .

That infernal tap-tap-tapping. It beat a tattoo in Claude's brain. He would get to the bottom of this. And when he did—

They passed the bent-backed man who tended the furnaces. His name was lettered on his coveralls: Bram Stoker.

With torches guttering, they swept by a beautiful scientist and his mad daughter. Some barbarous experiment was in progress.

They burst through a massive creaking door, older than time, and there it was.

Seated at a heavy desk enclosed in a scarlet pentagram was a bearded man. He was tap-tap-tapping on a toy typer. The echoes in the cavernous vault magnified the Noise.

"Kapital!" the bearded man chorted. "Kapital!"

"Your name?" Claude demanded imperiously.

"I belong to the family of Marx," the man said with some asperity. "Not one of those pitiful louts whose given names terminate with a vowel, but—"

"Karl," stated Claude knowingly.

"The same," Karl Marx admitted proudly. "Whoever *you* may be, I implore you not to touch that edifice." He gestured toward a precariously tilted structure that was bent over his desk. The thing seemed to be constructed of triangular slices of Italian cuisine. On top of it rested a balding head that fairly reeked of formaldehyde. "If it should collapse and come into contact with the pentagram, there will be Hell to pay."

"What is it?" Claude asked despite himself.

"It is the famous Lenin Tower of Pizza," Karl Marx explained. "A monument to my works."

"Balderdash," Claude commented.

"The word of an exploiter," Marx snorted. "The propertied classes are smug in their layers of lard. What do the downtrodden peasants know? I am the only one to divine the formula that will save them from their misery. By unleasing the plague of fantasy in the pitiless halls of the money changers, I have driven a wedge—"

"I did not come here," Claude said shortly, "to savor the rehashed fragments of a dreary lecture."

It was not simply that sociology bored him. The instant that Marx had opened his beard-stuffed mouth, Claude had realized that this was not the quarry he sought. To reach the true source of trouble, he must dig deeper.

Much deeper.

With Claude, to think was to act.

Grabbing Cleve's shrouded arm, he delivered a stout kick to the Lenin Tower with his right sneaker.

As the Tower fell, Marx screamed and clutched his toy typer to his bosom. The bowels of the Earth rumbled. Tongues of flame spat up from below. There was a distinct odor of brimstone, not unpleasant . . .

Holding tightly to Cleve, Claude leaped into the pentagram. While chaos sparked around him, he had a sensation of falling.

"Down, please," Claude murmured.

Claude found himself shoving a considerable boulder up an immense hill.

Momentarily curious, and ignoring the fearful means of

Cleve, Claude turned companionably to a fellow worker. "Tedious business," he observed. "How far to the top?"

The wretch could barely get enough room to speak. It was very crowded on the mountain. The heated rock was slippery with sweat.

"There is no top," the doomed soul lamented. "There is no bottom."

Claude was not without pity but he had never admired a quitter. He summoned a fork-tailed fiend. "There has been a slight miscalculation," he informed him.

"That's what they all say," the fiend said mildly.

"My companion and I," Claude went on, undaunted, "wish to be taken to Mr. Big."

The fiend shrugged. "Why not? We have an eternity before us. Go, come, stay. It is all the same to me."

"Get some starch in your ridgepole," Claude chided him. "It is not, I assure you, all the same to me. If you are a true fiend—a fiend in need, so to speak—you will transport us to Mr. Big."

"Nobody hurries here, lad," the fiend said. "Time, we have. However, who am I to add to your torment? In the final analysis, it can be neither better nor worse."

Sensing a growing impatience on Claude's part, the fiend escorted them to Mr. Big at something a tad faster than a snail's pace. The fiend then withdrew. He could wait. He could wait a long, long time.

Claude faced Mr. Big at last. Finally, an adversary worthy of his skills!

"I am Claude Adams," he announced, "and this is my friend. Not fiend. Friend."

The Devil had no horns. He was a short, fashionably-dressed man with thick glasses. He was quite busy. "Call me Tony," he said in a friendly, somewhat husky voice. "Be with you in a moment. Time! There is never enough time, even here."

Tony was awash in debris. He was surrounded by books, magazines, expense vouchers, comics, manuscripts, and opera records. He was writing a review. Claude peeked at the book's title: *The Corpse's Delight*, by S. Orbital Ridges. Tony didn't like it. Feeling that he had been too harsh in his criticism, he concluded: "Excellent side-lights on croquet playing in Wales."

"There," he sighed. "Not always easy to be fair, you know? Taste is such a personal matter. Now, what can I do for you?"

"We have come to make a deal," Claude stated.

"Flatly incredible!" Tony groaned. His voice seemed to emerge from the depths of his chest. "I had hoped for something more original. McComas and I—"

"Who is McComas?" Claude interjected.

Tony waved his manicured hand. "I always begin sentences that way. Pay it no mind. Your proposition?"

Claude did not hesitate. He who hesitated, as he had often, observed, was lost. "Do not mistake me for the callow youth I appear to be," he warned. "I am a man of no little experience.

"McComas and I understand that. Get on with it. I know you of old, Claude Adams."

Claude felt a pardonable pride. His reputation, then, had preceded him. "The essence of a good bargain," he said, "is that both sides profit from it."

"I agree with that. It is, indeed a platitude."

Claude was stung. "I will keep it simple. You are too clever for tricky clauses. I will state my case in plain terms, man to Devil. You will then have no choice."

"McComas and I," Tony said shiftily, "have many choices."

Claude seized the horns, as it were. "Try this one on for size. You are overworked and you are overcrowded. The commies are coming. They will try to organize everything, make you write reviews for the State—"

"McComas won't stand for it!"

"Perhaps, perhaps. But why face the problem at all? If you permit my companion and I to leave, I will eliminate the difficulty! I am no slouch at population control, as you know, and I can manipulate culture patterns. It will be like old times. No fuss, no bother, you in your kerchief and me in my cap—"

Tony's face flushed. "By gad, sir, you interest me! When McComas and I deal, we deal!"

Claude smiled slyly. "There is—uh—a way out of here?"

"There is a way," Tony assured him. "A bargain, as you say, is a bargain. But it will not be easy."

"It never is," Claude observed. He managed to contain his elation. He knew what was coming. "I am, I assure you, all ears."

"Oh my," said Tony in that distinctive deep voice of his. The Devil told Claude what he had to do. "There is one teensy condition," he concluded.

"Which is?"

"You must not look behind you on the journey. Remember that! Do not look back."

"I will not forget," Claude promised.

With his robed and hooded companion in tow, Claude took his leave.

The side-wheeler splashed through the miasmic murk of the River Styx. The river, of course, was full of stones.

A bewhiskered sailor leaned over the bow-rail, casting a long knotted line. "Ma-a-a-rk Twai-i-i-in!" he bellowed.

At exactly the proper moment, neither too early nor too late, Claude rolled the dice of destiny.

He looked back.

There was a shudder of silence, a skip in the heartbeat of eternity. Then came a blinding flash. Thunder boomed. It was like all the thunder there ever was, or ever could be, all wrapped up in the fireflies of an Illinois summer's twilight.

It rained strawberries.

Claude found the results quite gratifying. He stepped ashore on an Earth of desolation. He was up to his armpits in corpses and rotting strawberries.

"Unhappy world," he mused. "The paradox of the Solor System. For rebirth, we require abortion. To live in glory, it is necessary to become one with the worm."

"But what will we *do*?" quavered Cleve.

Claude gave no answer. He had been through this before. However, he was forced to concede that he was facing certain difficulties. He fingered his beanie. The Royal Atom-Arranger had done his work well. Lost and by the wind grieved . . .

Claude Adams was once more a white-maned old codger. Old, old and suffused with weariness. He noticed that his companion seemed dismayed.

"We must begin again," he intoned finally. He had never been one to shirk his duty, no matter what the odds.

His companion brightened. "It may be," the shrouded figure whispered, "that perhaps I can be of some assistance."

The tasseled robe fell to the shattered Earth. The hood was coyly slipped from golden curls.

Claude stared at her with surging fatigue. "I should have known," he sighed. "Cleve! You are not Cleve, as advertised, but rather you stand before me as—"

"Eve," she finished. She quivered expectantly.

"Not yet, child," Claude temporized. "Mercy, not yet. This has been a trying day, if day it was."

"When?" Eve pressed.

Claude squared his worn shoulders. He took refuge in his ancient briar, firing up the shag tobacco with the wooden stick match he always carried. There was great comfort in familiar things.

"Soon," he puffed. "In all the eons, I have never failed the Earth."

With infinite tenderness, he took her arm.

Together, they soared as though on gossamer wings, touching the grandeur of the silvered Moon, while billions and billions of cosmic stars smiled on the miracle of Creation.

APPOINTMENT
WITH EDDIE

IT WAS ONE of those bars that strike you blind when you walk in out of the sunlight, but I didn't need eyes, I could see him, the way deaf people can hear trumpets. It was Shecky, all right. But it also wasn't Shecky.

He was alone.

I'd known him for eight years, worked with him, traveled with him, lived with him; I'd put him to bed at night and waked him up in the morning; but never, in all that time, never once had I seen him by himself—not even in a bathtub. He was plural. A multitude of one. And now, the day after his greatest triumph, he was alone, here, in a crummy little bar on Third Avenue.

There was nothing to say, so I said it. "How are you, Sheck?"

He looked up and I could tell he was three-quarters gone. That meant he'd put away a dozen Martinis, maybe more. But he wasn't drunk. "Sit down," he said, softly, and that's when I stopped worrying and started getting scared. I'd never heard Shecky talk softly before. He'd always had a voice like the busy signal. Now he was practically whispering.

"Thanks for coming." Another first: "Thanks" from

Shecky King, to me. I tried to swallow but suddenly my
throat was dry, so I waved to the waiter and ordered a
double scotch. Of course, my first thought was, he's going
to dump me. I'd been expecting it for years. Even though
I'd done a good job for him, I wasn't the biggest agent in
the business, and to Shecky the biggest always meant the
best. But this wasn't his style. I'd seen him dump people
before and the way he did it, he made it seem like a favor.
Always with Shecky the knife was a present, and he never
delivered it personally. So I went to the second thought,
but that didn't make any better sense. He was never sick
a day in his life. He didn't have time. A broad? No good.
The trouble didn't exist that his lawyers, or I, couldn't
spring him out of in ten minutes.

I decided to wait. It took most of the drink.

"George," he said, finally, "I want you to lay some can-
dor on me." You know the way he talked. "I want you to
lay it on hard and fast. No thinking. Dig?"

"Dig," I said, getting dryer in the throat.

He picked up one of the five full Martini glasses in front
of him and finished it in one gulp. "George," he said, "am
I a success?"

The highest-paid, most acclaimed performer in show
business, the man who had smashed records at every club
he's played for five years, who had sold over two million
copies of every album he'd ever cut, who had won three
Emmys and at least a hundred other awards, who had, in
the opinion of the people *and* the critics, reached the top
in a dozen fields—this man, age thirty-six, was asking me
if he was a success.

"Yes," I said.

He killed another Martini. "Candorsville?"

"The place." I thought I was beginning to get it. Some
critic somewhere had shot him down. But would he fall in
here? No. Not it. Still, it was worth a try.

"Who says you aren't?"

"Nobody. Yet."

"Then what?"

He was quiet for a full minute. I could hardly recognize him sitting there, an ordinary person, an ordinary scared human being.

Then he said, "George, I want you to do something for me."

"Anything," I said. That's what I was being paid for: anything.

"I want you to make an appointment for me."

"Where at?"

"Eddie's."

"Who's Eddie?"

He started sweating. "A barber," he said.

"What's wrong with Mario?"

"Nothing's wrong with Mario."

It wasn't any of my business. Mario Cabianca had been Shecky's personal hair stylist for ten years, he was the best in the business, but I supposed he'd nicked The King or forgotten to laugh at a joke. It wasn't important. It certainly couldn't have anything to do with the problem, whatever it was. I relaxed a little.

"When for?" I asked.

"Now," he said. "Right away."

"Well, you could use a shave."

"Eddie doesn't shave people. He cuts hair. That's all."

"You don't need a haircut."

"George," he said, so soft I could barely hear him, "I never needed anything in all my life like I need this haircut."

"Okay. What's his number?"

"He hasn't got one. You'll have to go in."

Now he was beginning to shake. I've seen a lot of people tremble, but this was the fist time I'd seen anybody shake.

"Sheck, are you germed up?"

"No." The Martini sloshed all over his cashmere coat.

By the time it got to his mouth only the olive was left. "I'm fine. Just do this for me, George. Please. Do it now."

"Okay, take it easy. What's his address?"

"I can't remember." An ugly sound boiled out of his throat, I guess it was a laugh. "Endsburg! I can't remember. But I can take you there." He started to get up. His belly hit the edge of the table. The ashtrays and glasses tipped over. He looked at the mess, then at his hands, which were still shaking, and he said, "Come on."

"Sheck," I put a hand on his shoulder, which nobody does. "You want to tell me about it?"

"You wouldn't understand," he said.

On the way out, I dropped a twenty in front of the bartender. "Nice to have you, Mr. King," he said, and it was like somebody had turned the volume up on the world. "Me and my old lady, y'know, we wouldn't miss your show for anything." "Yeah," a guy on the last stool said. "God bless ya, buddy!"

We walked out into the sun. Shecky looked dead. His face was white and glistening with sweat. His eyes were red. And the shaking was getting worse.

"This way," he said, and we started down Third.

"You want me to grab a cab?"

"No. It isn't far."

We walked past the pawn shops and the laundries and saloons and the gyms and I found myself breathing through my mouth, out of habit. It had taken me a long time to forget these smells. They weren't just poor smells. They were kiss-it-all-goodbye, I-never-had-a-chance smells. Failure smells. What the hell was I doing here, anyway? What was Shecky doing here? Shecky, who carried his Hong Kong silk sheets with him wherever he went because that was the only thing he could stand next to his skin, who kept a carnation in his lapel, who shook hands with his gloves on? I looked down at his hands. They were bare.

We walked another block. At the light I heard a sound

like roller skates behind me. A bum without legs stopped at the curb. The sign across the street changed to WALK. I nudged Shecky; it was the kind of thing he appreciated. He didn't even notice. the cripple wiggled his board over the curb and, using the two wooden bricks in his hands, rolled past us. I wondered how he was going to make it back up to the sidewalk, but Shecky didn't. He was thinking of other things.

After two more blocks, deep into the armpit of New York, he slowed down. The shaking was a lot worse. Now his hands were fists.

"There," he said.

Up ahead, five or six doors, was a barber shop. It looked like every other barber shop in this section. The pole outside was cardboard, and most of the paint was gone. The window was dirty. The sign—EDDIE THE BARBER— was faded.

"I'll wait," Shecky said.

"You want a haircut now, is that right?"

"That's right," he said.

"I should give him your name?"

He nodded.

"Sheck, we've known each other a long time. Can't you tell me—"

He almost squeezed a hunk out of my arm. "Go, George," he said. "Go."

I went. Just before I got to the place, I looked back. Shecky was standing alone in front of a tattoo parlor, more alone than ever, more alone than anyone ever. His eyes were closed. And he was shaking all over. I tried to think of him the way he was ten hours ago, surrounded by people, living it up, celebrating the big award; but I couldn't. This was somebody else.

I turned around and walked into the barber shop. It was one of those non-union deals, with a big card reading HAIRCUTS—$1.00 on the wall, over the cash register. It was small and dirty. The floor was covered with hair. In the back, next to a curtain, there was a cane chair and a table with an old radio on it. The radio was turned to a ball game, but you couldn't hear it because of the static. The far wall was papered with calendars. Most of them had naked broads on them, but a few had hunting and fishing scenes. They were all coated with grease and dirt.

There wasn't anything else, except one old-fashioned barber chair and, behind it, a sink and a cracked glass cabinet.

A guy was in the chair, getting a haircut. He had a puffy face and a nose full of broken blood vessels. You could smell the cheap wine across the room.

Behind the bum was maybe the oldest guy I'd ever seen outside a hospital. He stood up straight, but his skin looked like a blanket somebody had dropped over a hat-rack. It had that yellow look old skin gets. It made you think of coffins.

Neither of them noticed me, so I stood there a while, watching. The barber wasn't doing anything special. He was cutting hair, the old way, with a lot of scissors-clicking in the air. I knew a bootblack once who did the same thing. He said he was making the rag talk. But he gave it up, he said, because nobody was listening any more. The bum in the chair wasn't listening, either, he was sound asleep, so there had to be a lot more. But you couldn't see it.

I walked over to the old man. "Are you Eddie?"

He looked up and I saw that his eyes were clear and sharp. "That's right," he said.

"I'd like to make an appointment."

His voice was like dry leaves blowing down the street. "For yourself?"

"No. A friend."

I felt nervous and embarrassed and it came to me, then, that maybe this whole thing was a gag. A practical joke. Except that it didn't have any point.

"What is his name?"

"Shecky King."

The old man went back to clipping the bum's hair. "You'll have to wait until I'm finished," he said. "Just have a seat."

I went over and sat down. I listened to the static and the clicking scissors and I tried to figure things out. No good. Shecky could buy this smelly little place with what he gave away in tips on a single night. He had the best barber in the business on salary. Yet there he was, down the street, standing in the hot sun, waiting for me to make an appointment with this feeble old man.

The clicking stopped. The bum looked at himself in the mirror, nodded and handed a crumpled dollar bill to the barber. The barber took it over to the cash register and rang it up.

"Thank you," he said.

The bum belched. "Next month, same time," he said.

"Yes, sir."

The bum walked out.

"Now then," the old man said, flickering those eyes at me. "The name again?"

He had to be putting me on. There wasn't anybody who didn't know Shecky King. He was like Coca-Cola, or sex. I even saw an autographed picture of him in an igloo, once.

"Shecky King," I said, slowly. There wasn't any reaction. The old man walked back to the cash register, punched the NO SALE button and took a dog-eared notebook out of the drawer.

"He'd like to come right away," I told him.

The old man stared at the book a long time, holding it close to his face. Then he shut it and put it back in the drawer and closed the drawer.

"I'm sorry," he said.

"What do you mean?"

"I don't have an opening."

I looked around the empty shop. "Yeah, I can see, business is booming."

He smiled.

"Seriously," I said.

He went on smiling.

"Look, I haven't got the slightest idea why Mr. King wants to have his hair cut here. But he does. So let's stop horsing around. He's willing to pay for it."

I reached into my left pocket and pulled out the roll. I found a twenty. "Maybe you ought to take another look at your appointment book," I said.

The old man didn't make a move. He just stood there, smiling. For some reason—the lack of sleep, probably, the running around, the worry—I felt a chill go down my back, the kind that makes goosepimples.

"Okay," I said. "How much?"

"One dollar," he said. "After the haircut."

That made me sore. I didn't actually grab his shirt, but it would have gone with my voice. "Look," I said, "this is important. I shouldn't tell you this, but Shecky's outside right now, down the street, waiting. He's all ready. You're not doing anything. Couldn't you—"

"I'm sorry," the old man said, and the way he said it, in that dry, creaky voice, I could almost believe him.

"Well, what about later this afternoon?"

He shook his head.

"Tomorrow?"

"No."

"Then *when*, for Chrissake?"

"I'm afraid I can't say."

"What the hell do you mean, you can't say? Look in the book!"

"I already have."

Now I was mad enough to belt the old wreck. "You're trying to tell me you're booked so solid you can't work in one lousy haircut?"

"I'm not trying to tell you anything."

He was feeble-minded, he had to be. I decided to lay off the yelling and humor him. "Look, Eddie . . . you're a businessman, right? You run this shop for money. Right?"

"Right," he said, still smiling.

"Okay. You say you haven't got an opening. I believe you. Why should you lie? No reason. It just means you're a good barber. You've got loyalty to your customers. Good. Fine. You know what that is? That's integrity. And there isn't anything I admire more than integrity. You don't see much of it in my business. I'm an agent. But here's the thing, Eddie—I can call you Eddie, can't I?"

"That's my name."

"Here's the thing. I wouldn't have you compromise your integrity for anything in the world. But there's a way out. What time do you close?"

"Five p.m."

"On the dot, right? Swell. Now listen, Eddie. If you could stay just half an hour after closing time, until five-thirty, no later, I could bring Shecky in and he could get his haircut and everybody would be happy. What do you say?"

"I never work overtime," he said.

"I don't blame you. Why *should* you, a successful businessman? Very smart, Eddie. Really. I agree with that rule a hundred per cent. Never work overtime. But, hear me out, now—there's an exception that proves every rule. Am I right? If you'll stretch a point here, this one time, it'll prove the rule, see, and also put some numbers on your savings account. Eddie, if you'll do this thing, I will personally see to it that you receive one hundred dollars."

"I'm sorry," he said.

"For a half-hour's work?" A cockroach ran across the wall. Eddie watched it. "Two hundred," I said. It was still fifty bucks shy of what Shecky was paying Mario every week, whether he worked or not, but I figured what the hell.

"No."

"Five hundred!" I could see it wasn't any good, but I had to try. A soldier keeps on pulling the trigger even when he knows he's out of bullets, if he's made enough, or scared enough.

"I don't work overtime," the old man said.

A last pull of the trigger. "One thousand dollars. Cash."

No answer.

I stared at him for a few seconds, then I turned around and walked out of the shop. Shecky was standing where I'd left him, and he was looking at me, so I put on the know-nothing face. As I walked toward him I thought, he's got to dump me. Any agent who can't get Shecky King an appointment with a crummy Third Avenue barber deserves to be dumped.

"Well?" he said.

"The guy's a nut."

"You mean he won't take me."

"I mean he's a nut. A kook. Not a soul in the place and, get this—he says he can't find an opening!"

You ever see a man melt? I never had. Now I was seeing it. Shecky King was melting in front of me, right there on the sidewalk in front of the tattoo parlor.

"You okay?"

He couldn't answer. The tears were choking him.

"Sheck? You okay?"

I saw a cab and waved it over. Shecky was trying to catch his breath, trying not to cry, but nothing worked for him. He stood there weaving and bawling and melting. Then he started beating his fists against the brick wall.

"God damn it!" he screamed, throwing his head back. "God damn it! God damn it!"

Then, suddenly, he pulled away from me, eyes wide,

hands bleeding, and broke into a run toward the barber shop.

"Hey," the cabbie said, "ain't that Shecky King?"

"I don't know," I said, and ran after him.

I tried to stop him, but you don't stop a crazy man, not when you're half his size and almost twice his age. He threw the door open and charged inside.

"Eddie!" His voice sounded strangled, like a hand was around his throat, cutting off the air. Or a rope. "Eddie, what have I got to do?"

The old man didn't even look up. He was reading a newspaper.

"Tell me!" Shecky pounded the empty barber chair with his bloody fists.

"Please be careful of the leather," the old man said.

"I'm a success!" Shecky yelled. "I qualify! Tell him, George! Tell him about last night!"

"What do you care what this crummy—"

"Tell him!"

I walked over and pulled the newspaper out of the old man's hands. "Last night Shecky King was voted the most popular show business personality of all time," I said.

"Tell him who voted!"

"The newspaper and magazine critics," I said.

"And who else?"

"Thirty million people throughout the world."

"You hear that? Everybody. Eddie, don't you hear what he's saying? Everybody! I'm Number One!"

Shecky climbed onto the chair and sat down.

"Haircut," he said. "Easy on the sides. Just a light trim. You know." He sat there breathing hard for a couple of seconds, then he twisted around and screamed at the old man. "Eddie! For God's sake, cut my hair!"

"I'm sorry," the old man said. "I don't have an opening at the moment."

* * *

You know what happened to Shecky King. You read about it. I knew, and I read about it, too, six months before the papers came out. In his eyes. I could see the headline there. But I thought I could keep it from coming true.

I took him home in a cab and put him to bed. He didn't talk. He didn't even cry. He just laid there, between the Hong Kong silk sheets, staring up at the ceiling, and for some crazy reason that made me think of the legless guy and the sign that said WALK. I was pretty tired.

The doctors ordered him to a hospital, but they couldn't find anything wrong, not physically anyway, so they called in the shrinks. A breakdown, the shrinks said. Nervous exhaustion. Emotional depletion. It happens.

It happens, all right, but I wasn't sold. Shecky was like a racing car, he operated best at high revs. That's the way some people are engineered. A nice long rest is a nice long death to them, because it gives them a chance to think, and for a performer that's the end. He sees what a stupid waste his life had been, working 24 hours a day so that people can laugh at him, or cry at him, running all the time—for what? Money. Praise. But he's got the money (if he didn't he wouldn't be able to afford the rest) and he's had the praise, and he hasn't really enjoyed what he's been doing for years—is it intellectual? does it contribute to the world? does it help anybody?—so he figures, why go on running? Why bother? Who cares? And he stops running. He gives it all up. And they let him out of the hospital, because now he's cured.

A lot of reasons why I didn't want this to happen to Shecky. He wasn't my friend—who can be friends with a multitude?—but he was an artist, and that meant he brought a lot of happiness to a lot of people. Of course he brought some unhappiness, too, maybe more than most, but that's the business. Talent never was enough. It is if you're a painter, or a book writer, maybe, but even there *chutzpah* counts. Shecky had it. Like the old story, he could have murdered both his parents and then thrown himself on the mercy of the court on the grounds that he was an orphan. And he could have gotten away with it.

The fact is, the truth is, he didn't have anything *except chutzpah*. His routines were written by other people. His singing was dubbed. His albums were turned out by the best conductors around. His movies and TV plays were put together like jigsaw puzzles out of a million blown takes. His books were ghosted.

But I say, anybody who can make out the way Shecky King made out, on the basis of nothing but personality and drive, that person is an artist.

Also, I was making close to a hundred grand a year off him.

What's the difference? I wanted him to pull out of it. The shrinks weren't worried. They said the barber was only "a manifestation of the problem." Not a cause. An effect. It meant that Shecky felt guilty about his success and was trying to re-establish contact with the common people.

I didn't ask them to explain why, if that was true, the barber refused to cut Shecky's hair. It would only have confused them.

Anyway, I knew they were wrong. Shecky was in the hospital because of that old son of a bitch on Third Avenue and not because of anything else.

All the next day I tried to piece it together, to make sense out of it, but I couldn't. So I started asking around. I didn't really expect an answer, and I didn't get one, until the next night. I was working on a double scotch on the rocks, thinking about the money we would be making if Shecky was at the Winter Garden right now, when a guy came in. You'd know him—a skinny Italian singer, very big. He walked over and put a hand on my neck. "I heard about Sheck," he said. "Tough break." Then, not because he gave a damn about Shecky but because I'd done him a few favors when he needed them, he asked me to join his

party, and I did. Another double scotch on the rocks and
I asked if he'd ever heard of Eddie the barber. It was like
asking him if he'd ever heard of girls.

"Tell me about it," I said.

He did. Eddie had been around, he said, forever. He
was a fair barber, no better and no worse than any other,
and he smelled bad, and he was creepy; but he was The
End. I shouldn't feel bad about not knowing this, because
I was one of the Out people. There were In people and
Out people and the In people didn't talk about Eddie. They
didn't talk about a lot of things.

"Why is he The End?" I asked.

Because he only takes certain people, my friend said.
Because he's selective. Because he's exclusive.

"I was in his shop. He had a lousy wino bum in the
chair!"

With that lousy wino bum, I was told, three-fourths of
the big names in show business would trade places. Money
didn't matter to Eddie, he would never accept more than
a dollar. Clothes didn't matter, or reputation, or influence.

"Then what *does* matter?"

He didn't know. Nobody knew. Eddie never said what
his standards were, in fact, he never said he *had* any standards. Either he had an opening or he didn't, that was all
you got.

I finished off the scotch. Then I turned to my friend.
"Has he ever cut *your* hair?"

"Don't ask," he said.

I had a tough time swallowing it until I talked to a half-
dozen other Names. Never mind who they were. They ver-
ified the story. A haircut from Eddie meant Success. Until
you sat in that chair, no matter what else had happened to
you, you were nothing. Your life was nothing. Your future
was nothing.

"And you go for this jazz?" I asked all of them the same

question. They all laughed and said, "Hell, no! It's those other nuts!" But their eyes said something different.

It was fantastic. Everybody who was anybody in the business knew about Eddie, and everybody was surprised that I did. As though, I'd mentioned the name of the crazy uncle they kept locked in the basement, or something. A lot of them got sore, a few even broke down and cried. One of them said that if I doubted Eddie's pull I should think about the Names who had knocked themselves off at the top of their success, no reason ever given, except the standard one. I should think about those Names real hard. And I did, remembering that headline in Shecky's eyes.

It fit together, finally, when I got to a guy who used to know Shecky in the old days, when he was a 20th mail boy named Sheldon Hochstrasser. He wanted to be In more than he wanted anything else, but he didn't know where In was. So he stuck close to the actors and the directors and he heard them talking about Eddie. One of them had just got an appointment and he saw that now he could die happy because he knew he had made it. Shecky was impressed. It gave him something to work towards, something to hang onto. From that point on, his greatest ambition was to get an appointment with Eddie.

He was smart about it, though. At least he thought he was. You don't get a good table at Chasen's, or Romanoff's, he said to himself, and to his buddy, unless you're somebody. For Eddie, he went on, you've got to be more. You've got to be a *success*. So the thing to do was to succeed.

He gave himself fifteen years.

Fifteen years later, to the day I'll bet, I met him at that bar on Third Avenue. Either he'd been thinking about Eddie all that time or he hadn't thought about him at all. I don't know which.

I turned the tap up, then, because he wasn't getting any better. I found out the ones who had made it and talked to them, but they weren't any help. They didn't know why they were In or even how long they'd stay. That was the lousy part of it: you could get cancelled. And putting in a word for Shecky wouldn't do any good, they said, because Eddie made his own decisions.

I still had a hard time getting it down. I'd been around for fifty-four years and I hadn't met anything like this, or even close to it. A Status Symbol makes a little sense if it's the Nobel Prize or a Rolls Royce, but a *barber*! Insanity, even for show business people.

I started out with money and didn't make it, but that didn't mean he didn't have a price. I figured everybody could be bought. Maybe not with dollars, but with something.

I thought of the calendars on the wall. They're supposed to be for the customers, but I wondered, are they? You never knew about these old guys.

I found the wildest broad in New York and told her how she could earn two grand in one evening. She said yes.

Eddie said no.

I told him if he'd play along, I'd turn over a check for one million dollars to his favorite charity.

No.

I threatened him.

He smiled.

I begged him.

He said he was sorry.

I asked him why. Just tell me why, I said.

"I don't have an opening," he said.

Two weeks and two dozen tries later, I went back to the hospital. The Most Popular Show Business Personality of All Time was still lying in the bed, still staring at the ceiling.

"He'll give you an appointment," I said.

He shook his head.

"I'm telling you, Sheck. I just talked with him. He'll give you an appointment."

He looked at me. "When?"

"As soon as he finds an opening."

"He won't find an opening."

"Don't be stupid,. Sheck. You're just nervous. The guy's busy all the time. I was there. He's got people lined up halfway down the street."

"Eddie's never busy," he said.

Christ, I had to try, didn't I? "I was there, Sheck!"

"Then you know," he said. "Eddie's kind of customer, you don't get many. Just a few. Just a few, George." He turned his head away. "I'm not one of them."

"Well, maybe not now, Sheck, but some day. You can talk to him . . . ask him what he wants you to do. I mean, he's got to have a reason!"

"He's got a reason, George."

"What is it?"

"Don't you know?"

"No! You've stepped on a few heads, sure, but who hasn't? You don't get to the top by helping old ladies across the street. You've got to fight your way up there, everybody does, and when you fight, people get hurt."

"Yeah," he said, "you know," and for a second I thought I did. I sat there looking at him for a long time, then I went out and got drunker than hell.

They called me the next morning. I was in bad shape but I had my suit on so it only took fifteen minutes to get to the hospital.

It was a circus already. I pushed through the cops and the reporters and went into the room.

He was still lying on the bed, still staring up at the ceiling, looking no different from the way I'd left him. Except for the two deep slashes in his wrists, the broken glass and the blood. There was a lot of that. It covered the Hong Kong silk sheets and the rug and even parts of the wall.

"What made him do it?" somebody said.

"Overwork," I said.

The papers played it that way. Only a few guys knew the dirt, and they were paid for, so Shecky was turned into a martyr. I forget what to. His public, I think. I have most of the clippings. "In his efforts to bring joy to the people of the world, The King went beyond the limits of his endurance; he had gone beyond ordinary human limits long before . . ." "He had no ambition other than to continue entertaining his fans . . ." "Following the old show business motto, 'Always leave 'em laughing', Shecky King departed this world at the height of his popularity. No other performer has ever matched his success . . ." "He is a legend now, the man who had everything and gave everything . . ."

I don't think about it much any more.

I just lie awake nights and thank God that I'm bald.

THE CRIME OF
WILLIE WASHINGTON

THE SECOND AFTER Willie Washington put his knife in George Manassan's stomach, he knew he'd done a bad thing. But all the demons in Hades put together couldn't have made Willie run or lose his head, so he stood around very quiet, waiting to see what would happen. He figured deep inside his head that he'd done an evil deed, although he wasn't exactly sorry. George had told tales about Cleota and as far as Willie knew, there wasn't a man alive who'd stand for another man telling tales about his wife. He wasn't sorry and he wasn't glad and there was a sharp thing eating at his insides, sharper than the knife that had cut George.

Willie waited for a considerable time, but George only groaned and wheezed. And since the blood didn't stop oozing out over the rug, Willie finally decided that he must do something. He put on his hat and walked quickly down the street until he came to an apartment like his own.

He knocked hard on the door, several times.

The old woman who opened the door was very withered and dried up with the years, but when she heard the news she moved faster than she had for quite a while. She flew about the rooms, gathering all the clean rags she could find and muttering under her breath and Willie had to trot to keep up with her when she hobbled out the door and back up the street.

When they got to the room, however, there was no sign of George Manassan except for the blood left on the rug and floor.

The old woman looked around and when she was convinced that George had left, the fear in her face disappeared.

"You cut him deep, boy?" she asked.

"No'm, Aunt Lucy, I didn't. I don't think he got hurt too bad," Willie answered.

Then Willie went to the sink and wet a large cloth. He bore down and managed to get the blood off the floor, but it wouldn't come out of the rug.

"You send that to the cleaners, boy. You never get that out alone."

The old woman sat down and breathed heavily. Her face and arms were shiny with perspiration.

Cleota got off work at the bakery at eleven-thirty and when she got home Willie told her everything that had happened. She said she was sorry and that she thought Willie had done right.

Aunt Lucy later learned that Doctor Smith was the one who fixed up George. She was more relieved than she let on, to hear that the wound had been a minor one; and she sermoned to Willie and to Cleota for months afterwards when she was positive that George had left town.

Now this was the only bad thing Willie ever did in his entire life, up to the time the policemen came to put him in jail for something else, so he didn't forget it right away. He didn't miss a day on his job and he didn't spoil his record by doing poor work, but most of the fellows on the line noticed that Willie Washington was not quite himself again until almost a half year had passed. It was then that he forgot about cutting George Manassan and that Cleota once more took up smiling at men in the bakery.

It was a great surprise to Willie when they shook him out of bed and carried him off to jail.

The night was sticky and hot but the pillow hadn't turned damp yet. It was soft and cool and he sank into it grate-fully. Cleota was already asleep, silent, as always, like a cat. Willie had never slept with anyone else so he had the impression that only men snored. It struck him as a very masculine thing.

He finished his prayers to the Lord and fell into a pleasant languor that soon turned into sleep.

The sound of voices outside in the hall was not disturbing because there were frequently voices in the hall. Willie had gotten used to lovers' goodnights and sleepless women's babble as a soldier gets used to sleeping amid gunfire. He didn't even hear the door tried and opened.

What did awaken Willie finally was a rough hand on his shoulder, pressing hard and shaking. He heard the voice halfway through consciousness.

"Come on, you're not kidding anybody. Get the hell out of that bed."

And when he came to completely he saw three men in his room, two of them with flashlights and the third with a gun in his hand. He did not understand.

The men were all white. They were very energetic looking men, with sharp chins and unblinking eyes. There was no hesitation.

The one with the gun pulled Willie to his feet.

"Okay, let's go, fella."

Cleota awakened with a nasal little cry. She clutched the sheets to her breasts and said nothing.

"Go where?" Willie's mind was not clear.

The man with the gun looked over his shoulder and laughed.

Willie looked angry. He didn't understand, but he knew he didn't like these men. He hated to be called a nigger in Cleota's presence.

The man with the gun grabbed Willie's undershirt and twisted it in his hand. He turned his head towards the door and took out a police credential.

Willie started to move, but the gun was pushed into his stomach. The two other men edged closer.

So Willie turned his eyes to Cleota and got dressed quickly. The men kept their flashlights on even though Cleota had switched on the lamp.

In a short time Willie was shoved into the waiting police car and taken to the city jail. He was then put into a moderately crowded cell.

No one told him exactly what he was supposed to have done, but through constant questioning he learned that he was being held for the rape and murder of a white girl. He didn't know why they had thought of him, but he did not know what the charges meant. He thought and thought and could provide no good proof of where he actually had been at the time of the crime.

He had been home, reading, but of course no one would believe that.

Cleota came to see him whenever she could and so did Aunt Lucy. They both made him feel good, though it was actually Aunt Lucy who gave him hope.

During the long days before the trial she would say to him, "Willie, it's bad trouble but they won't hurt you. We both know you ain't done nothin' wrong, an' when you don't do nothin' wrong the law can't hurt you. You gonna be all right, boy. You gonna get out of this all right."

And Willie would smile until one day he stopped being afraid. He was offered a lawyer but he said he didn't want one. He ate well and looked forward to the day of the trial, because he felt sure that would be the day they would let him go.

All this time he made prayers to the Lord that he'd get his job back and that he would be forgiven for hating the people around him and the people who came to ask him deep questions he couldn't figure out. Then he stopped worrying about his job and didn't hate.

And whenever he would get confused, Aunt Lucy would come by and say, "Now rest easy, boy. Everything gonna be all right. You a innocent boy and the law ain't gonna hurt you," and he'd smile and feel good again.

When the day of the trial came at last, Willie sat in the courtroom without a fear or a doubt. He thought of the stories he'd be able to tell the gang on the Line when he went back to work, so he didn't hear much of the proceedings.

They asked him where he was on the night of the crime and he told the truth. "I was at home, readin' a magazine, your Honor," he said. They asked him other questions and the tall man in the gray suit talked so fast and so loud Willie couldn't hear him clearly. Only the words 'society' and 'justice' sounded so that he could hear.

And after a time, the people in the brown stall filed back to their seats. Willie folded his hands and craned his head to hear what would be said.

". . . do you find the defendant: guilty or not guilty?"

Willie wasn't nervous. He kept grinning, wondering whether or not to look back at Cleota.

"We find the defendant guilty, your Honor."

The words were spoken slowly and clearly, but with some emotion. The thin man with the furrowed face who spoke the words looked directly at the judge and then sat down.

Willie wanted to scream but then something pierced his stomach and held his insides tight. He couldn't move or say a word. Confusion swam in his head, in great hot waves. He rose with difficulty when commanded.

". . . sentence you, Willie George Washington, to the supreme penalty prescribed by law . . ."

These words were a haze out of which only one came clearly. *Dead*.

". . . to be hanged by the neck until you are dead . . ."

Willie struggled and pulled out the thing in his heart. He screamed.

"No, your Honor, you don' understand! I didn't kill nobody! I didn't do nothin' wrong! I'm innocent, your Honor!"

And two men had to hold Willie's arms and pull him back to his cell.

No one paid much attention to the old Negro woman who cried "No, Lord!" or the young one who smiled strangely.

It wasn't easy for Willie, but he had plenty of time to think and so after a while he started to smile again. Aunt Lucy was able to see him upon occasion during the months and Cleota came by a respectable number of times. They both said that everything would be all right.

And since Willie had been conceived of the strongest hope there is—a woman's hope—it took only the merest spark to ignite his courage. He told himself that he had not for a moment lost his faith in the ultimate rightness of things, not even in the courtroom that day he was told solemnly he must die, for a crime he did not commit.

And so the days passed and Willie grew stronger instead of weaker, all the while certain that the Lord would not permit him to be wrongfully punished.

So it was that on the morning designated as the time of execution Willie spoke lightly with the somber looking man in the black frock coat who wore such a long face.

"Reverend," Willie said, "I knows your intentions is good, but they ain't really much sense in your being here."

And the Reverend shook his head and opened his book. "No sir, Reverend, they ain't nothin' gonna happen to me. It say so right here in the Good Book—here, let me show you the place where it say—"

And Willie took the book and thumbed quickly through the pages.

"Y'see, Reverend, the Lord say it: 'As ye sow, so shall ye reap.' It put different in your book, but it mean the same thing."

The man in the frock coat sighed.

"But my son, you have been proven guilty of the sin of murder."

Willie grinned.

"Yes, sir, but they got that wrong. It wasn't me what did that to that little girl. You gots to be honest bad 'fore you can do a thing like that! And Aunt Lucy can tell you— I ain't honest bad, Reverend. I studied hard all I could, when I was a kid, and I been workin' for the railroad since I was thirteen. Never missed a day—up to this, I mean. Never missed a Sunday at Church, neither. An' I got me a good woman too. No sir, I jus' never did this thing, Reverend, and you knows the Lord ain't gonna cast me down for somethin' I never did."

The man in the frock coat looked perplexed as he studied Willie's face. The prayers he said were not the ones he had previously considered nor could Willie hear them.

Not too long afterward other men came and walked with Willie down a long hall and into a small yard. The sun was shining but the yard was dark with shadows. The cement was clean and smelled of soap and water.

The men led Willie up some steps and onto a small door out into the planks. Directly above dangled a rope, the end of which had been formed into a noose. The rope was sturdy and strong; the fibers were close and smooth.

They asked Willie if he had anything to say and he told them yes, he did.

"You folks is really wastin' your time," Willie said. "I

told you, I never did nothin' wrong and the Lord ain't gonna let you hurt me.''

Then a man walked up and fitted a black cloth bag over Willie's head. After that he pulled down the rope and put the noose about Willie's neck. The noose was tightened somewhat.

No one could see, but Willie was still smiling. He couldn't think clearly about anything except what Aunt Lucy had told him. Her words roared in his ears and he knew that they couldn't be wrong.

Willie waited. He didn't know what he waited for, but he waited. A long time he stood, with the handcuffs heavy on his wrists, but nothing happened.

All was silent and then, as suddenly as if it had always been, loud with the hum of voices. Words Willie couldn't hear, words that pierced the air, words that were filled with fear and awe.

After a long while the bag was taken off and Willie was led back to his cell. Later he learned what had happened, why everyone had looked so strange. The lever that controlled the trapdoor had been pulled but the trapdoor had remained fixed. It did not fall away, allowing the body that stood upon it to sink into the yielding air. It did not suddenly become the mouth of death, which was its function. The trapdoor simply had not worked. And this was strange because it had been tested according to routine a few minutes before the actual time of execution, and stranger still that it operated with the greatest efficiency a few moments after Willie was taken from the platform.

Willie thanked the Lord and thought that would set him free, but he was wrong. Someone told him that they would try to hang him again, and Willie shrugged and said that it was very foolish.

It was Aunt Lucy who told him the laws of the state, which required a man condemned to death to be subjected to three attempts at execution before he be freed. The old woman whose face looked older and more withered than ever Willie had known it to be, still spoke confidently and Willie believed her. The Lord would not desert him now.

When he asked about Cleota he received answers he somehow didn't like, although they meant nothing in themselves. He put it aside and continued to write her letters. The answers were cheerful and evasive and so Willie was not disturbed.

He spent his time praying, in between executions.

And when it came time for them to try to hang Willie again, the same somber man in the frock coat dropped into the cell to mumble; the same walk and the same tiny yard. The same dark shadows, but a different rope and a more thoroughly oiled trapdoor mechanism.

Willie got up to the scaffold unhesitatingly. He was stood to one side as the trapdoor was tested for good measure. He watched it drop swiftly and saw the blackness below, without relaxing his smile. Then the hood was fastened securely.

A man started to say, "Any last words," but he stopped. The man nodded to the executioner.

And when the lever was pulled all the way back, a great murmur went through the crowd. The trapdoor had not moved.

Some time later, Willie read in the newspaper about how he was fooling death but, of course, he knew that was wrong. They didn't understand. They didn't understand that the Lord protects his own and that an innocent man can't die for something he didn't do.

Time passed slowly after this. And when he realized that he had been a prisoner for over a year, Willie became bored and restless. His prayers became routine and he wished mightily that they would hurry up with whatever they were going to do, so he could get back to his job and wife. Aunt Lucy told him he looked tired these days and he agreed with her.

Cleota wrote more frequently and visited more frequently now that they had tried to hang Willie twice already. It scared her, but only this far. She found it remarkably easy to lie to Willie now, so the sacrifice was not a great one. She had fallen in love with a number of people since her husband was first put in jail. A man named Frank Jones wanted her to go to Detroit with him. She was considering it.

Time crept, the boredom of the minutes filling Willie with a growing urge to leave the prison and have it all done with. The game had lost its amusement; it was like waiting interminable hours on a streetcorner for someone you know will show up, eventually.

So he finally stopped praying and thanking the Lord and began to pace restlessly in his cell. Even the newspaper reports had lost their interest. Everything had lost its interest, except getting out. Willie thought and the more he thought the more he wanted to have this foolishness over.

Sometimes he thought about his job; relived pleasant hours when work was not so hard. He'd had the job for seventeen years, and although he'd never risen in rank, neither had he ever been docked or rolled.

And he thought about stories of poor Negroes constantly out of work and how nobody would hire you if you were black. He didn't believe it. He was black and he had a job. He was black and he had a wife. What else, he wondered, could there be in life?

Time dragged, stood still, waited, inched, stopped.

Then the day arrived, the day Willie so longed for: his last execution.

The attendant delicacies were hurried this time and somewhat embarrassed. The man in the frock coat had refused to come and so another man like him came instead. Willie listened politely to the Last Prayers, but he was feeling too good to really hear them. Aunt Lucy had seen him the afternoon before and he hadn't noticed the fear in her eyes. He had only heard the kind, happy words that came from the friendly face. He knew them by heart now, every word and every nuance.

"You gonna be home little while, boy. They gonna let you go and you gonna be home. The Lord has taken care of his young lamb."

The yard was filled with many people this time. It was a special occasion; rules were relaxed. Many had notebooks open and pencils in their hands. Some looked afraid—those faces he recognized, they looked afraid. Others looked interested or expectant.

There was a slight breeze, so the rope swung gently backward and forward from the scaffold. Its shadow on the wall was many times enlarged and grotesque.

When Willie came in, everyone stopped whispering. There was absolute quiet, the quiet that is born of a beating heart. Willie grinned widely and tried to wave his hands so they could see.

He knew the way by now. He knew how many steps it was from the door to the platform of the scaffold. He knew the moment the hood would be lowered. Willie smiled at the blackness as the trapdoor was dropped five times. He smiled at the executioner, but the executioner didn't smile back.

Then the long wait. Through the coarse black cloth over his head, Willie heard the frightened gasps and the sharp little cries. He heard someone say:

"My God, it didn't work! It didn't work!"

He was carefully led from the platform back to his cell. He remembered to thank the Lord and then he went back to sleep.

The following week Willie was told exactly when he would be released, and until that time he found many interesting things to read in the newspapers.

Aunt Lucy and the men from the newspapers were waiting for Willie the day he walked out of prison a free man.

Many pictures were taken of him and many questions asked
and Willie was polite to everyone. But when he would ask
Aunt Lucy where Cleota was, Aunt Lucy would turn her
head and someone else would say something. After a time,
Willie got worried and told the people he would talk with
them tomorrow.

When he got home, Willie learned that his wife had left
him. He didn't grasp it at first. Cleota had run off with a
man named Frank Jones. She had left him.

Aunt Lucy remarked that she never did care much for
Cleota and had told Willie so the day he married her. She
reminded him of George Manassan and asked him why he
had never blamed Cleota. But whenever Aunt Lucy would
say anything bad about Cleota, Willie would tell her to be
quiet. He wanted to think.

Alone in his room, he lay on the bed and wept. He
understood why he had felt strange about those letters and
why he had put the feeling aside. Cleota would never sleep
with him again; she would never come back.

He fought the tears until his eyes hurt and then he slept.

The next morning he rose early, put on the clothes that
had hung in the closet for almost a year and a half and took
a bus to his work terminal.

The sight of the huge ornate building restored Willie's
spirits. He forgot about Cleota. This was the other of the
two important things in his life; he proposed to marry himself completely to his job now.

The foreman shook his head at Willie.

"Sorry, fella, but the Line's full up now. Union tightening up . . . letting off help . . . sorry."

The foreman had to talk a long time to convince Willie
that he had no job. The big man, with his black arm-sleeves
and green head-shield, was puzzled that anyone could have
the nerve to ask for a job after an absence of a year and a
half. That a murderer could expect to have his job back.

Willie walked out of the building slowly, trying to put things together in his head. He asked the Lord what had happened, but the answer was indistinct. He boarded the bus and got off before it started. He walked the three miles to Aunt Lucy's apartment.

The old woman was crying.

"Boy, I don't know 'zactly what could he'p you now. You got no job and you got no wife. But you got to live, 'cause that's what the Lord say you got to."

And Willie knew she was right. He had to live.

He went home and put on his suit. It was wrinkled where it had draped across a wire hanger, but it still had class. Willie had never worn it much, but he always felt good in it. He put on his flamingo tie and polished his shoes with an old shirt. He sat down to decide what to do.

He walked down Government Street and entered an S.P. ticket office. He asked for a job and was quickly refused.

He went to every ticket office, steamship, railroad and freight line in the city. He didn't pause to eat. At nightfall, when he returned home, there were smiling newspapermen waiting for him. He admitted them and talked politely.

". . . you got to live, boy . . ."

The next day he went to garages, filling stations, and miscellaneous stores. He went through the factories and warehouses, to the Civil Service building and to the employment agencies. He was not even asked to fill out forms.

". . . there isn't a thing for you . . ."

"No use to fret, Willie Washington, you had it good most of your life. The Lord took good care of you. You just got to scrounge a little now . . .", was what Willie said to himself.

He went to large office buildings, print shops, frame makers, construction companies, the city hall, grocery stores.

Some grimaced at him, most recognized him from the pictures in the paper. But no one gave Willie a job.

He went to Aunt Lucy and she just told him to keep looking.

He put an ad in the paper, he answered all the ads. He went to janitors and street cleaners, to airports and railroad stations.

He walked until his feet hurt and turned numb to pain. And when he looked at his money he started to become a little frightened. But he didn't stop walking and he didn't stop talking.

And then one day, when the newspapermen had had enough of Willie's story and he was left entirely alone, Willie sat in his room a whole day, thinking. He asked the Lord numerous questions and waited for the answers that did not come. He looked in his pockets and saw that his money was nearly gone.

He remembered the looks of hate on people's faces when they saw him, how they whispered when he left. He had done nothing, and had proven it, but he began to see that there was no one who believed him. No one but Aunt Lucy.

Everyone thought that he had actually killed that little girl. Didn't they realize that he would have been hanged, that his neck would have been broken and that he would have died, if he'd been guilty?

Or did they care . . . ?

For the first time in his life, Willie Washington really hated. He hated the people who hated him; he hated everything around him. He had forgiven them and their wrong, but they would not forgive him his innocence! Hate surged and churned in his heart. It did not have time to mature. It was now and it was full-grown.

Aunt Lucy was afraid. She sensed in her old heart what had happened, so she got out of bed and went over to Willie's room.

She said, "Boy, you got to get that look out of your eyes. It ain't good."

And Willie said, "But they won't give me work an' I'm runnin' out of money,"

They sat.

Then the old woman looked very deep inside Willie's heart and she left in fear. It had dried up in her but she recognized the budding shoot. She remembered it and how it had conquered her. But she had been a woman, and Willie a man, and that is why she was afraid.

Willie didn't say very much to anyone the next day. He'd ask for a job and he'd be refused and he'd walk out, looking so grim and confused people would stare.

The black flower began to press his throat and his breast, so that he shook when he asked the question, defeatedly, under his breath.

"Lord, it ain't right what you're doing to me. I been good and look at me! I got no money, no job, no wife . . . And it wouldn't none of it a happened if you hadn't put me in that jail. Why'd you let it happen, O Lord!"

Willie had a mind full of confusion, a mind full of angry hornets.

When he heard the white woman say "There's the murdering nigger they couldn't hang," hot vomitous acid rose in his throat and eyes and he went back home.

He spoke directly to the Lord.

"It ain't been right, you *know* it ain't been right! My money's all gone, Lord, an' I can't get any more! What am I gonna do? Tell me, Lord, 'cause Willie Washington, he's slippin'."

He waited, hunched and silent, for an answer that did not come.

He waited for sleep, but that didn't come either.

He thought of the little murdered girl, who lay in the rain with a cruel cross carved in her stomach.

"What about the man what did that, Lord? Is you punishing *him*? Why do you gots to punish me—what did I do? Lord, tell me, tell me, WHY! If I knew that then it'd be all right, but I don't know! I don't know why!"

Willie raised his voice and called into Heaven.

"Why, Lord God?"

Then he tore at his shirt and rolled on the dirty bed, sobbing and moaning. The night went and the day came, but Willie did not sleep. He was hungry and tired.

He walked out the door, feeling dirty.

People stared at him, whispered at him and around him.

"Aunt Lucy! What am I gonna do? I got no money! You got money?"

"No, boy, you know that. I got twenty-seven cents. Here, take that. And let me fix you a little food. Boy, you look poorly!"

Willie fell in a chair and put the cereal to his mouth.

"Aunt Lucy, what do the Lord say to you?"

"He been kinda quiet lately, boy."

"The Lord ain't with me, Aunt Lucy. He against me!"

"Hush now! Don't you let me hear you talk like that. That's you daddy's blood talkin'! The Lord works in wonderful ways, boy, don't you know that?"

"He wouldn't get me a job."

"He kept 'em from hangin' you, didn't He?"

Willie put his head on the old woman's breast.

"Now don't that mean somethin', Willie boy?"

Willie cried.

"No, it don't! It don't mean nothin'!"

Willie straightened and went out of the room quickly. The old woman called for him to come back, then she fell on her knees and cried to the Lord.

Willie almost ran to his room. He looked through two dresser drawers and got his small pocket knife. He looked at it for only a few moments, remembering how he had cut a human being and why he had cut a human being.

The black flower covered him. He was full: his stomach and his heart and his soul were full.

He put it in his pocket and went into the street.

"Lord, remember. You left, me. You did it. Wasn't me left you!"

Willie walked all the way to the railroad tracks without knowing why. He sat in a small clearing until it got dark, thinking. About the faces and the mouths and breathing hot that the Lord had left him.

Then he walked on down the tracks, hating. He walked for miles, walked till his legs refused to move. He took out the knife, opened it and looked at the blade.

He walked back into town and hid behind a warehouse. He held the knife tightly and perspiration coursed down the handle.

Willie waited and he was afraid he knew what he waited for, this time. The whole world started to pound in his ears and his body shook.

And then the tears came. They fell from his eyes as if they would never stop, and he turned his back to the street, weeping onto the wooden slats of the warehouse. The knife dropped to the ground and as it struck, Willie knelt with both knees on the cement.

"Lord, Lord God, I'm sorry. I'm sorry. I'm sorry! I'll not leave you again, not ever again!"

Willie walked back to Aunt Lucy's. And when the old woman saw his face, she smiled broadly. The vise around her neck relaxed and she felt young again.

"Well, boy, you get the hate cut out of you!"

"Yes'm."

"You ain't no different from any of us, boy. It jus' come to you late, that's all. You never saw what you was, boy, that was your trouble."

Willie looked up and smiled.

Aunt Lucy hurried to fix coffee.

"You know, Willie boy, we mus' be the Lord's favorites, 'cause we got the biggest cross of all to carry. You know what I'm talkin' about, boy?"

"Do you suppose the Lord'll forgive me, Aunt Lucy?"

"I kinda think He will. He's a mighty understandin' person."

Then Willie began to laugh and the old woman laughed with him.

They laughed for a long time.

THE MAN WITH
THE CROOKED NOSE

HE WAS VERY small. And, he was invisible. Or almost: there and not there, existing and not existing—like a shadow just before the lights come on, or a face you see in the window of a speeding train, or birds at midnight. He lived in the corner of your eye. Turn around, quick! and stare and—he's gone, he's somewhere else.

After a while I stopped trying to find him. It made things easier. In at nine: "Good morning, Mr. Gershenson!" (a quick silent grin from the little man); out at six: "Good night!" (the same) and repeat. A few requests: Bring that set of Dickens up front, please; don't forget to dust the A secton, will you?—Nothing more.

And it seemed to work all right. Actually, it didn't. Because he was there and we worked together, eight hours a day, and it isn't very pleasant, ever, to give orders to a man who is twice your age and then watch him jump and run like a monkey set on fire. Yet so quietly.

He was always running. Even when he swept up, as though his life depended on it—Switch! Switch! with the broom down the aisles, getting the dirt off the floor, Switch! billowing it over all the books, and then off, fast, to another chore. I never saw a man work with such speed. Or so hard. Or do such a poor job—poor Martin, and he had the world's easiest. An idiot could have done it better.

The others got a big kick out of him. They called him "Pop"—although he wasn't very old: maybe fifty, maybe sixty, no older—and they pulled fancy gags, thought out days in advance, planned in secret conclave. Once Berman called from New Books downstairs and asked for Martin and double-talked until he had the little man shaking. They laughed at him all day long.

It wasn't easy not to laugh, I suppose. He was pretty funny; right from the first, from the day Steinberg hired him. In a lot of ways: the quick-padding Mandarin's walk he had, feet barely touching the floor; the outsized mixed-up clothes he wore; and all those boxes and phials and bottles of medicine! It seemed that every time you looked, he was popping a pill into his mouth or swigging cough syrup. Which is funny to watch, although I didn't feel much like laughing, somehow. He was always so intense about it. As if he thought, if I don't take all this medicine, I'll die, almost certainly. I'll catch a horrible disease and die.

And that made you wonder—well? Why should he want to stay alive to the point of fighting death every five minutes? An old man with most of his years behind him, and what is he now? A stockboy in a bookstore, without a hope of anything better.

But he didn't frown any oftener than he smiled. He just worked. Gently and quickly and poorly and quietly—always quietly: I never heard him speak a word, then. It gave rise to the rumor that he was a mute, but I don't think anyone actually believed that.

Maybe it was his eyes that kept me wondering. It probably was, at first, because there wasn't anything else. They were so bright beneath those black-clumped John L. Lewis brows, so bright and full. While he fumbled about like the wrong machine for the wrong job, I watched his eyes, and sometimes they seemed about to fly loose from their sockets and sometimes they rested there like milk-glass marbles, looking, beyond the shelves and beyond the walls.

Of course, after a few weeks the newness wore off. We all got used to Martin's quick little movements and his silence. Business picked up over the holidays, so there wasn't much time for finding him. Gradually, pieces floated in. Not many, not enough to make a picture—but some.

For one thing—and we should certainly have guessed it—Martin had been in America only a few months. The reason he never talked was that he hadn't learned English; he could understand it, but not speak it. And the fact that he was a foreigner explained, for almost everybody, the other peculiarities.

The "Pop" label stuck. As the days passed, he melted into a fixture, like the rest of us, as if he'd always been with the store, ever since it was built. I covered his mistakes and didn't push and he smiled good morning and good night and that was that. We had a funny little foreigner working in Used Books. He was quiet. He took medicine. He put in his hours. That's all we knew, that's all we needed to know.

But I was the one who worked with him. I was the one who saw his eyes. And "that" couldn't be exactly that, with me.

I went back on the hook when I first heard his music. It was near closing time and we were alone. He was pulling books from the F section, I was pricing some Americana. I could see his short little monkey's body scrambling up and down the ladder, and in the dusty murk between aisles, the whiteness of his skin was like white wax. Especially then, climbing, he reminded me of a newsreel I'd once seen of some man who had lived in a cave for a year, without any of the civilized comforts, and who had then been brought before the cameras, shaved and bathed, hair combed but not yet cut, cheeks scrubbed—nervous and unnatural, a little terrified and colorless as a slug.

It was very quiet and still that afternoon.

Then, suddenly, Martin began to hum. It surprised me, I don't know why exactly, but it was as if he had just ripped off his shirt and turned around and showed me his wings; or an extra pair of arms. I was careful not to look up: I knew there wasn't anybody else upstairs.

The melody swam through the heat and dust. But it wasn't ordinary humming, not at all. Each note was hit accurately and the piece was continued from its beginning to its end. When the notes got too high, or too low, he simply switched octaves. And it sent a shiver through me, because what he hummed was Beethoven's *Pathetique Sonata*. Right straight through, transposed beautifully.

After a pause it began again, this time the fugue from Bloch's *Concerto Grosso*. And then some Bach I couldn't recognize.

This little man, who couldn't even put a book on a shelf right, who ran around like a half-killed chicken, like a scared mouse, singing to himself now, his eyes lost completely— they couldn't *actually* belong to the sad bundle of wet sticks and white skin!—this little man, singing and humming, so powerfully, so lovingly, that you forgot about him and you heard the music as it was written, the pianos, the violins, the flutes; and you heard every note, every note.

I never let him know that I heard, of course. I just listened, and whenever there were no customers, he would start. Today, *In the Hall of the Mountain King*; tomorrow, *Adoramus Te Christe*; the next day, *Liebestod*. Giant music and small music, Beethoven and Chopin, Moussorgsky and Jannequin and Mozart and Mendelssohn.

Finally, I couldn't take it any longer. I wormed a lunch out of Steinberg, the boss, and I pumped him, discreetly.

It was disappointing, in a way . . . I'd hoped for more. In another way, it was not so disappointing.

Steinberg told me about how Martin Gershenson had once been the leading music critic for a newspaper in Germany.

About how he had once been married and how, one day, he and his family had been carried from their home and put into different concentration camps; and how Martin had escaped and learned, much later, that his wife and his two children had been executed.

How he had wandered the cities of the earth, afterwards . . .

From music critic to stockboy. I began trying to find him again, and once I tried whistling, something by Rachmaninoff. I got half-way through. He didn't pause for a moment. But he stopped singing.

Dust carefully, Martin! Go unload that shipment of Rand McNalley's, please, Martin! Don't forget to turn out the lights!

A smile, a jump, a running.

And a little reproachful look in those eyes, asking me why, why did I have to take his music away from him?

Gently and quietly—maybe once or twice a murmured, "Schnell? Oh, ja ja!" Gently and quietly, as quaint and funny as Gepetto, a funny character out of the comic pages, always rushing, taking the jokes of others, and smiling only at the children who came up with their mothers.

When he learned a little English, we tried him on a few customers. But he got red and frightened and nervous, and the cash register terrified him—he wouldn't touch it—so we had to take him off the job. He didn't complain.

And I kept wondering, why? With eyes like those, why was he so beaten and so frightened, so willing to fit any mold like hot lead?

"Don't *worry*," they used to say to me. "Forget it—he's happy. Leave him alone."

So I did.

Until I heard his music again. Something by Bloch, slow
and full of sadness. He twisted each note and squeezed it
and wrung out its sadness.

Outside, the rain washed over our thin roof like gravel.
I was listening to the rain and to Martin's music, and thinking, when I heard the heavy footsteps on the stairs. At the
same instant, Martin Gershenson quieted, and there was
only the sound of those footsteps, slow and heavy.

The man wasn't unfamiliar to me: he'd been in a couple
of times before, I remembered dimly. Now he wore a thick
checkered overcoat, soggy with rain, and a wet gray hat.

"Yes, sir," I said to him. "Can we help you?"

"Perhaps," he said. There seemed to be a slight accent;
that, or his English was too perfect. "I am looking for a
nice set—I mean in good condition—of Eliot. George Eliot. Do you have that?"

He was a large person, thick-handed and rough-fleshed.
Chinless, the neck fat drooled over his collar and swung
loosely. His lips were dry and white and seemed joined
by membrane when closed. But I think it was his nose
that made me dislike him. Crooked, set at an angle on
his face as if not quite tight on a pivot, the bridge broken and mashed against the white fat of upper cheeks.
His eyes were merely eyes, soft as eggs. Perhaps a trifle
small.

"I'll see," I said. Then I called, "Martin! Would you
please see if we have a mint set of Eliot?" By this time the
little man could understand English quite well.

"Ja—" His feet padded quickly over the floor, stopped,
turned, were still.

The man was smiling. "Personally," he said, "I think
the old lady is very funny, but there is a friend of mine
that fancies her. A woman friend, of course. You know?"

Martin came running. Halfway across the room, he
stopped. He appeared to stare, for a moment.

"We do not have this in stock," he said to me.

"No Eliot at all?" I asked.

"No," he said, paused another second, staring, and then went rushing back down the aisle into the back.

The big man was chuckling. "Well," he said, "perhaps no Eliot at all is the better present to my friend!" He thumbed through one of our special hand-tooled copies of Tristram Shandy.

"I'm sorry, sir," I said. "We're usually not so low in stock. But if you'd care to leave your name and address, we'll let you know when it—"

"It's all right," the man said, not lifting his eyes from the book. "I will come in again some time."

"If there's anything else we can do for you . . ."

"Sangorsky," he said. "Good leather." His fat hands rubbed the red morocco binding.

"Yes. As you can see, we have the book marked at a considerable reduction—"

"You don't have this Eliot that I want, do you?"

"No sir. But, I tell you what. We can order it and it would only take a few days. Why don't you let us have your name and address and we'll contact you?"

He walked about examining the books. Then he lit a cigarette.

"Pencil," he said.

I gave him a pencil and he wrote down his name—John S. Parker—and his address.

"Yes, sir, we'll let you know the minute—"

"All right. You let me know." He pulled down a large Skira volume, glanced at it, put it back. He rubbed his nose. "It is wet out," he said.

"It sure is. Not bookstore weather."

"You let me know, young man."

He turned and went down the stairs.

It was soon very quiet again, except for the rain.

Martin was padding about in the back. Slowly; not fast, like always before.

I thought about the look on his face when he had caught sight of the new customer, about the man's strangeness, his accent; I thought about concentration camps.

Then, suddenly, I knew. I knew beyond all doubt.

Martin had found what he was looking for.

Later, at home, I built the story in my mind. I dressed it up, gave it plot and structure.

I even wrote the newspaper headline:

MAN BRUTALLY SLAIN IN APARTMENT!

And the picture, not a good one, but clear enough to make out the fat face and the crooked nose.

I composed the story with a sick feeling, the feeling you get when you hear of the death of someone you know—not necessarily a friend—just anyone you've ever seen or spoken with.

> A man identified as John S. Parker was found dead in his apartment at 734 No. Sweetzer early yesterday evening by his landlady. Parker was the victim of a brutal attack by an unknown assailant. According to the police report, he was hacked fifty-three times with an axe about the face, neck and chest. There were evidences of other atrocities: cigarette burns about the legs and armpits, deep bruises in the abdominal region. No motive for the crime known . . .

Later reports—it was Sunday: I had plenty of time to construct the drama—revealed further information. The murdered man's name was not John Parker. It was Carl Haber. And he was in America illegally. Hiding. Because he had once been Colonel Carl Haber, and he had once run the show at one of the smaller concentration camps in

Germany—one of the missing cogs in that well-oiled machine, the Third Reich. Missing until now.

The papers had the full story for their evening editions.

Haber, nee Parker, had slipped into the country by the kind offices of a friend in Venezuela. He had some money. He loved books. He had taken an apartment, a small bachelor's, and lived the quiet life of a retired businessman, a widower, perhaps.

And this man with the crooked nose and the fat neck had waited, for the world to forget about the millions of human beings he had helped consign to the lime kilns and the brick ovens and the shower rooms with hot-and-cold running carbon monoxide.

But somebody hadn't forgotten.

One of the city's sensational sheets got a hold of a picture of Haber's body. You couldn't look at it for long.

It was impossible to believe that one man could have had the strength or the fury or the hatred to do what was done to Haber.

The blood-smeared thing in the photograph—I saw it as clearly as if I had been holding it in my hand—wasn't human. It was a pile of carrion, like a dog after a truck has run over it, or like meat that's been picked over by hawks.

And the unknown assailant . . . Who could tell?

I thought of nothing all day but this one thing, of Martin, little ineffectual Martin, with his musician's hands bloody, the vengeance out of him.

Next day I scrutinized the papers. They told of a disaster at sea. They spoke of senators and dogs and starlets. But they did not speak of John S. Parker.

Well, I thought, not even aware of my disappointment, well, perhaps he's biding his time. Perhaps tomorrow.

Things were the same at work. I recall that I considered that ironic—that things should be the same. Martin was there as usual, not smiling, not frowning, hurrying up and

down the aisles of books with his broom, hurrying just as
fast as his short legs would carry him—Switch! Switch!—
and the dust clouds after him, plumed and rolling. Martin,
with his clown's suit and his bushy brows and his bright
ferret's eyes caught in their pasty prisons . . .

Outside, it was raining, the same rain that had fallen
when "John S. Parker" came to buy his set of Eliot. It was
a gravel-spray on the roof, a steady monotonous dripping,
drumming.

"Good morning, Martin," I said.

Stop; turn; silent smile; then, quick, back to the sweeping.

Somehow, I don't think I was surprised to hear him
sing—although I ought to have been surprised. He did,
softly, from the back of the store. Melodies in a minor key,
sad, haunting, and so full of these things that when the
customers came in they stopped and looked up from their
books and listened, strangely moved.

All day he sang, as he might breathe. The second movement from the *Eroica*, the Allegretto from the Seventh
symphony, Block and Dvorak and Tchaikovsky and Mah-
ler, over and over, while he worked.

And I wanted to go to him and shake his hand grimly
and tell him that I knew and understood, understood completely, and therefore did not blame him. I wanted to let
him know that he could trust me. I would betray his secret
to no one, and John S. Parker's unknown assailant would
remain unknown, forever . . .

But, of course, I didn't say these things. I merely waited,
watching the little man, listening to him, studying his face
to see if it would give any hint of what lay beneath. I
thought of him with the axe in his hands, swinging the axe,
repaying the beefy German in full.

And the day wore on.

Next morning I got the first paper off the stand. I'd

spent a sleepless night, tossing, arguing that it was better this way; that I must not call the police and spoil things.

But there was nothing in the paper. Or in any other paper.

And the day was the same.

I decided then that Parker's body had not been discovered yet. That was the answer. It was lying crumpled where Martin had left it three days ago! So I suffered through the hours and drove straight to the address Parker had given me.

It was a small stucco apartment, neat, old, respectable.

I knocked on the door, trembling.

John Parker opened the door. "Yes?" he said, his voice heavily accented. "Yes?"

"We have a lead on those Eliot's," I said. "I happened to be passing by and thought you might like to know."

"Thank you, young man. That was nice. Thank you."

I looked at him as one would at a corpse suddenly brought to life, his wounds made well, his torn flesh whole.

Then I went home and tried to laugh.

But laughing is a lonely thing when you've no one to share the joke. So I went back outside and drank whiskey until I couldn't think about the little man.

Next day Martin didn't show up for work. He called up and said he was sick.

He never came back.

But John Parker did. The big man with the crooked nose still comes up to browse through the books, every now and then. I chat with him: he even calls me Len now. But I don't like him. Not a bit.

Because he makes me think of Martin. Because he makes me wonder if I'd been so wrong, after all, if my imagination had run quite so wild.

Perhaps Martin did find what he had been looking for. And perhaps, once finding it, he had decided it was not worth having, or that he lacked the strength to keep it.

And perhaps John S. Parker is something more than John S. Parker.

And perhaps not.

I'm afraid I'll never know. But I'm also afraid that I'll never forget the little man with the bright eyes and the hurrying feet and the sad face.

I hope he's still taking his medicine, wherever he is.

THE CARNIVAL

THE COOL OCTOBER rain and the wind blowing the rain. The green and yellow fields melting into grey hills, into grey sky and black clouds. And everywhere, the smell of autumn drinking the coolness, the evening coolness gathering in leaves and wheat alfalfa, running down fat brown bark, whispering through rich grass to tiny living things.

The cool rain, glistening on earth and on smooth cement.

"Come on, Lars, I'll beat you!"

"Like fun you will!"

Two boys with fresh wet faces and cold wet hands.

"Last one there is a sissy!"

Wild shouts through the stillness and a scrambling onto bicycles. A furious pedaling through sharp pinpoints of rain, one boy pulling ahead of the other, straining up the shining cement, laughing and calling.

"Just try and catch me now, just try!"

"I'll catch you all right, you wait!"

"Last one there is a sissy, last one there is a sissy!"

Faster now, flying past the crest of the hill, faster down the hill and into the blinding rain. Faster, small feet turning, wheels spinning, along the smooth level. Flying, past outdoor signs and sleeping cows, faster, past strawberry fields and haystacks, little excited blurs of barns and houses and siloes.

"Okay, I'm going to beat you, I'm going to beat you!"

A thin voice lost in the wind.

"I'll get to the trestle 'way before you, just watch!"

Lars Nielson pushed the pedals angrily and strained his young body forward, gripping the handlebars and singing for more speed. He felt the rain whipping through his hair and into his ears and he screamed happily.

He closed his eyes and listened to his voice, to the slashing wind and to the wheels of his bicycle turning in the wetness. Whizzing baseballs in his head, swooping chicken hawks and storm currents racing over beds of light leaves.

He did not hear the small voice crying to him, far in the distance.

"Who's the sissy, who'll be the sissy?" Lars Nielson sang to the whirling world beside him and his legs pushed harder and harder.

His eyes were closed, so he did not see the face of the frightened man. His ears were full, so he did not hear the screams and the brakes and all the other terrible sounds. The sudden, strange unfamiliar sounds that were soft and quiet as those in his mind were loud.

He pushed his young legs in the black darkness, harder, faster, faster . . .

The room was mostly blue. In the places where it had not chipped and cracked, the linoleum floor was a deep quiet blue. The walls, specially handpattered, were soft greenish blue. And the rows of dishes on high display shelves, the paint on the cane rockers, the tablecloth, Mother's dress, Father's tie—all blue.

Even the smoke from Father's pipe, creeping and slithering up into the thick air like long blue ghosts of long blue snakes.

Lars sat quietly, watching the blue.

"Henrik." Mrs. Nielson stopped her rocking.

"Yes, yes?"

"It is by now nine o'clock."

Mr. Nielson took a large gold watch from his vest pocket.

"It is, you are right. Lars, it is nine o'clock."

Lars nodded his head.

"So." Mr. Nielson rose from his chair and stretched his arms. "It is time. Say goodnight to your mama."

"Goodnight, Mama."

"Goodnight."

"So."

Mr. Nielson took the wooden bar in his big hands and pushed the chair gently past the doorway and down the hall. With his foot he pushed the door open and when they were inside the bedroom, he pulled the string which turned on the electric light.

He walked to the front of the chair.

"Lars, you feel all right now? Nothing hurts?"

"No, Papa. Nothing hurts."

Mr. Nielson put his hands into his pockets and sat on the sideboard of the bed.

"Mama is worried."

"Mama shouldn't."

"She did not like for you to be mean to the dog."

"I wasn't mean."

"You did not play with it. I watched, you did not talk to the dog. Boys should like dogs and Mama is worried. Already she took it away."

Lars sat silently.

"I'm sorry, Papa."

"It isn't right, my son, that you should do nothing. For your sake I say this."

"Papa, I'm tired."

"Three years, you do nothing. See, look in the mirror, see at how pale you are getting. Sick pale, no color."

Lars looked away from the mirror.

"I tell you over and over, you must read or study or play games."

"Play games, Papa . . . ?"

Mr. Nielson began to pace about the room.

"Sure, certainly. Games. You can, you can make them up. Play them in your head. You don't have to run around and wave your arms to play games!"

Lars looked down, where the carpet lay thin and unmoving.

"But you do nothing. All day I work, and *hard* I work, lifting many pounds, and I come home tired. All day I use my arms and feet and back and I do not want to any more, when I come home, so I don't. I sit in the chair and read. I *read*, Lars, and I smoke my pipe and I talk to Mama. I sit still, like you, but I do something!"

With Mr. Nielson's agitated movement, the room started to pick at the Feeling. Lars concentrated on white.

"And it don't take my arms and legs to do it. They are tired, they are every way like yours. I am you at night, Lars. And I am old, but I don't sit with nothing. I am always playing games, *in my head*. I don't move, but I don't worry Mama who loves me. I don't move, but I don't say nothing to my Mama and Papa, ever, just sit staring!"

"I'm sorry, Papa."

"Yes, for *yourself* you are sorry! You are sixteen years old and should be thinking about how to live, how to get along when Papa is no more here to take care of you and there is no money."

"Yes, Papa."

"Then begin to think, Lars. When I come home at night, let me see you talking to Mama, planning things with your brain. The big men are big because of their brains, my son, not their arms and legs. Nothing is wrong with your brain, you didn't hurt it. You have time to learn, to learn anything!"

"I will begin to think, Papa."

Mr. Nielson rubbed his hands together. They made a rough grating sound.

"All right. Tomorrow you tell Mama you are sorry and want to play with the dog. She will get it back for you, and you should smile and thank her and talk to the dog."

"I—I can go to bed now?"

"Yes."

Mr. Nielson leaned forward and slid one arm behind Lars' back, another beneath his legs.

"We are not like others," he said slowly. "When I am gone, there will be nothing, no money. Don't you see why you got to—are you ready?"

Mr. Nielson lifted Lars from the wheelchair and laid him on the bed. He sucked on his pipe as he removed shirt, trousers, stocking, shoes and underwear; grunted slightly as he pulled a faded tan nightgown over heavy lengths of steel and rubber.

Then he smiled, broadly.

"You should say big prayers tonight, my son. You have worried Mama but even so, tomorrow is a surprise."

Lars tried to lift his head. Father stood near the bed, but in the corner, so the big smiling face was hidden.

"Tomorrow, Papa?"

"I tell you nothing now. But you are a young man now, nearly, and you have promised me that you will begin to think. Isn't that what you promised, Lars?"

"Yes."

"So. And I believe you. No longer coming home to see you sitting with no thoughts. I believe you and so, tomorrow you get your reward. Tomorrow you will see happiness and it will clear your head; then you will be a man!"

Lars stopped trying to move his head. He closed his eyes so that he would not have to stare at the electric light bulb.

"Hah, but I don't tell you. Say *big* prayers, my son. It is going to be good for you from now on."

"I will say my prayers tonight, Papa."

"Goodnight, now. You sleep."

"Tell Mama—that I'm sorry."

Mr. Nielson pulled the greasy string and the room became black but for the coals in his pipe.

Lars waited for the door to close and Father's footsteps to stop. Then he moved his lips, rapidly, quietly, fashioning the prayers he had invented. To a still, unmoving God, that he could stay forever in the motionless room, to fight the Feeling. That he could think of colors and nothing and keep the Feeling—the feet across meadows, the arms trembling with heavy pitchforks full of hay, all the parts of life—in a small corner in a far side of his mind.

Lars prayed, as Father had suggested. His head did not move when sleep came at last.

"You did not tell him, Henrik?" Mrs. Nielson rocked back and forth in the blue cane chair, breaking green beans into small pieces and throwing the pieces into an enamel wash-basin.

"No."

"He never was to one—there never was one in Mt. Sinai since I can remember."

"Once when I worked for the fruit company it came here but we were very busy and I could not go."

"Henrik, do you think, will it *really* be good for him?"

"Good? Mama, you do not know. When I went to that one in Snohomish I did not have a job to work or money. I just went to look and I didn't spend anything. But there was all the people, everybody in the town, and all laughing. Everybody, laughing. And so much to see!" Mr. Nielson began to chuckle. "Shows and machines and good livestock like you never saw. And funny, crazy people in a tent. Oh Mama, when I went home I was happy too. I didn't worry. Right after, I got a job and met you!"

Mr. Nielson slapped his knees.

"How many? Twenty years ago, but see, see how I remember! Lars will be no more like this when he sees all the laughing. He will come home like I did. But I didn't tell him. He don't know."

A cat scratched at the screen and Mrs. Nielson rose to open the door. She sniffed the air.

"Raining."

Mr. Nielson took up his newspaper.

"Henrik, he can't go on the rides."

"So? I went on no rides."

"What can he do?"

"Do? He can see all the people laughing. And he can see the shows and play with the dice—"

"No!"

"Mama, he is sixteen, almost a man. He will play with the dice, he will say, and I will throw them. And he will see the frogs jump. And I will take him to the tent with the funny people. The brain, Mama, the *brain*! That is what enjoys the carnival, not arms and legs. That is what will make Lars understand."

"Yes, Henrik. We must cheer him up. Maybe after, we can bring him the dog and he will play with it."

"Sure, certainly, he will. He will be happy, not alone in this house, feeling sorry for himself."

"Yes."

"It will start him to think. He will think about how to make for himself a living, like anybody else. And he will read books then, you'll see, and find out what he wants to do. With his brain!"

Mrs. Nielson paused before speaking.

"Henrik."

"Yes?"

"What *can* he do, like you say, with his brain, without arms and legs?"

"He has arms and legs!"

"As well not, as well no back, no body."

"Hilda! He *must* do something, something. Look at that

blind woman who can't hear, like we read in the magazine—she did something. Can't you see, Mama, can you not understand? I would take care of Lars, even if it is wrong. But you know the railroad will give only enough for you when I die, and I am not young. We married late, Mama, very late. If Lars does nothing, how will he live? Is it an institution for our boy, a home for cripples where he sees only cripples all day long, no sunshine, no happiness? For Lars? No! At the carnival tomorrow he will see and begin to think. Maybe to write, or teach or—something!"

"But he has not been from the house, since—"

"More reason, more!"

Mrs. Nielson broke beans loudly. Kindling crackled in the big cast-iron stove.

"This blind woman you say about, Henrik. She has feet to walk."

"Lars has eyes to see."

"This woman has hands to use."

"Lars has ears to hear, a brain to think, a tongue to talk!"

The cat scratched sharp sounds from the linoleum.

Mrs. Nielson rocked back and forth.

"This woman has money and friends. She never saw or heard, she cannot remember."

Mr. Nielson went to the sink and drew water from the faucet, into a glass. He drank the water quickly.

"So, then Lars has a heavier Cross and a greater reward."

"Yes, Henrik."

"You will see, Mama, you will see. After the carnival, he will know what he wants to do. He will begin to think."

Mrs. Nielson rose and dusted the bean fragments from her lap, into the wash-basin. She picked up the cat and went outside onto the porch. Then she returned and snapped the lock on the door.

"Maybe you are right, Henrik. Maybe anyway he will like little dogs and talk to me. I hope so, I hope so."

Mr. Nielson wiped his hands on the sides of the chair and listened to the rain.

Lars felt his body pushed by strong invisible hands, felt himself toppling over like a woolen teddy bear onto Father's shoulder. He bit his lip and closed his eyes.

Mr. Nielson laughed, applying the brake.

"There now, the turn too sharp, eh Lars? I will be more careful."

The car began to move again, more slowly, jerking, rattling. Lars looked out the windshield at the fields and empty green meadows.

"Papa, is it far?"

"Hah, you are anxious! No, it is not far. Maybe five miles, right over the bridge."

"Will we have to stay long?"

Mr. Nielson frowned.

"I told Mama we would be back before dark. Don't you want to go, after what I told you, after what you said?"

Two children playing in a yard went by slowly.

"Don't you want to go, Lars?"

"Yes, Papa. I want to."

"Good. You don't know, you never saw anything like a carnival, never."

Lars closed his mouth and thought of colors. The children touched his mind and he thought of the blue dishes in his home. He opened his eyes, saw the pale road and thought of black nothing. Wind came through the open windows, tossing his brown hair and clawing gently at his face and he thought of the liquid green in a cat's eyes.

Mr. Nielson hummed notes from an old song, increasing pressure on the accelerator cautiously. Soon the road became a white highway and other cars went whistling by.

Signboards appeared, houses, roadside cafes, gasoline stations and little wooden stands full of ripe fruit.

And then, people. People walking and leaning and playing ball and some merely sitting. Everything, whirling by now in tiny glimpses.

Lars tried to force his eyes shut, but could not. He looked. He looked at everything and pressed his tongue against his teeth so the Feeling would stay small in his mind. But the meadows were yards now, and they were no longer quiet. They moved like everything in them moved.

And the people in the automobiles, laughing and honking and resting their elbows out the windows.

When he saw the girl on the bicycle, Lars managed to pull his eyelids down.

"Oh, such a beautiful day, Lars! Everyone is going to the carnival. See them!"

"Yes, Papa."

The car turned a corner.

"Different than all alone in a cold room, eh my son? But, see—there, there it is! Oh, it's big, like when I went. Look, Lars, this you have never seen!"

Lars looked when his eyes had stopped burning.

First, there were cars. Thousands and millions of cars parked in lots and on the sides of the highway and wherever there was room, in yards, gasoline stations, the airfield. And then there were the people. So many people, more than there could be in the world! Like ants on a hill, scrambling, walking, moving. Everywhere, cars and people.

And beyond, the tents.

"Oh, Mama should have come, she should have come. Such a sight!"

The old car moved like a giant lobster, poking in holes that were too small for it, pulling out from the holes, seeking others. Finally, beneath a big tree in a yard, stopping.

Mr. Nielson smiled, opened the back door and pulled the wheelchair from the half-seat. He lifted Lars and put

him in the chair and stood for a moment breathing the air
and tasting the sounds.

"Just like before, only even better! You will enjoy yourself!"

Lars tried to feel every rock beneath the wheels and every
blade of grass. He turned his eyes down as far as he could,
to see the earth, but he saw his body. The sounds grew
louder and as he glided on the smoothness he began to see
beyond the crawling, moving people. It all grew louder and
Father's voice faster so Lars cut off the feeling and returned to the bottom of the ocean.

The hard-rubber wheels turned softly on nothingness . . .

*Heyheyheyhey how about you, Mr.? Try your luck, test
your skill, only ten cents for three balls . . . Now I'll count to
five, ladies and gentlemen, and if one of you picks the right
shell, you win a Kewpie Doll . . . All right, sir, your weight
is one-fifty-three, am I right? . . . Right this way, folks, see the
wonders of the Deep, the dangerous shark and Lulu the Oc-
topus . . . The Whirlagig, guaranteed to scare the yell out of
you . . . Fun, Thrills and Excitement, only twenty-five cents
on the Flying Saucer . . . Fresh cotton candy . . . Spooktown,
Spooktown, ghosts and dragons and lots of fun, ten cents for
adults, a nickel for the kiddies . . . How about you, Mr.? . . .*

Lars kept his eyes still, but the Feeling was there. It was
small at first and he could think yet of colors and beds that
did not move. But it was growing, in the shape of baseballs
and bicycles and gigantic leaps, it was growing.

Mr. Nielson took his eyes from the iron machine and
turned the crank until it clicked. The sign read Secrets of
the Harem and Mr. Nielson sighed.

He put the huge ball of pink vapor to Lars' mouth and
Lars put his tongue about the gritty sweet.

"Ah ah ah, you are happy, I can see, already! What shall
we do now? The fish, we will look at the fish!"

Peculiar grey creatures swimming in dirty water in a big glass tank.

"Now you wait here for Papa."

Father stuffed into a small box and the box falling fast down a thin track, then up and later down again. Screams and laughter and movement. Movement.

"Watch, you see. I'll break the balloon!"

Pop! And a plaster doll covered with silver dust and blue paint.

Inside for the thrill of the century, ladies and gentlemen, see Parmo the Strong Man lift ten times his own weight . . .

A man with a large stomach and moving muscles, pulling a bar with a black ball at either end, hoisting the bar, holding it above his head. Laughs and cheers.

Yahyahyahyah! See her now, folks, the most gorgeous, the most beautiful, the most (ahem!) shapely little lass this side of Broadway. Egyptian Nellie, she's got curves on her yahyahyahyah . . .

"Lars, you wait—no, you don't. It wouldn't be right."

The candy and the peanuts and the little dirty faces. The rides and the planes and the exhibits and the penny arcades. The stale, excited odors and the screaming voices. And the movement, the jerking, zooming, swooping, leaning, pushing, running movement.

Last one there is a sissy, last one there is a sissy . . .

"Good, good, good. Mama should be here! But now we must eat!"

An open arena, with fluffballs of red and yellow and green hanging from the ceiling. On the floor, popcorn and peanut shells and wadded dirt.

"It's all right, Lars, it's good meat. Maybe not like Mama makes, huh? So. Open your mouth."

The people's eyes, staring, pitying, a million eyes, and hums of voices in the colored restaurant. Then a kind of quiet, like sharp prongs in the Feeling. In the little Feeling, coming awake.

"Now, so? You are finished. No, the milk, the milk to make you strong."

Off out of the arena, back into the movement.

And out into the very heart of the shining motion.

Lars stopped fighting. He let his eyes see and his mind fill.

Last one there is a sissy and Father seated in a small car, bumping the car into others and howling. First one to the trestle and the slow circling ferris wheel with the squealing dots.

Just try and catch me, just try . . .

"Come now, Lars, we rest."

The horror in the washroom and out again, feeding the Feeling, sending it along the spiral. The music bellowing and even in the little car in the blackness of the Fun House—movement there. Sudden lights on painted monsters, cotton bats squeaking along invisible wires.

And then—

Here we go, folks, the experience of a lifetime. Yah yah hear! See 'em all—the Frog Man, Queenie the Fat Girl (three hundred pounds of feminine loveliness!), Marco the Flame-Eater, yah, yah, all inside, all inside . . .

"Come, Lars, after this we will go. But if it is like last time—you never saw anything like it. Funny looking crazy people. It's good, good."

And as a special attraction, ladies and gents, we have Jackie the Basket-case. No arms, no legs, but he writes and plays cards and shaves, right before your very eyes. Science gave him up as lost, but you'll see him now. Jackie, the Basket-Case. And the headless girl, who defies doctors throughout the universe! Nurses in attendance! Heah heah heah! Only ten cents, the tenth part of a dollar.

Square canvas flags with strange pictures on them. A man with a sword in his mouth, a woman with an orange beard, a ferocious black man with feathers. And in front, high on the platform, a man with a striped shirt and a cane, hitting a pan.

"So, we go in."

Lars said nothing. He listened to all the sounds and how they seemed like the swift rush of cold wind and rain across his face. His heart beat and his blood pounded against his temples.

I'll beat you, Lars . . .

Lars felt his chair being pushed forward. Out of the sunlight and quickly into the dimly lighted interior, he could see nothing at first. Only what he had been seeing for hours.

There was the sudden quiet, for one thing. Nothing to see yet, but like dropping from a close, hot hay-loft to freshly watered earth. Damp and cool, like perhaps a grave.

The Feeling stopped growing for a moment as Lars focused his eyes. He wondered where all the people had gone, what had happened, if he were back in the silent unmoving room. The cold stillness and then the soft muttering of voices, strange and out of place.

"Here, Lars, don't you see?"

Mr. Nielson ran his hand through Lars' hair and touched his shoulder. The chair moved over ploughed ground.

"Papa, what—"

Mr. Nielson giggled no louder than the other people in the tent.

"Ha ha! Look, boy, look at the woman!"

Lars saw the object that Father had called a woman. The product of mutant glands, a huge sitting thing with mountains of flesh. Flowering from the neck down the arms and looping over the elbows, dividing like a baby's skin at the hands; the thighs, cascading flesh and fat over the legs down to the feet. And over all this, a metallic costume with purple sequins attached and short black hair, cut like a boys'.

"Have you ever seen anything so big, Lars!"

Lars looked from his wheelchair into the eyes of the fat
lady and then quickly away from them.

Over the ground. Stopping.

The sign reading The Frog Man, and four people staring.
"Look! Ohhh!"

Shriveled limbs with life sticking to them. Shriveled,
dried-up, twisted legs, bent grotesquely. And the young
man with the pimples on his face crouching on these legs,
leering. Every few moments, the legs moving and the small
body hopping upwards.

Lars tried to shake his head. The Feeling started from
where it had left off, but it traveled elsewhere now. It
traveled from his mind to his eyes and from his eyes out-
ward.

"Come, it will be late. We must see everything. Oh,
look, have you ever seen such a crazy thing!"

Lars leaned his head forward painfully and looked.

The face of a very old man, but smooth along the creases
and over the wrinkles. Wrinkled hands, thin hair. An old
man standing three feet from the ground. But not merely
small. Everything dwarfed. The false beard and the gnome's
cap and the stretched-gauze wings.

The Feeling went into the eyes of the midget.

"There, over there! There was no such last time!"

Over the ground, slowly, past the man with the pictures
on his skin, the black creeping thing, the boy with the
breasts, slowly past these, slowly so the Feeling could be
fed and gathered.

And now, the Feeling reaching across the tent to the
other side, reaching into the woman with seventeen toes,
the boy with the ugly face, the alligator girl, the human
chicken, reaching and bringing back, nursing, feeding,
identifying. Identifying.

Then ceasing.

"Lars, look. Never was there such a thing."

Mr. Nielson's voice was low and full of deep wonder as he craned his head over the people's shoulders.

Lars tried one last time to see the blue of the linoleum, the grey of his room, all the quiet things his mind had made so carefully. But his eyes moved.

It was large, made of wicker, padded and made to look like an egg basket on the outside. There was in front of it a square card with writing, which gave dates and facts, but the card was dirty and difficult to read. The thing in the basket lay still.

A knitted garment covered the midsection and lower part. Above, the pale flesh stretched over irregular bumps and lines, past the smooth armsockets on up to the finely combed black hair, newly barbered.

The face was handsome and young, clean-shaven and delicate.

When it lifted Mr. Nielson and the other staring people gasped.

In the mouth was a pencil and with this pencil, the thing in the basket began to write upon a special pad of paper. The lead was soft so that those nearby could make out the words, which were "My name is Jack Rennie. I am very happy".

Lars saw his father's hands about his side, lifting and pushing.

"Look, see what it does!"

Lars' body trembled, suspended above the basket, held in air. Everything trembled and shook, as teeth held a moving pencil and the pencil made words. The limbless man thought, it—he—*thought* . . .

The automobile came straight at Lars, and he saw it now. Saw it speeding over the trestle for him, bellowing its warning. The brakes screeched in his head and he saw the car swerve and careen in the wet road. And then floating down the trestle, below it, onto sharp hard things.

Lars looked from his wheelchair at the armless, legless man in the cheap basket and in one explosion, the thoughts sprang from the Feeling and scattered through his brain, moving, dancing, swinging arms, jumping on legs, moving, moving with all the ecstasy of a dead child brought suddenly to life.

"It shaves, sees, talks, it writes!"

Lars rode his bicycle in the sunlight down through the fields near the river and never stopped, for he was never tired. He rode past laughing people and waved his arms at children blurring in the distance. He pushed his young legs on the pedals and flew past all the things of the country and then of the world, all the things best seen from the eyes of a young boy on a bicycle.

The thing in the wicker basket ceased to exist. The grinning gasping people ceased to exist and Father was someone sitting in a chair, smoking his pipe.

Lars had reached the crest of Strawberry Hill and he lifted his feet, drifting and floating downward, letting the wind and rain and sunlight whirl past.

Mr. Nielson gently pulled Lars back in the wheelchair and rolled silently from the darkened tent into the afternoon.

The people were sparse. They straggled by hoarse vendors and still rides, yawning and shuffling.

Mr. Nielson forgot about the tent and began to talk.

"Well, we go home now. All day at the carnival, what, my son? Ah, Lars, I tell you, Mama should not have stayed home. Now you feel good, you will be a fine man and think, eh Lars?"

Mr. Nielson picked leaves from overhanging branches as he walked, feeling good and pleased.

When he got into the car, he looked at his son's eyes.

"Lars, there is nothing wrong? You don't look like you feel so good."

Lars was going too fast to hear Father, the wind was

shrieking too wildly. The green hills turning golden, the leaves from orange to white, and all the boys and girls riding behind him, chasing, trying to catch him.

He turned, laughing. *"Who's the sissy now, who's the sissy now!"*

Mr. Nielson scowled.

"You'll never catch me, you'll never catch me!"

"What, what is that you say?"

Lars sang into the wind as the children's voices grew faint. He waved his arms and pedaled with his legs and saw the beautiful hill stretching beneath him.

"You just watch, you just watch!"

The beautiful hill sloping gracefully downward and without an end.